BROOKE MONTGOMERY

Copyright © 2025 Brooke Montgomery
www.brookewritesromance.com

Take My Name
Willow Branch Mountain, #1

Cover designer: Qamber Designs
Cover photographer: Wander Aguiar
Cover models: Jerryn & Ella
Editor: Lawrence Editing

willow branch mountain

suggested reading order

Take My Name (#1)
Take My Love (#2)
Take My Kiss (#3)
Take My Soul (#4)
Take My Hand (#5)

Each book can be read as a stand-alone and ends in a happily ever after. However, for the best reading experience, read in order.

I'm still holdin' on to you
    But I know you're already gone
    I'm still wakin' up to you
    I've been holdin' on for too long

When was it over for you?
    When was it over?
    When was the moment you knew
    That you were gonna walk out eventually?
    It's still not over for me

when was it over?
Sasha Alex Sloan, Sam Hunt

playlist

Listen to the full *Take My Name* playlist on Spotify

Take My Name | Parmalee
When was it over? | Sasha Alex Sloan, Sam Hunt
Versions of Forever | Matt Hansen
Can You Die From a Broken Heart | Nate Smith, Avril Lavigne
Once in a Lifetime | Landon Austin
Mercy | Brett Young
Slow Dancing in a Burning Room | John Mayer
I Miss You | Clean Bandit, Julia Michaels
Plot Twist | Ashley Kutcher
loml | Taylor Swift
I Hate That It's True | Dean Lewis
Not Over You | Gavin DeGraw
You Happened | Knox
Dear God | Tate McRae
Die With A Smile | Lady Gaga, Bruno Mars
Someone You Love | Lewis Capaldi

author's note

There are some NSFW art inside, so please be aware of that when you flip through.

Willow Branch Mountain is a fictional town set in northeastern Tennessee. The characters speak in a Southern dialect, which is reflected through their dialogue and inner thoughts. Outside of that, the narration is written in standard American English to ensure clarity and a smooth reading experience.

Take My Name is about two people who are still legally married but have been estranged for seven years. During their time apart, the FMC gets engaged to another man. While they're married on paper, there's no actual cheating between the MCs. When the couple reunite to discuss divorce plans, they participate in some "sexual couple activities" while she's still engaged. The MCs do not cheat on each other when they're officially back together, but depending on your own preferences regarding cheating, this may or may not be for you.

If you choose to continue reading their book, I hope you enjoy their journey to falling back in love!

Welcome to Willow Branch Mountain Equine Ranch & Luxury Camping Resort

The town of Willow Branch Mountain, Tennessee is home to twenty-five hundred residents and is nestled in the Appalachian Mountains between Doe Mountain, Forge Mountain, and Iron Mountains—a landscape surrounded by peaks. Willow Branch Mountain is one of the highest valleys in the state. We're just a few miles from the Virginia and North Carolina state lines.

Enjoy a cozy couples getaway in the mountains with luxury cabins, domes, glamping tents, or leisure treehouses. Spend the day horseback riding, trail walking, cliff diving, biking, or ziplining and then enjoy a romantic dinner at the Summit Views Restaurant! We have massage therapists on-site, ready to turn your room into a sanctuary, and a hot tub for you to enjoy after. Relax and reunite with your partner during your stay!

Don't forget your welcome basket loaded with self-care essentials, including goat soap from our family-owned goat soap business—Langston Soapworks, a spa-inspired candle, snacks, and books. If you need anything while you're here, don't hesitate to reach out to The Branch Haven so someone in guest services can bring you whatever you need.

Meet the Langston family:

Grady & Lindsey Langston
the parents

Aunt Josephine "JoJo" Langston
paternal aunt

Warren Langston
the oldest child and son

Posey Langston
the oldest daughter

Colton "Colt" Langston
the middle child

Bodie and Bellamy Langston
twins, the youngest

Job titles:

Grady & Lindsey
Owners

Aunt JoJo
Restaurant manager at Summit Views

Warren
Ranch Operations Manager

Posey
Goat farm manager at Langston Soapworks

Colt
Resort Operations Manager

Bodie
Ranch hand

Bellamy
Resort Concierge

Find all of our current information at
http://willowbranchmountain.com

We hope you have the best time!
-The Langston Family

See map on the next page!

Willow Chalet
Willow Peak Stables
Zipline Area
The Branch Haven
Ranch
Resort
Willo

Summit Views Restaurant
Willow Falls River
lls Bridge

prologue

Warren

"I CAN'T BELIEVE you talked me into this." Maisie laughs, treading water and glancing around to make sure no one's around. The sun's about to set, so most of the guests from the resort are at the restaurant for dinner or they're in for the night.

Wrapping an arm around her bare waist, I pull her closer into my chest. She wraps her limbs around me, and I hold her up in the river with my body.

"Skinny dippin' is a rite of passage," I tease, cupping her ass cheek and squeezing.

"Yeah, right. You find any excuse to get me naked." She tightens her grip, causing her abdomen to rub against my cock that's half hard between our bodies.

When she rocks against me, I groan and she chuckles at my discomfort.

"You're gonna pay for that," I warn, reaching up to pinch her nipple.

She yelps, then splashes water on my face, distracting me long enough to get away. I swim after her, easily catching up, then dive under the water to yank her ankle.

"Warren!" Her scream is muffled when I bring her down with me.

We aren't submerged for long before I release her and meet her back up above the surface.

"That was mean!" She splashes me again, but her smile is wider than before.

The sounds of crashing water off the cliff echo around us as I pull her toward me. She fits against my chest in a familiar way that calms my heart.

"I'm gonna miss you so much," I tell her softly.

She tangles her legs and arms around me, hugging me closer. "Gonna miss you more."

"Impossible," I breathe out, holding in my emotions the best I can.

Maisie returns to college in New York City for her third year tomorrow. She's majoring in English and hopes to get an internship before she graduates. We've been doing long-distance for two years, and though she comes home during the summer and holidays, it's not enough. Not when I got used to seeing her every day since we were twelve.

"I'll be back for Thanksgiving," she reminds me. "And we'll still video chat and text."

I tip up her chin so I can see her gorgeous hazel eyes, but they look more brown than green during the golden hour. "It's not enough. I want you here with me."

"Only a couple more years."

"Yeah? And then what?"

Her tongue peeks out, wetting her bottom lip, and she hoists herself up higher on my waist as I stand in shoulder-deep water.

"Then we…" She lifts a shoulder. "Start a life together."

"Hmm…" Her words swirl in my head. "Why wait another two years to do that?"

"Whaddya mean?"

"We should get married."

"After graduation?"

"No." I tighten my grip on her. "Next summer."

The area around her eyes creases when she flashes a white, toothy grin. "Are you proposin'?"

"Would you say yes if I were?" I drawl, unable to contain my own smile.

"Maybe you oughta ask and find out…" Her calm, taunting tone sends my heart into overdrive because we've talked about our future plenty of times but discussed getting married after she moved home permanently.

I walk us slowly through the water to keep warm, but I don't release my hold on her when I brush my thumb over her cheek and cup her face. "Maisie Callaway, will you be my wife?"

"Hmm…" She twists her lips, her brows furrowing as she contemplates her answer. "You really wanna marry me?"

"Been wantin' to since I was fifteen, darlin'."

"That's when we started datin'."

"Exactly."

She beams, unable to hide her excitement, although she's trying to act unaffected.

"Give me one good reason why I should," she says in a playful tone that means she's not going to make this easy for me.

My fingers flex into her ass, pushing her against my cock so she can feel how much I want her.

"Besides that." With her arms around my neck, she lifts slightly to purposely rub her stomach against my growing erection.

"Because Maisie Langston sounds so fuckin' good on you."

"You do have a point..." Her teeth graze her bottom lip again, and I'm tempted to lean in and bite it.

"Is that a yes? You'll take my name?"

"On one condition..." Her cheeks flush. "You build me a house like the one we discussed."

"The two-story A-frame cabin with the large deck?"

"And a fireplace in front of the large windows, a cozy living room, big enough kitchen for us to cook together, a reading nook I can fill with my books, and a room for a nursery. Oh, and a master room big enough for a king-sized bed with an en suite that has a large tub for us to fit in together."

Smiling wide at her excitement, I can hardly contain my own at the thought of us living under the same roof. When we were still in high school, I told her my dream was to build a house on my family's property when we got married and she started looking at ideas the next day. She created a whole dream board of pictures and ideas, and I loved every single one.

"I'd love nothin' more than to build that for us, baby."

She leans her head back toward the water, her arms stretched out while they stay wrapped around me and as her legs tighten around my waist, she laughs up at the darkening sky. It's a beautiful sight.

"Then yes, Warren Langston..." She returns her eyes to mine, pressing against me. "I'll be your wife."

My hand wraps around her neck, pulling her mouth to mine, and I devour her. My tongue slips between her lips, tasting the country air and waterfall ripples, and moaning against them.

"So, next summer?" I ask between kissing down her jaw.

"What's the hurry? Am I pregnant?"

I chuckle against her neck. "I would've asked you years ago if I knew it wouldn't have freaked you out. Or our parents."

Considering we're only twenty, they definitely would've freaked out.

Hell, they still might.

Her parents aren't my biggest fans, but that's never stopped me from showing how much I love her. Mine, on the other hand, adore her.

"Why do ya wanna marry me so badly?"

I meet her eyes and they're filled with sincere curiosity.

"Besides how much I enjoy being with you, you're my best friend and the love of my life. Why wait when I already know who I'm meant to be with for the rest of my life?"

"Are you callin' me your soul mate?" She wiggles her nose against mine, her voice softening. "Because I feel the same."

"Good, because I wanna wake up next to you every day, snuggle you in my arms as the coffee brews, and kiss your neck until the sun rises and we're forced to get outta bed. In the evenings, we'll dance in front of the fireplace while we wait for the oven timer to go off, then we'll feed each other dinner and spend the rest of the night soaking in the tub, washing each other." I thumb her chin, finding her gaze. "I want forever."

"That sounds...heavenly." She sighs happily. "Like a dream."

"And soon, it'll be our reality."

She crashes her lips to mine, sucking my bottom lip into her mouth and pressing into me. "I can't wait," she whispers, resting her forehead against mine. "I would've said yes either way. The house is a bonus."

"I know. You can't resist me."

She rolls her eyes, reaching between us and grabbing my cock.

"Maze..." I warn, swallowing hard.

"You don't wanna celebrate our engagement?" she asks in her seductive teasing tone that always makes me fold.

Fuck.

She strokes my shaft and my balls tighten.

"That's it. Time to go." I walk us out toward the shore and carry her to my truck, where our towels and clothes are waiting. "Don't get dressed. Just wrap a towel around you."

"Where're we goin'?" she asks before I sprint around to my door, buck naked.

"The Chalet."

The Willow Chalet is only a few-minute drive. It's a large two-story cabin with a wraparound deck and has ten bedrooms and fourteen bathrooms. We reserve it for large family gatherings, wedding receptions, or high-profile guests.

And the best part, the showers are always stocked.

"It's not reserved?" she asks.

"Not until Friday."

Which means, we can easily sneak in without anyone finding out.

We usually hook up in my truck or I sneak her into my bedroom, but this way we can shower together without the fear of anyone overhearing or interrupting.

Once I park, I grab our clothes and lead her through the back entrance that's usually left open for the staff.

"We're gonna get caught!" she whisper-hisses when I flick on a light.

"By who?"

"I-I dunno. Your parents? Or siblings?"

Considering I'm the oldest of five kids, I doubt it. They're probably at home getting ready for bed since it's a weekday.

"Stop worryin', sweetheart. We're celebratin', remember? Plus, doesn't the thrill make it that much hotter?" I smirk over my shoulder before pulling her into one of the bathrooms.

It's spotless as usual, with fluffy towels and robes folded for the guests. Since I work on the ranch side, I'll tell Posey, my eighteen-year-old sister, who works part-time on the resort side, to make sure the bathroom gets re-cleaned.

She owes me a favor anyway after I caught her sneaking a boy out of her room at three in the morning on a school night. She claims they fell asleep, but I've used that excuse too many times to count. If our parents had caught her, she'd still be grounded.

Turning on the hot water, I nod at Maisie. "Lose the towel, baby."

When we step in, the stream falls over us under the rainfall showerhead. We wash one another from head to toe, slowly massaging shampoo in each other's hair and rinsing off. Neither of us can stop smiling at our secret engagement and sneaking in here, but it's equally exciting and romantic to get this time with her before she leaves.

"What size ring are you?"

"Six, I think."

"I'm gonna get you the biggest and most beautiful ring I can afford."

"You don't have to spend a fortune. I'll be happy with anythin' you pick out."

"There ain't no way your parents are gonna be happy with something small."

"Who cares what they think?"

"Uh...me. They're already gonna be pissed I didn't ask for their blessin' first."

"That's an outdated tradition. They'll be happy as long as I am."

The expression on my face causes her to roll her eyes in disagreement. As much as I love her, she's blind to the way her parents look at me. Her father owns an investment firm where he grows and flips Southern businesses in healthcare, manufacturing, and more. Her mother is from old money, so I wouldn't be surprised if that's why they got married in the first place. Rich families wanting to stay rich and all that. They're well-known and prestigious around here, but they've always given me the impression they don't want their only daughter to marry a rancher.

It's why I'm certain they encouraged Maisie to go to college seven hundred miles away.

I never had plans for college because working on my family's horse ranch and resort is all I've ever wanted to do. Although we have a full staff for the ranch and resort, I'm certain my siblings will follow suit and stay here too. I love it here. Even if it's hard work, it's the only kind I know.

And I wouldn't change it for anything.

Although my parents are respected by the community for their successful luxury camping resort, they're not valued in the same light. We stay booked and busy year-round, minus a couple winter months over the holidays where it slows down, but they do well for themselves. Most of my checks go into my savings since I still live at home, so if I have to prove I'm worthy of marrying their daughter, I will by making sure she has the ring she deserves.

I already know her mother will want full control of the wedding planning.

Assuming they don't ship Maisie overseas or some shit to get her away from me.

"Either way, when you come back for Thanksgiving, I'm gettin' down on one knee and proposin' with a ring."

She wraps her arms around my waist, peering up. "I don't think you're supposed to tell me ahead of time."

"We're already engaged. This'll be the formal engagement, where I propose with clothes on."

Laughter echoes through the shower as her shoulders shake. "I much prefer you being naked."

I kiss the tip of her nose, sliding my palm down to smack her ass. "Good, because I'm about to fuck you against the wall until you lose your voice from screamin' my name."

"Warren!" she squeals.

"That's the one." I wink. "You agreein' to be my wife unleashed a new side to me, baby. And if this is the last night I get with you for three months, we're makin' it a memorable one."

"We don't have condoms."

Although we don't always use them and she's on birth control, we've been extra careful since she's in school, but I can't help the smile that takes over my face at the thought of her pregnant with my baby.

"Not-uh." She shakes her head at my devious grin, pointing a warning finger toward me. "No knockin' me up before we get married. Or before I graduate."

I chuckle, grabbing her wrist and repositioning her until her back presses against my chest. Then I plant her palms on the wall farthest from the showerhead.

"I'll pull out and paint your ass with my cum. How's that?"

"Fuck," she groans, arching her back until my cock slides between her crack.

"Spread your legs for me, Maze," I demand in her ear and she does until her feet are next to mine. "And keep your palms there until I say otherwise. Don't wanna have to explain a sex injury to our parents."

She looks over her shoulder, meeting my gaze with her lust-filled ones. "Then don't let me fall."

"Never." Squeezing her hip, I press my lips to hers, grab my shaft with my other hand, and give it a few strokes. Sliding my cock between her legs, I find her opening and slowly push inside.

"Jesus, you feel so good," I murmur, not even halfway in. Her breath hitches and when she relaxes, I slide the rest of the way. "Doin' okay?"

"Mm-hmm." Her head falls against my chest and she bites her lip. "You can move now."

I pull out to the tip, then thrust back inside her tight cunt and groan at how hard she squeezes me.

Heavy breathing, the water hitting my back, and her little gasps echo around us as our bodies slap together in perfect harmony.

"Oh my God, you're so deep," she blurts around a long moan.

"Hang on, my love."

Releasing my grip on her waist, one hand slides between her legs to find her clit while the other slides around her throat. My fingers squeeze the sides of her neck the way she loves and she nearly loses her balance when waves of heat burst through her.

"That's my good girl. Come on my cock."

She gasps when I slap her greedy clit. "I'm close..."

"So fuckin' beautiful when you're flushed with need. My future wife."

My cock drives into her, over and over, until I slam into her G-spot.

"Oh God, Warren. Yes, right there. Don't stop." Her shallow pants cause her breasts to rise and fall. I'm tempted to pinch her nipples, but she's so close, I don't want to make her lose focus.

"Jesus Christ, you're takin' me so good."

I've always been vocal during sex, but the more I talk, the harder and faster she orgasms. And any chance to do that, I take it. Hearing and watching her respond to me is enough to make me explode.

I can't hold back the growl that rips through me when her pussy pulsates and she screams through her release. She shakes against me, her neck fully exposed as her head falls back and she meets my gaze.

Her pupils are blown out with pleasure, and I love that I'm the one who caused it.

"I changed my mind, baby. Get on your knees."

As soon as I release my hold on her, she turns and obliges. I pump my shaft as tingles shoot down my spine and settle in my balls.

"Open up, Maze." She stares at me and draws out her tongue. "So goddamn gorgeous."

I barely get the words out before my release takes over and ropes of cum shoot across her face, incidentally, missing her mouth.

She wipes her fingers over her cheek and slides them between her lips, sucking them right off.

"Fuckin' hell," I growl at the sight of her licking my cum. "That's hot."

"Your aim sucks."

I bark out a laugh, helping her up. Then I clean her face with some water and crash my mouth to hers. "But I hear it's a great skin serum."

She makes a gagging noise. "Never say that again."

"I dunno. Might have to include it in the welcome baskets for the guests. Special skin treatment. Locally harvested."

"And I change my mind about marryin' you."

"Take it back!" I lift her up, nuzzling my face in her neck and tickling her side with one hand.

"Warren!" she squeals, her limbs clinging around my body. "Don't drop me!"

"Then say what I wanna hear," I prompt, poking her other side. "Say you're gonna marry me."

"No, you weird cum freak!" She giggles out the words as she tries to smack my hand away.

I tickle harder, and when she manages to get back on her feet, I don't let her go.

"Stop, you're gonna make me pee!" Maisie laughs as she tries to escape.

"Didn't know you were into that, but I'll try anythin' once."

"Warren!" She continues wiggling, and I release her so she doesn't fall. But then she drops to the ground as if that'll stop me from getting what I want.

I tower over her as she faces me, the water turning cold as it hits my back, but I don't care.

"Fine, fine! I take it back," she relents when she can no longer take it.

"Take what back?" I grab underneath her knees, finding a tickle spot there too.

She tries kicking me away. "What I said!"

"Say it." I cup her chin, holding her gaze.

She wrinkles her nose that she lost this round. "I'll marry you."

I soften my touch to give her a moment to breathe, but we're both laughing frantically at our positions. Me straddling her waist and trapping her with my thighs. Considering I'm a good seven inches taller and weigh more than her, she ain't going anywhere without me getting up.

Sometimes I let her win by pretending I'm too weak to fight back or too slow to chase her, but this isn't one of those times. Especially since I let her win the last tickle fight and she nearly had me crying with how much she had me laughing.

"You're gonna take my name?" I grab her wrists, holding them above her head. "And live in our dream house together?"

"Yes! Maisie Gracelyn Langston. Your wife." She grins wider and her cheeks heat. "That sounds good, doesn't it?"

My smile reaches my temples, and I lean down to kiss her. "Fuckin' perfect."

chapter one

Warren

PRESENT DAY

"KICK ME ONE MORE TIME, you little shit…"

Shaking my head, I stifle a laugh and walk toward my brother Bodie, who looks ready for a fight. His brows are drawn and sweat lines his forehead as he tries to lift her hind leg. Each time he attempts to pull her hoof between his thighs, she whinnies and jerks out of his grip.

"I dunno if I'm rootin' for you or Lilith." I stand next to the quarter horse who's giving him hell and pat her back.

Bodie glances at me, his lips in a hard line. "No wonder she's named after an evil demon. She nailed me in the balls twice already."

This time I do laugh. "Yikes. Hope you didn't wanna have kids."

He's been learning how to become a farrier so he can do our horses when our current one retires. He's only been practicing for six months, so he needs a bit more experience before he'll be ready to take over the job. Considering he's eight years younger than me and only twenty-one, he's got time to figure it out.

"At this rate, I'm gonna be down a testicle."

I snort, taking pity on him. "Want some help?"

"Gee, ya think?"

"Damn, settle down. No wonder you're makin' Lilith anxious as hell. She can sense your nerves."

Sliding my palm down her rear and leg, I motion for him to move.

"Nice and easy," I say calmly. Once I'm in position, I pull her hoof into the farrier stand and when she doesn't move, I pat her again. "That's my good girl."

"Well shit. Didn't know I was supposed to talk dirty to get her cooperation." He shoves his hands in his pockets and huffs at how easy I made it look.

I lift a shoulder, crossing my arms. "It's what every woman wants to hear."

"Pfft. How would you know?"

Rolling my eyes, I don't bother engaging. It's not the first time he's given me shit for staying single for seven years and it won't be the last. I may not be with Maisie anymore but she's still my damn wife. I'm nothing if not loyal and faithful to the vows we said to each other eight years ago.

Even if she's not.

"Get outta the kick zone and stop being squirmy, then she'll do exactly what you want," I tell him, handing him the rasp.

"Another woman tip?" he mocks.

"Yeah, consider it a freebie," I deadpan, leaving the grooming stall and heading toward my office at the back of the barn.

It's been a long week, and I'm ready to wrap it up. One more day and then I can take it easy for the weekend. Not that there isn't work to be done, but we save the hard shit for the weekdays when we have more workers. As the Ranch Operations Manager, my tasks include a lot more than ranch hand duties.

It comes with a bullshit amount of paperwork and emails.

Bodie's the only other sibling who works exclusively on the ranch side with me. Posey manages the goat farm and the family soap company, Langston Soapworks. Colton and Bellamy work on the resort side dealing with operations and guest services.

My parents couldn't pay me enough to deal with people every day. It's bad enough I have to manage the employees and their half-assed excuses on why they're late or how they forgot to request off—usually the day before they need it, too. Most of them text me instead so they don't have to see the disappointment on my face or get told no in person.

I wasn't always this way, but certain life experiences made me bitter and less tolerable.

Like after my wife and I did long-distance while she went to college, all for her to leave again four months later for an apprenticeship in New York.

I supported her the best I could, hoped she'd gain the experience she was after, then return and find a job here. Or hell, work remotely or start her own business.

But then—

I shake my head to get rid of the dark thoughts threatening to consume my mind. There's no use going down that path again when I know where it always leads me—drinking until I pass out and sending her drunken voicemails she'll never listen to.

The only response I'll get is another certified letter with divorce papers inside.

Over my dead fucking body am I signing those.

She can face me instead of being a coward if she wants one

that badly. Until then, I'll continue writing *return to sender* and let her eat the cost of her lawyer's fees.

"Hey, boss!" Nicky pops in through the doorway while I sit behind my desk and read through emails.

Hesitantly, I glance up and grimace at his too-wide grin that's probably meant to butter me up before he tells me something I don't want to hear.

"Whaddya want this time?" I grumble, shifting my gaze back to my screen.

"It's not as bad as it sounds..." His eager tone tells me otherwise and he continues without waiting for me to respond. "I need a couple weeks off."

"When?"

"Um, see...that's the thing." He sits in the chair across from me.

"Nicky," I bark. "Get on with it."

"Starting Monday."

That's four days from now.

"You know the rules. Thirty days' notice for anything over five days."

"I do! And normally, I'd give proper notice, but to be fair, I didn't know Darla thirty days ago."

That grabs my attention. "Excuse me? Who's Darla?"

"My fiancée! We're getting married this weekend, and I promised her a honeymoon in Mexico. Hence...the short notice."

My lip curls. "*Hence*...being denied. I'll give you one week, that's it."

"But—"

"I don't have coverage for two weeks." He should be thankful I'm even giving him that on a four-day notice.

"What if I—"

"Nicky." I blink away from the screen and shift my eyes to his panicked ones. "What the hell are you marryin' a woman you met less than a month ago?"

"She's my dream girl." His gaze with heart-shaped pupils stares back at me.

It makes me sick.

"It's never gonna work out. You know that, right?"

"Yes, it will. Not everyone's as cynical as you. When you find *the one* you don't let her get away."

Poor sucker is living in a delulu world.

"You think a ring and piece of paper is gonna keep her from runnin' off with the next guy?"

Or moving to another state.

"She won't if you let me take her to Mexico for two weeks!" He scoffs as if I'm to blame.

I roll my eyes at his dramatics. "Since I doubt you'll leave the bedroom, tell her one week in Mexico and one week here at the resort won't make a difference."

"Are you serious?" His face lights up and he nearly leaps out of his seat. "You'll let us stay there?"

"Assumin' I can find something available, yes. But it's comin' out of your vacation pay and your ass *will* be here workin' while she stays there. No excuses."

It's the middle of May, the start of our busy season, but I'm sure Colton can put them in one of the cabins or domes undergoing a remodel. As long as the bedroom and bathroom are available, they won't need much else.

"Deal!" He jumps to his feet.

I shake my head at becoming a softie.

Twenty bucks says he sneaks off for a quickie at least once a day.

"And you're gonna love her. She was a belly dancer at a hotel in Vegas and can spin around me in two seconds flat. She's also *very* flexible…if you know what I mean."

I wait to see if he's fucking with me or not.

"So any time the resort needs extra entertainment…"

"I'll let Colt know," I blurt, letting it become his problem since he's the resort operations manager.

"Thanks, Warren. I owe ya!"

"Mm-hmm," I murmur.

Once he vacates my office, I finish my work and then check-in with Bodie.

"Almost done?" I ask, noticing he's cleaning out the grooming stall.

We muck the stalls every morning, so it's rare he has to do it again in the evenings.

"Blythe took a shit right as I was cleaning her back hooves and got it all down my back and in my hair."

It's then I realize he's shirtless.

"Well…*shit*." I cough through a laugh, unable to hold back. "I mean, that sucks."

"Yeah…it fuckin' does. I had a date tonight, but instead, I'll be showerin' horseshit outta my pores for three hours."

"I'm sure it ain't that bad."

"Come closer and smell for yourself," he bites out. "Nicky nearly threw up when he came to help me and said I should soak in vinegar. Pretty sure that'll have my date runnin' for the hills."

"Coulda been worse." I shrug, walking toward the exit. "Coulda gotten it in your mouth!"

"That's very reassurin'!" he calls out.

I walk backward as I shout, "Try baby shampoo!"

"Seriously?"

"Yep! There should be some travel bottles in the stock room."

We store everything needed for the resort at The Branch Haven where the guests check-in. The staff grab what they need and restock after check-out.

"Thanks!"

I wave, heading toward my truck.

It's only a ten-minute drive to my house. Mostly because I have to drive slowly through the ranch and up into the mountains where I built my A-frame cabin, but the view from my deck is well worth it. Even better is the peace and quiet.

When I park and get out, I head toward my chickens. They cluck and swarm me as soon as I walk through the gate.

"I'm comin', hold your feathers."

I only have half a dozen of them and one rooster, but it's more than enough for fresh eggs every day. My siblings usually sneak over and steal my extra ones like the freeloaders they are.

If they're not taking my eggs, they're helping themselves to my fridge and robbing my food they're too lazy to go buy on their own.

I need to get better at locking my patio door on the lower level. They know if they can't get through the front, the other one is probably unlocked.

"Who's got some eggs for me?" I check their nests and find six fresh eggs.

In the mornings, I let them out so they can wander in the fenced-in area, then at night, I sprinkle out more food and water before tucking them into bed.

Which is a fancy way of saying I lock them in their coop so they can sleep on their roosts or nesting areas.

There are too many curious animals that come around at night, so I keep them safe inside.

"One, two, three…" I count as they go in and realize I'm missing one. "Kelly Cluckson, time for bed. Where're you?"

The moment I call out her name, I regret caving when Bellamy begged me to let her name a couple of them. She and Bodie are twins and the babies of the family, so they've grown up always getting their ways.

She finally struts in, and I close the door. "G'night girls and Chucky."

Charles got his nickname after he chased Bodie around the yard, then nearly pecked off his face when he tripped and face-planted the ground.

He hasn't tried to steal my eggs since then.

I strip out of my work clothes and get in the shower to wash off the barn smell. The hot water feels good on my achy muscles, and although it wasn't a labor-intensive workday, they still get stiff. Constantly lifting, moving, or even sitting behind my desk with tense posture makes me feel like I'm sixty instead of twenty-nine.

My after-work routine is simple. Put on comfy clothes, listen to music or an audiobook as I make dinner, and eat on the couch while catching up on the news. Most nights, I'm passed out before nine.

When there's a knock at my door, I sit up and stare at it. I'm not in the mood to deal with any of my family members tonight, but considering the wall is covered in floor to ceiling windows and they can see inside, there's no use pretending I'm not here.

Except when I open it, it's the last person I expect.

My wife.

chapter two

Maisie

STARING into the same gray eyes that've been ingrained into my memory since I was a teenager makes my heart race.

Or rather, it's *pounding*.

I'm positive he can hear it.

My chest aches at seeing his face in person again and sweat forms over my palms. It's painful to see how much he's changed and how grown he looks. He's no longer the boy I fell in love with at fifteen, or even the man I married at twenty-one. He's all man—more muscular and a defined jawline with light scruff over it. The thicker hair above his lip is...*new*. But the hair on his head is shaggier, more unkempt than I remember. Aging lines crease around his mouth and in between his brows, which means he frowns more than he smiles.

Blinking away the fog being near him puts me in, I straighten my stance and inhale a confident breath.

It's now or never.

"Hi, Warren," I greet when he doesn't say anything. I fold my hands in front of me, my thumb rubbing over my engagement band mindlessly and the papers burning a hole in my purse.

His jaw tenses, eyes narrowing as his gaze burns through me. Darkness surrounds him although the lights are on behind him. This isn't the Warren I walked down the aisle to. The charming, sweet man who couldn't wait to get us back home so we could celebrate our nuptials in private is long gone.

He's stone cold.

His gaze lowers down my blazer and pencil skirt, the corner of his lips curl as his hand grips the side of the door. "You must be lost. The stuck-up resort is down the road."

My breath hitches at the cruelness of his words, but I'm not going to sink to his level of bitterness, so I speak with all the confidence I can muster. "I'm not stuck up and you know it."

Blinking, his hard eyes find mine again. "Coulda fooled me. You hate skirts."

He's not wrong, but some things have changed, and me wearing professional work clothes is one of them. I grew to tolerate them since I was no longer spending my summers on a ranch.

"I *used* to hate skirts." I'm not giving him the satisfaction of being right. He doesn't get to pretend he still knows me after seven years.

But I didn't come all this way to argue about that, so I blurt the words I should've said to his face years ago. Pulling out the manilla folder, I hold them out to him. "I want a divorce."

The fire behind his gaze could burn me alive. "No."

Then the asshole yanks the folder out of my hand and slams the door in my face.

I pound on it, screaming his name. "Open up, Warren!"

"No one's home."

"This ain't funny." I bang my fist some more. It's a good thing I have several copies in case he tosses them. "You can't force me to stay married to you!"

I should've taken care of this after the third time he sent them back. It's a process to do a default divorce, but I kept hoping he'd come to his senses and make it easy on me.

It appears I was wrong.

"C'mon, let's talk like adults!" I shout louder.

Then he blasts music and turns off the lights.

"Real fuckin' mature," I mutter.

There's gotta be a way into this house.

Although it's nearly pitch black out with no motion lights, which is stupid, I use my phone flashlight to walk around the deck to check for a back door, but it's locked. Not wanting to give up after what it took for me to find his house in the first place, I go down the steps and find a patio door that leads to the lower level.

And it's unlocked.

Bingo.

Slowly, I slide it open and step into darkness. My flashlight leads me toward a staircase and I tiptoe up the stairs as quietly as my heels allow. Once I get to the top, I walk into what looks like a mudroom. Jackets and hats hang on the wall with dirty work boots on the floor.

I hold my breath, making my way into a hallway and searching for a light switch. The music blasting has me covering one side of my face while I hold my phone with the other hand.

"Whaddya think you're doin'?"

The deep, rough voice in my other ear causes me to jump out of my skin. "Jesus Christ, Warren!"

Spinning around too fast, I lose my balance when my heel

twists and has me reaching out for support. Warren grabs me before I can fall to my knees and holds me up.

"Shit," he mutters. "You alright?"

"Can you turn that down?" I shout once I'm standing confidently.

He yanks out his phone and presses an app on the screen to shut it off, then the only sound left is the blood rushing to my ears.

With a few more taps, the hall lights come on.

He's only six inches from my face and it's the closest we've been in years, yet there's a pang of familiarness that seeps into my heart.

"I think you woke up my chickens," he finally says once the silence lingers too long.

"Your music did that," I retort, hearing them make noise from the coop.

He huffs, but I catch his gaze dropping to my mouth before he asks, "What're you doin' here, Maze?"

"It's *Maisie*. And we need to talk."

He scoffs at me for correcting him. Maze was a special nickname only he called me and hearing him say it like we're twenty-one again doesn't feel right.

"And what?" He stuffs his hands in his pockets, looking smug. "You lost my number?"

"Would you have picked up if I'd called?" I cross my arms over my chest, matching his attitude.

He lifts a shoulder, keeping his gaze on mine. "Depends."

I blow out an exasperated breath. "Look, I don't wanna fight with you. But this—" I wave a finger between our bodies that somehow feel closer than a moment ago. "—is long over. Why drag it out longer than it already has?"

"'Cause we promised *forever*, and unlike some people, I take my vows seriously."

My brows pull together as I wonder *how seriously* he's been taking them. "Warren…" I pinch the bridge of my nose. "We've been separated longer than we were married. We're two completely different people now. Isn't it time we move on?"

"Looks like you already have." He nods toward my left hand with my engagement ring on it.

"Yes," I murmur, dropping my arm and swallowing hard. "He doesn't know I'm still married, so that's why I need you to sign the papers this time and get it finalized quietly."

"So…" The corner of his lips tilt up in a taunting grin. "You need me to sign the divorce papers so you can marry another man, who doesn't know you're married to me? Did I get that right?"

His amused tone makes my heart sink because I can tell he's going to fight against it even harder now. I debated on telling him but it didn't sit right with me to lie about it either. He would've eventually found out anyway.

I'm already being dishonest to my fiancé, which makes me feel like a horrible person as it is. He has more traditional values and is sixteen years older than me. I panicked he'd end things if he knew I was legally married, so I didn't say anything. The longer time went by without telling him, the harder it was to figure out how to tell him. It wasn't until he unexpectedly proposed last year that it became a bigger concern.

"We haven't been together in seven years, Warren," I remind him. "I sent you divorce papers five times!"

Twice since I've been engaged.

"And you finally figured out I wasn't gonna sign 'em. What makes you think I'll sign 'em now?"

My shoulders slump, sucking in a breath to calm my nerves so I don't lose my cool.

"'Cause I'm askin' you to let me go," I say above a whisper, hoping he'll see how much this hurts. "Let me move on."

His jaw ticks and my gaze lowers to his stretched-out hand before he balls it into a fist.

"I can't."

"Why not?" I ask sincerely. "Don't you wanna be happy again?"

"I was happy. You made me happy. *We* were happy."

"That was a long time ago, Warren. We aren't those people anymore."

"You didn't—" He blurts before abruptly stopping, inhaling a sharp breath, and turning away from me.

It's then I look around him and notice our wedding photos hung on the wall. Beaming smiles and heart eyes. We were so in love.

Why would he put those up?

My heart races remembering that day.

The perfect summer wedding.

My parents fought me every step of the way, but I was determined to marry the love of my life. Although they tried to talk me out of it, they paid for everything, and made sure it lived up to the Callaway standard—over-the-top flashy and expensive.

"You didn't gimme a chance. *Us* a chance." His pained eyes meet mine. "We were married for just over a year before you left —nine of those months long-distance. Then, you left four months later. Hell, we were still in the honeymoon phase when you packed your things!"

"I begged you to come with me!" I throw up my arms, defeated that we're arguing about something long over.

"To do what?" He raises his voice slightly. "What the hell was a rancher gonna do in a big city?"

"You could've gotten a different job, if you wanted us to stay together, you woulda tried harder."

"Oh, now I didn't try hard enough? Callin' and textin' all the time, supportin' your dream while mine were being crushed, that wasn't tryin' hard enough?"

"You know what I mean," I say between ragged breaths. "You only visited once."

He flew up a month after I moved there and only stayed for four days.

"And you worked most of the time I was there," he deadpans. "What woulda been the point?"

"To be with me when I wasn't workin'. To let me show you what our lives could be if you gave it a chance. You woulda grown to like it. If it meant stayin' together, you woulda put in the effort, but you didn't."

This isn't the first time we had this fight. But it's exhausting, nevertheless.

After two months of not seeing each other and rarely speaking, I came home for Christmas and told him if he had no plans of trying to make it work long-distance, then we were over. There was no point in dragging it out seven hundred miles apart.

He admitted he hoped I'd get the job "out of my system" and return home.

That's when I knew we were over for good.

I wanted to pursue my dream and he refused to leave his family's ranch.

"We talked about our future for years and none of the possibilities had us movin' to New York. You threw me a curveball, then made me the villain when I didn't immediately jump on board."

My nostrils flare. "That's not fair and you know it."

He *knew* I wanted that apprenticeship and to find a long-term job in publishing, but I had to start at the bottom and you can't do that in a small mountain town. I got lucky that they offered me a social media marketing position a year later. That one turned into finding my career path as a literary agent at an agency, which led me to start my own company last year. It was all about in-person networking and that couldn't have happened here.

"Neither is life, darlin', but here we are."

I roll my eyes at his harsh tone.

"Now that we've rehashed why our marriage failed, why won't you sign the papers? Besides being engaged to someone else, I'm not movin' back here, so there's no chance for us. If you don't, I'll end up filin' for a default divorce anyway." My voice cracks as I continue, "Either way, it's over."

But since I waited too long, I risk it not going through before the wedding date. There's also a thirty-day period where Warren could appeal the divorce decree, which is why this will go so much smoother if he'd sign them.

Looking back, I should've done it years ago. Although I continued sending him the papers, I wasn't in a rush since I wasn't actively dating. Starting my own business and being with my fiancé didn't leave me a lot of free time to focus on it. Warren was being stubborn for no reason, but once I got engaged, I had to get it figured out.

He pops his lips, then gives me a wicked smile. "You do that then."

"Warren, *please*." I grind my molars, resisting the urge to lash out. "I'm not askin' for anything from you but this one thing. It should be a simple process. Hayes and I are gettin' married in four months, so can't we be adults about this?"

Warren's brow arches at the sound of another man's name I hadn't meant to let slip. He bows his head, locks his hands behind his back, and leans in. "There's the door…" He nods around me. "Let yourself out, would ya? It's past my bedtime."

"I'll come back, ya know? I'm not leavin' without those papers signed," I say firmly.

He walks backward, looking smug as shit as he creates more distance between us. "Just to be safe, you might wanna wait on sendin' out Save the Date's."

When he winks, I want to scream.

This isn't over. I'll make him *beg* to divorce me once I inconvenience his life the way he's done to me.

I walk down the hallway and into the darkness of another room that leads to the front door before his voice catches my attention.

"Oh, and Maze?"

I turn around at the sound of my old nickname and wince that I do it out of habit.

"I'll be lockin' my patio door from now on, so don't try to sneak back in."

chapter three

Warren

I WATCH as her rearview lights disappear through the trees and wonder if she'll make good on her threat of coming back or not.

But most importantly, do I want her to?

No.

Yes.

Maybe.

Not to force those papers on me, but to see *her* again? Even if we're arguing, it's better than nothing.

Staring at the manilla folder I swiped from her, I leave them on the coffee table, not sure what to do with them. I read them the first time they were delivered, but didn't bother the next four times she sent them.

I've thought about this day countless times. What it'd feel like seeing her again after all these years apart and if the spark between us would still be there.

She's changed some, but overall, she's still my Maze— headstrong, determined, fiery.

Her soft hazel eyes that compliment her brown hair, which always looked lighter under the sun, and pouty lips I struggled to look away from, were all familiar. She's changed in the way she dresses, but I don't necessarily hate it. However, it surprised me.

Maisie was always ready to go on horseback rides, hiking, or swimming, which means she'd never wear skirts. Sundresses maybe, but mostly jean shorts and boots.

Grabbing my phone, I call my cousin before I do something I'll regret—like get wasted and drunk dial her.

Landen lives two hours away on his own family's ranch and retreat. Where our resort focuses more on relaxation and helping couples reconnect through outdoor and indoor activities, theirs is for family getaways and kid-friendly.

Being the same age, we grew up close, but I also get along with his four siblings. When we were kids, they'd visit every summer for a couple weeks and we'd camp out in tents or sleep in our trucks—causing trouble most of the time.

During spring break our senior year, he came with a group of friends to hang out for the week. Unfortunately for him, his ex-girlfriend tagged along and what was supposed to be their final night of fun, turned tragic when Angela pushed their other friend off the fifty-foot cliff. We were taking turns jumping into the waterfall and when Talia wouldn't jump, Angela took it upon herself to push her over the ledge.

When she didn't swim up to the surface, we knew something was wrong.

Her body was found two hours later.

It rocked our community and everyone here at the ranch. Although I'd only met Talia that week, it still affected me knowing she died on our property.

I've swam in the Willow Falls River for nearly my whole life.

It's the same location I proposed to Maisie.

To make matters worse, Talia's boyfriend ended his life from the immense guilt and grief he felt. Guilt for not protecting her from Angela, who kept pressuring Talia to jump, and grief for losing the love of his life.

Tucker was also Landen's childhood best friend.

He lost a lot that summer and it affected him for years.

Fortunately, Angela was charged with voluntary manslaughter and sentenced to fifteen years in prison.

But then nine days ago, we found out Angela's eligible for parole after only serving eleven years. The lawyers suggested everyone who testified against her and made character witness statements should write a letter to the parole board, so we've been making plans to write a joint statement. He and his other friends who were also there that summer are supposed to come up here soon, but now I'm not sure that's going to happen.

"Which planet is outta sorts right now makin' everyone extra crazy?" he picks up without a proper greeting and it throws me so off-guard, I stumble over my words.

"Um...Earth?"

He barks out a laugh. "Touché."

"Should I even ask?"

"Just a rough day. So what's goin' on?"

"Maisie just showed up at my door," I blurt without thinking. Though I don't plan to tell him every detail since I've hardly talked about her to him in the past several years. If I do, the rest of my family and cousins will know within twenty-four hours. Landen loves to gossip.

"Excuse me?" He chokes through a coughing fit. "*Maisie*? Your ex-wife, Maisie?"

"Yep…" Now here's the part he's going to flip over. "Except, she ain't my ex-wife. We're still married."

"I'm only on my first beer, so I know I ain't drunk and heard ya wrong. Y'all didn't get divorced?"

"She wanted to. I didn't."

I never announced it because I didn't want to deal with the line of questioning that'll prompt me to admit I've never gotten over her.

"She coulda filed without you. There's laws or some shit that'd allow her to get one even if you don't sign," he responds.

"I know. And yet, she didn't."

Which is why I still think there's a chance although she's convinced we're over for good.

"So why is she back? Did you tell her about Angela's parole hearing?"

"Not yet. She's engaged and needs me to sign so she can go marry another man. Doesn't want him to know she's been married all this time, so she needs me to sign and get it finalized quietly," I explain, not even bothering to hide the pain in my voice.

"Fuck. I'm sorry, Warren. What'd you say?"

Blowing out a breath, I give him the quick version. "I said no and slammed the door on her."

"I can only imagine how pissed off that made her."

"Shoulda heard her screamin' at me and poundin' on the wood. Really fired her up when I blared my music and turned off all the lights in the house. Pretty sure she woke up my chickens."

I leave out the part where she snuck in or how close we were before I walked away. He's pitying me enough as it is.

"Jesus Christ." He chuckles. "But it's been like what, seven years? Why do you wanna make her stay married to you? She has her own life seven hundred miles away."

Inhaling a shaky breath, I contemplate his question and how to answer without sounding like a sappy idiot.

"'Cause she's the love of my life." I go with pure honesty. "The only woman I've loved or will love. How can I just let her go?"

"Maybe it's time for you to move on. She's livin' her life. You should be, too."

"I wish I knew how." I sigh because it's easier said than done.

Wanting to take the attention off me, I ask, " "How're things goin' with you?"

"Well..." He half-laughs, and I'm intrigued before he continues. "The girl I've crushed on for four years still hates my guts. No matter what I do to get her attention or simply talk to her, she always finds a way to make me feel two-inches tall. And the worst part? I have no idea why."

"There must be a reason. What'd you do?"

"I dunno, and she refuses to tell me. I was flirtin' with her a few days ago, ya know being my charmin' self..."

I snort because I do know.

Landen Hollis is a playboy who gets every girl he wants. Except this one, apparently.

"And she snapped at me. Told me to leave her alone, she's not playin' hard to get and she's not gonna tell me why she hates me."

"Sounds like she knocked your ego down a few pegs."

He scoffs. "Maybe."

I laugh and it feels good after what happened within the past hour.

"Except, when we all ended up at The Lodge for lunch that

afternoon, she started chokin' on her food. In that millisecond of seein' the panic in her eyes and her face go red, I forgot every mean thing she's ever said to me and went into action. I rushed over and gave her the Heimlich maneuver."

"Oh shit." I gasp. "She alright?"

"Yeah, a bit in shock, but overall she's fine."

"What happened after?"

"We finished eatin', but later when I went into the barn, she stopped to thank me."

"Oh, did she?" I taunt.

"She attempted to anyway…" He cackles. "But I made her say what she was thankin' me for since she was actin' so weird about sayin' the words. That earned me an eye roll."

"Gee…I wonder why she hates you," I deadpan.

"Mhm. Well, I didn't want her thinkin' she was special or anythin' since she loves to tear me down, so I told her it was my oath to help anyone in need 'cause of my EMS trainin'. Couldn't let her know I was panickin' about her chokin' to death."

"Of course not 'cause that's not manly at all," I drawl, amused at Landen's definition of *flirting*.

"It doesn't matter anyway. After thankin' me, she let it be known she still didn't like me."

"Ouch."

"Yeah, but then I responded how I didn't like her either."

"Which was obviously a lie…"

"Obviously."

"So what's your next step in makin' her fall for you?" I ask, leaning back on my couch and propping my feet up on the coffee table. I'd rather hear about his shitty love life than think about mine.

"The northeast pasture still needs the fence fixed," I tell Bodie, looking through my checklist the next morning. It's not one we use very often so we've been putting it off but whenever there's time in our schedules to work on it, the sky opens up and downpours. The metal posts along the property line are rusty and need to be replaced up there as well, but that's an even bigger job.

"I'll put it on my list for next week," he tells me the same thing he said last Friday.

"Don't forget," I say firmly.

The one time we're going to need it is when it won't be fixed and then we'll be screwed.

"I'll ride out there today and check what we need so I can make sure we have the supplies." It's off-road so it's easier to horseback up there versus driving. I could take the four-wheeler, but riding helps me clear my head.

"You want me to go with you? It might be a swamp and a little dangerous."

"Aw...you worried about me?"

I huff a laugh when he rolls his eyes.

"Nothin' I haven't done before," I reassure him.

Since Bodie and I work on the ranch side, we look out for each other, but with him being younger, it's usually me keeping an eye on him.

"Can you grab me some horse tack while I get Priest out?" I ask him.

He's one of the best trail horses we have at the stables, but I often use him for riding when I need to go further up the mountains. So even if the conditions of the pasture aren't ideal, he won't be fazed by it.

The Willow Peak Stables are between The Branch Haven and the Willow Chalet. There's a corral in the front of the barn and an area behind it with horse rails for the guests to saddle up before they go riding. They're required to go with a tour guide, so there's always staff and ranch hands walking around the area, but guests are free to ride whenever they want within riding hours.

The other horse barn is on the ranch side where we board other people's horses. Some are for racing or show, but the majority are personal horses for people who live in the city or don't have land to keep them.

It brings in a good chunk of extra income but can be a pain in my ass in terms of paperwork and sending invoices.

Since my office is located at the stables, that's where I spend most of my time, although I go back and forth as needed.

"Uh...Warren?" Bodie's hesitant voice grabs my attention, and when I look at him with the tack in his arms, he's staring at something near the doors.

"What is it?"

The spell finally breaks and he blinks. "It's...Maisie, I think?"

He hasn't seen her since he was fourteen, so I'm not surprised he'd be hesitant.

My gaze darts to where he was transfixed a moment ago, and sure enough, there she is looking like a lost puppy as she scans the area for me.

I'm hunched down on the other side of Priest where he's cross-tied in the aisle, so she can't see me, but I can see her.

"What's she doin' here?" Bodie murmurs, tossing the saddle blanket over Priest's back.

I lower my body so she's no longer in my view. "She showed up at my house last night, but I sent her away."

He doesn't need to know the specifics either.

"Does she wanna reconcile?"

Blowing out a stressed breath, I shake my head and keep my voice down. "No, she wants a divorce."

His eyes widen to saucers, and it's then I realize how many people don't realize we're still married. To be fair, it's not like I announced it either.

"Warren?" she calls out.

"He's over here!" The traitorous asshole shouts.

"What the fuck, man?" I hiss, standing to my full height.

He doesn't respond, but the wicked grin across his face tells me everything I need to know.

He wants to witness this shit-show front and center. He's as much a gossip as Landen.

"What're you doin' here?" I bark once we make eye-contact.

She licks her lower lip before coming toward me, and it's then, I notice her outfit.

"What the fuck are you wearin'?" My eyes scan down the length of her in a pantsuit and heels. The complete opposite of what you should wear inside a barn.

Her eyes lower to her brown blazer and navy-blue dress slacks.

"It's casual chic," she says as if I should know what that means.

I snort. "If you say so."

"Never mind my outfit. We need to talk." She puts her hands on her hips as if that'll make her look more intimidating.

"Too bad, I'm workin'." I make a show of attaching the saddle to Priest's back and then grab the rest of what I need so I can leave.

"I'm here for two weeks, Warren." The bite in her tone makes the hair on the back of my neck stand up. "Which means I'll continue showin' up and buggin' you until we discuss our divorce."

"Hard pass." I continue what I'm doing without making eye contact, but she pushes herself between me and the horse, forcing me to take a step back at her close proximity.

"Or you can sign the papers now and I'll get outta your hair." She raises a brow, crossing her arms.

Pinching my lips to the side, I pretend to contemplate her offer. "Temptin', truly...but I'm gonna have to go with *no*."

"Goddammit, Warren!" She hisses between her teeth. "Why do you make me be mean to you?"

"It's my kink." Shrugging, I wink before I un-tie Priest and guide him away from her.

"You're seriously gonna leave right now?"

"I'm workin', Maze!" I face her, my neck getting hot. "Did you expect me to drop everythin' for you? I can't just take a break 'cause you finally returned after seven years." My words come out harsh, but I can't seem to stop the anger from pouring out.

"Fine. Let me go with you and we can talk while you..." She waves her arm toward Priest. "Do whatever you're doin'."

"You're gonna ride in those atrocious heels?" I raise a challenging brow.

"There's extra boots in the tack room," Bodie blurts, and I avert my gaze to his, hoping he sees the daggers I'm shooting at him.

"That works for me," Maisie says.

"Fine," I spit out between clenched teeth. "But you better keep up. I'm headin' north to check the fence."

"This ain't my first rodeo, cowboy." She plants her hands on her hips. "I've been on horses plenty of times before."

"Coulda fooled me," I say, scanning my eyes down her outfit again.

"Yes, I know I'm not dressed for it, but that doesn't mean I can't do it."

I shake my head, taking the boots from Bodie when he brings them over. "As long as you don't complain about 'em gettin' dirty or some shit."

"I'm not the stuck-up city girl you think I am. I can handle it."

I nod my head toward the stall behind her. "Lean back and gimme your foot."

She furrows her brows until I'm kneeling in front of her, motioning for her to lift a heel.

When she does, I pull off her shoe and slide on the boot, then stare up at her while she watches me tighten the strings.

She swallows hard when we don't break eye contact. "I coulda done this myself."

Instead of responding, I finish that boot and then set it down. "Next one."

Licking her lips, she lifts her other foot, and I go through the same process. Except this time, I keep my eyes transfixed on hers while my fingers do the work.

There's a thickness in the air and it's not from the dust blowing up.

"How do they feel?" I ask once both feet are on the ground.

She shifts from side to side. "They'll do."

I stand and find a horse for her to ride.

"This is Lilith," I tell her, shifting my gaze to Bodie who's shaking his head at me for giving her the demon horse. "Do you remember how to put on a saddle?"

"I'm sure I'll figure it out," she bites out.

Bodie returns with more tack and we watch as she fumbles her way through attaching it. Every time she attempts to put the bit in Lilith's mouth, she gets nipped.

"Should we help her?" he leans over and whispers.

"Nope," I pop out the word, keeping my attention on her.

"I thought you were in a hurry," he muses, and I nudge him with my elbow to shut up.

A few other ranch hands walk around, giving us weird looks, but I subtly shake my head for them not to ask.

Another five minutes go by before I take pity on her.

I spin my ball cap around and murmur in her ear, "Need an assist?"

She jumps at the sound of my voice.

"Jesus. You scared me." She blows out a breath. "Yes, I-I can't remember all the steps. I think I put the reins on backward."

Instead of gloating that she needs my help, I talk her through the rest of the steps and double-check everything before she climbs on.

"Good?" I ask, handing her the reins.

She wiggles in the seat and nods. "I think so."

"Great." I pet Lilith before jumping on Priest. "Let's go."

chapter four

Maisie

ADMITTEDLY, I might've oversold how much I remember about riding horses, but I wanted to prove him wrong.

I might be a city girl now, but I'm a country girl at heart.

Warren's determined to do this the hard way, so I have to keep up with his antics if I want him to sign the damn papers.

He's stubborn and I don't want to hurt him, but I only have a couple weeks to convince him. My brother and sister-in-law's baby shower is next weekend, so I already planned to come for that. Since Hayes and I are getting married in the next town over, being here makes it easier to coordinate with my mom and the wedding coordinator on things we still need to decide. This was the best time to fly down and face Warren without Hayes getting suspicious.

When he got down on one knee and proposed, I hadn't expected it. It was a lovely surprise, but I knew I could no longer drag my feet on getting it done.

There's a real fear that Warren won't sign. If I go the default divorce route, it's a risk he'll appeal it and drag it out even longer. Most people wait for that period to pass before getting married again, but I might not have a choice—assuming it goes through on time.

At that point, I'd tell Hayes the truth so he's not blindsided if things go to shit. He'll be pissed and disappointed, but if our love is as strong as I think it is, he'll understand and forgive me.

Hayes is an established epic fantasy author and his online fanbase is protective of him. When he shared a photo of us on his social media for the first time, some of his fans were brutal. They commented about my looks and age while others made threats if I became the reason he didn't finish a series or didn't release his next book fast enough. Or if it was bad, they'd point the finger at me for being bad juju.

It's why I never revealed the truth because if people found out that I'm still legally married while dating him, they could use it against him and it'd tarnish his beloved reputation. After all the sacrifices to get where he is, I couldn't risk his career.

Or mine.

I use my maiden name for my literary agency, so there's no connection when people search me online, but it's why I'm careful not to post too many personal details. Living in New York City, he attends book events for each release tour and his readers usually recognize me when I tag along.

He hired a professional photographer to hide nearby to take our proposal pictures, and as soon as he posted them, his circle of the internet blew up.

Everyone was noisier than usual about who I am, where I'm from, and what I do for a living. It was invasive, to say the least. My anxiety has spiked each day since then wondering if today's the day someone goes all detective mode to find out the truth.

It's why I need to get this done.

Following Warren out of the barn, I try to relax on the saddle and move with the horse, but I think she can feel me tense. She abruptly stops as we approach the trail.

I click my tongue, encouraging her to go, but she stomps a hoof and stays in place.

Warren glances over his shoulder, noticing my predicament, and slows down.

"Give her a little kick," he tells me.

I do and nothing happens.

"C'mon, Lilith. Let's go," I say, squeezing my thighs to encourage her to move.

Warren comes over, riding next to me. "Get movin', girl." Then he gives her ass a slap.

Without warning, Lilith takes off and in my scramble to hang on, I lose my grip on the reins. I tighten my legs and fall forward, holding on for dear life, and forgetting everything about what to do when a horse runs off like this.

My heart races at the thought of being thrown off or falling to my death and I squeeze tighter.

Warren whistles at his horse to catch up and then he's next to me, keeping the pace, and reaching over to grab the fallen reins.

"Whoa, Lilith." He gains control, and we slowly come to a stop.

His gaze finds mine, but his are hard to read.

"You okay?" he asks, but before I can respond, he adds, "Squeezin' your thighs tells her to go faster. You need to relax."

I release my death grip, then push myself back up into a sitting position and take the reins from him.

"I think she has a death wish for me."

Warren's horse starts walking, prompting mine to do the same. But this time I remember to keep my legs loose over her.

"Well, we don't call her Lilith for no reason."

My eyes widen at the realization he gave me a spitfire on purpose and he cracks a smile, the first real one I've seen on him.

"I figured you hated me but didn't realize you wanted me dead."

His expression softens. "I could never hate you, Maze." Then he smirks. "*Loathe*, maybe."

"Well...I definitely loathed you every time those papers returned without a signature."

"Figured you woulda gotten the hint."

I swallow down the lump in my throat. "Why're you makin' this so difficult?"

His gaze shifts and he stays silent, making me think he's not going to answer that, until he looks over. "You ever think you're the one makin' this difficult for *me*?"

The trail takes us higher into the mountains as his question simmers in my mind.

"I thought you knew it was over when neither of us were willin' to budge on the long-distance or movin' thing."

"I wasn't ready for it to be over. We didn't get a real shot."

My throat goes dry and words are caught in there before I can say them aloud. "Sometimes things don't work out. You can't hold onto the past forever. At some point, we need to move on with our lives and accept that it didn't go as planned."

His jaw twitches, but he doesn't speak again until we get to his destination.

"Careful, the ground is uneven up here."

Lilith follows his horse's lead as he trots near the fence.

"Shit, it's worse than I thought."

Glancing over to see what Warren's looking at, I notice metal posts bent in half and some tilted in the wrong direction. It's probably not a huge deal since they don't keep the horses up here anymore, but it's still dangerous to keep it that way with guests trail riding up here.

Warren takes some pictures and then leads us to another area that's closer to the property line. It's not much better.

"I'll probably yank out those other posts so no one gets hurt," he mutters more to himself. "These others I can replace."

"When are you plannin' to work on it?" I ask, wondering if he'll use it as an excuse to avoid me.

"Bodie said next week, but I'd be surprised if he does it. He's been puttin' it off, so I might do it myself if I can find the time."

I nod, riding next to him down the trail.

"Are—"

"Do you—"

We blurt the words at the same time when the silence gets awkward.

"Go ahead," I tell him.

"I was gonna ask if you wanted a tour."

"Of what?"

"The ranch. A lot has changed since you've been here."

"Really?"

He shrugs. "Posey started a goat soap business and we built a new shed for 'em all."

"You have goats? Oh my gosh, yes. I'd love to see 'em."

He chuckles. "Shoulda known that'd work on you."

"Well…who doesn't love goats?" I hesitantly laugh because we're not fighting for once, but I doubt it'll last. "How many do y'all have?"

"I think she's up to a dozen now."

"Wow. A whole goat farm."

"Posey will probably be there, if you're okay with that," he tells me cautiously.

"I am if you are."

He lifts a shoulder. "I'm sure Bodie's texted the sibling group chat by now anyway."

Not sure what to think about that, if that's good or bad, but I don't ask.

It doesn't take long to get to the shed, and I beam at how cute it is. Some of the goats are grazing and unphased by our arrival, but as soon as Warren and I climb off our horses, Posey bursts out and rushes toward me.

"Oh my God!" She wraps me in a hug before I can brace for it and nearly fall to the ground.

Laughing, I cling to her and pull back when she does.

"Maisie! I can't believe you're here."

With her only being two years younger, we became friends when Warren and I started dating. She was thirteen, but we went to the same high school and had some classes together. Whenever I'd come to see Warren, she'd fight for me to hang out with her instead. She was the little sister I never had.

But we didn't stay in contact after I left for New York the second time.

That's the sad reality when your relationship ends.

His parents and siblings were like a second family to me, and I haven't seen them in years.

"You're all grown up!" I beam.

In one word, Posey's adorable. She's petite with long blonde hair and a baby face. Although I'm certain she gets highlights to lighten her hair because it wasn't always this blonde.

Either way, she looks amazing.

"Yep...but in my case, twenty-seven and still single."

I snort when she pouts.

"No one's put a ring on your finger yet?"

As soon as the words come out of my mouth, Warren tenses next to me.

Shit.

"Nope, not even close. Every time I go out with my friends, the only eligible bachelors we meet are forty-year-old men who 'aren't ready to settle down yet.'" Her eye twitches as her fingers do air quotes.

"That's unfortunate. Maybe you need to branch out of your small town."

"You're probably right, but I'm booked and busy." She casually lifts her shoulders. "I've tried datin' apps a couple times but they're worse than the men I meet in real life."

I wince remembering the one time I tried a dating app before I met Hayes.

"Gonna show her around?" Warren asks, getting impatient. "I still have work to finish."

"Relax, grumpy pants." Posey scrunches her nose at his growly tone, but she takes my hand and drags me away while Warren stays by the horses.

"Batman, no!" Posey scolds one of the goats chewing on a boot.

"Batman?" I muse.

"Yep, and Robin's here somewhere. They're trouble-makers."

Posey shows me her soap making area and gives me a brief summary of the process. It's quite fascinating and honestly sounds fun.

"If you ever move back, I could always use the help..." Posey singsongs. "I need like four extra hands at this point."

I'm not sure what she knows about why I'm here or that I'm engaged, but I don't want to be the one to burst her bubble.

"I'll keep that in mind."

Walking around, I pet some of the goats, but then I'm hit with Déjà vu. Warren used to take me to street fairs and farmer's markets where they had petting zoos. It's probably why he knew I'd want to see their goats. Although my parent's house is on a good chunk of land, we never had any farm animals, and that's why I loved coming here. There was always something fun to do.

Before we say goodbye, I give her another hug.

"It was so good seein' you. Thanks for showin' me around. Looks awesome."

"Thank you! And it was so amazin' to see you too. Don't become a stranger."

"I won't," I say sincerely.

"Oh wait, Warren…" Posey grabs his attention before he climbs on his horse. "Did you show her the house?"

Warren tenses, shaking his head firmly.

"What house?" I ask.

"Warren built it after you moved away. It took him years to finish, but it's gorgeous. The large wraparound deck is my favorite, but there's a huge library room on the lower level, a ginormous tub he *never* shares, a fireplace in the living room and big kitchen. Oh, and—"

"Posey, zip it."

My heart plummets into my stomach at the descriptions she mentioned.

I think back to when I walked through his house last night but it was too dark to see anything. The only light was my phone's flashlight and in the hallway once he turned it on. But when I walked to the front door, the rest of the house was pitch black.

Did he build our dream house?

It'd explain why he hung our wedding photos on the wall, but it's hard to comprehend why he'd do that after I left.

Warren gets on his horse and starts moving before I'm on Lilith. Once I'm settled, I give her a little kick to catch up to them.

"Hey, wait up."

He glances over, his expression unreadable, but he lifts a brow.

"You built the house we talked about?"

"Yeah." His voice is low, but there's a roughness in his tone.

"Can...I see it?"

He averts my gaze and nods.

There's something in his features that makes my chest ache. Like his guard is no longer up and all that's left is...pain.

chapter five

Warren

SHOWING the woman the house I built for her after all these years is harder than I thought it'd be.

I can't get my heart to settle down, but I push down the nerves and follow through.

Maisie's dream board stuck with me, and although she left, I still wanted the house we discussed.

And a part of me hoped it'd bring her back to me.

She'd see what a life together could look like and pick us over her career hundreds of miles away.

But I never found the courage to tell her I built it.

When we got married, we lived in a small trailer behind my parent's house. We were adjusting to living together for the first time since she graduated and moved back. It wasn't much, but we made it our own while we dreamed up what our future home would be.

Her parents hated it. They wanted to buy her a new construction with zero charm or character, and as much as they tried to convince her, we said no.

It's another reason I think they encouraged her so hard to take the apprenticeship. I know Maisie wanted it, but they helped her pay for whatever she needed that was out of her budget. We had a joint bank account but not even my monthly salary would cover her rent. If her parents weren't so willing to pay her way, she would've had to stay.

And yeah, that's a douche thing to think about when it was her dream, but when she got a permanent job offer, they're the ones who sent her even more money to make sure she had the fancy clothes and nicer apartment.

I couldn't compete with that.

I could only hold onto the hope that she'd realize starting a life with me was once her dream too.

"Wow, Warren…" Her eyes widen when the A-frame comes into view. Now that it's daylight, she can see the large windows and deck. "It's even more stunnin' than the photos on my board."

"I agree. Pictures don't do it justice."

"You built this by yourself?" She looks at me in awe.

"Well, after a developer came out and got the land ready. My dad helped with the framing and floors, then I hired contractors for the electrical and plumbin'. Then I did the rest."

The corner of her lips tilt up sweetly. "Can I see the inside?"

Inhaling deeply, I nod.

We climb off our horses, and I tie them to a tree before walking up the staircase that leads to the front door. I lift one of my plants and reveal the hideaway key.

"Seriously?" she deadpans.

I grin, laughing. "Don't get any ideas. I'll hide it under a different plant now."

She snorts.

Once I get the door open, I hold it for her and motion for her to go inside.

I follow as she walks into the living room and takes it all in.

"I can't believe how beautiful this is. It's so much better than I imagined it'd be."

Even though it has the cozy vibes and fireplace she wanted, it's still cold without her warmth added to it. She loved decorating, candles and picture frames, but the only photos I have are the ones of us.

I lead her to the kitchen and get a similar reaction.

"Do you cook here a lot?"

"Yeah, I taught myself after Aunt JoJo kept bringing frozen lasagnas and casseroles 'cause she was worried I wasn't eatin' real food. Finally decided it was time to learn, so I took an online class and bought some cookbooks."

Aunt Josephine's a chef and manages the Summit Views Restaurant on the resort side. It's a classy place for couples to have a romantic evening, and since each reservation includes one free dinner, it's always busy.

"That's awesome. I bet you're a good cook too. I can only make food that comes out of a box or can."

She was the one who wanted a kitchen big enough for us to cook together, so that surprises me she never learned. It's not her fault she never did growing up since she was raised with housekeepers and chefs in her parents' house.

I walk up behind her and murmur close to her ear, "Want me to cook somethin' for you? A Southern home cooked meal. You remember those, dontcha?"

She shivers before looking over her shoulder and meeting my

hard gaze. Hers drop to my lips and she swallows hard before her eyes find mine again. "I don't wanna inconvenience you."

My head's screaming, *inconvenience me! Do it! Stay here and never leave.*

"I'm the one who offered," I reply instead. "C'mon, I'll show you the rest of the house and I'll make us lunch."

"Okay," she says softly.

Deciding against my better judgment, I grab her hand and lead her down the hall to the rooms. When she doesn't yank it away, I squeeze tighter and a shiver rolls down my spine at touching her again.

"This is the spare room that we said we'd use as a nursery, but since you wanted to work in publishing, I made it into an office instead."

There's a desk and chair facing the large window with bookcases on either side of the plain walls.

"Why's it empty? You don't use it?"

"'Cause it was meant to be yours. I use the one at the stables and leave work at work, so I don't need one here."

She blows out a breath. "Wish I knew that feelin'."

That makes me wonder if she ever does anything for herself or if her life revolves around her job.

"You should put some books in there. Or paintings on the walls," she suggests.

"I keep my books downstairs in the library."

She spins around, her wide eyes locked on mine. "You really built a library?"

"It's not full or anythin', but I put in built-in shelves so that you had room to store all your books. I figured you had so many already and will continue to buy 'em, so I wanted you to have the proper space."

She chews on her bottom lip, and I'm tempted to pluck it and ask what she's thinking.

"I have most of mine in storage at my parents'. My apartments never had enough room and it seemed silly to keep movin' 'em around."

"Do you live with your fiancé now?"

"Yeah, but I didn't wanna go through the hassle of gettin' 'em shipped up there and takin' up space. Plus, they're from when I was in high school and college. Most of the books I read now are from submissions and queries."

"Hm. Interestin'..." I hide my disappointment.

The Maisie I knew would never be far from her books. Even when she didn't read 'em anymore, she always felt comforted with them around her. She'd pull them off her shelves, flip through the pages, and bring it to her nose to inhale the scent. When we'd hang out and she'd read, I'd smile at her expressions when she'd get to a big plot twist or reveal of some kind. I could watch her read for hours.

Every time she finished a book, she'd give me a full summary of everything that happened and if her theories were right or not. I loved that time we spent together, and even if we weren't talking, being near her was all I needed.

Considering she'd reread her favorites over and over, it's sad to know she's no longer near them.

"What is?" she asks, furrowing her brows.

Clearing my throat, I say, "Nothin'. C'mon, this way."

I walk down the hallway toward the master bedroom and into the en suite.

"Holy shit, this is huge!" She steps into the bathroom, her eyes focused on the deep tub. "I think this is bigger than my first apartment."

"Had to make it large enough to fit the tub."

"Do you use it a lot?"

"Only a few times."

"That's it?" She gasps, laughing, and the sound of it has me smiling wide. "I'd never leave. You'd have to pry me outta there."

That was my hope.

She walks around, looking at everything, opening drawers and cabinets, as if she's trying to find something. I silently follow when she goes into the walk-in closet.

"What?" I finally ask, curious about what she's thinking.

"There's no sign of another person livin' here. No extra toothbrush or clothes."

"No."

"I'm surprised."

"Why?"

Her shoulders lift casually but she averts her gaze as she continues snooping through my things. Not that I mind, so I don't bother stopping her.

"You're a catch, Warren. Figured you woulda had a special someone in your life by now."

"I've never brought anyone here. Besides my family, you're the only woman who's been inside my bedroom."

That grabs her attention, but her hard stare is hard to read. "Never?"

"Why would I bring another woman to my bed that was meant for my wife and me?"

"Warren…" The sound of my name on her lips sends a jolt of electricity through me, and I hate how badly I crave to hear it again.

Stepping closer, I bring my hand to her face and brush a

loose strand behind her ear. "I'd burn it down before I let another woman live here with me."

Hazel orbs burn through me but the wheels are turning through her mind.

"You have to move on," she demands above a whisper. "This ain't healthy."

I inch closer again, unable to keep my distance. "I can't."

"You deserve to be happy. But that can't come from me."

"Then I don't want it."

"Warren, please. I don't wanna hurt you more than I already have. We're not compatible anymore. Don't you wanna find—"

"I'd rather die alone than be with someone else."

"That's dramatic."

"It's the truth."

"You've not been with anyone else?"

I arch a brow at her question because I thought I was being fucking clear.

"No, Maze. I've only been with you. You were my first and last."

Her throat bobs and my own tightens. We're a breath apart, but I don't move, hoping she'll take the half-inch step to press her lips to mine.

"I should go."

She moves to step around me, but I grab her arm. "Wait, I owe you lunch."

"I'm not hungry."

"You don't wanna see the library?"

That causes her to pause. "Okay, but then I need to get home."

She's full of shit, but I don't call her out on it. Considering she's the one who sought me out and is on my ass to sign those papers, her wanting to bail means being near me is giving her conflicting feelings.

Seven years apart, and I can still tell when her body reacts to mine.

She follows me down to the lower level and when I flick on the lights, there's a sharp gasp behind me.

"Oh my God, Warren…" She walks ahead of me and toward the floor to ceiling shelves I painted a matte black.

Lights on top of each shelf angle down to spotlight the shelves, not that I have any books on there, but for when there is. On the far right is an attached sliding ladder so she could easily reach the top shelf.

"This is stunnin'…I—" She spins around, her mouth agape. "I love it."

It's impossible to contain the smile that takes over my face. "I hoped you would. You said you wanted a readin' nook but I knew you'd fill that up in no time."

"It's a shame it doesn't get used."

I point to my small stack of books on the table next to my recliner. "I'm too slow of a reader to fill it. I've been workin' on those for the past year."

Curiously, she lifts the first book and looks through the others but stops on the Hayden Wills novel I'm in the middle of reading.

"That's one of my favorite authors," I murmur, walking up behind her. "But it takes me a couple months to get through his since they're thicker."

His epic fantasies are over eight hundred pages with small ass text, but it means I always have something of his to read because there are several I haven't gotten to yet.

"Oh," is all she says before setting it down without going through the rest.

"I needed something to help me get out of my own head," I blurt.

She knows I wasn't much of a reader in high school but it got lonely sitting in this house all alone.

"He's a good writer," she says but there's a weird hesitancy in her voice.

"You know of him?"

She turns so we're facing each other. "Mhm. I'm a friend of his agent."

"Ah." That makes sense. She probably knows a lot of authors besides the ones she represents.

Her gaze finally lifts to mine. "You built this house as if you hoped it'd bring me back."

"Of course I did." I scratch over my scruffy cheek, contemplating how much to reveal when we're this close. "We made plans for our future, and I made a promise to build your dream house. Split up or not, I wasn't going back on my word."

Her teeth drag along her bottom lip as if she's trying to keep up with her thoughts. "I need you to understand that I'm not comin' back. You know that, right?"

I will hold onto hope until the day I die. "Sure."

"You need to decorate, fill up the empty space, and make it a home...*for yourself.* Open your heart to someone and give yourself permission to be happy. It's not too late."

Instead of telling her that'll never happen, I come up with an idea.

"I'll make you a deal."

She takes a small step back, crossing her arms and looking less than amused. "What kind of deal?"

"I'll do those things you said *if…*"

Her shoulders slump because she knows I'm about to make it harder for her to get those papers signed. *Good.*

I don't want to spend the rest of my life wondering about the what-if and if this is the only chance I get, I'm taking it. It's this or she files for a default divorce anyway.

"You gimme seven days to prove there's still somethin' between us."

Her arms fall to the side as she gapes at me. "That's ridiculous."

"It's only a week. We deserve the chance we never got after you left and shit hit the fan."

"A week isn't gonna change being apart for seven years or that I'm engaged to another man."

"How do you know if we don't try?" I challenge, hoping she'll take the bait.

"You think you can make me change my mind and fall back in love with you in seven days?"

When she says it like that, I sound as delulu as Nicky.

But fuck it.

"No, but I think I can make you second guess your decision in that timeframe. We aren't startin' from scratch. We have history. You fell in love with me once before, and I have no doubt I can remind you what it was like. I can show you what life would be like if you had stayed. Maybe I'm wrong, and it'll backfire, but maybe I'll be right. And hell, if I'm not, I'll sign those papers and you'll never hear from me again."

Her breath hitches but then something flashes across her face.

"You have nothin' to lose unless you're afraid I'll prove you wrong," I prompt when she doesn't give me an answer.

"You'll sign those papers after seven days? No bullshit?"

"No bullshit."

"I'm not cheatin' on my fiancé."

"I don't recall askin' you to, but if you wanna get technical, you were my wife first. Still *are* my wife. You're the one who's been cheatin' on me."

She resists rolling her eyes, but I can tell she wants to by her glare. "We're separated."

I purse my lips. "I don't remember agreein' to that or gettin' any documentation that you filed for a separation…"

She sucks in a slow breath, squeezing her eyes closed for a moment. "I didn't."

"So…accordin' to Tennessee law, we're legally married."

"By the law, yes…but I think not talkin' or seein' your spouse for years implies the separation."

"I'm just sayin'…there must've been a reason you never filed for one," I probe.

"There is, but it's not 'cause I didn't want one."

"How do you think your fiancé's gonna feel if he finds out he's been the homewrecker this whole time?"

She swats my chest, but there's no force behind it. "Can you stop being insufferable? You're the one who wouldn't sign the damn divorce papers!"

"Give me seven days and I will…" Then I smirk because getting a reaction from her is better than the silence she gave me for years. "But I'll be citin' adultery as the reason."

Her eyes harden, and I know I've pushed too far.

"Jokin'!" I hold up my palms in surrender, but I can't help the cackle that releases from my throat. "I'll sign whatever you want as long as you gimme this one chance."

Her tongue pokes through her cheek. It's one of her tells

she's thinking or frustrated. "As long as you're aware nothin' will happen between us."

The corner of my mouth tilts up slightly. "If you say so."

I don't give a fuck about her fiancé or the giant rock on her finger. Maisie was mine first and if she's agreeing to give me one week, I'm doing whatever it takes to get her back.

And if it blows up in my face, at least I'll be able to say I tried everything. Maybe then, I'll be able to let her go and move on.

chapter six

Maisie

I'M HAVING A NEUROLOGICAL EPISODE.

It's the only logical reason to explain why I agreed to his stupid deal, but it was also the only way he'd finally agree to sign the papers.

I can do this. It's only a week.

Then I'll get to relax and spend the rest of my time with my family before I fly home. I'll file the papers before I leave and wait for the settlement agreement to go through. Since we don't have kids and we're not splitting assets or asking each other for alimony, it should be a simple process. And hopefully quick. With an act of God, it'll be granted before Hayes' and my wedding date.

He's almost finished with his current novel, so being away for these two weeks will give him uninterrupted time to write, but he promised to check in at least once a day. He gets locked in for hours and doesn't always realize how long he's gone without eating or sleeping, so I always made sure to set timers.

Both of us being workaholics is why we mesh so well

together. Unless we have something specific planned in the evenings, we take a break to eat dinner together and sometimes watch a movie, but then we're back to working until bedtime. When he's in deadline mode, I usually sleep alone while he stays up for a few extra hours. Once he emails the manuscript to his editor, he can breathe easier and we'll make up for the lost time.

"Where've you been?" Mama asks when I walk through the front door and find her in one of the sitting rooms. My childhood house is the epitome of old Southern money and always felt more like a museum than a home.

"Had some errands to run."

"Mm. Did you see *him*?" Her eyes catch mine over the magazine she's reading.

I resist the urge to roll my eyes at her unwilling to say his name.

My parents are the only ones who know we're not divorced. They were never huge fans of him but even more so not after he continuously sent the papers back to their lawyer.

"Yes. We talked and went horseback ridin'."

She drops the magazine to her lap, brows raised. "You what?"

"He was workin' and it was the only way to get him to talk to me."

"In that?" She nods toward my outfit.

"He let me borrow a pair of boots," I explain quickly, not wanting to share the details of how he knelt in front of me and kept his hard gaze on me while he took off my shoes and tied on the boots. His stare was a mixture of loathing and lust.

"Okay, and what happened durin' this *talk*?"

The entire drive home I contemplated what to tell them because I knew their reaction wasn't going to be a good one.

"He said he'll sign 'em in a week." I hold my breath before blurting the rest. "As long as I spend time with him each day."

"I beg your pardon?"

My shoulders fall, taking the chair across from her. "He wants me to give him seven days to prove why we should get back together. I told him it was a wasted effort but it was the only way he'd agree to sign 'em."

"*Maisie.*" Her tone is sharp, the same way she'd say my name when I'd get into trouble as a teenager. "Why would you agree with his obvious attempt to manipulate you?"

I'm wondering the same damn thing.

"'Cause seven days is better than waiting another four to six months for a default divorce to go through. An uncontested divorce would take three. This way, he gets closure, and I can move on for good with Hayes."

I leave out the parts where Warren admitted he's not been with anyone else since me. The less she knows, the better. My parents mean well, *usually*…but they're known to be judgmental and that's the last thing I need from them right now.

She tsks, reclining back in her chair. "I knew that boy was trouble."

I snort. "He's not a boy anymore, Mama."

Oh no, he's a fully grown man who looks like he's never skipped a day at the gym. Except, the ranch are his machines and all the hard work he puts in has only added to his build.

I've always been attracted to him and we were mutually obsessed with each other, so that was never a problem in our relationship, but his unwillingness to budge at moving with me is what ultimately ruined everything.

"Don't tell your father about this," she warns. "He'll march over there and set him straight."

"Well, that wouldn't be a good idea," I say dryly. Not because I think Warren would fight him but it could prompt him to appeal the divorce and prolong it.

"I won't say anything," she says, mimicking buttoning her lips. "But you better be sure he signs 'em when the week is over. Movin' the weddin' date this close would humiliate the family. And you'd have to confess everything to Hayes. He might not be so forgivin' when he finds out the whole truth."

That's my worst fear.

Standing, I lean over and kiss her cheek. "I'll make sure he signs 'em, Mama."

Or at least he better.

I walk to the kitchen because I lied about not being hungry. After realizing how hung up on me he still is, I needed distance and room to breathe. He was too close, almost touching, and it was suffocating.

It's why I had to make it crystal clear I had no interest in reconciling our relationship nor was I leaving my fiancé. My life is in New York and we're happy.

"Hi, honey." I answer my phone when Hayes calls a few hours later.

"Hello, sweetheart. How're you?"

"Good. Readin' in bed." I stretch back against the headboard, setting the open book face down across my chest.

"A new manuscript?"

"No, actually. A book I used to read in high school. My parents have all my old ones and I was feelin' nostalgic."

"It's nice you're reading for yourself."

"Yeah." I smile.

Books have always been a healthy escape for me. Living under the pressure of my parents growing up, I needed an outlet that was just for me. Between the extracurriculars they pushed on me so my college applications looked good and countless charity events they dragged me to, I looked forward to sticking my nose in a fictional world I could pretend was my own.

"How's writin' going?"

"Great. I'm takin' a break to eat and then I'll probably continue until bedtime."

"I can't wait to read it," I gush. He doesn't let anyone see it until his editor goes through it, but it's always a treat when it's ready for me.

"Me too. I think it's my best work to date."

"Doesn't every writer say that?" I tease.

"But this time, I'm serious." He chuckles lightly. "Hoping to be done in a couple weeks, maybe sooner."

My mind goes back to the moment I saw his book in Warren's stack. It's one Hayes released before we started dating, but since then, I've managed to read all of them. It took a while since there's almost thirty. As soon as Warren said his favorite author is my future husband's pen name, the words caught in my throat and my heart pounded in pure panic.

If Warren found out, he'd be devastated.

I didn't want to give myself away or ruin his reading experience, so I tried not to react.

"Perfect, that means I'll get my fiancé back when I return."

"At least until I get my editorial letter."

That'll be at least a month, so I'll take what I can get.

"Just in time to finish some weddin' stuff when I get back."

"What's left that the event planner can't do?"

He's not been super active in the plans, but I don't mind. Since we're getting married here versus New York and both busy with work, it made sense to hire Nicola and let her handle the bigger details down here, but there are some things we need to do ourselves.

"Well…you still need to get fitted for your tux. We need to pick out our weddin' bands. Write our vows. Decide on which weddin' party gifts we wanna give the groomsmen and bridesmaids. Finish our registry. Maybe book our honeymoon?"

"As soon as I have my next tour dates," he reminds me.

The book he wrote last year releases in a few months. We'd already booked our venue when the release date was announced, so until his tour dates are set, we haven't been able to make plans. But I'm hopeful he'll find out soon.

"Right."

"Sorry, Maisie. My dinner's here. Talk tomorrow?"

"Sounds good. I love you."

"Love you."

I pick up my book again and read until my eyes close.

WARREN

Meet at my house at 5. No heels.

I roll my eyes. Of course he'd say that.

MAISIE

Are you gonna tell me what we're doing?

WARREN

Nope.

MAISIE

How do I know you're not going to take me
out to the woods, force me to dig a six-foot
grave, and push me inside it?

WARREN

Because it'd take you the whole week just to
dig the hole and I wouldn't waste seven days
on that.

MAISIE

Are you calling me weak?

WARREN

More like a city girl. You showed up on a ranch
in six-inch heels.

MAISIE

They were only four-inches, thank you.

WARREN

And my point is made. No. Heels.

I glare at my screen, hearing his grumpy tone in my head.

MAISIE

Give me a hint.

WARREN

I'll have you screaming my name within a few
seconds.

He's gotta be fucking with me.
He knows exactly how that sounds.

MAISIE

That only adds to my murder theory.

WARREN

If that was my plan, I would've let Lilith throw
you off instead of saving your ass.

MAISIE

I knew you gave me a bad horse on purpose!

WARREN

She's usually an angel. She must've sensed a
bad vibe.

MAISIE

You're insufferable.

WARREN

So I've been told.

5pm. Don't be late.

Considering I don't have anything without a heel and don't want to borrow another pair, I get dressed and drive one of my parents' cars into town.

I have a dozen old cowboy boots from high school, but I'm not sure that's what he had in mind either, so I go to the only shoe shop in Willow Branch Mountain. I have countless memories growing up here, walking around the town square, and hanging out with Warren and our friends on the weekends.

"Maisie Callaway?" a voice calls, and I turn to find where it came from.

"Delia?" My spine straightens at seeing the girl who tried to steal Warren from me our junior year of high school.

Just my luck I'd run into her.

And I was so close to opening the door of the store.

She opens her arms, and I let her hug me.

"I haven't seen you in a hot minute! How're ya?"

"I'm great. Visitin' my parents and going to Aaron and Collins's baby shower."

Aaron's two years younger than me and his wife's family is as prestigious as ours. They grew up together, but they could barely stand each other, so I was surprised when they got engaged a couple years ago. I thought for sure ours and her parents forced them together like some royal arranged marriage, but then she got pregnant only a few months after the wedding, so I guess that hate turned into passion.

"Oh how sweet. Is it a boy or girl?"

I shift my feet, inching closer to the steps. "They've decided not to find out until it's born."

"Henry and I did that with our first, but then I couldn't wait with the next two."

"You have three kids now?"

She rubs a hand over her belly. "Recently found out we have one more on the way."

Four?

If I didn't already feel behind in life, I would now. Not because twenty-nine is old, but most of our friends from high school got married and had kids a couple years after graduation.

"That's so great. I bet your hands are full."

"Yes, but so is my heart. They're so precious."

"Well, it was great—"

"Whatever happened with you and Warren?" she asks, cutting me off.

"Just went our separate ways when I got a job in New York."

I'm not giving the gossip queen any juicy details to share with everyone else.

"Oh, what a shame. You two were the *it* couple in high school. If I'd bet money on anyone makin' it last, it woulda been y'all. I'd never seen a more protective and in love man than Warren when it came to you."

She would know considering she tried to seduce him and he shot her down.

"Mhm." I force a pained smile. "So sorry to run, but I gotta—"

"Oh no, of course! It was so good seein' ya. Send my best to your family." She smothers me in another unwanted hug. "Bye-bye."

"Bye," I punch out, rushing up the steps and swinging open the door.

After finding appropriate shoes for the ranch, I go to one of the boutiques to find a couple sundresses and other casual outfits. I needed something nicer to wear to the baby shower anyway, so it was a good excuse to shop.

Luckily, I don't run into any more people from high school and make it home with plenty of time to get ready before I have to meet Warren. Considering it's Saturday, I'm surprised he didn't utilize the full day of torturing me.

But now that makes me wonder if he saved it for the evening on purpose. That usually implies something more romantic.

Grabbing my phone from the bed, I shoot him a message.

MAISIE

I'm assuming no heels means no skirts or dresses too, right?

WARREN

Not unless you wanna give me a show.

I grind my teeth.

MAISIE

What the fuck does that even mean?

WARREN

It means wear comfortable pants, Maze.

If I wasn't already having a crisis about what clothes I need, I'd scold him for using that nickname again. I don't hate it, but it means something more to him than it does to me.

MAISIE

Can't you just tell me what we're doing?

WARREN

Reminding you of your roots and where you came from.

Well that could be anything coming from him.

MAISIE

You said you weren't going to murder me.

WARREN

Pretty sure I only implied I wasn't gonna make you dig your own grave.

MAISIE

You're not as funny as you think you are.

WARREN

Who said I was joking?

MAISIE

I'm not coming until you can promise I'm not going to die.

My nerves are on fire as I think about what he's planned. Admittedly, I've gotten used to living in the city and haven't stepped foot on a ranch until two days ago. Anxiously, I wait for his response, which takes him a solid three minutes.

WARREN

You should know by now, I'd never let you get hurt. We're going to have fun, and you're going to get rid of the stick up your ass, so prepare yourself.

MAISIE

What kind of half-ass backward compliment is that?

WARREN

You're wound tight, Maze. I saw it the moment I opened the door.

MAISIE

I have a stressful job, but that doesn't mean I have a stick up my ass!

WARREN

Guess you'll have to prove me wrong.

Goddamn him.

chapter seven

Warren

I DON'T USUALLY work on the weekends unless there's an emergency or project that needs to get finished, but I needed something to keep myself busy before I go stir crazy.

Unfortunately, I could only find enough stuff to do at the stables until noon, so I texted my childhood best friend, Silas, to meet me for lunch. We've been through everything together, so he knows all about the rollercoaster that is Maisie's and my relationship. He's going to give me so much shit when I share the details.

"Hey, man!" His face lights up, sliding out of the booth to give me a hug.

"How's it goin'?" I ask, then sit across from him.

We met at Willow Branch Grill, a bar and restaurant downtown that we've been to dozens of times since before we could legally drink alcohol.

"I've been on edge since you texted that you had to tell me somethin'. What is it?"

Before I can respond, our server approaches and asks for our drink order.

"Budweiser on tap, please."

Silas orders the same and then his gaze is back on mine. "So?"

"Impatient much?"

I'm stalling for the inevitable freak out, but I need to talk about this with someone I'm not related to. My siblings have been blowing up our group chat now that they all know she's here and that we're still married. They've been relentless, so I had to mute it.

Mom and Dad haven't said much since finding out she's here, but I know what they're thinking. They want me to move on so I don't get hurt.

A little too late for that.

"Well, yeah. The last time you told me you had news, it was about Maisie sendin' the divorce papers again and you sendin' 'em back again…"

Lowering my gaze, I nod to confirm his suspicions.

"Oh shit, she sent 'em *again*?"

"Worse."

He arches a brow. "How much worse?"

I might as well get it over with and tell him what he wants to know.

"She showed up at my house two nights ago, asked me for a divorce so she can marry another man, but I said no and slammed the door in her face. A few minutes later, I caught her sneakin' in through the patio door and said I wasn't signin' 'em 'cause we never got a real chance to make things work. The next day, she showed up to the stables in heels, demanding we talk. Told her I didn't have time, and if she wanted me to listen, she could ride out to the pasture with me. So I gave her some boots and put her on Lilith, who ran off before I caught up to her, then took her over to see Posey and the goats. My loud-mouthed sister blurted about the house, and Maisie asked to see it, so I took her there next," I reply quickly, hoping he catches it all.

When I look up, his jaw is on the floor and eyes wide as saucers.

"She...saw the house?" He blinks. "The whole thing?"

I lick my lips. "Yep."

"Then what?"

The server brings our drinks, we quickly order our usuals, and then Silas' attention is back on me. "What'd she say about it?"

"She seemed to like it but was surprised I built it for her. Then, told me I needed to move on."

He grimaces. "Shit."

"And I told her I couldn't."

"She's engaged to someone else?"

"Yeah, some guy from New York. Asked me to let her go and that I deserved to be happy, so I needed to let someone else in."

"Well..." He shrugs cautiously.

"That's not all."

"Why am I not surprised?"

"I told her I'd let her go, sign the papers, and move on if she gave me seven days to prove we deserve a second chance."

"Even though she's with someone else?" He looks at me as if I've lost my mind, and maybe I have, but I'm not going to admit that.

"She's still my wife," I remind him. "If I have to give her up for good, I need to know I tried everythin' first. That means showin' her what we could be if we stayed together."

"I dunno, Warren..." He scratches the back of his neck. "That sounds like a recipe for disaster. Especially if she's gettin' married to someone else."

I lift a shoulder, not caring about that part. "She ain't married to him and we ain't divorced. That means I still have time to make her doubt her decision."

"You're sure about this? It could, and probably will, backfire on you."

"What other choice do I have? Let her walk away with my heart while she gives hers to someone else?"

"You think one week is gonna make a difference?"

"It's my last resort to remind her how in love we used to be. I'll be respectful of her *relationship*—" I nearly choke on the word. "—if it's clear there's nothin' left between us. But if there's even a sliver of a chance she's indecisive about the divorce, then I'm not lettin' her walk away again."

"Do you know who her fiancé is?" He cracks his knuckles. "Could we take him?"

I snort out a laugh. "Just that his name is Hayes."

"*Hayes*? Sounds like a tool."

"He's probably some guy who works in a stuffy office and has never gotten his hands dirty."

"Most likely," he agrees.

Silas works with his fiancée's dad as a contractor and mostly works on new construction homes throughout the state, so he's as familiar with hard work and getting dirty as I am.

"So what're you plannin' for your seven days?"

When our food arrives a few minutes later, I'm still telling him my ideas and ask him for any other ones. I'll have to work during the weekdays, but in the evenings, she'll be all mine.

"You know I love ya." He pulls me in for a hug when we stand. "Good luck. Keep me updated."

"Thanks, and I will."

"And hey if it works out, we can go on double dates." He smirks, and I laugh.

"Give Aundrea my love." I pat his back as we walk outside. He proposed last year and they'll tie the knot this fall.

"I will."

We go our separate ways, and I get into my truck. My heart rate spikes when I check my phone and find a new message from Maisie. After I texted her this morning to meet at my house this evening, I've been anxious as hell, which is why I word vomited all over Silas.

But I'm looking forward to seeing her without the hostility looming between us.

MAISIE

I'm assuming boots means no skirts or dresses, right?

WARREN

Not unless you wanna give me a show.

MAISIE

What the fuck does that mean?

I bark out a laugh because getting under her skin the way she's been under mine is a thrill I haven't felt in years.

We text back and forth a few times and when I tell her she'll have to prove me wrong she's not wound up with a stick up her ass, I set my phone down and drive home.

"You've gotta be kiddin' me." Maisie's head lifts to the ladder that leads to the zip line.

"You scared of heights now?" I ask because she wasn't before.

We have a zip line for the guests that offers a beautiful view of the river and mountains. We used to do it all the time and try to beat each other's times.

"I haven't done this in forever."

"Exactly. Let's get suited up." I nod for her to climb up and follow behind her.

The guests go through a mini training session before staff let them go, but since it's just us and we aren't first-timers, we're going straight up.

"You better not be lookin' at my ass." She tries to glance over her shoulder, trying to catch me.

"It's right in my face. Where do you want me to look?"

"At the ground. The sky. The trees."

"Nah, none of 'em are as appealin' as the view in front of me."

I wasn't even staring at her ass...until she mentioned it.

"Warren!" she scolds.

"You act like I haven't licked hot fudge off that ass. Relax."

"Oh my God, no!" She climbs on top of the hut where we'll get ready. "You're not allowed to talk like that. If I have to suffer through seven days of this, no sex talk or mentions of what we used to do."

"Shit, I wish you woulda told me that sooner. Kinda puts a

damper on the plans I had for later of watchin' our old dirty home movies."

She swats my arm when I reach her. "That's not funny."

"Jesus, Maze. Is this you tryin' to convince me you're *not* stuck up? Where'd your sense of humor go?"

I'm usually the one being told to lighten up, so this is a weird change of pace.

"Can we set some boundaries, please? I agreed to this so you'd see we're over and that you need to move on. But I'm not gonna listen to you reminisce about our past sex life. That's off-limits."

"Okay, fine." I tower above her, lifting a brow as she meets my gaze. "But that goes both ways. No lookin' at my ass either."

She rolls her eyes, crossing her arms. "Not gonna be an issue on my end."

"Great." I smirk. "Am I allowed to help you into the harness or is that breakin' some unspoken rule you haven't told me about yet?"

Her tongue pokes out between her lips and I can tell she wants to respond with a smart-ass comment. "As long as you keep your eyes and hands above my waist."

My eyes lower to her chest, purposely taunting to get a reaction out of her.

"Not there either."

I chuckle, shaking my head.

Grabbing the harness, she avoids my gaze as I help her into it and make sure she's secure.

"Feel okay?" I ask, giving the ropes and belts a tug.

"I think so."

"Hey, sorry I'm late!" Asher meets us on the platform, one of the staffers from the resort. I gave him a heads up I'd be bringing someone before he took his last break.

"No worries. Asher, this is Maisie."

"Hey, nice to meet ya." He shakes her hand, then grabs two helmets and two sets of gloves.

While he double checks Maisie's good to go, I put on my gear.

"Y'all ready? Who's first?" Asher asks.

"She is."

Maisie narrows her eyes like she wants to murder me, but she should've known I'd want to make sure she gets to the other side safely. There's another staff member waiting for us over there.

Once Asher clips the harness to the cable and double checks everything, I lean into her ear and whisper, "Don't forget to scream my name."

She turns her head, our faces inches apart, and I shoot her a wink.

"Just for that, I'm gonna beat your time to the other side."

"Game on, city girl."

I back up out of the way as Maisie grabs the handle and inches closer toward the edge.

"Bend your knees and lean back," Asher reminds her.

"Oh my God!" she screams the second she steps off and Asher and I burst out laughing. "*Warren!*"

I might've forgotten to tell her there were some updates since she was on it last and we made the cable longer.

"She sounds like she wants to kill you." Asher chuckles.

"Oh trust me, she does."

I wait for the confirmation she's made it across before I get into position and take off.

It takes less than thirty seconds before I meet her on the other side. Jake grabs me before I crash into the pole, then unhooks me from the handle.

Her conflicted expression either means she had a blast or she's ready to push me off the mountain.

"I knew you'd scream my name," I tease Maisie once I'm next to her. "You have fun?"

Her fingers grip around the belts of the harness as she glares. "You didn't tell me it was a longer line."

I scratch my cheek, holding back a grin. "Slipped my mind."

"Mhm."

"Ready to go again?" I ask, motioning for her to get back into position so Jake can hook her back up.

"Fine," she breathes out the word but I'm fairly certain she's trying not to smile. "At least this time I know what to expect."

She screams again, not my name this time, but it's funny, nevertheless. Jake gets a kick out of it too.

We end up going back and forth three times before calling it quits.

"What's that?" I point to her face when we walk toward my truck.

"What?" She brushes her cheek.

"I think I saw a smile."

"Dammit, Warren," she says, laughing this time.

"Admit it, you had fun." I nudge her with my elbow.

She pinches her thumb and forefinger together, leaving a tiny space between them. "Just a little."

I smirk. "I'll take it. Are you hungry?"

"Depends. You gonna make me eat something weird like raccoon or skunk and then not tell me until after?"

I smack my palm to my heart. "You know me so well after seven years apart."

She rolls her eyes, and I snicker at her inability not to grin when she does it.

Opening the passenger side door, I help her inside and then rush around to my side.

"Since I don't have to work tomorrow, I was thinkin' we could drive out to Marley's Barrel House."

Her whole face lights up. "Oh wow, I haven't been there in ages."

It's an hour's drive, but they have the best smoked barbeque and live music on Saturday nights.

"You wanna go?" I double check before starting the engine.

"Sure, I'm hungry."

I let her pick the music and try to think of something safe to talk about on the way.

"So tell me about your job. I dunno what you do now."

I assume she stayed in publishing, but I never knew for sure.

"I'm a literary agent. Started my own agency last year."

"What's that exactly?"

She explains it to me like I'm five, which I appreciate, and I learn she represents authors so they can sell their manuscripts to publishers. She continues to talk about the specifics and what her day to day is like.

"What do you love most about being an agent?" I ask, glancing over as she grins.

"So many things, honestly. I love that I get to find rare gems of brilliant writers and help make their dreams come true. I love findin' books I woulda never picked up otherwise. I love readin' pitches and gettin' excited for fresh material. I love hearin' my authors cry tears of joy when I tell 'em their book got a deal, sold to auction, or made a bestseller list. I love hearin' their stories about how becomin' an author changed their lives 'cause they were stuck at meaningless jobs until they could focus on their writin' dreams."

She beams with each word she says, and it's hard not to smile as she speaks.

"I also love networkin' with other agents and learnin' about their process and which authors they've signed. The community as a whole…it's big but small at the same time. I love bringin' new stories' into the world and seein' readers' reactions to cliffhangers and plot twists. It energizes me to get up and work each day. It's never boring or gets old. It brings me joy in a way nothin' else ever did."

I'm stunned by her honesty and feel a wave of relief that her job makes her this happy. It would've been worse had she left her life behind and hated it. At the very least, she did what she set out to do and it wasn't for nothing because she got her dream career.

"Wow, Maze. That's…incredible. I'm so glad you got what you wanted. Sounds like you get to do somethin' really special for others, too."

"I do. So many people strive to work in publishin' compared to those who actually get to, even less when it's this level of work, so it's a blessin' I was able to start so early and branch out on my own."

"You must work long hours then, huh?"

"Yeah, usually. I'm kinda obsessed with keepin' up with the industry and makin' sure I reply to emails in a timely manner. Readin' through manuscripts take me the longest. I tend to work until my stomach growls and I realize I haven't eaten all day."

"Maze…that's not healthy."

"I know, but I love makin' goals and being able to check 'em off my list when I finally hit 'em. Makes it worth it. When I sold my first film rights for a debut author, I celebrated so hard, I had to take off the next day." She laughs. "And then to hear about the progress of a movie being made was also fun. Bringin' art to life…it's not somethin' everyone gets to experience or be a part of, so I try not to take it for granted."

I can't help asking, so I do. "What does your fiancé think about you workin' so much?"

When I briefly glance over, she visibly stiffens, and I worry she'll tell me that's another topic off-limits.

"He's quite the workaholic, too," she replies. "He's also in publishing."

"Oh…" I swallow hard, hating myself for needing to know more about him. "Is that how y'all met?"

"Mm-hmm," is all she responds and it's obvious she's holding back, so I don't push her on it.

Once we arrive at the restaurant, we sit across from each other in a booth and place our orders.

"So I told you about my job. Tell me more about yours." She sips her Coke, looking up at me as she does.

"You probably know plenty about my job considerin' not much has changed in the ranchin' world."

"Well…you're like the boss now, right? Under your dad, I assume."

I nod, grabbing my Sweet Tea and taking a drink. "I manage the ranch staff and deal with the day-to-day operations. I'm usually at the stables or out in the pasture fixin' shit. Bodie works with me, so he helps with makin' sure tasks get done."

"I can't believe how grown up he is. He must've been fourteen when I moved."

"Sounds 'bout right. Little shit went through a growth spurt and passed me up a few years ago."

She laughs. "And he has a whole face of hair! He was a smooth-skinned baby face back then."

That has me chuckling. "Should see his arm. It's all tatted up."

"*Bodie?*"

"Yep. A full arm sleeve or whatever it's called. Couldn't tell ya what they're off 'cause they all blend together, but I swear he gets a new one every month."

"Wow. Bodie the badass. Who knew?"

"Don't tell him you said that. It'll go right to his head."

She grins and the sight of it warms me from the inside out. "Why do I have a feelin' he's a bit of a player?"

"You'd be correct." I smirk, remembering how he said he had a date the other night but had to cancel 'cause Blythe shit all over him.

Our food arrives and we shift to small talk. Her favorite restaurants in New York and what she loves and hates about living in the city. I eat my sandwich and onion rings, nodding along, but secretly dying inside that she'll never want to leave a city that offers her much more than I ever could.

If a second chance between us became a real possibility, could I move up there for her? It's not like the ranch can't run without me, especially now that Bodie's older and my parents aren't busy raising teenagers in their house.

Back then I didn't want to leave the only home I'd ever known or abandon my responsibilities on the ranch, especially being the oldest child. But now knowing what it feels like to lose the love of my life, my perception has changed.

Could I live in a big city?

If it meant I got my wife back…I think I could.

By the time we get back to my house, it's after dusk. We managed to keep a flow of conversation going while we ate and on the drive back. I even had her laughing a few times until her phone rang and she told me it was Hayes calling to say good night.

I told her to go ahead and pick it up. When she explained to him that she was out with an *old friend*, my jaw nearly snapped in half. I wanted to ask her why she never told him about being married, but I have a feeling she wouldn't tell me. We've had a fun evening with no fighting, so I didn't want to ruin it.

"I actually had fun," she says when I walk her to her car.

"You sound surprised." I shove my hands in my pocket so I don't reach out and touch her.

My heart's been pounding all night at getting to be around her again. Being this close confuses my brain that she's not mine to kiss when I spent years pulling her toward me and spreading her lips with my tongue.

"Honestly, I am. I wasn't sure what to expect but it was a nice break from sittin' behind my computer or thinkin' about work. Sometimes it's hard to turn off my brain, so I end up workin' even when I'm not."

"Sounds like you needed the reminder that you work to live and not live to work."

"I know," she whispers.

"Hopefully you find time to have fun and live your life too?"

"Sometimes."

Opening the driver's side door, I stand in front of her. "Is it okay if I ask for a hug? Or is that not appropriate for an *old friend*?"

"Stop it," she says playfully, swatting my chest. "We were friends before we started datin', so technically that wasn't a lie."

"Mhm."

She can keep telling herself that, but we both know she's full of shit.

When she opens her arms, I wrap mine around her and pull her to my chest. She settles against me, and fuck, it feels good. My chin rests on top of her head, and I inhale her shampoo. Rainforest something.

It smells heavenly.

I want to bottle it up and inject it into my veins so I never have to be without it.

"Drive safe, Maze." I kiss the top of her head without thinking but don't apologize for it.

"Thanks, I will."

I feel the loss of her as soon as she steps away. Watching until she drives away, I drag my feet and force myself to go inside.

My mind's racing too much to fall asleep, so I call Landen to give him an update.

"Fuck, I'm so in love with my wife," I blurt the moment he picks up.

"I..." He pauses. "Is this a new revelation?"

"Not exactly, but a part of me wondered if I was holdin' onto the Maisie I knew and if I had built her up to be somethin' more in my head, especially since I hadn't seen her in years."

"And I'm guessin' that wasn't the case."

"Nope." The girl I fell for is still there somewhere.

Underneath the skirts and workaholic, my Maisie exists. She just needs a little help remembering where she came from. "My feelings for her never left and are stronger than ever."

Though I'm trying not to show it so I don't scare her away—at least not right away.

I recap what happened since the last time we spoke and about our seven-day deal.

"After zip linin', we fell back into our old selves and spent the rest of the night talkin' and laughin'. It's like the time apart didn't exist. Does that make me crazy?"

"Pft. No crazier than me pinin' for a woman who spent most of the day ignorin' my existence and would rather drive to the Franklin Rodeo alone than go with me."

I wince. "Ooh, ouch."

"Antonio, the kid I'm trainin', has big heart-eyes for her and she purposely goes outta her way to be extra nice to him. I swear, she does it on purpose. Meanwhile, I'm like a dog takin' any scraps she'll gimme."

Barking out a laugh, I shake my head. "Woof."

"Exactly."

"Fuck...we're so doomed."

chapter eight

Maisie

WAKING up with a smile on my face and sore muscles is the last thing I expect, but I don't let myself get into my head about it. Zip lining was fun, even if it wreaked havoc on my body, which is used to sitting all day. But revisiting a restaurant we used to love was a different kind of fun—familiar and comforting. The live band was entertaining, and Warren and I managed to hold a conversation without any arguing—so I'd call that a win.

"You look lovely, dear." Mom grins when I come down for breakfast.

Sunday's are church days, rain or shine, and since I'm home, I'm expected to tag along.

"Thanks, Mama. So do you."

She beams, and I wonder if my father remembers to compliment her after three decades of marriage.

"Hi, Daddy." I go to the front of the table and kiss his cheek.

"Mornin', sweetheart. You got in late."

I drag my sweaty palms down my dress and hope he can't hear my heart thumping. The blood rushes to my ears as I contemplate what to say.

Pulling out my chair, I sit and fan my napkin out on my lap. "I met up with an old friend in Jonesborough for dinner. We got to talkin' and stayed to watch the band."

My gaze shifts to my mother who's trying not to act obvious at knowing who I'm talking about. It must be enough to appease my father because he quickly drops it and starts talking to the housekeeper to get him another plate of pancakes.

Mom blurts that he doesn't need more carbs, but Dad ignores her and stuffs them down his throat anyway.

Meanwhile, I recap everything in my mind that happened yesterday and wonder how I'm going to survive the next six days with Warren. Things started rocky in the beginning but it transitioned into one of the most fun evenings I've had in a while.

It reminded me I need to do better at taking breaks and not working myself to death.

Especially since I'm not even thirty and am waking up with sore muscles from being active for less than an hour.

While Dad drives us to church, I text Hayes since we didn't talk much last night. By the time I got home, I was exhausted.

MAISIE

Morning, honey. How'd writing go last night?

HAYES

Still going.

My eyes widen. It's almost nine in the morning.

MAISIE

You've been up for twenty-four hours. Go to sleep.

HAYES

I'm finishing up this chapter and then I will.

MAISIE

Okay good. Call me when you're up.

HAYES

I'll text so I can stay focused.

My stomach drops, but this is how he gets during his deadlines and I can't take it personally.

MAISIE

Alright. Good luck.

HAYES

Thanks.

MAISIE

Love you!

HAYES

XO

He's reached the point of overexhaustion, but I wish he'd listen to his body and rest instead of pushing himself to the brink. Although I can't talk much given my own unhealthy habits, but writing is a different beast where it wears on him mentally as well as physically.

When he's in the drafting phase, he's constantly thinking about his book and will abruptly get up from the dinner table to go write something down so he doesn't forget it.

I'm not a writer, so I don't get those sudden bursts of creative energy, but I understand it's part of his process.

After shaking strangers hands and getting pulled into random hugs from my parent's friends who haven't seen me in a few years, I'm relieved when we get back in the car.

My lips twitch when I find a text from Warren about his day two plans.

WARREN

Up for a picnic?

MAISIE

Is this another no heels outing?

WARREN

I wouldn't recommend wearing them, no.

I roll my eyes knowing he's probably rolling his too.

MAISIE

Sure. When?

WARREN

Around noon.

That gives me enough time to get home, change, and drive over there.

MAISIE

I'll be there.

I don't know why I'm nervous, especially after how well

yesterday went, but maybe that's why I am. Warren and I being best friends and attracted to each other was never a problem in our relationship. But I buried my feelings for him and that's where they need to stay.

Getting over him was the most heartbreaking experience I went through.

And it took *years*.

I can't go through that again.

We need to leave the past in the past, and I need to prove that to him during these next six days.

There's no reason to confuse our familiarness with chemistry. He lives here and enjoys the slow-moving life. I did too at one point, but now I thrive on staying busy and having a packed schedule.

Even though he said no heels, I think cowboy boots and a sundress will work for a picnic. Assuming he's not making me climb up a mountain to get to said picnic.

"Where're you headed?" Mama asks before I can sneak out the front door.

Well, not so much as *sneaking* as I didn't want her to notice.

Licking my lips, I avert my gaze. "He's takin' me on a picnic. No big deal."

She purses her lips but the disappointment flashes across her face.

"As friends," I add. "I told him nothin' was gonna happen between us."

"And you believe that?"

Crossing my arms, I nod. "Yes, Mama. I told you why I'm doin' this, so you need to trust me."

"I do, sweetheart. It's *him* I don't trust."

I blow out a breath, drop my arms, and lean in to kiss her cheek. "I'll see you when I get back."

As soon as I pull into Warren's driveway, I find him waiting for me—on a four-wheeler.

"Please tell me we're not…" I motion toward the death-machine.

His eyes lower down my body, to my boots, and then back up to my face. They're full of heat and confusion.

"You said no heels," I explain. "You didn't say no dress."

He bites the inside of his cheek, holding in a laugh. "Fair point, but you're gonna wanna tuck your dress in between your thighs."

I don't know why that makes my neck go hot, but I ignore it.

"I'm sure I'll be fine." I drag my palms down my sides, hoping like hell I can tame it enough so it doesn't blow up in the wind.

"Alright, well hop on." He scoots forward.

"I thought we were goin' on a picnic."

"We are. I brought everythin' up there already."

"Up where?" I ask, grabbing onto his shoulder so I can climb on behind him.

He glances over his shoulder, smirking. "You'll see."

When the four-wheeler rumbles to life, the vibrations shake against my exposed legs, and I quickly tuck the material underneath them as much as I can.

"Ready?" He speaks loudly over the noise. "You're gonna need to hang onto me."

"Um…where?"

Without responding, he grabs my hands with both of his and wraps them around his waist. Then he pulls them tighter around him until my chest is pressed against his back.

"Hang on and don't let go," are his final words before taking off down his driveway.

I haven't been on one of these since before we got married. High school, probably. He'd take me on rides all around the ranch and resort, up the trails into the mountains, and sometimes race with his best friend who'd come over and add to the chaos.

It's impossible not to smile at how much fun it is riding with him. Although he's going fast and moving up and down little mounds throughout, I feel safe with him. He knows exactly what he's doing to stay in control while making it fun.

"Is that laughter I hear?" he taunts, smirking over his shoulder.

Grinning wide, I reply by jabbing a finger in his rib cage.

"Hey, cheap shot." He covers my hand with his but doesn't remove it. Instead, he continues driving one-handed while softly rubbing a finger over my knuckles.

My words to ask him to stop doing that get caught in my throat. It shouldn't feel as comforting as it does.

Warren slows us down, and I notice we're close to where he took me to when he first asked me to be his girlfriend. He'd packed us lunches of PB&J sandwiches and little bags of chips. At fifteen, I thought it was the most romantic thing ever.

It was pretty sweet, though.

"We're here." He turns off the four-wheeler, then shifts until our gazes meet. "Do you want help gettin' off?"

I realize my grip on him has tightened. "Oh, um no. I think I can manage."

I, in fact, cannot manage.

Forgetting I tucked my dress under my thighs, I nearly fall to my death when I stand to slide my leg over. Luckily, Warren catches my waist and pulls me into him before I steady myself on the footrest.

Wrapping my arm around his neck, I hold onto him tightly, breathing through the panic.

"Oh, shit." Our faces are close—*too close*—so I pull back and try to brace myself to step down.

"You alright?" The look of concern on his face makes my chest ache.

I nod. "Yeah, thanks for catchin' me."

"Always." Then he fucking winks.

Was he always this charming or did I forget?

Once I've safely mastered putting two feet on the ground, Warren climbs off next.

"Ready?"

"Depends...are you gonna make me BASE jump next?" I shiver at the thought of jumping off a cliff with a parachute.

He chuckles, grabbing my hand and leading me up the trail. "Haven't done that, but maybe I should add it to my bucket list."

I'm not even surprised.

"Ugh, I forgot how outdoorsy you are." I groan when the heel of my feet rub against my boots.

"Outdoorsy?" He snickers. "You used to be adventurous, too. Cliff-jumpin', swimmin', horseback ridin', campin' in tents and passin' out in sleepin' bags. You never wanted to be inside."

"I was a teenager who wanted any reason to stay out of my parent's house. Even now, it's tense and cold in there."

The Langstons' home was the complete opposite. Warm and inviting, we'd hang out in the living room with his siblings and play games or watch movies, laughing most of the night. It was a contrast to the way I grew up.

"Speakin' of your folks, do they know?" he asks, glancing at me before shifting back to the trail in front of us.

Sighing, I nod. "Only my mother knows about the...*deal*. She warned me not to tell my father, so he's only aware that you haven't signed the papers."

"Well...I never was on their good sides, no point in tryin' now."

I snort. "That's one way to look at it."

When we finally get to the top, my mouth falls open at the *picnic* Warren set up for us. Instead of a blanket over grass, it's a full set up on the flat gravel overlooking the other side of the mountains.

A table, two chairs, a vase of purple and pink roses—my favorite colors— and a spread of food.

"Wow, Warren...this is—" I look at him in awe, shocked he'd go to so much trouble for a lunch date.

"This is what I thought I was doin' when I first brought you up here to ask you to be mine. My resources were a smidge limited back then."

I can't help smiling. "It's quite the upgrade from PB&J sandwiches."

He smirks, shrugging. "Thought it'd be fun to revisit, even as *old friends*. But I also wanted to show off my cookin' skills."

"What'd you make?" I walk closer but he stays next to me.

"It's nothin' fancy..." He lifts one of the plate covers and reveals something that looks delicious. "Homemade croissants with walnut chicken salad."

"You—" I point at him. "Made that?"

"All from scratch."

"When did you have time to do all this?"

"I can never sleep in, even when I have the day off." He

shrugs it off like it's no big deal, but I think this is one of the sweetest things I've ever experienced.

It's not flashy, which I appreciate considering how over the top my parents are, and how every time Hayes and I go out to a restaurant, I have to be in full glam or I'll stand out for being under dressed.

Warren pulls out one of the chairs for me and waits for me to sit before pushing me in.

"The view hasn't changed though. It's so beautiful." The sun's high in the sky, reflecting over the trees and rivers that travel through the valleys.

"It really is." His voice is so low, I almost don't hear him, but then I find his gaze on me instead.

He lifts the other plate covers and reveals a fruit and dessert platter.

"Damn, you're gonna have to carry me back after makin' me eat all of this." But it looks so good, I wouldn't even care.

We dig in, and I moan at how good the croissant tastes, then make him tell me how the hell he made it. I always wanted to learn to cook, especially since my mother never did. We always had a personal chef to cater all our meals.

But my job always came first, so I never made time.

"Maybe one of our *dates* can be you teachin' me how to make something."

His brow arches, and I laugh at his shocked face. "You'd wanna learn?"

"Assumin' I can…" I drawl.

. "If I can figure out how to use an oven, I have no doubt you can."

"I appreciate the confidence, but I smoked out my entire apartment floor when I hit the broil button instead of bake."

Warren chokes on the grape he popped into his mouth and has a coughing fit trying to get it out.

"Shit, are you okay?" I'm halfway out of my seat when he holds up a hand and nods.

"That—" He takes a drink, swallowing hard. "—is impressive work, even for you."

"Yeah, they sent me an eviction notice the next week."

"I'll make sure to have a fire extinguisher on hand."

"I appreciate that," I say, laughing, and he does too.

We continue talking while we eat. I gush about some of the Broadway shows I've seen and he tells me about Silas and his soon-to-be wife.

"How'd they meet?" I ask because I don't remember anyone local named Aundrea.

"You're gonna love this." He smirks, shaking his head. "A sugar daddy datin' app."

My jaw drops, but I cover it with my napkin since I just took a bite of food.

"*Silas*? A sugar daddy?" I burst out laughing, unable to control myself.

"To be fair, he was dared to sign up."

"Who would da—" I pause when he grins wider. "*You* dared him?"

"We were drunk."

"Clearly."

"It worked though. He met Aundrea a few days later and they've been together ever since. That was two years ago."

"Wow...that's hilarious."

"Don't worry, he got me back with his own dare."

"Do I wanna know?"

"Nope."

Silas was a skinny, nerdy kid in high school and never had girlfriends. But it's safe to assume he's changed since I've seen him.

"She made her father hire him at his home construction company and pay him a higher salary so he could spend more money on her."

I can't stop laughing at this whole story. "Can't hate her for findin' a loophole."

chapter nine

Warren

I'M up earlier than usual because after the most amazing afternoon lunch date with Maisie yesterday, my mind hasn't been able to shut off long enough for me to sleep.

But I'm on too much of a high to even need it.

Getting my hopes up for anything happening between us again is stupid considering how different our lives are now, but I can't help how happy it makes me to spend time with her. Being near the woman who was once my best friend and who will always be the love of my life is giving me a false sense of hope that maybe, *just maybe*, she'll remember how good we were together.

I should prepare myself for the worst, but I can't. Not yet anyway.

Bodie's brows furrow and he squints as he stares. "Why're you smilin'?"

"Whaddya mean?" Even as I say the words I can't stop the smile from spreading across my face.

Bodie's face lights up and he points at me. "You got laid! Fuckin' finally! Who is she?"

I roll my eyes at his obnoxiousness. "Not even close."

Walking toward my office, Bodie catches up to me. "Is it about Maisie?"

I'm about to open my mouth to tell him the truth when I remember he can't be trusted. "I'm not tellin' you shit. You'll tell the group chat."

He mimics zipping his lips and throwing away the key.

"I'm not Bellamy, that doesn't work on me."

"Oh, c'mon! I'm your favorite brother."

I scoff. He wishes.

"I bet you use that on Bellamy, too."

"Well, obviously. I'm her twin, so she has to say it's me. But I swear I won't tell 'em."

"Fine."

He follows me into my office and sits in the chair in front of my desk. I log into my computer and click my emails tab.

"I don't have all day, man. Spill it already."

Rolling my head back on my shoulders, I give my neck a few cracks.

"Text me an embarrassin' pic first."

"Wait, what?"

"I need leverage. You spill the beans, I plaster your photo all over a datin' app of my choosin'."

His jaw drops in shock. "So much for being *my* favorite brother." Instead of arguing like I assumed, he pulls out his phone and sends me a shirtless mirror selfie of him in a cowboy hat. Except, he looks good.

"This is the worst ya got?"

"Yeah, I ate carbs that day." He pats his abs like he doesn't always have a six-pack.

I roll my eyes. "Fine, whatever."

Instead of drawing it out, I share every single detail of our seven-day deal and what happens once the week is over. I tell him about each date we've had so far and what I have planned for the rest of the five days.

Shit, that feels good to get off my chest.

When I stop talking, Bodie's expression is frozen.

"Gonna tell me what you're thinkin' or keep starin'?"

He mimics reaching down to pick up his jaw off the floor, and I lean back in my chair, crossing my arms while I wait for his dramatics to be over.

"Well that...was unexpected. She's engaged, though?"

"So? What does that matter when she's *married* to me?"

"Do you truly think she'll change her mind?" His face softens, concern etched in his features.

"I-I dunno. We're gettin' along as well as we always have, minus the touching or intimacy. I'm not pushin' for any of that anyway. I just want her to realize what she's givin' up before she does."

He nods, squeezing the back of his neck. "And if she doesn't? You'll finally move on?"

I lift a shoulder because who's to say at this point? "I'll have to."

"You know I want you to be happy. If you two get a second chance, I'll support y'all and be the ring bearer again at your vow renewal." I laugh at that. Considering he was thirteen at the time. "But if not, we'll get shitfaced at the bar and find you a freak-in-the-sheets."

"Why does she have to be—"

"Hey, boss…"

My head falls at Ricky in the doorway, grinning like a fool.

He's Nicky's younger brother. And yes, their names rhyme.

"We'll chat later," I tell Bodie.

He stands but rests his palms on my desk, leaning closer and lowering his voice. "Since I promised to keep this between us, does that mean I get updates during the week?" He waggles his brows. "So I can prepare."

"Prepare for what?"

"Champagne if we're celebratin' or some Mad Dogs to drown your sorrows. Or if you're feelin' really down, Four Lokos."

I snort because there's no way I'm drinking that shit. "Sure, I'll text ya."

Once he leaves, Ricky enters and plops down in front of me.

"Don't tell me you got married, too?"

After dealing with Ricky and going through emails, I check in with Bodie and see where I can help. I'm trying to stay focused instead of thinking about Maisie, but it's nearly impossible.

Our picnic yesterday went so well, I'm half-way worried I won't be able to top it. Although that's not the point of spending this week with her, but since I have to be here during the day and she's spending time with her parents or working, we'll only get a few hours in the evening. And I want them to be memorable.

WARREN

Wanna go for an evening swim tonight?

It's nothing major, but not being able to sleep is catching up to me. I'd rather do something lowkey tonight since I have other late-night activities planned this week. We used to swim under the waterfall all the time when we were younger, but I haven't been able to go there since the last time we went together.

It'll also give me the opportunity to tell her about Angela since I didn't want to do that in a public space.

MAISIE

I didn't pack a bathing suit.

WARREN

That's never stopped you before.

MAISIE

Warren! I'm not going skinny-dipping again…

I laugh, unable to hold back the rush of emotions hitting me at her remembering the one and only time we did was the night I proposed.

WARREN

You have until 7 to get one. Bring extra clothes to change into after. I made your favorite dessert.

MAISIE

You bake too?

WARREN

Just one thing, nothing special.

Cheesecake was always her favorite, so over the years, I watched videos and taught myself how to make it. It took a while to get it right, but I finally got it down after several failed attempts. I started making one yesterday after I got home from our picnic so it'd be cooled in time for tonight. Once we're ready to eat, I'll top it with berries and salted caramel drizzle.

MAISIE

Okay well, you won me over with dessert, so
I'll be there.

WARREN

Glad to see nothing's changed with your sweet
tooth.

After work, I shower and crawl into bed for a quick nap. I'm dragging ass and will have to chug an energy drink before we go tonight.

The moment my body sinks into a deep sleep, a loud pounding at my door wakes me.

"Ugh, go away," I mumble, grabbing the pillow to cover my head.

"Warren Grady Langston! Open this door!"

Oh fuck.

My mother.

"We know you're in there!"

Double fuck.

Aunt JoJo.

They know where the hideaway key is, so there's only a few more seconds of them shouting my name before they barge inside.

"Hope you're decent, we're comin' in!" Aunt JoJo shouts.

"No one is home!" I yell.

"Nice try," Mom says, walking into my bedroom without knocking.

"I coulda been naked in here," I grumble, sitting up.

"I saw your mother give birth, nothin' I haven't seen before," Aunt JoJo blurts, sitting on the edge of my bed.

"I think we need to have a discussion about boundaries." I pull the sheet over my waist since I'm only in my boxers.

"Speakin' of discussions…" Mom grins, folding her hands in front of her. "We want an update on Maisie."

"And you couldn't have called or texted?"

"We did call," Aunt JoJo says. "Straight to voicemail."

"And that was an invitation to interrupt my nap?"

"We didn't know you were sleepin', honey." Mom shrugs. "But since we're here…"

"We want the juicy details," Aunt JoJo blurts.

"Jesus, y'all are worse than Bodie." I sigh, knowing they won't drop it until I tell them everything. "Can you at least let me get dressed?"

"Sure, sweetie. We'll be in the kitchen." Mom nods to Aunt JoJo to follow her out.

"Don't touch the cheesecake," I warn, knowing they're little snoops.

"*Cheesecake*?" Aunt JoJo's mouth opens before it forms into a mischievous grin.

"Don't," is the last word I get out before my mom drags her out the door and closes it behind them.

You'd think living up the mountains away from the ranch and the main farmhouse would award me some privacy, but Aunt JoJo and my mom are the biggest gossips in town. They were best friends before Mom married Aunt JoJo's older brother, so they have decades of getting in trouble together.

Once I have pants and a T-shirt on, I meet them in the kitchen.

"Sorry, honey. Bodie let it slip that you have seven days to win her back, so we needed to know what's goin' on."

"That little shit," I murmur.

I should've gotten a worse picture of him. He's probably hoping I do leak it because it'll make girls his age go crazy. Especially the ones with a cowboy fantasy.

"If I tell you everythin', do you promise to leave and keep tight-lipped about it?"

"Yes!" they agree in unison.

I blow out a breath, then lean against the kitchen counter as they sit at the breakfast bar. Starting at the beginning, I go back to last Thursday when she showed up at the house and continue with my plans for tonight. Finally, I explain what'll happen after the seventh day if she still wants a divorce—I'll sign the papers and never see her again.

"Wow..." Aunt JoJo murmurs in a daze.

"You're gonna let her rip out your heart a second time," Mom says, the disappointment written across her face.

"Maybe that's what it'll take for him to move on from her for good," Aunt JoJo says, speaking as if I'm not in the same room as them. "Unless she changes her mind and they give their marriage another chance."

"Assumin' she's willin' to move here." Mom presses her lips into a firm line.

"She's her own boss, so she can work remotely anywhere," Aunt JoJo replies.

I cross my arms over my chest as they go back and forth, discussing my marriage as if they're picking out an outfit for a random night out versus my actual life.

"What if he moves there for her instead? At least he'd be happy…" Aunt JoJo continues.

"I don't like that idea," Mom replies. "If they have kids, I'll never see my grandchildren."

"Oookay…" I drawl, interrupting the shitstorm of possibilities. Pushing off the counter, I wave my hand between their faces. "Only Maisie and I will be discussin' what happens next, and that's only *if* she wants to give it another shot. The deal was I had to make her change her mind about the divorce, so there's no point in talkin' about what's next unless she does."

"We wanna see you happy again, honey. You've been a shell of yourself for too long. You deserve to find someone who wants to be with you as much as you wanna be with 'em."

"I know, Mom. And if she still wants a divorce, I'll give it to her, and find a way to move on, then."

I grind my molars because the thought of *moving on* makes my stomach twist.

She rounds the counter, wraps her arms around me in a hug, and I give her one in return.

"Just guard your heart, okay? You're still in love with her, but she's in love with someone else, and that scenario never ends well."

Even though I'm well-aware of the consequences I could face after spending time with her this week, Mom's words stab a dagger through my chest. It's one thing to go through the pain in secret, but the more people who find out, the more will witness the aftermath—which is why I didn't want anyone else to know.

"You can say no, but…" Aunt JoJo drawls, glancing between my mom and me. "Invite her to the restaurant tomorrow night and I'll make sure it's in a private area for the two of you."

"That sounds awfully romantic," Mom says in her disapproving tone.

"I thought the whole point was to make her fall in love with him again?" Aunt JoJo scowls. "What better place to take her than the Summit Views Restaurant, which was designed to help couples reconnect? Plus, tomorrow's special is lamb chops." She grins proudly.

It's obvious my mother isn't on board but it does sound nice.

"If I bring her, do you promise not to embarrass me?" I ask, pinning my gaze to hers.

"Of course! I'll even leave my Warren hearts Maisie T-shirt at home."

I roll my eyes, already regretting this, but I can push my original plans to another day.

"Alright, fine. Can you get us a table for six?"

Mom opens her mouth like she wants to say something but then clamps it shut.

"Yep, I'll make it work. It'll be the most romantic table in the whole place. Fairy lights, roses, a private violinist—"

"Okay, that's not necessary."

"—chocolate-covered strawberries, candles, and a view of the mountains that'll have her wishin' she never has to leave." Aunt JoJo sighs in delight at her obnoxious ideas.

Mom stares at her and Aunt JoJo furrows her brows in confusion. "What?"

"Keep it simple, okay? I'm not tryin' to scare her."

Aunt JoJo gives me a thumbs-up. "Sure, okay, yeah."

Why do I have a feeling she's gonna do the exact opposite?

After we say goodbye and I gently push them out of my house, I grab my phone to text my least favorite brother.

WARREN

You. Are. Dead.

BODIE

THEY FORCED IT OUT OF ME!

WARREN

If you have plans in the near future, cancel them. You'll be too busy working overtime and sore from what I'm about to make you do.

BODIE

OH COME ON! I didn't tell them anything bad!

WARREN

Emptying all the water troughs and scrubbing them clean with a toothbrush, picking rocks in all the pastures and corrals, and sheath cleaning all the stallions.

BODIE

DUDE. No fucking way am I doing all that or touching a horse's dong. You act like I rented out a billboard and told the entire town!

WARREN

This will remind you to shut your pie-hole next time, won't it?

BODIE

Seven years of no sex turned you into an asshole. The punishment doesn't fit the crime!

WARREN

Mom and Aunt JoJo barged into my house while I was trying to sleep and wouldn't leave until I told them everything, so I think the crime fits perfectly.

BODIE

Not like you wouldn't have told them
eventually.

I roll my eyes, no longer in the mood to argue with him. Instead, I check on my cheesecake before making myself something to eat since there's no chance of me falling back asleep.

When my phone vibrates with a text from Maisie, I choke on my food at the near naked photos on my screen.

MAISIE

Which one? I'm mildly freaking out about
being in a swimsuit around him and can't
decide which one is less slutty.

It's obvious this message wasn't for me, but I can't help teasing her and replying as if it was.

WARREN

The sluttier the better in my opinion.

My phone immediately rings.

"Well hello…" I can't help the smile on my face.

"Oh my God, that was not meant for you!" she spits out in one breath.

"No way?" I gasp in shocked amusement. "'Cause I thought the mirror ass selfie of you in that purple skimpy string bikini made perfect spank bank material."

"Warren," she grinds out between her teeth. "Delete 'em."

"No."

"Warren, *please*. I sent 'em accidentally."

"And who did you mean to send your half-naked ass to?"

"My agent friend, Jessica. I haven't worn a swimsuit in years, so I was panickin' about how I looked in one."

"Why? And I'm askin' genuinely 'cause you look amazin'.""

I had to tell my cock to calm down the second I saw them.

She's quite for a moment before she clears her throat. "My body's changed a lot over the years, especially the more I worked and the less active I got. I know it's normal for things to change as we get older, but it doesn't make me any less self-conscious when it comes to wearin' a bikini around a man who saw my body at fifteen."

"Maze, you have nothin' to worry about with me. And for what it's worth, I much prefer your womanly body over a teenager's going through puberty. That'd be criminal if I preferred that at my age."

She chuckles and the softness of it sends a wave of relief through me.

"That's true. I'm overthinkin' this, aren't I?"

"I want you to be comfortable, so if a swimsuit is too much, then don't wear one."

"I already told you I'm not skinny-dippin'…"

"No!" I bark out a laugh. "That's not what I meant. Wear shorts and an oversized T-shirt for all I care. I just thought it'd be fun to swim where we spent a lot of our summers. Plus, you can't beat the sunset views from there."

"Okay, well thank you for talkin' me off the ledge. There's a cute one-piece that I tried on earlier that I'll buy instead."

"Perfect. Can't wait to see it."

"Well, don't look *at* it."

"Okay…" I drawl, trying not to laugh. "I'll keep my eyes above the neck at all times."

She snorts. "Yeah, right."

I smirk, licking my bottom lip because I can't even argue that it'll be a constant battle not to check her out.

"See you soon," I say.

"Yeah, be there at seven."

We say goodbye and hang up, then I stand in my kitchen wondering how much it's going to hurt when I have to say goodbye to her for the last time.

chapter ten

Maisie

"JUMP!" Warren shouts for the second time, but he's grinning.

"I'm too scared!"

"I'm right here to catch you."

Glancing down from the boulder I'm standing on, a nervous shiver runs through me. It's twenty-five feet high, half the height of the cliff we used to jump off from, but that was me as a careless teenager. Now I'm ready to shit my pants.

"Okay, I'm gonna do it..." I try to amp myself up and shake out my arms. We've done this countless times. I can do it.

Warren's already done it three times to prove it was safe.

I back up a few feet, then run off and scream until my body crashes into the water. Before I can swim to the surface, Warren's pulling me up.

"Holy shit!" I suck in a breath and then hang onto Warren's shoulders as he keeps me afloat.

"That was some jump." He laughs. "Your legs and arms were floppin' all over the place."

"Shut up!" I giggle, pushing against him.

"I'm kiddin'. You did great for your first time in years."

"And my only time."

"Oh c'mon...we'll go together."

"Fine, *once* more," I compromise.

We swim to the shore and climb higher than before, my nerves on fire at being even more scared.

"Stop lookin' down," he says, grabbing my hand and interlinking our fingers. His unexpected touch sends heat down my neck, and I try not to overthink it since we're having fun. "On the count of three, we'll go."

When we step back, he counts down.

"3...2...1...*go!*" We continue holding hands as we jump, and I scream the entire way down.

Our hands lose contact when we sink into the water, and I fight my way to the surface. But when I wipe my eyes, I don't see him.

"Warren?" I frantically look around, shuffling my arms back and forth to search for him. "Warren!"

My voice cracks but then I'm yanked down when I call his name a third time. "War—"

I barely have a moment to grasp what's happening when I reapproach the surface and can breathe again.

Warren appears and smirks.

"You asshole!" I splash water at his face and he grabs my wrist, pulling me closer.

"What? Were you worried about me?" He arches a brow, a wicked grin etched across his face.

I push against his chest, putting distance between us. "That was rude."

"You forget I was practically raised in this river. I can hold my breath for over a minute."

"That doesn't mean you're invincible from drownin' or smackin' your stupid brain."

He tilts his head into the water, slicking it back and laughing. "Glad to hear you care about my stupid brain."

I roll my eyes, struggling to stay afloat.

Warren closes the gap between us, and my heart stutters anticipating his next move, but then he spins around. "Climb on my back. I'll swim us to shore."

Though I should argue about wrapping my bare arms and legs around him, I could use the relief. Except when I do, I feel every muscle against me that he didn't have before. Warren's built solid and swims like my added weight hardly fazes him.

Once we reach land, he hands me a towel, and I try not to watch as he dries off with his. His swim trunks are low on his hips, revealing a deep V he most definitely didn't have before. He has a smooth chest, which only accentuates his lean six-pack abs that were built from working on the ranch.

"Ready?" Warren's voice snaps me out of my haze, and I quickly nod, wrapping the towel around my body.

I follow him to his truck and he blasts the heat for me since it's after sunset and I'm wearing next to nothing.

"I've been waitin' to bring this up, but Landen and I are supposed to talk tomorrow, so I figure it's now or never."

"What is it?"

"Angela's up for parole and Tucker's family's lawyer suggested we write a letter to the parole board to hopefully influence their decision on lettin' her out."

My throat goes dry as his words digest in my mind.

"I-I can't believe she's eligible already..."

"Yeah, it's bullshit but not much else we can do if they

approve it. She's had good behavior and served her minimum time so far."

"Truthfully, I blocked that week out of my mind 'cause it kept givin' me nightmares for months after, but I'll think of something to write. She deserved longer."

"Agreed. Tonight's the first time I swam there since the night I proposed."

My head snaps toward his, brows furrowed. "Whaddya mean?"

He proposed nine years ago.

"The night you agreed to marry me…that's the last time I swam in the river. You left for your third year of college at the end of summer. The next summer we got married and spent most of our free time in bed. After you graduated, you were applyin' for jobs, and I had that big job helpin' my dad build another barn and more treehouses. Then, you left that September. Never had the urge to swim there until tonight."

Warren's life didn't stop when I left, but it's clear he stopped living.

I draw my lips into my mouth, trying to wet them since the humidity—or maybe it's the tension in the air—made them dry.

"I'm sorry."

He glances at me before shifting his eyes back to the road. "For what?"

"For leavin' the way I did. Had I known how hard you took it, I woulda thought twice about it. We were married, and I shoulda taken your concerns more seriously. I convinced myself you'd change your mind once I moved away, and you'd come up and see how great it could be. I shoulda considered your feelings more."

Warren parks the truck in front of his house, then turns

toward me. "You're not the only one to blame, Maze. You were right when you said I coulda tried harder and given it a real chance instead of writin' it off so quickly that I'd hate it there."

"But that's the thing, you woulda hated it. Livin' in as big of a city as New York isn't for everyone. It took me months to adjust, hell, maybe years, but I had tunnel vision about gettin' my dream job. It was selfish."

He leans over and rests his palm on my towel-covered thigh. "I think we both were, if I'm being honest."

I swallow hard before blurting my next words. "I waited over four years for you."

He pulls back slightly, blinking before his gaze hardens on mine. "You did?"

"I had no interest in datin', which is why I wasn't that persistent at first about the divorce papers. My parents' lawyer drafted 'em up before they told me about it. They said four years was long enough. After you sent 'em back unsigned, I didn't think too much of it 'cause I wasn't in a serious relationship so there was no urgency. Hayes and I were casually datin' at the time, but we were both too focused on our careers to make a real commitment. But after I brought Hayes home to meet 'em, they got pushy. Once he proposed, that's when they sent the papers twice more."

"I wish I'd known that..." He scratches his cheek before rubbing the back of his neck. "I woulda changed my mind."

"About what?"

"About not wantin' to leave here. After four years of knowin' what it was like to be without you, I woulda jumped on a plane and moved my whole life to be with you again. Instead, I got obsessed with buildin' my house, and every time I got those papers, it fueled me to work harder. Hopin' that each time I sent 'em back, you'd come and change your mind once you saw what was waitin' for you."

My throat burns as tears prick the corner of my eyes. "I wished I'd known you hadn't moved on."

"Why?" he asks softly, leaning closer.

Swallowing hard, I focus on his lips as I force out my words. "I woulda come sooner."

Before he can ask me to elaborate, a loud knock on the driver's side window causes us both to jump.

"Jesus Christ." Warren inhales a sharp breath before rolling the window down.

"Hey!" His sister pokes her head through the window, then finally notices me. "Oh, hey Maisie!"

"Hi, Bellamy." She looks more mature than the last time I saw her, but her long dark hair and dimples when she smiles are the same.

"Sorry to interrupt your…" She waves her hands, unsure of what to call this. "But I heard you had cheesecake?"

That's the dessert he made for us? That's more impressive considering that's not an easy recipe.

"Please be jokin'…" Warren blows out a harsh breath, his head falling against the seat in defeat.

"What?" She feigns innocence and it's hard not to crack up. "Like you two are gonna eat a whole one? You can share with your favorite sister. C'mon, I'm hungry." Then she skips away toward the staircase that leads to the deck.

"Movin' seven hundred miles away ain't lookin' so bad now," he mutters, and I snort.

We get out of the truck and walk together into the house. A cold rush of air hits my skin, and I shiver. Even though I wore a one-piece, it still barely covers anything. I wasn't as self-conscious as I thought I'd be, but being in the water helped since he couldn't see anything below my shoulders.

"Would you mind if I quickly warmed up in your shower?"

"Yeah, of course. Go ahead. I'll grab some clothes and change in my room."

"Thanks." I give Bellamy a quick wave before grabbing my bag of clean clothes and dipping down the hallway.

Bellamy's loud whistle echoes and then there's a muttered "shut up" from Warren.

Their relationship has always been hilarious because Bellamy's the baby of the family and Warren's the oldest.

Although I've been in Warren's bathroom before, I'm still in awe that he did most of it himself and picked everything out. It's clean and tidy, almost like no one ever comes in here. The tub is tempting to say the least, but then I'd never want to leave.

I try not to take too long but the rainfall showerhead has me wanting to stay under the hot water forever. Once I've warmed up, I wash my body with his soap and use his two-in-one shampoo and condition so my hair doesn't smell like the river. Stepping out, I dry off and wrap a towel around my hair, then put on my leggings and sweatshirt.

Looking for his hamper, I realize there isn't one in the bathroom, so I open the door with one towel on my arm and lower my head to shake out my hair before grabbing that towel next.

But when I lift my head, I'm met with Warren's bare ass.

"Oh shit," the words fall out of my mouth at the same time he turns and shows me a whole lot more of him.

I'm frozen as I take in all of his skin and muscles, and it takes a few more seconds before I realize he doesn't cover himself.

Is that...*a piercing?*

Warren clears his throat and my gaze snaps to his.

"Sorry, I—" I finally spin around but it's too late—the image of his half-erect pierced cock is forever burned into my brain.

That's a *new* piece of jewelry. If he's not been with anyone except me, why would he get *that* pierced? Better yet, why am I wondering what it'd feel like inside me?

I mentally slap myself.

"You were takin' a while so I figured there was time to change before you came out," he explains.

"Yeah, no, of course. I didn't mean to take so long, but I fell in love with your showerhead, and well, we're quite friendly now."

He chuckles, then a drawer opens and closes. "You can turn around now."

I squeeze my eyes, my cheeks flaming hot, and cover my eyes before facing him. Peeking through my fingers, I make sure he's decent before I drop my hand. He's in gray joggers, which is somehow worse.

That's a man's slutty version of a mini skirt.

No way he doesn't know it conceals *nothing* in the crotch area or the outline of his barbell.

And now he's caught me looking *there*, twice.

"Um..." I clear my throat, unable to meet his gaze. "Do you have a hamper for towels?"

"In my closet, but I can take 'em," he offers, putting on a plain white T-shirt before rounding the bed. My breath hitches as he approaches.

Why am I having this kind of reaction when we've slept together countless times? I'm familiar with every inch of him.

But his body *now* is not his body from years ago.

No. I need to snap out of it. Warren's much more than his physical appearance, but Jesus Christ, it doesn't hurt.

"You alright?" he asks once he's in front of me, grabbing the towels from my grip.

"Yeah!" My eyes shoot to his too quickly and are too wide, there's no way he didn't see me checking him out.

"Here, let me get that for ya…" His thumb wipes underneath my bottom lip. "Had a little drool."

My mouth parts to say something, but then the asshole winks and walks away.

Instead of trying to defend myself, because I can't, I follow Warren to the kitchen and find Bellamy sitting at the breakfast bar.

"Finally! This jerk wouldn't cut into the cheesecake until you came out."

I chuckle nervously. "Sorry."

"Don't be," Warren says in his deep, rough voice. "Freeloader number four shouldn't even be here."

"Hey!" Bellamy scowls. "Bodie's more of a freeloader than me."

"I'd say it's a tie," Warren counters. "You're just more annoyin' about it."

Warren grabs the cheesecake from the fridge and sets it down on the platter. "I added the fruit and drizzle already."

"It looks delicious," I say honestly. "You made this from scratch?"

"Mm-hmm. I worked on it yesterday after our picnic and let it cool overnight."

"You took her on a picnic?" Bellamy gushes. "How 1960s of you."

I can't help the snort that escapes me.

"It was very sweet," I tell her. "I'd forgotten how beautiful the views were from up there."

"Oh you took her up *there*?" Bellamy eyes Warren cautiously before shifting to me. "He takes all his ladies there so he can impress 'em with the view and cookin' skills. Did it work on you?"

My heart has no right to nosedive into my stomach but it does at the thought of him being with other women.

Warren grabs a knife and drops his fist on the counter. "If I give you half the cheesecake *to go*, will you leave?"

Bellamy folds her hands on top of the counter and smirks. "Deal."

"And she's lyin' by the way," Warren tells me, focusing his attention on cutting through the cheesecake. "I've never taken anyone but you up there."

And just like that, my stomach somersaults again.

"Warren!" Bellamy scolds, widening her eyes. "That's jealousy 101. Read my cues."

"Oh, you were tryin' to make me jealous? Why? I'm engaged to someone else." I regret my words as soon as I blurt them, especially when Warren winces. But I couldn't help it because the way it made me feel for that split-second had me second-guessing everything, and not for the reasons it should be.

"Yeah, so? You know how many men use the *I'm engaged* or *I'm married* line to get other women into bed? It doesn't mean anything. Marriage is a contract between you and the government. It's bullshit patriarchy crap to control women. It doesn't change anything between a couple. If anything, it makes men more attractive 'cause it implies they can commit and settle down, meanwhile, their wives get more bitter that even though they got the big white weddin' and shiny ring, it's not enough to keep a man's pryin' eyes."

"Wow, I'm shocked you're single," Warren deadpans.

"I *choose* to be single, thank you very much."

"You're too young to be that jaded," I tease.

She's only twenty-one.

The same year Warren and I got married.

"No, I'm not stupid enough to give half my assets to a man who will promise me the world in one breath and ask me what's for dinner in the next."

I bite back a laugh. "You can be a feminist and still wanna cook for your husband."

Warren looks skeptically from the corner of his eye.

"Okay, well not in *my* case 'cause I can't cook, but you get the gist."

Even though he's looking down while he cuts into the dessert, I notice the corner of his lips tilt up in amusement.

"Does that mean your fiancé cooks for you?" Bellamy asks.

"No, he's not much of a cook either." We're both too busy to remember to eat half the time.

"So what do y'all do?"

"We order in, mostly. Or go out."

"Every day?" Her mouth falls open. "I can't imagine that."

"There's endless options in New York, so you never get sick of it."

Warren puts half the cheesecake into a container, snaps the lid on it, then places it in front of Bellamy.

"Here. You and your anti-marriage views can go now."

Bellamy picks up the container, hops off the chair, and beams. "Thanks! You're the best big brother ever."

"Mhm." He shakes his head but blows out a breath when she finally leaves. "And now it's your turn."

"Huh?"

I shift and find a fork an inch from my face. "Try it."

My gaze falls to the cheesecake and I lick my lips before parting them. The salted caramel drizzle hits my tongue and I moan at how good it tastes.

"Wow..." I bob my head. "That's good. Really good."

"Yeah?" He takes a bite for himself. "Mmm."

"How many times have you made this?" I ask, stealing the fork so I can have more.

"Probably a dozen times or more. Took me a while to perfect it."

"Well, it was well worth it 'cause this is the best cheesecake I've ever tasted, and I've had a lot." I smile, stealing another bite.

"You're supposed to be sharin' that," he taunts, stepping closer.

I grab another forkful and put it in front of his lips, but when he opens his mouth, I shove it into mine instead.

"Too slow!" I laugh, swallowing it down.

"Maisie Gracelyn!" His fingers dig into my sides, causing me to laugh harder as he tickles me. I jump out of his reach and run around the counter, but he's quick to catch me.

"Where do you think you're goin'?" He wraps his arms around me, pressing his chest to my back, and for a moment, we're teenagers again. Having tickle fights, laughing and teasing each other, like we've done dozens of times before.

Warren buries his face in my neck and inhales. "I love that you smell like me."

His warm breath against my cool skin causes an electric current to shoot down my spine and my heart beats wildly out of control. I wouldn't be surprised if he can feel it against my pulse point.

"You had limited options in the shower," I manage to say.

He chuckles against my cheek. "Sorry 'bout that. You're the first woman to use it. I'll make sure to have a better selection next time."

Next time?

I want to ask what he means by that, but instead, I step out of his hold and face him.

"It's gettin' late. I should get home before my parents scold me for stayin' out too late again." I roll my eyes so he doesn't think I'm leaving because I want to.

Rather, I *need* to.

The more time I spend with him, the more I'm having conflicting feelings. I need to walk away before my head gets confused even more.

"Sure." He rounds the counter. "Do you wanna take some of this home? I can put it in a container."

"That'd be great." I smile. "I'm gonna grab my bag while you do that."

I stare at our wedding photos hung in his hallway and wonder how he can stomach seeing them every day. So many *what-if's* linger in the air if things had gone differently.

Would he have built this house still? Would we be as happy together as we were before? Would we have started a family?

We had so many talks about the future, and yet, somehow ended up here.

On the brink of a divorce, living seven hundred miles apart, but not really living at all.

Twisting my engagement ring around my finger, I wonder if

it's proper etiquette to give back your wedding bands when you're the one who asks for the divorce.

I wore mine from Warren during my first year in New York and can't help wondering how long Warren wore his before permanently taking it off.

It got exhausting having people at work ask where my husband was and why he didn't move with me. It was easier to keep it off, but I still held onto hope that someday I'd get to wear them again.

Breaking out of my trance, I walk to the bathroom and grab my wet swimsuit hung over the tub and stuff it into my bag.

By the time I return to the kitchen, Warren has the container set out for me.

"How do you feel about dinner at Summit Views tomorrow night?"

My eyes lift to meet his and there's hesitation in them.

We've been there several times, but it's a place for couples. A *romantic* place.

"My mom and Aunt JoJo stopped over this afternoon and JoJo insisted I bring you, but if you don't wanna—"

"I do," I blurt without thinking. "It'd be nice to see her again too."

Assuming she doesn't hate me.

"Great. And you can wear your heels without it being a death trap." He winks and it makes me laugh. "But if it's overkill, just know it was Aunt JoJo's doing."

I grin, already looking forward to it. "What time?"

"Reservations are at six."

"I'll meet you here at quarter to?"

"Works for me." He tilts his head toward the door, grabbing the cheesecake. "I'll walk you out."

134

When he presses his palm to my lower back, those damn butterflies resurface. He walked me to my car the past two times I've been here, so there's no reason I need to be this nervous.

"Thanks for swimmin' with me," he says when we get outside.

"It was fun," I say genuinely. "But maybe don't wait another nine years before going again."

"I won't if you don't." He gives me that boyish grin that used to work so well on me to get what he wants.

And dammit—it still does.

"Fine," I give in. "No yankin' me under water, though!"

He bites his lower lip before releasing it. "No promises."

I roll my eyes, unable to contain my laughter at his blunt honesty.

Warren reaches around me, grabs the handle, and opens the door. "Drive safely."

"Thanks, I will."

He holds out the container, but when I reach for it, he leans in and presses his lips to my cheek.

"See you tomorrow night. Wear a dress."

I'm in such a state of shock, an "mm-hmm" is all I can get out before climbing into the driver's seat.

"Thank you for the cheesecake." I hold it up stupidly.

"It was my pleasure." He smirks. "G'night, Maze."

"Night, Warren."

He closes the door, and as usual, waits for me to drive away.

My heart races the whole way home with jumbled thoughts as I try to make sense of these suppressed feelings.

Warren and I didn't separate because we stopped loving each other. Had I never moved, we'd probably still be madly in love, and living happily.

But I did move and met Hayes.

Who makes me happy.

And I promised to marry him because we're in love.

However, if that were true...would I be having doubts after reuniting with my husband who never moved on from me?

This would be so much easier if he had.

But the thought of him with someone else makes me sick to my stomach, so maybe that's all the answer I need.

chapter eleven

Warren

TALKING to Landen on the phone for a couple hours was a nice break from the thoughts roaming freely in my head. We decided to write our letter to the parole board together, and by the end, we had a strong case. It's weighing heavily on his mind, as it is for me too, but the majority of my focus is on Maisie and the way my heart hasn't stopped beating rapidly since she showed up on my doorstep.

She's a constant loop in my head.

The way she smiles and a crimson blush covers her cheeks and neck.

How she smelled like me after her shower and I had to actively think of something else so I didn't pop a boner.

The way she laughed when I tickled and chased her around like we'd been doing it for years.

Something changed yesterday, and I know she felt it too.

Swimming in the river brought me back to the night I proposed and how happy we were together. And maybe it did for her too. She opened up a bit more and let loose. Her stuck-up exterior is dissolving with each passing day we spend with each other.

We're nearly halfway through our week and I'm doing whatever it takes to make the most of it. That might not be fair of me considering she's engaged, but I'm not going to make her picking him over me an easy choice. I want her conflicted and confused so she finally has to admit her feelings for me.

Before I leave work early for the day, I check with Bodie who's having an animated conversation with Ricky.

"Everythin' okay?" I approach them.

"Tryin' to convince him to go to Ladies' Night with me tomorrow at Honky's since we're both painfully single. Tryin' to teach him how to line dance." He grabs his belt and pops his hips, mimicking the moves, but doing a poor job at it.

"You think that's gonna get you girls?" I taunt, cackling.

"At the very least, drunk girls with daddy issues." Bodie grins. "You should come!"

I snort. "No thanks."

The Honky Tonk Tavern is a college-aged bar, and I haven't been there in years given that I'm well above the age bracket.

"Bring Maisie!"

"I don't think so." I'm about to walk past them when I get an idea. "You said there's line dancin'?"

"Yep, and girls eat that shit up."

I have a feeling Maisie could use a night out drinking and dancing. Plus, it'll give me an excuse to hold her close while we slow dance.

"Alright, ya know what? I'm in. I'll bring her."

"Hell yes!" Bodie pumps his fist in the air, then turns to Ricky, jerking a thumb over his shoulder toward me. "Now you gotta go. You're not gonna wanna miss these *old folks* tryin' to find their rhythm."

I cross my arms and glare. "Funny."

Bodie grins.

Ricky sighs. "Fine, but you better teach me how to do that line dance thingy so I don't look like an idiot."

Bodie puts his arm around Ricky's shoulder and I walk away, shaking my head at him giving dancing lessons in the middle of the barn. It's a good thing I can trust Bodie to make sure his tasks are done before leaving.

Although I showered after Maisie left last night, I need to take another one before our dinner date tonight. I stop at the Branch Haven and stock up on some floral soap, shampoo, conditioner and a couple other things—in the event she's ever in my shower again.

By the time I get home, I only have an hour to get ready, but when my phone rings with Silas' photo on my screen, I pick it up.

"Kiss her yet?" he blurts when I answer.

"Is that seriously the reason you called?"

"That's a no. You sound too grouchy for a guy who got some action."

"That's a none of your damn business."

"Hmm…" He ponders. "Nah, that's still a no."

I scoff, setting my phone down on the sink counter and putting the call on speaker so I can get undressed.

"I kissed her cheek," I admit, deciding to give him something.

"Oh God! Alert the pope!"

I pinch the bridge of my nose. "I hate you."

He laughs and it echoes through my bathroom. "You love me. What're your plans for tonight?"

I've been texting him updates but just the bare minimum, nothing too personal. Although he was reluctant about my seven-day deal at first, he's been supportive and encouraging me to win her back after each date.

"I'm takin' her to eat at Summit Views. Aunt JoJo's idea."

"Oh, shit. Does that mean you're takin' out the big guns?"

"If you mean my black suit, then yes. I told her to wear a dress."

"Thatta boy!"

I snicker at his overeagerness. "Calm down."

"I want a full report tomorrow, k?"

"Mhm," I respond dryly.

"C'mon, I'm livin' vicariously through you right now."

"How so? You're engaged!"

"She's been workin' overtime for the past month so we hardly see each other during the week."

"Doesn't she work at her dad's company with you?"

"She's in the office, so we rarely cross paths."

"Maybe you should meet her for lunch, be a little spontaneous, if ya get what I'm sayin'. Bring back the spark."

"Hm...like bend her over the desk?"

"Jesus Christ," I huff out a laugh. "Pick her up, drive somewhere secluded, and get in the backseat."

"Ahh...a quickie. That means I gotta clean out my truck, but totally doable. Wait, have you had backseat sex before?"

"Maisie and I did all the damn time before we moved into the trailer. Since we both lived with our parents, we had to sneak around if we wanted to hook up."

"And y'all both fit without smackin' your heads or your legs crampin'?"

I regret bringing this up. "Yes, if she rides you, spread your thighs wide and y'all will fit."

"Thanks, man. We'll try it and I'll report back."

"No, that's not necessary…" I deadpan, shaking my head. "I'm about to hop in the shower, so I'll text you tomorrow."

"Alright, go fuck your wife. Bye!"

He hangs up before I can tell him off. *Motherfucker.*

Once I've showered, I trim my beard and mustache, then add a little gel in my hair to slick the sides down.

Shit…do I look like I'm trying too hard?

I haven't felt this uneasy since I asked Maisie to be my girlfriend fourteen years ago or when we slept together for the first time six months later.

And I can't help wondering if she's as nervous as I am right now.

Taking a bathroom selfie for a quick check, I send it to Bodie and Silas in a group chat.

WARREN

Without being assholes, do I look okay or does it look like I'm trying too hard?

SILAS

Looking good, man!

BODIE

Trim your nose hairs.

I roll my eyes.

BODIE

Otherwise, you look good!

SILAS

Don't forget the ears, too! (That's what Aundrea always tells me anyway).

WARREN

Nose and ears, got it. Anything else?

SILAS

Did you trim below the belt?

BODIE

Girls don't want hairy balls in their mouths either!

Jesus fucking Christ.

WARREN

I regret asking y'all.

SILAS

Don't forget to wrap it.

WARREN

Please be joking.

BODIE

Safe sex is no joke! Unless you have a breeding kink, but even then, no glove no love.

WARREN

Considering I'm the one who gave you the safe sex talk when you were fourteen, I'm well-aware how to wear protection.

SILAS

Do you? Hasn't it been a while?

BODIE

Maybe give it a test run and make sure the equipment still works...

WARREN

I'm blocking both your numbers.

SILAS

It's like riding a bike!

BODIE

Or scooter!

WARREN

Goodbye.

BODIE

Do you need me to bring you some condoms??

SILAS

Or lube?

WARREN

I'm good, thanks.

BODIE

Okay, good luck!

SILAS

You got this

I can't help laughing at their obnoxious support, but I do what they say and trim my nose and ears. Below the belt will have to wait for my next shower.

Once I'm groomed, I put on my black slacks, black button-up shirt, and black tie but omit the jacket. It's too hot for that.

I wish I could pick her up like a proper date, but her parents would never allow that, and since her father doesn't know about our deal, he wouldn't be happy to see me.

Right on time, Maisie knocks on my door, and I nearly lose my breath when I open it.

She's in a black floor-length, V-neck dress that fits her like a second skin and the slit up one of her legs has me reaching down to adjust myself. Her hair is halfway pulled up into a clip with long curls flowing down her back. And her heels, *goddamn.* I've never been a fan of them, but her open-toe black stilettos that strap around her ankles are giving me some very bad ideas.

I'm so fucked.

"Holy. Shit." The words fall out of my mouth before I can stop them, my gaze covering every inch of her exposed skin. "Maisie, you're—"

The word doesn't exist for the way my stomach flips at seeing her.

"So fuckin' gorgeous. Jesus Christ." I blink a few times to make sure I'm not hallucinating.

Her face goes red and the blush dips between her breasts.

I snap out of my gaze and realize what I said. "I'm sorry, that was inappropriate."

But when I meet her hazel eyes, they slide down my body and check out every inch of me just the way I was doing to her.

Clearing her throat, her gaze meets mine. "Thank you. I like this look on you. Very handsome."

She gestures toward me with her black clutch gripped in her hand.

I smooth my palms down my chest, willing my heart to slow down. "Yeah? I haven't gotten it out in a while. Wasn't sure it'd still fit."

"Oh, it fits…" Her eyes lower again, and I can't help the way my body buzzes at her actively checking me out.

I halfway wonder if she'll prefer this over my cowboy get-up I plan to wear tomorrow night at the bar.

"Should we go?" I ask, breaking the trances we're both under.

She blinks. "Yes. I'm starvin'."

I grab my wallet and keys before locking up, then help her walk down the stairs. "Those heels are killer."

"They tried to kill me a few times already tonight."

Pressing my palm to her lower back, I lead her to my truck and help her climb in. Then I carefully tuck in her dress and make sure she's comfortable before hopping into the driver's seat.

I drive us toward the restaurant but since it's on the resort side and up the mountain, I have to go slow.

"So I have to ask, and feel free not to answer if it's outta line, but does your fiancé wonder where you are each night?"

This is our fourth night together, but I've not seen her check her phone once during those times, so I wondered if she told him something or if he doesn't reach out for hours at a time.

"No." She pauses but I don't miss the quiet sigh she releases. "Truthfully, we haven't talked much since I've been here. He's on a tight deadline for work."

"Oh." I lick my lips, contemplating my next words. "You said he's in publishin'? What does he do?"

She stiffens a bit, and I worry I've hit a sore topic. "He's a writer, actually."

"An author?" I confirm.

"Yeah."

"Are you his agent?" I ask, but it comes out more accusing than curious.

"No, he was agented long before I became one."

"How'd you meet?" She didn't exactly tell me last time, but I'm too curious not to ask.

"I was at a book event and he was there. His agent is a mutual of ours and she introduced us. Things were casual between us for a long time," she says as if she needs me to know they didn't rush. "I was still uncertain about datin' again and he respected that. It was a slow progress of gettin' to know each other, and little by little, my heart opened up a bit more until I was ready to accept that I had to move on. We didn't put a label on us until he met my parents a year into datin' and they adored him."

Of-fucking-course.

"How long after did he propose?"

"Another year. I wasn't in a rush but as soon as my mother heard the news, she was already callin' the best venues in the area."

Wait a minute…

"You're gettin' married *here*?"

"Thirty minutes away, but yeah. Mama wanted a Southern weddin' and Hayes said it was fine."

"And what do *you* want?"

Her shoulders lift slightly but she looks defeated. "I loved our wedding day. I hope you know that. But it wasn't me. It wasn't *us*. I woulda been happy with a romantic and intimate ceremony, some dancin', and good food. When I brought up the Willow Chalet as a possible venue idea, my dad scoffed and said it wasn't to their level, but that's what I woulda wanted."

"Why didn't you ever say anythin'?"

"I didn't wanna fight with 'em, especially since I'm their only daughter and it seemed important to 'em. Plus, I was up at school and they were here makin' all the plans, so it was easier not to argue. At the end of the day, I wanted us to get married, so I went along with it."

"Fuck, Maze. The only reason I went with it is 'cause I thought it's what you wanted."

"Well…Mama doesn't seem to care what I want, so she and the event coordinator have been doing most of the plannin'. *Again*."

"Not that I'm wantin' you to get married to another man—just makin' that clear—but why don't you stand up to her? You don't need their approval anymore. Does Hayes even want that?"

She scrunches up her face as if to say she doesn't know. "I think he'd be fine goin' to the courthouse and elopin'. He doesn't like a lot of fuss."

"So you're both goin' along with whatever makes your parents happy instead of what makes y'all happy? That makes a whole lot of no sense."

"Yes, I know." She groans. "Why do you think I was so eager to get outta here? She's controllin' and judgmental. I give her an inch, she takes a whole damn football field."

I knew they were hard on her growing up, but I hadn't realized how bad it still was as an adult. When they wanted to buy us a new house, and we said no, I think they knew I was the reason she was gaining a backbone. Seems like Hayes doesn't know her all that well if he can't see when she needs someone to support her in standing up for herself.

"Well…if you ever need someone to intervene, let me know. She already hates me. Pissin' her off wouldn't make me lose a lick of sleep," I say, pulling into the parking lot and finding a spot.

She chuckles but quickly covers her mouth as if she's surprised herself.

"Thanks, I'll remember that."

I shoot her a wink, then jump out of my truck and usher her out of the passenger side.

The moment we enter, my stomach growls at how good it smells.

"Wow…this is so different," she whispers, leaning closer to my ear.

"It went under a remodel a few years ago. Aunt JoJo went a little overboard."

The dim-lighting makes it hard to see deeper into the restaurant, but it's a large cabin-style building with a wraparound deck for outside seating. There's a brick fireplace that adds to the mood, candles on every table, and decorative cloths. The servers dress up in three-piece suits and all the guests are required to be in formal wear.

"Mr. and Mrs. Langston," the hostess' eyes light up as if she didn't know we were arriving but clearly does. "Welcome! Your table is ready."

Resting my hand above her ass, I guide her to follow while the hostess leads us to a back area that's secluded from the rest of the guests.

I pull out a chair and motion for Maisie to sit, then help push her in before taking the seat across from her. It's hard to pull my eyes away from her, especially when I catch her looking at me too.

Once we're settled, the hostess hands us our menus and tells us the specials. "Your server will be here shortly. Enjoy."

"Thank you," we both mutter.

"Wow…" Maisie scans the room in amazement at what I can only assume was Aunt JoJo's doing.

Fairy lights hang from the ceiling, an ice bucket with a bottle of red wine is on one side of the table, and candles spread around a vase of purple roses.

"Hello, hi!" Yani enters, greeting us with a warm smile.

She's worked here for the past five years and is one of their best servers, so I'm not surprised Aunt JoJo gave her our table.

I smile in return and ask how she is.

"Have y'all had the chance to look through your menus or have any questions about the specials?" she asks, pulling out a corkscrew and then takes the Cabernet Sauvignon out of the ice.

"I think we're still lookin'," I tell her since Maisie hasn't opened her menu.

"No problem," she singsongs, popping the cork and pouring it into our glasses. "I'll be back with your bread."

She returns a few minutes later with a basket of hot rolls and butter.

"You look extra muscular in this, by the way." Yani squeezes my bicep.

I chuckle. "Thank you."

Her gaze shifts to Maisie and slowly lowers down her dress before swallowing hard.

"Are y'all ready to order?"

We both get the lamb chop special and extra waters.

"Great choice." Yani winks. "JoJo's recipe is the best I've ever had, and I rarely eat meat, so that should tell ya how good it is."

"I can't wait to try it," I say, grinning at Maisie who's jaw looks ready to snap in half.

"Be right back with your soup and salads."

After she leaves, I unfold my napkin and place it in my lap. I organize my silverware so I have room to rest my arms on the table.

"Stop lookin' so jealous. I'm not her type."

Maisie's gaze snaps to mine, her brows furrowed with guilt at getting caught.

"I wasn't. And how do you know?"

Trying hard not to smirk, I bite my lower lip. "I'm not the one she was eye-fuckin'."

It takes her a second but then she realizes. "Oh." Her eyes shift to where Yani exited. "Really?"

"I mean, can you blame her? You look sexy as hell."

That embarrassed blush reappears, and I can't help wondering what else on her body I can make red.

We drink our wine and make small talk during our appetizers. Maisie tells me she's been rereading her old books, and I beam at that.

"What's your favorite book?" I ask once our dinner is served.

As expected, the lamb chop is cooked to perfection.

"Whaddya mean?"

"What I just said…"

"Like my favorite book currently? In a specific genre? Or trope?"

I chuckle at her little panicked voice. "Like…your favorite book of all time. The one you think about regularly or one you could reread for the rest of your life and never get tired of. The top-tier book of all books."

"You know it's criminal to ask a book lover her favorite book. I have several."

"Nope, you can only pick one."

"That's cruel."

"You gotta do it," I tease.

"Fine." She dabs her mouth with her napkin, then takes a drink of her water. "It's a book that got me into readin' in the first place. I wouldn't say it's *good* in terms of literary prose, but it made me happy every time I read it. And it's always stuck with me. Even now."

"Okay..." I'm intrigued. "What's the title?"

"Dr. Seuss' Green Eggs and Ham."

My fork hits the plate and she grins.

"I was five, don't judge me."

"I'm tryin' not to..." I mock.

"I was so obsessed, I asked Jerald, our chef at the time, to make me green eggs. Of course my mother said absolutely not, but I refused to eat regular eggs. Finally, one day, Jerry surprised me with a plate of 'em. I was so happy and scarfed 'em down. But whatever he put in 'em to make 'em green made me sick. I threw up for hours and never asked for green eggs ever again."

I nearly choke on my food from laughing. "I can't believe I never knew this about you."

"It's my first tragic story."

"You poor thing. Now tell me your favorite *adult* book."

"Oh, now you're specific."

I continue eating as she gushes about a book I've never heard of, which doesn't mean much since I'm out of the loop on most things. She explains how it's a love story between a couple who would've never met if fate hadn't brought them together at just the right time. They don't like each other at first, but because they're forced to live in the same house for a few weeks, their walls eventually come down and they become friends. Except, she's keeping a secret.

"She finally reveals that she's sick and her body didn't respond to the treatment. It was makin' her sicker and the doctors couldn't guarantee the treatment would work. She decides she's not gonna continue and instead writes a bucket list of everything she wants to do before she dies. But since she's a bridesmaid in her friend's wedding, that's how she ends up in the same house as the guy 'cause he's a groomsmen. But had she continued doing treatment, she wouldn't have been able to be in the weddin' since she lived across the state and wouldn't have been able to travel."

"Oh...so kinda like the butterfly effect?"

"Right! And it goes deeper than that. Her friend is marryin' the guy's brother and the bride and groom almost didn't meet 'cause of a whole event that led to 'em being in the same place at the same time but nearly missing each other. So, if they never met or got engaged, the two main characters woulda never had the opportunity to meet either."

"Wow..." I say with a smile. "I can see why you love this book."

"It's much deeper than how I'm explainin' it, but it's main message is livin' your life like it's your last day, and not takin' it for granted that you'll get another chance to do the thing you've been puttin' off 'cause that day may never come. It's why she made the bucket list. Her chance was now or literally never."

My heart pounds against my rib cage at the words that hit too close to home.

"Safe to say, I sobbed and think about that book all the time. If I ever manage to get my hands on a signed copy, I'd display it like an Olympic medal in a bullet-proof case."

I chuckle at that because I'm not surprised. Even in high school, her bookshelves were always neat and organized, and she rarely let anyone touch them.

"How's it end?" I ask solemnly.

"They fall deeply in love, he helps her complete her bucket list—except one—and when she's too sick to travel, he stays by her side until she takes her last breath. I cried uncontrollably."

"Damn, that is sad. What was the one thing on her list they didn't complete?"

She sucks in a sharp breath as if she's holding back tears. "She added to it after they fell in love and it was to find another woman to love him after she passed 'cause she didn't want him to be alone or grieve her for too long."

"Jesus...that's..." I shake my head, unable to form the words as I get choked up.

"The epilogue though...I was unwell for weeks."

"Oh no. Did he die too?"

"No, but we get his point of view for the first time and we get his perspective on the first time he met her, when he first confessed his love to her, and some other little bits that were really heartwarming. Then it skips to three years later and he's back at one of the beaches they went to where she wanted to collect seashells. He had this...urge. This feelin' that he needed to go there that exact day, so he packed up his car and drove four hours down the coast. When he arrived, there wasn't anythin' noticeable about why he felt drawn to go, but he sticks it out and wanders about for a while before deciding to leave. Just then, a little girl runs up to him crying that she lost her mommy. He's freakin' out like, oh my gosh, did her mom get swept up in the water or somethin'. He starts walkin' around but doesn't see her."

"Well that's weird..."

"Right? Finally, the little girl points to a woman exitin' a restroom, frantically searchin' for the child. He calls out to her and she rushes over, quickly grabbing the little girl and thanking him over and over. Once she's calmed down, they exchange names and he realizes he knows her."

"Oh shit…why do I have goose bumps?" I can't help being invested.

Maisie laughs. "Guess who she is?"

"Pff…no clue."

"The girl's sister!"

"No way."

"I swear! They'd only met a couple times and once was at the funeral. The little girl was only two at the time so he didn't recognize her either."

"So…were they brought together so he'd find the child instead of someone else who coulda taken her or were they brought together 'cause they were meant to fall in love?"

"Exactly."

"What do you mean? Which is it?"

"We don't know…the book ends after they realize who each other are."

"What do you mean it *ends*? Do they fall in love or not?"

"It's up for reader interpretation."

I lean back in my chair, frustrated. "That's some bullshit."

Maisie laughs, shrugging. "And that's why it's my favorite book. There isn't always a straight answer. Like…did the female main character add that to her list on purpose so she felt less guilty that he fell in love with a sick woman who couldn't give him a future or did she do it so he knew it was okay to move on? Or both? Did the guy feel pulled to go to that beach that day to find her sister so they'd fall in love or to help the child? And did the sister also get the feelin' she had to go to the beach that day? Or does she always go to that beach and they happened to cross paths that specific day? What if they both felt that pull but only one had shown up? Or neither did and never got the chance to meet again? It's all about choices and how one small decision can alter the rest of your life."

"That is truly wild, Maze. I think I need this book."

"Well I told you most of the plot."

"Don't care. Is there a second book so we see what happens between him and the sister?"

"There were talks about it at one point, but the author never published it."

"But you're in publishin'...can't you reach out to her agent and give her a little push?"

She snickers. "Doesn't quite work that way."

"Damn. I need closure. What happens? Do they fall in love? I mean, it'd be kinda weird considerin' it's the dead woman's sister..."

But who am I to judge?

"But what if that was the whole point the entire time?" Maisie counters. "The sister and the guy were supposed to meet 'cause they're fated to fall in love but the circumstances to 'em meetin' was through the sick sister."

That makes me pause for a moment. "Nah...that's too twisty for me."

"I'm just sayin'...it's a possibility."

I don't like that there's no straight answer, but I can appreciate how it makes you think twice about your life circumstances and how small choices can lead to big outcomes.

When Yani returns, we're both laughing.

"How was your food?" she asks.

"So delicious," I tell her.

"That's great to hear! Dessert is on the way, so I'll get your plates outta the way," Yani says, reaching in front of us to grab them.

"Dessert? What'd you order?" Maisie asks.

"Not me. Must've been Aunt JoJo."

"Yes…and it comes with a surprise, so don't go anywhere." She winks, but this time it's directed at Maisie.

Her mouth parts, looking bashful, and her cheeks flush.

"Told ya," I gloat, taking a sip of the wine. "Neither of us can stop starin' at you."

chapter twelve

Maisie

WARREN'S GAZE drops to my chest as he finishes his glass of wine, not even trying to be subtle. I figured he'd like it but his reaction to seeing me for the first time was better than I imagined it'd be.

And truthfully, it felt nice to have him openly show his fondness of it. Even after years of being together, he always expressed how beautiful he thought I looked.

Meanwhile, I've been actively trying not to stare at his arms. The very ones Yani squeezed before I realized she wasn't interested in him. He has the sleeves rolled to his elbows and the shirt is tight enough to make his biceps pop through the fabric if he's not careful.

God, he looks delectable in all black.

Even his tie. He could wrap it around my wrists and then—

Oh.

Where did that thought come from?

Nope, not going there.

I'm ovulating. That's the only explanation why my body's reacting to him.

And he's familiar.

Of course my body recognizes his touch, as subtle as it is, but it doesn't mean I want to jump into bed with him.

We can be friends without it turning intimate.

Yeah, divorced besties.

That's definitely a thing.

Besides trying to keep my hormones in check, dinner with Warren has been magical. The romantic setting, the delicious food and wine, the amazing conversation about my favorite book—it's been one of the most fun nights I've had in a while.

Warren makes it easy to talk about anything because he listens intently and wants to know everything I'm thinking about it. I've missed that.

It dawns on me that Hayes doesn't know my favorite book nor has he ever asked me. For being in publishing, we don't talk much about books besides his or the authors' I'm representing.

"Oh my goodness, look at y'all!" JoJo gushes, walking toward us.

Warren stands, pulling her in for a hug. "That was a delicious meal."

"Yes, it was so good," I gush. "You're gonna have to roll me out on a stretcher after all that food."

"So glad y'all liked it." She smiles wide, wrapping me in a hug next before I can get to my feet. "You look so beautiful."

"Thank you."

"I hope y'all don't mind…" JoJo says, looking up to no good. "But I made something super special for dessert."

Yani returns and places two white round dishes on the table. Then she sets down two spoons and grins before leaving.

"Is that crème brûlée?" Warren asks.

"It is. I don't make it often 'cause it takes over six hours, but I wanted y'all to have some."

"It smells incredible," I say, leaning over to inhale it.

"I also have some strawberries comin'. And maybe one more thing," she quickly adds. "Enjoy."

She winks at Warren, and I can't help wondering what else she's up to.

"I don't think I've ever had this," I admit, grabbing one of the spoons and scooping a small amount.

"Oh my God…" I moan, my eyes rolling to the back of my head as the rich and creamy vanilla custard hits my tongue.

"Probably one of the best things you'll ever have in your mouth," he teases, taking a bite at the same time as me, but his words have me choking.

"Warren!" I scold, swallowing.

"Well…was I wrong?"

"It *is* good." I grin, taking another bite.

A moment later, Yani returns with a bowl of chocolate covered strawberries and then a violinist appears behind her.

"This is Francis." She holds up a hand toward him. "If you have any requests, feel free to ask him."

My mouth opens, unable to form words as he starts playing.

"I'm sorry about this," Warren says above a whisper. "I told her not to overdo it."

I can't even be upset because it's sweet.

"Do you wanna dance?" he asks, raising a brow.

"Here?"

He glances around, noting that we're alone in a private room. "Why not?"

Good question.

"Okay, sure."

Before I stand, Warren's behind my chair pulling it out for me. He offers his hand and I gladly accept it.

Warren mutters something to Francis, he nods and starts a new song.

He leads me to the other side of the table and pulls me into his chest. My fingers intertwine with his and my other hand rests on his chest.

"Is this Celine Dion?" I ask, recognizing the melody.

His gray eyes stare into mine and he nods. "You remember."

"Our weddin' song? Of course."

"I listen to her a lot when I'm cookin'."

"You do?" That surprises me considering he always had country music playing when we were together.

"Posey walked in while I had *My Heart Will Go On* blastin' and loves to gimme shit for it. When I let her name a couple of my chickens, she picked Jack and Rose just to fuck with me."

My head falls back with laughter. "Considerin' she has two goats named Batman and Robin, I'm not surprised."

"Maybe tomorrow night I can introduce you to 'em. You'll adore Kelly Cluckson."

The smile on my face somehow gets wider. "Do I wanna ask how she got her name?"

"Nope, you do not." He chuckles. "Or how my rooster, Chucky, got his from Bodie fallin' on his ass after he tried stealin' my eggs."

The crease lines around his mouth have me staring at his lips and wondering if I remember the last time we kissed. You never think it'll be your last, and yet, I can't remember when it was or how it felt.

"What're you thinkin' about?" he asks, and I decide to be honest with him.

"Tryin' to remember when our last kiss was and if I knew it would be." My voice unexpectedly cracks at the end, and I try to cover it up with a cough, but he notices.

"It was the day you left after the holidays. January second. You had to get back to work. We fought most of the time, you were beggin' me to move and said if I didn't, then we might as well end things. Your bags were packed and you stormed out of the trailer. I was furious you gave me an ultimatum, but I couldn't let you leave without kissin' you. So I rushed outside as you were throwin' your suitcases in the trunk. I pushed you against the door and kissed you."

His gaze lifts to the ceiling for a moment before finding mine again.

"That was the last time," he whispers.

Tears well in the corner of my eyes, but before I can stop them, they fall down my cheeks.

"I remember that," I choke out, the vivid memory now resurfacing. God, he looked so hurt when I drove away. "I think deep down I knew it'd be our last time."

"I suspected it too," he says softly.

I lean into his touch when his thumb brushes over my cheek to wipe away the tears. When my vision clears, I notice his eyes are glossy too.

Without exchanging another word, Warren pulls me in closer until my head rests on his chest and my arm wraps around him. His heart pounds against my cheek, and I wonder if he can feel mine beating rapidly too.

Warren and I dance for another few minutes before we decide to finish our desserts. The conversation shifts to something more light-hearted and once I'm physically unable to stuff anymore food in my stomach, I tap out. Warren smirks, then steals the rest of my strawberries.

"You ready to go?" he asks when I groan at being this full.

"I'm gonna have to be cut outta this dress."

He chuckles, pulls out my chair, and bends down to lift me.

"What're you doin'?" I ask frantically, grabbing my clutch before wrapping my arms around his neck.

"You said earlier you needed to be rolled outta here, so I'm helpin' ya out."

"I didn't mean *literally*, Warren. Put me down."

"Too late. I like carryin' you." He winks and walks out of our private room.

"Everyone's gonna see us!" I whisper-hiss.

"Sweetheart, the restaurant's been closed for an hour. No one's out here."

I look around the main room and see he's right.

How long have we been here?

JoJo's at the hostess station, waiting and watching us with a devious grin.

"Thanks again, Aunt JoJo."

"You kids have a good night…" she says, but I don't miss the suggestive tone in her voice.

I give her a little wave of gratitude and then Warren's walking us to his truck. He sets me down briefly to open the passenger side door before helping me climb inside.

"Good?" he asks after I buckle in.

Good? Sure, if you consider the pit in my stomach *good*, then I'm freaking great.

"Yes, thank you."

My thoughts are jumbled while he drives us to his house and

I pretend to play with the music, not sure how to end our evening without breaking down. The conflicting feelings are becoming too much. I wish there was a clear vision of how this was going to play out.

Especially when it's costing him his heart.

And mine.

Warren helps me out of his truck once again after he parks next to my car.

"Would it be okay if I hugged you goodnight?" he asks, almost nervously.

"Of course." I reach for him and he smothers me in his big arms. He's so warm and comforting.

To hell with it.

"Warren…" I breathe out his name.

One syllable is all it takes for him to read my mind.

"Are you su—"

I cup his face, pulling him closer, and crush his mouth to mine. My tongue breaches his lips, and I sink inside, seeking his warmth. He lowers his hands to my ass, picks me up, and presses my back against the side of his truck. His hips pin me in place as my legs tighten around his waist. A moan releases from deep in my throat when I feel his erection jab into my stomach.

This kiss is desperate, needy, and somehow gentle—it's everything at once. I can't keep up with the emotions bubbling inside me,

"Fuck, Maisie," he drawls, sliding down my jawline. "I'm gonna cum in my pants if you don't stop grindin' against me."

I hadn't realized I was doing it.

"Sorry," I say breathlessly, untangling my legs from his waist.

He helps set me down, both of us panting.

"Shit, I'm the one who's sorry." He scrubs a hand through his hair, causing some of the strands to stick up.

"Don't be. I'm the one who kissed you."

"Yeah, but I went overboard."

"No, it was perfect." I swipe a finger under my eye, wishing I'd worn waterproof mascara. "That was a much better last kiss. One I'll never forget."

My throat burns getting those last words out, but I had to say them.

"R-Right," he stammers, taking a hesitant step back. "Me neither."

"I'm sorry, I shouldn't have—"

"Stop apologizin'." He tilts up my chin, forcing our gazes to meet. "We have three more days together. Let's enjoy 'em, alright?"

I suck in my lower lip, nodding. "Okay."

"I'm takin' you dancin' tomorrow, so wear your cowgirl get up."

"My what?"

The corner of his mouth lifts. "Ya know—a pretty dress, cowboy boots, and hat. We're goin' to Honky's."

A laugh bubbles out of me, remembering how crazy that place was years ago. "Seriously?"

"Bodie talked me into it and I figured you could use a fun night out."

I smile wide because that does sound like a good time. "Can't wait."

This time when Warren opens my car door, he leans down and presses his lips to forehead. "Drive safe, Maze."

Although it's a twenty-minute drive to my parent's, it's hardly enough time to clear my head, but my brain's working overtime to try and make sense of how I feel.

Once I've parked, I do my best to wipe my face and fix my makeup before walking inside the house.

"Maisie." My mother's booming voice catches my attention after I cautiously shut the door.

She's in the sitting room in her nightgown and sipping tea.

"You're still up."

"As are you," she says pointedly.

"Dinner ran late." I grip my clutch in front of me, needing to get out of these heels and away from this conversation before she says what I think she's going to say.

She sets her mug down, stands, and walks toward me to close the gap between us. Without a word, she brushes her thumb over my cheek, and tsks at my smudged makeup.

"This has to stop," she warns. "You're actin' foolish. Stayin' out late and comin' home with smudged lipstick. It's no way for a lady to act, especially one engaged to another man."

A man who doesn't mind going days without hardly talking to her.

I swallow hard, amping myself up to express the thoughts that consumed my mind on the way home. "I'm goin' to tell Hayes. He deserves the truth about why I came home and—"

"Absolutely not," she snaps. "You're not goin' to ruin your relationship over a few days with Warren. Get him out of your system once and for all or whatever it is you're doin', then you go back to Hayes and marry him."

I wince at the verbal slap. "Mama—"

"You will not embarrass this family, do you understand me? After everythin' we've done, you can do this one thing for us."

"Providin' me with food and shelter as a child isn't the same as askin' me to marry a man just 'cause you approve of him."

"What about your career, then? You worked your ass off to get where you are. Why would you give that up for some young love you once had?"

"Young love?" I huff, ignoring the part about my job. She knows I work from home and could live anywhere if it came to it considering I've been on my laptop since I got here. "We were together for seven years."

"And apart for another seven," she snaps. "He can't give you what you need, Maisie. You're thrivin' in New York. You felt suffocated here, don't you remember? Your dreams were bigger than Willow Branch Mountain."

"Doesn't mean things can't change," I say weakly.

And it's clear to me they have.

"Sure, but not about this. Hayes is your future. Warren is your past. Finish up the week, get the divorce papers signed, and move on. It's time to grow up."

She walks past me without saying another word, and I'm left standing frozen in shock at my mother's harsh words.

Swallowing down the urge to cry, I go to my bedroom and fall apart against the door until I collapse to the floor. She's always had a problem with Warren's family being ranchers, although they run a successful resort, nothing's ever good enough for my parents if it doesn't involve fame or loads of money.

When they found out Hayes was a well-known author, they latched onto the idea of me being his wife, and how it'd make them look better to their friends and community of rich snobs.

I do love Hayes. We have a lot in common and our relationship's been easy for the most part. We aren't codependent and each stays busy focusing on our work without worrying about the other person getting upset. He got me out of an emotional spiral I couldn't snap out of and rescued me when I thought I lost hope of being in a happy relationship. He's good to me, even if he doesn't always make time for us, but it's not because he doesn't want to. He has deadlines to meet, as do I.

But it's clear I'm still in love with Warren. The boy I fell for at the age of fifteen who experienced all of my firsts with me, and made me feel special, not because I came from money, but because he truly adored me. If anything, he helped me feel normal in a family who tried their hardest to be above everyone else. As much as I didn't want to admit it, I can't deny the way he makes me feel when we're together. Kissing him only reminded me of how compatible we are and how our intense passion comes naturally.

Two very different men—who have my heart for very different reasons.

And no matter what I do, one of them will get hurt.

Myself included.

chapter thirteen

Warren

WAKING UP THE NEXT MORNING, I still taste Maisie's lips on mine. My cock ached all night because I refused to touch myself when there's so much uncertainty in the air between us. I'm not letting myself have too much hope, as much as I want to, but I have to protect my heart after not being able to get over her.

I want to believe she feels the undeniable chemistry between us too, but when she implied that kiss was a rewrite of our last one, I lost faith she'd ever admit it.

But I'm going to use these next three dates to show her why we're meant to be together, even if I get crushed at the end, I have to stay all in.

Maisie's the love of my life, and even if she doesn't pick me, I'll always pick her.

"You look like shit," Colton says, barging into my office without knocking and plopping down in the chair across from my desk.

"Thanks," I mutter.

"Are you not sleepin'? You have under-eye bags. And some puffiness..." He smacks his cheeks, smirking.

I stare, willing him to vanish into thin air. "Is there somethin' I can help you with or did you come all this way to rag on me about my face?"

"Well..." He leans back and kicks up his boots. "A source tells me you're going dancin' tonight with your ex-wife, who's actually still your wife, and I wanna know why I didn't get an invite?"

Standing, I push his filthy boots off my desk. "A source? You mean, Bodie."

Colt's four years younger than me but an older version of Bodie who loves getting on my nerves.

"Ricky."

"Of course." I shake my head. "I dunno when they're goin', but I'm takin' Maisie around eight."

"Eight?" He snorts a laugh. "Are the doors open that early?"

Early?

I roll my eyes. "I'm guessin' we'll run into you when we're leavin' and you're just gettin' there."

"I'll get there at ten and probably leave at one, unless I find a lady to dance with until closin' time." He smirks like I can't read into what he's saying.

"Well, it is Ladies' Night after all, so I'm sure you will." I grab my phone, checking if Maisie replied to my text. "As long as you show up to work on time."

He scoffs. "You're not *my* boss. How would you know?"

"I'm sure one of our siblings will rat you out in our group chat and then I'll tell Dad."

"You wouldn't."

He's right, but that doesn't mean I can't threaten him. It's my duty as his older brother to keep him in line.

I shrug, pinching my lips together. "Anythin' else or can I get back to work?"

"Is it true y'all are gettin' back together?"

Averting his gaze, I look at my laptop screen. "I'm not sure," I say honestly. "Obviously, I wanna, but it's not up to me. She's engaged."

"But you're fightin' for her, right?"

"All damn week, yeah."

"No, I mean *really* fightin' for her. Puttin' on that thick Langston charm."

"And what exactly does that entail?" I glance above my screen.

"You gotta throw out the baby's, sweetheart's, darling's. Kiss her knuckles. Only have eyes for her, and if another woman hits on you, pretend it doesn't faze you."

But it wouldn't faze me.

"Is that so?" I deadpan.

"Girls eat that shit up, I'm tellin' ya! Then, when you're dancin', you whisper sweet-nothings in her ear about how you can't keep your eyes or hands off her sexy body, how you're desperate for her, and *beg*."

An aspirated laugh escapes me. "Beg?"

"Yeah, beg to kiss her or eat her out. Tell her you'll die if you don't taste her. Shit like that."

I stare at him, unblinking.

"If she has a praise kink, holy shit. Tell her how good she takes your big cock. She'll be putty in your hands."

Pinching the bridge of my nose, I can't believe I'm getting sex advice from my younger brother.

"And this works for you?" I ask, more curious than anything since I've never been in the dating scene and have only slept with my wife.

"Every-fucking-time!" he gloats, and I shake my head at his confidence. "In fact, they love it so much, they end up beggin' on their knees for me."

And now I regret asking.

"You seriously sound like a douche."

"Hey, if they wanna meet Colt Jr. who am I to say no?" He throws up his hands like it's such a hardship having so many women want him. "But never be pushy about it. The more I tell 'em nothin' has to happen and we can move slowly, the more they're beggin' for it."

"How in the world haven't you knocked up a girl by now?"

"I'm horny, not stupid. I wrap it every time, thank you."

"Glad to hear it," I say dryly.

"Trust the process, it's foolproof."

"I think I'm good…" I drawl. "But thanks."

He stands. "Alright, well…don't come cryin' to me when she realizes you have no game."

"I can't wait for the day you're obsessed with a girl who doesn't give you the time of day and you're wonderin' why your *process* ain't workin' on her."

"That'll never happen."

"Pfft." I snicker. "Okay."

"Well, not anytime soon. Maybe when I'm like forty and ready to get married."

"Forty? Fuckin' hell."

"Or fifty."

"You're as bad as Bodie, I swear."

"'Cause we didn't marry the first girl who showed us their tits?"

"Dude." I scowl. "Fuck off."

"And look how that turned out?"

"You can leave now."

"See ya tonight! I'll come early so you can watch me in case you need to know how it's done."

"Please don't."

"I gotta say hello to my sister-in-law!"

"You don't."

"Maybe I can convince her to upgrade to the better Langston." He waggles his brows like an asshole.

I point my finger toward the entrance. "Out!"

He leaves but his laughter can be heard down the hallway.

That little shit. Now I'm even more nervous than I was before.

Checking my phone again, I'm relieved she responded.

MAISIE

7:30 works for me.

WARREN

Perfect. Make sure to eat enough if you plan on drinking.

MAISIE

I will. My parents make such a fuss about dinner, I eat everything on my plate so the chef doesn't get insulted.

WARREN

The chef gets insulted??

MAISIE

According to my mother, yes.

I shake my head, seriously wondering how Maisie can stand to be with her parents for two weeks.

WARREN

Well if you want me to rescue you, we can have dinner here first.

MAISIE

I already told her I'd be here and if I cancel at the last minute, she'll throw a fit.

Jesus Christ.

WARREN

Oh…then you might wanna know I planned on cooking dinner for you Friday night. In case you have to…give notice?

MAISIE

Haha, thanks. I'll let her know.

WARREN

And hell, if you want an excuse for tomorrow night, make something up and come over early.

MAISIE

What do you have planned?

WARREN

You wanna know?

MAISIE

As long as it's not skydiving or scuba diving with alligators…

WARREN

Damn, well onto plan C. How about the drive-in movie theatre? Thursday's are 80s-themed and it's a double feature.

MAISIE

OMG, really? What's playing?

I grin, knowing she's going to freak out.

WARREN

Back to the Future I and II.

MAISIE

YES AND YES!!

Laughing, I reply.

WARREN

Thought you'd say that.

I plan to turn the bed of my truck into a cozy place for us to lay together. Even if nothing can happen, I'll be in heaven being next to her.

MAISIE

I'm so excited.

WARREN

Me too. I can't wait. But until then, see you in a few hours.

MAISIE

Sounds good 😊

When I see that little blushing-smiley emoji at the end of her text and my heart immediately starts beating harder, I know I'm so fucked.

Maybe Colton's right and I should lay the charm on thicker. Why make this easy for her when she's the one who showed up and agreed to the deal? Not that I've been purposely making it easy, but up until last night when she kissed me, I've been respectful of her wishes not to cross those boundaries and act as friends.

However, that kiss was anything but friendly.

MOM

I made some fresh banana bread for you.
Come over after work.

Staring at the text, I wonder if it's some kind of trap.

Knowing my mother and how often she talks to Aunt JoJo, she wants details.

WARREN

Okay, thanks. I can't stay long though.

I need to get home and ready for tonight before Maisie arrives.

MOM

It won't take long!

So she says.

Once I've finished feed inventory and reordering what we need, I do an equipment maintenance check. With the peak summer season approaching, it's better to get everything stocked and looked over before we get too busy.

We get regular orders of hay and straw bales delivered and it's all hands-on deck to get it put away.

Before leaving for the day, I walk through the stables and check how everyone's doing. There's a nice breeze coming through the barn doors, which helps when it's a cloudless hot day.

"Hey," Bodie calls, rushing up behind me. "Ready for tonight?"

I scowl at his hand on my shoulder. "I guess."

"Colt and I will be your wingmen, Ricky too. We'll make sure y'all have fun."

"Great," I deadpan.

Three single party boys third-wheeling my date.

Exactly what I need.

"Don't worry!" He smacks my shoulder again. "It'll be fun."

"Mhm. I already regret lettin' you talk me into this."

Before leaving, I peek into a few stalls and make sure the water buckets are full.

"Alright, see ya later," I tell him and walk to my truck.

When I pull up to the two-story white farmhouse with a wraparound porch and a million plants, I let myself in and inhale the scent of fresh bread.

"Is that my favorite nephew?" Aunt JoJo calls out.

"Are you allowed to say that?" I tease, entering the kitchen.

After her divorce ten years ago, my parents converted their garage to an apartment so she could stay on the property and manage the restaurant. But when she's not working, she's usually baking with my mom.

"As long as the three of y'all aren't in the same room at the same time." She winks, drying her hands off on her apron to give me a hug.

"Thanks again for last night," I tell her. "It was incredible."

"You're so welcome, sweetie. Looks like y'all had a great time."

Oh, we did.

"Hi, honey!" Mom walks in and quickly wraps an arm around me.

I lean down to kiss her cheek. "Hi, Ma. Smells good in here."

"Glad you think so 'cause I have three loaves for you."

"Three? I'm one person."

"Give one to Maisie." She grins like I can't tell what she's doing or that she didn't get the full breakdown of last night's dinner from Aunt JoJo.

"*Mom…*" I drawl, crossing my arms and leaning against the counter.

"What?" she asks innocently.

"Gettin' Maisie back is a family effort," Aunt JoJo defends.

"Oh, so if I can't convince her, maybe your banana bread will?"

"Exactly!" Mom pinches my cheek like I'm five-years-old. "I was hesitant at first, but I haven't seen you this happy in years."

My heart sinks because while it's true, if Maisie still wants me to sign those papers, it won't only be my dreams she crushes. It'll be my whole family's too.

"Don't get your hopes up, please," I say.

"She's hopin' y'all will get back together and give her grandchildren," Dad blurts, walking in the front door.

Although we have enough staff, Dad prefers to get his hands dirty and work outside than stay in a stuffy office, so he's covered in dirt and straw. Most likely working in the barn with the boarded horses. They get rotated out to the pastures to graze.

"Grady! Hush," Mom scolds, but accepts his kiss when he leans in.

"Or just one…" Aunt JoJo adds. "We're not greedy."

I huff a laugh, pushing off the counter. "Right. Anyway…I gotta go home and feed my chickens before Maisie comes over."

"And may I suggest a shower?" Mom grins, setting a bag filled with goodies on the counter in front of me.

I frown. "I planned on it...if I'm ever allowed to go home."

Even though I didn't spend much time out of my office today, the barn smell still soaks into my pores and hair.

"Of course, sweetie. What're tonight's plans?"

I debate telling her because she'll come up with her own conclusions, but she'll bug me about it until I do. "Goin' line dancin' at Honky's."

"Oh my gosh!" Mom's eyes brighten. "I haven't gone dancin' in forever. Grady, why don't you ever take me?"

"Here we go..." He grumbles, washing his hands in the sink. "Fine, you wanna? We can. I'll get changed."

"Please be jokin'." I scowl, shaking my head.

"Honey, you won't even know we're there."

"Highly doubtful," I say dryly.

"Wait...is Honky's the one with the big flashy sign in the front?"

"Yes."

"Okay, maybe not there." My mom grimaces. "But the other one...with the Bingo hall attached."

"The nursin' home?" Dad gapes.

"Well, that's on the other side."

"If you're goin', so am I," Aunt JoJo says. "I won fifty bucks last time!"

Shaking my head, I grab my bag and walk backward out of the kitchen. "Thanks for the bread again. I'm gettin' outta here before y'all make me late."

"Have fun, sweetie!"

"Wait, hold up. I'll walk ya out," Dad says, grabbing something from his back pocket.

He rests his arm on my shoulder, then discreetly hands me a small box. "I figure it's been a while since you've needed these and you don't wanna use expired ones…"

I finally look and realize he gave me a three-pack of condoms.

Jesus fucking Christ.

"Better to be safe than sorry until you're ready to have a baby, ya know?" Then he pats my chest and walks away.

chapter fourteen

Maisie

THE BEST PART of my job is that it keeps me busy and distracted when things in my personal life are going to shit.

And then I have to face reality.

I can easily drown out the thoughts when I'm reading manuscripts and contracts, replying to emails, video chatting with my assistant, or negotiating offers.

But as soon as I close out of my thirty-seven tabs, I'm forced to face reality and contemplate what the hell I'm doing.

After a perfect night with Warren and my mother scolding me to grow up, I need to do the right thing and confess to Hayes. He deserves to know the truth of why I came here, besides the baby shower, and that I have feelings for both of them.

Telling him while he's on a deadline isn't ideal, but the longer I wait, the more I'm hurting him by lying. Truthfully, I'm not sure how he's going to react, but I'm also not sure how I want him to.

The decision between Warren and Hayes is more than deciding which future I want—it's either going back to the place

I've called home for seven years or moving my whole life back to Willow Branch Mountain—and risk regretting making the wrong choice.

The worst part is having no one to talk to about this.

I'm not super close with my brother, so I wouldn't be surprised if he hasn't a clue what's going on. The only other person I trust is my friend Jessica, who happens to be Hayes' agent and the one who introduced us. Before I flew here, I told her what I was doing and she promised to keep it between us, but considering she cares deeply for Hayes, I'm not sure she'd be on my side once I tell her I kissed another man.

My parents will be furious if I call off the wedding, but that can't be why I go through with it. However, I've gone almost thirty years trying to please them, so the thought of disappointing them makes me sick.

I'm so grateful for everything they've done, paying my way through college, and supporting me early on in my career. It'd kill me to lose them.

But I have to be able to look myself in the mirror every morning, which means I need to be honest with Hayes before this continues. I'm supposed to meet with our wedding coordinator in a couple hours, and I can't do that without getting this off my chest.

"Hello, honey," he picks up on the fourth ring.

"Hi, are you busy?"

"No more than usual, but I can take a short break for you. It's nice to hear your voice. How're things going?"

My heart pounds harder, and I swallow down the vomit threatening to surface.

"There's somethin' I need to tell you about my past that I never shared and the real reason I came here."

A brief pause and then he clears his throat. "Okay. What is it?"

"I got married when I was twenty-one to my high school sweetheart and we never got a divorce. After I left for New York, I hoped he'd move with me, but he never did. I served him divorce papers several times but he'd never sign 'em and at the time I wasn't in a huge rush to file for a default divorce, so I kept waiting and hoping he'd sign 'em the next time. I sent 'em twice since we got engaged and decided to ask him in person since he sent those back unsigned too."

"Okay..." He breathes out slowly. "Did you get him to sign now?"

"Not yet, but..." I lick my lips, confused. "You don't sound surprised to hear that I'm married to another man."

"I'm not."

I wait for him to elaborate.

"I knew you got married young."

"You *knew*? Why didn't you ever say anythin'? And how?"

"I figured if you wanted me to know, you would've told me. I hired a PI to do a full background check on you before things turned serious and he found your marriage record but no divorce decree or obituary that he had passed."

"Wait..." I blink hard, not believing what I'm hearing. "You did a background check on me?"

"Of course. I had to make sure the woman I was bringing into my life wasn't a secret obsessive fan or someone with a criminal record that would make me look bad. I had to make sure I was making the right decision."

"So this whole time...for three years, you knew I was married and still proposed to me?"

"I hoped it'd help move things along. I figured there was a

reason you never told me, so I thought maybe a little push would help get it done. I didn't like the idea of the woman I love being someone else's."

I'm speechless, too shocked to fully comprehend his words. My chest is so tight, I can't breathe.

"Maisie?"

Squeezing my eyes, I lean back in my bed to stop the stars from taking over my vision.

"Honey, speak to me."

"I-I don't even know what to say to you right now."

"You're not upset, are you?"

My mouth falls open. "That you did a background check on me? No. I understand needin' to be cautious. But the manipulatin' me part...I'm upset about that, yes."

"Well...I could say the same about you for not being honest with me, and yet, I'm not mad."

"If you knew, why didn't you ask me about it? Why act like you wanna marry me just so I'll get divorced?"

"Like I said, I figured you had good reason for not telling me, but I don't wanna share you, Maisie. I want you as *my* wife."

"I dunno if that's gonna happen, Hayes."

"Which part?"

"The gettin' married part."

"I take it he hasn't signed them?"

"No, he hasn't. But he will in a few days...if I ask him to."

"That's great." There's hope in his voice. "What's the problem, then?"

"I—" I gather the courage to say the words I need to say. "I'm not sure I want him to."

The line goes quiet, so I continue explaining.

"When he wouldn't agree to signin' and I threatened going

the default divorce route, he offered to make a deal with me, and if I still wanted a divorce, then he'd sign."

"What kind of deal, Maisie?" His tone is harsh, filled with suspicion.

I explain in detail about Warren's seven-day deal, that we've gone on four dates so far, and have three left, including tonight. I tell him that Warren thinks he can make me doubt my decision to get the divorce and then I admit it's working because I am second guessing it.

"You can't stay married to him and be engaged to me," he says after I spill everything.

"I know," I say softly. "That's why I'm tellin' you. It didn't feel right deceivin' you, even though my mother seemed to think it was, but I respect you more than that. At the very least, I couldn't continue with these last three dates without you aware of 'em."

"I don't want you going on them."

"Whaddya mean? You don't want him to sign the papers?"

"File for a default divorce and we'll push the wedding date until after it's finalized. I don't want him getting more time with you than he's already had."

I stay quiet, trying to organize my thoughts, but I can't think straight. When it's Hayes and me, I feel like one person, but when I'm with Warren, I feel like a completely different one.

And I can't decide which person I'm meant to be.

"Unless you aren't sure you want him to sign them because you're choosing to stay married to him?"

"I dunno..." I confess, my breath hitching before I say my next words. "I kissed him last night."

"Is that all that happened?" he asks after a long beat of silence.

"Yes."

"Do you still love him?"

I gulp. "Yes."

"And do you still love *me*?"

"Yes," I say with certainty.

"Then I guess you have a decision to make."

"I dunno that I can," I admit.

"I don't want to have to convince my fiancée to be with me, so do whatever you have to do these next few days to make up your mind, and I'll see you on Saturday."

"You're comin' here this weekend?"

"I was gonna surprise you since I'm on the final two chapters of my book. That way I could be there to help with wedding plans, go to the baby shower with you, and spend some quality time together since I'd been so buried in writing."

My heart aches. "Hayes…"

In any other circumstance, I'd be excited for him to come down and spend a week together without worrying about his deadline.

"I'll fight for you—if that's what you need for me to prove I want us—but I'm not going to be made a fool either while you string me along. I love you and want to be your husband, but if you don't make a decision by the time I arrive, I'll make it for you."

Guess that means I'm the one with the deadline now.

A dagger pierces my heart because while I don't blame him for not wanting to be strung along, the thought of losing him and the home we made together has my stomach in knots.

Three days ago, I was confident that my life was perfect with Hayes. I knew it deep in my bones, and not because he's in New York, but because there's a level of mutual respect that I cherish. We have similar goals and the determination to hit them.

But after that kiss with Warren? That confidence evaporated into a layer of dust that appears after a bomb gets destroyed and all that's left is the fallout.

He's reminding me of things I forgot—my roots, how much fun we had, how to laugh at myself. When I'm with him, I'm my true self again.

I should hate him for making me second guess my plans, and for a while, I loathed him for complicating my life every time he returned those papers. But all those feelings of frustration have long vanished.

"Is the music super loud or are we gettin' old?" I lean into Warren's ear so he can hear me over the bass.

"Both?" he muses, then tightens his grip on my hand and leads us through the crowd toward the bar. I can't remember the last time I've been to a place like this, but only after a few minutes, I feel out of place.

After my call with Hayes, I did a lot of thinking and decided I'm going to spend these next three days doing what I set out to do from the start—give Warren what he wants in terms of trying to change my mind. Then come Saturday, I'll make my decision. That way no one's left wondering and everyone can move on. No more second guessing or wondering about the what-if's.

"What do you want to drink?" Warren asks once we find a spot at the bar.

"I'll have…" I chew my lower lip, contemplating. "A Mai Tai."

"Okay."

"And tequila shots," I quickly add when the bartender approaches.

I've also decided I need to get wasted tonight.

He does a double take, narrowing his eyes in question. "Alright…"

Then he leans over the bar to give her our order.

I'll probably regret it tomorrow, but I can't focus or have fun with my mind going a million miles an hour. I need something to help me let loose so I'm not a Debby downer.

"I like this on you…" Warren thumbs the fabric of my purple dress covered in a cherries print. Then he flicks my cowboy hat. "This too."

"Just know I had to go to three stores to find somethin' cute."

"*Three*? Oh the hardship."

I playfully punch his stomach and immediately regret it because it reminds me about his washboard abs.

"The boots too," I say, giving his a little kick. They're light purple with a cute floral design.

"You don't look so bad yourself, cowboy." I smile up at his cowboy hat that admittedly does things to my ovaries.

He's in dark wash Wranglers with a western belt buckle and an eggplant purple button-up. The top two buttons are open and his sleeves rolled up, which also makes my stomach flutter.

It's not often he wears the cowboy getup, but when he does, I swear my clit piercing vibrates and my breathing halters.

"What was that you said to me about your outfit that day in the barn? *Casual chic?* So I guess this is *cowgirl chic?*" he taunts, laughing.

"Very funny." I kick him again, harder this time. "But if you must know, it's *flirty cowgirl*."

"Is that so?" He grabs the two tequila shots from the bar, then hands me one. "Show me whatcha got, city girl."

We clink our glasses before shooting them down, and I choke as it burns down.

"Oh fuck." I cough, setting the glass on the bar. "I can't remember the last time I had that."

"Same."

He hands me the Mai Tai and takes his beer, then grabs my hand. "Let's find a table."

"Are your brothers here?" I ask once we find somewhere to sit. He told me on the way here Colton was coming out with Bodie.

He checks the time on his phone. "Doubtful. They're probably still gettin' ready."

I sip my drink, letting the fruity combination hit my taste buds and moaning around the straw.

Warren's gaze catches mine over the rim of his beer bottle as he takes a swig.

Neither of us has brought up our kiss from last night, and I'm not sure if he's purposely not wanting to talk about it or if he thinks I won't want to. But I feel like I should say something.

"You wanna go out there?" he asks before I can speak up, pointing toward the middle of the bar.

"You wanna line dance?" I ask, surprised he'd offer.

"Sure or we can wait for a slow song if you prefer."

Warren was a good dancer even if he acted shy about it, so hell yeah I want to.

I gulp down the rest of my drink and pop the cherry into my mouth. "Let's go."

He cackles. "One second."

Tipping his head back, he empties the rest of his beer. Then he grabs my hand and pulls me onto the dance floor just as Alan Jackson's *Chattahoochee* starts playing.

I burst out laughing. "Oh my God, I haven't heard this song in ages!"

But the memories of us dancing surface as soon as I hear the lyrics. We begin by tapping our heels two times to the right and then two more times to the left before we stomp both feet forward and slap our boots behind our knees.

I'm a little rusty, so I go the wrong direction during the serpentines, but straighten myself out once we scuff our heels and do a quarter turn to the left.

By the third time, I have it down and manage to add in the clapping without messing up.

"There ya go!" Warren chuckles, not missing a beat.

"Are you sure you haven't practiced this?"

He smirks. "I may have taken a crash course after work."

"Thanks for the heads up!"

"Bodie was teachin' Ricky so I stayed to watch for a few minutes."

I wish I'd thought to look it up beforehand, but I was a bit preoccupied with talking to Hayes and trying to find the right outfit.

"Don't worry. You're doing great, darlin'." His genuine smile makes my heart melt but it's the *darling* he let slip that has everything below my waist throbbing.

Halfway through the song, the dance floor is packed and we're closer than before. Everyone hoots and claps when the song ends, half of them leaving when *Tennessee Whiskey* starts playing—an obvious beloved song here.

Warren's hands find my hips when I face him and the look he gives me can only be described as *hunger.*

"Dance with me?"

Unable to form words, I nod and let him pull me to his chest. Other couples find their way to the floor, but I can only focus on him and how good it feels to have my arms around him.

My boots give me a few extra inches of height, so when he leans down, his mouth easily brushes my ear.

"I'm strugglin' to keep my hands off you, baby. You look so beautiful in this dress."

Is he trying to fucking kill me?

His fingers tighten on my waist, and I step closer until his boots cage mine. Our bodies sway together in smooth harmony, but when I bury my face in his neck and inhale his earthy cologne, his hands clasp above my ass. A small gasp releases from my throat and when my breasts press against him, I'm positive he can feel my heart pounding.

Just as Chris Stapleton sings about strawberry wine for the final time, Warren's deep voice is in my ear again.

"Do you want to get another drink?"

I lift my head so he can hear me over the music, but he moves his face toward me at the same time, bringing our lips an inch apart. His gaze drops to my mouth and I swallow hard, begging him with my eyes to put me out of my misery.

"Sure."

But neither of us moves.

When my tongue swipes along my lower lip, his gaze tracks the movement, then flicks to my eyes as if to ask permission. I confirm by tilting my head closer.

"Hey, love birds!" I nearly jump out of my skin at the voice before I realize it's Colton. He's definitely grown up since I've seen him last. A full face of facial hair and a too-tight shirt reveals how muscular he is.

"Colt," Warren mutters between gritted teeth.

"We came early for y'all. Let's get some drinks! Bodie and Ricky are at the bar already."

I release my hold on Warren, stepping back to give Colton room to wrap his arms around us. "First round's on me!"

Warren glances over, an apologetic expression on his face, and I smile at how annoyed he looks. He's a good brother, though and tolerates Colton's eagerness to hang out with us.

He orders a round of shots for everyone, and I get another Mai Tai. While we drink at the bar, Bodie introduces me to Ricky and then I chat with Warren's brothers and catch up with them.

I don't know how many drinks deep I am, but the jumbled thoughts in my head are gone, so I'm relieved. We spend the next couple hours dancing and my ability to line dance drunk is proven wrong at me having two left feet.

"Maze, we should get you home," Warren says in my ear from behind.

Colton and Bodie have been taking turns getting me drinks, and each time Warren glares at them and tells them no more.

But I can't remember the last time I let myself have this much fun and let loose, so I'm taking advantage.

"Nooo..." I whine, spinning around to face him, but I trip over his boot and fall into him. He catches me, holding me up against his chest.

"You can't drive home like this. You're gonna have to sleep it off at my house," he tells me.

"Ooh, like a sleepover?" I waggle my brows, but I'm disoriented so my eyes twitch instead.

Warren stopped drinking a few hours ago, so he's not having

as much fun as the rest of us are. Which is a shame. Warren could use a night to let loose.

"Sure," he deadpans. "Let's say goodnight to my brothers and get outta here."

He leads me off the dancefloor to the game area where they went to play a game of drunken pool.

"We're headin' out. Y'all gonna sober up before you go?"

Ricky lifts his hand. "I stopped drinkin' an hour ago and will get 'em home."

"Thanks, I appreciate it." Then he points his finger at Colton and Bodie. "Don't stay up too late."

They both give him a mock salute and taunt him.

I snicker at them calling him *dad*.

"Bye, boys!" I go to wrap my arms around them, but Warren yanks me back and lifts me over his shoulder. "Hey! I was gonna hug 'em good night."

"Say it without touchin' 'em."

Colton and Bodie danced with me earlier when Warren told them to keep an eye on me so he could use the bathroom. When he returned, I was sandwiched between them, and that's when he yanked them away and told them to go play pool.

"Is that jealousy I hear?" I tease, hanging onto my hat as he carries me toward the exit.

He smacks my ass in response.

"You're ridiculous. They're like my little brothers."

Considering how young they were when we first met, I'd never see them as anything else than family.

"Mhm."

"Are you mad?" I ask once he puts me in the passenger side and stick out my lower lip.

"Fuck," he mutters, scrubbing a palm down his face. "No, I'm not mad. But you're gonna be hungover as shit tomorrow, so it's better to get you close to a bathroom before you throw up."

"You didn't seem to be havin' fun tonight."

"Why do you say that?"

"You have that frowny grinch look on your face."

"What's that mean?"

"You look irritated."

He tips my chin, forcing our eyes to meet. "Not at you, sweetheart."

"Your brothers?"

"A little, yes. But it's fine."

"Is that why you wouldn't kiss me?"

"No."

He makes sure my belt is buckled before shutting the door and rounding the front of the truck to get into his side.

"Then why?" I ask. "I was waitin' all night for one."

"You've been drinkin, Maze. A lot."

"So?"

"I didn't want to take advantage."

"Even if I wanted it?"

"Especially that."

"Well…" I huff, leaning back in my seat. "You're no fun."

"'Cause I won't kiss you when you're wasted and could wake up regrettin' it?"

I sigh, pressing my cheek against the cool window and unable to keep my eyes open. "I regret a lot of things, Warren. But never that."

"Alright, I'll allow it if you can say the alphabet. Then I'll know you're cognitive enough to know what you're askin' me."

I snort. That's easy. "A…B…"

"Backwards," he clarifies.

"Warren!" My eyes pop open and I scowl. "I can't do that sober."

He lifts a shoulder, starts up his truck, but doesn't put it into gear.

"Rude."

He chuckles lowly. "Don't worry, sweetheart. I plan to make up for it tomorrow when we go to the movies, assuming you're not sick or hungover."

"Really?"

"Yep."

"What exactly are you gonna do to me?"

"Maze…"

"C'mon, tell me! I'll probably forget by tomorrow anyway since I'm *too drunk* to consent."

His tongue peeks out, shaking his head at my sass. "You really wanna know?"

"Yes, please."

He undoes his buckle and reaches across the center console until we're face-to-face. Then his finger brushes softly over my collarbone. "I'd start here…" Then his finger slides up the side of my neck. "Then, kiss right underneath your ear and tell you how crazy you make me. I'd suck on your lobe and give it a little bite before moving to the other side, kissing up your neck until I reached your lips. I'd sink my tongue inside and inhale every breath and gasp."

"Holy. Shit."

I'm already gasping.

"Eventually…" He slides his finger down my chest and dips below my dress, between my breasts. "I'd make my way down here, lick and suck your pretty nipples, then kiss every inch of your perfect breasts."

"Warren…" I can't breathe. "*Please.*"

He plucks my lower lip from between my teeth. "Not tonight, darlin'. Not until you're sober and can gimme your consent."

My hazy eyes are blissed out, needing more, his hands and mouth all over me.

"I'm not above beggin'."

His breath feathers over my cheek as he chuckles lightly. "Fuckin' Colton."

"Huh?"

"Nothin'…I'm just gonna have to admit he was right."

"About what?"

"That you'd be beggin' for more."

Not exactly sure what he's talking about, but I don't care enough to ask. "So what're you waitin' for, cowboy? Give in."

Instead of giving in like I desperately need, he leans in and presses a tender kiss to my forehead. "Not tonight, baby."

"I hate you." I hiccup, sinking deeper into the seat and letting my eyes close.

"Mhm." The truck vibrates underneath me as he drives us out of the parking lot.

"No, I really, really do. Loathe you, actually. How dare you tease me after years of waitin' for you? Do you know how many times I played with my vibrator to memories of us? You were always so good at givin' me what I want and need. And now you're danglin' it in front of me and tellin' me I can't have it? So yeah, I hate you so much." I'm a rambling mess, not even sure what I'm saying, but he doesn't give me shit for it or respond. Just an amused chuckle.

I give up trying to talk him into kissing me, but it's not until he lifts me out of the seat I realize we're at his house. I must've fallen asleep because that felt like thirty seconds.

"Don't be mad." I tighten my arms around his neck, inhaling his scent.

"I'm not. Gonna tuck you into my bed so you can sleep it off."

"Not about that," I murmur, barely awake.

"Then what about?"

"Hayes Williams," I blurt.

His body stiffens against me. "What 'bout him?"

I whine when he lays me down and lose his warmth. "He's your favorite author."

"What?" The word comes out harsh, probably louder than he expected since his next words are softer. "What're you talkin' about?"

"Hayden Wills," I murmur. "That's his pen name."

I shift to my side, getting comfortable against his pillow. "Mm, this smells like you."

"Maze?" His voice comes closer, but I can't open my eyes. "Hm?"

He curses under his breath. "We'll talk tomorrow."

"You're not mad?"

"Well...I'm not happy. But we'll deal with it later."

"Are you gonna lay with me?"

"I'll be on the couch. Gonna put a bucket next to the bed in case you need it." His voice is distant, and I reach out for him.

"No, stay. Please? What if I need you?"

"I'll be in the livin' room."

"You can't sleep on that tiny couch. You're a big, big, big man."

He huffs a laugh. "Fine, I'll take the floor."

I try to argue that the floor is too hard, but I can't make my lips move as sleep threatens to take over.

I'm not sure how much time passes before the bed dips next to me and Warren's hand brushes the hair out of my face.

"If you can hear me, I'm gonna sleep next to you 'cause that floor is hard as fuck…"

Told ya. Well, in my head I did.

"So don't freak out if you wake up and you find me up here."

I'm too sleepy to speak, so I arch my back and rub my ass against him in response.

He groans. "Go to sleep, Maze."

Then he kisses my temple, and I do just that.

chapter fifteen

Warren

CHUCKY CROWS BRIGHT and early as he always does, waking me for the day, even when I'm not ready to face what might be in store.

Glancing across the bed, Maisie sleeps soundly, and I'm thankful she didn't get sick. I hate to leave her here alone, but I have to be at work in an hour.

I take a quick shower to help me wake up, then head to the kitchen to whip up a smoothie for her inevitable headache and some breakfast for myself. Grabbing some pills and a glass of water, I go back to my room and see she's not moved.

"Maze..." I kneel next to her, rubbing the pad of my thumb over her cheek. "I gotta leave for work soon, but I brought you some stuff."

My eyes lower to her shoulders and the white T-shirt she's wearing instead of her dress. I left it out on the chair next to my dresser in case she needed it and she must've changed in the middle of the night. I vaguely remember hearing her get up to use the bathroom at some point.

"Hm?" She nuzzles into my pillow, which is now going to smell like her, and wrinkles her nose. "What?"

"Hangover smoothie and water is on the nightstand with some meds. New body scrub and hair products in the shower for ya if you wanna use 'em before you go. An extra toothbrush, too."

She flutters one eye open, finally looking at me. "You finally stocked your bathroom?"

"For you."

"Wow, that was very sweet." A shy smile stretches across her face. "Probably more than I deserve."

"Well…" Unable to resist touching her, I brush loose strands of hair behind her ear. "I'm in this to win you back, especially now knowin' who I'm up against."

Her eyes widen as if she forgot she shared that little tidbit.

"Oh my God!" She smacks a palm to her forehead. "I shouldn't have blurted that."

"Not the best way to find out my favorite author's engaged to my wife, but I'm glad I know now. The chickens will enjoy the ripped pages in their coop."

She gasps, and I chuckle. Did she really think I'd keep those books in my house? At the very least, they can be used for bedding.

"I was gonna tell you…eventually. There was no easy way to mention it without makin' things tense."

I shrug, agreeing that it probably put her in a difficult situation once she saw my books.

"Drunk off your ass was one way to go."

She squeezes her eyes shut. "I'm so sorry for last night. I fucked up."

"You needed a night where your brain could shut off for a

few hours. I'd rather you do that with me than by yourself anyway."

"My stomach and head are cussin' me out, but I had fun dancin' with you. Felt like we were twenty-one again."

"I did, too." My grin forms into a scowl. "Until my brothers stole you."

She groans, digging deeper into the mattress and pulling the covers over her face. "Any chance we can forget last night happened?"

"Not a chance," I say, yanking them down so I can see her beautiful eyes. "Forever ingrained into my memory. Especially carryin' you out over my shoulder and you beggin' me to kiss you in my truck."

"And now I'm gonna die of humiliation." She reaches for my pillow and plops it over her face.

"So dramatic." I chuckle, pushing it away, then cup her cheek and rub the pad of my finger over it. "As long as you stay sober enough tonight to gimme permission, I'll kiss you—assumin' you still want me to."

A blush covers her face and neck.

"We can talk later. For now, rest and take it easy." I press my lips to her forehead, tempted to slide them lower.

"You have to leave?"

"In a few, yeah. But stay as long as you want, okay? I made your favorite smoothie, assumin' it's still your favorite, or if you want to eat somethin' else, help yourself to the fridge. There's also three loaves of banana bread from my mom and Aunt JoJo."

"Mm…that sounds delicious." She smiles wide but then pushes herself up and leans against the headboard. "You should know I told him about you."

That has me arching a brow and contemplating my next words carefully. "What did you say?"

"The truth." She swallows hard, but it's her expression that concerns me. Guilt, maybe? Or hesitation. "When I confessed some things to him, he told me I had a decision to make by the time he arrived on Saturday."

"He's coming...here?"

Nodding, her gaze drops to her hands. "He was gonna surprise me. He said if I can't decide by then, he'll decide for me."

Well fuck.

"Oh." I scratch over my cheek, the two-day old scruff feeling rough under my nails. I'm about to tell her we can cut the seven-day deal short so she has more time to make her decision, but then I remember my brothers' advice and my parents' and aunt's encouragement—they're rooting for me to remind her why we should be together.

I didn't suggest this deal to make it easy on her. The purpose is to help her realize what could be and how in love with her I still am. If I don't give it my all, it'll be a missed opportunity I'll never get again.

"Guess that means I better make sure these next two dates are unforgettable." I wink, grabbing her hand and kissing her knuckles. "'Cause I'm still in this, no matter who he is or what he says."

Sucking in her lower lip, her teeth drag over it. "Well, I did agree to seven days."

She's trying to hide her excitement, which means she wants them as much as I do.

"Good. You still have to meet my chickens, so come at seven and we'll head out after."

"Is this another no-heels situation?"

Standing, I bark out a laugh. "Honestly, wear whatever you want. I'm puttin' an air mattress with blankets and pillows for the bed of my truck so we're comfortable. You probably won't even keep your shoes on."

"Sounds perfect after dancin' all night. My body's not moved like that in a long time."

That makes me wonder how vanilla hers and Hayes' sex life must be, but then I shake my head to get that thought out of my brain.

"Quick question though…" One I haven't been able to stop thinking about all night. "Isn't Hayes like fifty-something years old?"

"Um…" She coughs as if she hadn't expected that. "Forty-five."

Well…that confirms my vanilla theory. Curious if he can even get it—

Nope, not thinking about that.

"It's not what you're thinkin'," she says, and I snap my gaze to hers wondering if I said my thoughts aloud. "That I must have daddy issues, right?"

"No…" I am *now* though.

Leaning down, I swipe my finger along her lower lip, plucking it out from her front teeth. "I was thinkin' how it's been seven years since you've been thoroughly fucked that wasn't in missionary."

Her mouth opens but then quickly closes, swallowing down her gasp. "What's wrong with missionary? We've done that."

"Sure, in between a dozen other ones." She loved being flipped around, pressed into the shower wall, or ride me in the back of my truck.

I stand to my full height, no longer touching her. "You're tellin' me you get off being in one position the whole time? Does he make sure you come first?"

"That's pretty bold comin' from someone who hasn't had sex in years! Just 'cause he's a little older—"

"A little?" I bite out. "He was gettin' his driver's license when you were exitin' the womb."

She rolls her eyes, crossing her arms as if it's not the first time she's heard comments about their age gap. Honestly, it only bothers me because it's *him*.

A person I idolized because of how much I enjoyed his books and now each one I've read feels like a stab to my chest. Every word a lie.

And fuck yeah, I'm being petty, but I no longer care.

"Well it's a good thing we didn't meet until I was twenty-six."

"You're not worried that you'll only be forty-four when he's sixty? Does he have to take Viagra to fuck you?"

"Warren!" She slides out of the bed, then pushes me out of her way, but I barely move.

"That's an honest question. Men tend to lose their ability to get it up naturally as they age."

"So what? Women go through menopause and sometimes lose their sex drives. It's not supposed to be a deal breaker."

"But you'd usually go through it together being from the same decade."

"Well sometimes people fall in love with older or younger people. Why is this any of your business?"

My jaw tenses and reality slaps me in the face. I'm being a jealous dick.

"You're right. It's not."

Oh except, you're my *wife*. And the thought of another man

touching her makes me feral. Perhaps it was better when Hayes was a faceless person I had no connection to.

A little too late for that.

I grab my wallet and phone off my dresser but then pause at the thoughts taking over.

"How do you know you're not his midlife crisis? You met three years ago? He woulda been in his early forties when a lot of men have affairs or buy expensive cars."

She stomps until she's in front of me, tilting her head to meet my hard gaze, hands plastered on her hips. "Are you that insecure you're goin' to nitpick everythin' about him to justify how I could possibly be with a man like him when I was with a man like you first?"

"Maybe, and yeah, I don't get it."

She pokes me in the chest, glaring with fury. "You don't have to get it! It's not your life, it's mine."

"Your boring and miserable life?" I blurt, no longer able to stop the words coming out of my mouth. "It's why you work yourself to death. It's why these past few nights have made you come alive for the first time in years. Why you could let loose— you knew you were safe with me."

"I already told you I work a lot 'cause I love my job." She huffs, throwing her arms up and pacing. "So which is it now? I work too much 'cause I'm bored or 'cause he's not sexually satisfyin' me?"

Both?

"You don't need to work as much as you do, it's not like you need the money! You have a trust fund for fuck's sake. Your parents paid for your apartment and everythin' else you needed, which means you work yourself to death 'cause you're missin' something in your life. You work to fill the void instead of admittin' work is all you have to live for. Do you even have friends outside of the industry?"

Her nostrils flare, face beaming red as narrowed eyes glare at me.

"You know that's not fair. I just started my own agency last year, so of course it takes a lot of time to get it up and runnin'. I focus on it so much 'cause it's my passion. Not that you'd know anythin' about that."

Ouch. Except my passion was her and building this house for us.

"Would you be honest with yourself for once? There's passion and then there's an unhealthy obsession to avoid reality. If you were truly happy in all aspects of your life, your job wouldn't come first. You can love it and still have some sense of work-life balance. It doesn't have to take over your whole world."

"Oh and what…you're livin' life to its fullest? Out here in your secluded cabin with chickens for neighbors! Do you know what it took to find you in the first place? One person I spoke to in town thought you had moved away to another state 'cause she hadn't seen your face in three years. Another for sure thought you had died. Even pointed me in the direction of a cemetery. The man livin' in our old trailer wasn't quite sure where you lived, but he knew it was on the property somewhere. If it wasn't for drivin' up and down these back mountain roads and seein' your old truck parked by a tree, I woulda never found you. And why do you have that ole thing anyway? Does it even work?"

My gut flips. I wondered how she found me, although I figured she checked there first. There are a couple ranch hands who live in the trailer during the summer. They only work at the resort during our busy season, so they're not locals.

"No, but it holds a lot of memories I didn't wanna let go."

Namely, all the memories of her and me.

"Right, 'cause you're stuck in the past. I might be glued to my computer for fifteen hours a day but at least I'm workin' toward a future that I can be proud of. That I built, on my own! It's not always about goin' out with the girls for brunch or makin' love all night long. Sometimes it's about growin' up and facin' reality. And hopefully findin' someone to match your goals and dreams."

I tense, jaw locked at how angry she is. It's clear we're at a stalemate.

"Then maybe you should go back to your fiancé who can give you what you want 'cause I won't watch you work yourself to death and forget what's truly important in life."

She stumbles back, her chest rising and falling as her breath hitches. "W-what?"

"There's supportin' your dreams and there's enablin' you to *only* think about those dreams. A career isn't supposed to take over your whole goddamn life."

"It doesn't—" She promptly stops as if she lost her train of thought on whatever argument she was going to make, so I pour out my soul and hope it's enough to help her understand.

"Maisie, I want a family with you. I wanna wake up on the weekends with you in my arms. I wanna make breakfast for you and our kids. I wanna get 'em ready for the day and take 'em hiking or horseback ridin'. I wanna snuggle with you on the couch or read in bed. Then I want you to tell me all about your book when we're in the shower together. I don't want my partner to care more about her job than her family—'cause at the end of the day, it is just a *job*. You're not gonna look back on your deathbed and wish you worked more hours, you're gonna wish you spent more time with your loved ones. But if that's the kind of man you want—the one who'll put his job first and not care that you're doin' the same thing—then I'm man enough to admit that's not me and I'm not the one for you."

She swallows hard, licking her lips, thinking hard about her next words. "Why didn't you ever say any of this before? It's not like I didn't make it obvious what I wanted to do in New York."

"'Cause I couldn't compete with your parents and their lifestyle they wanted for you. I'd always thought that didn't matter to you, the flashy and expensive shit, but as soon as they could fund you movin' up there, you left everythin' behind. Chasin' you wasn't an option, so all I had was buildin' the future we planned together and hope like hell one day you'd come back to see what you were missin'.'"

She blinks up at me, on the verge of tears, and I wish I could comfort her. Lean in and wipe her cheeks, then kiss away the pain.

"Being born into my type of family meant my life's been planned out since day one. What was expected of me, where I'd go to university, the type of man I should marry. I needed to prove to myself and everyone else that I was more than their daughter or someone's wife. Just once, I wanted to make my own plans and take care of myself. And yeah, I needed their money to help at first, but I've paid 'em back every penny they gave me since I moved to New York. I haven't touched my trust fund. I wanted to be with you, but I wanted to do this for myself more. Build my own legacy that was founded on my own merit. I didn't expect to fall in love with another man. And I sure as hell didn't expect to still have feelings for you after all these years."

My heart pounds uncontrollably and the blood rushes to my

ears as I wrap my brain around each word she says. We were so young, so desperately in love, but too young to realize the future we had ahead could change at any moment. My tunnel vision only showed me her. Us. Together. Nothing else mattered.

And I should've seen it sooner.

The way her parents pressured her to be what they wanted and then I started doing the same. Expecting her to be happy being my wife when she wanted so much more.

I understand more than I want to admit, but I do.

She needed to experience life on her own terms.

Although I stand by what I said, her perspective changes everything.

"Why didn't you tell me this before when I fought so hard against movin' there?"

She shifts nervously between her feet, rocking back and forth. "I didn't know how to explain it back then. A part of me felt silly for needin' to leave my hometown or that no one would understand. Poor rich girl wants to fly from the nest to prove she's not the stereotype everyone assumes she is. I thought it'd make me sound ungrateful for what I had but it had nothin' to do with that. I had to prove to myself I was more than my family name."

"I get it now, Maze. I really do. And I shouldn't have manipulated you into spendin' a week with me just to get somethin' in return." My mouth goes dry before I say my next words but I force them out. "You're off the hook. I'll sign the papers."

Before she can respond, I exit the bedroom, my heart lodged in my throat as I find the manilla folder that's been on my coffee table for the past week. Grabbing a pen from the kitchen, I flip through the pages until I reach the last one awaiting my signature.

Staring at it, I contemplate what this means.

I'm letting her go. It's time.

And then I sign it.

chapter sixteen

Maisie

WHEN THE FRONT door slams closed, I know he's left.

My feet are still frozen in place from where he bolted his bedroom. I couldn't find the words to speak up and stop him.

I can hardly breathe. My chest's tight and head's dizzy.

Rubbing my sweaty palms down the T-shirt, my vision goes fuzzy.

I'm having a panic attack.

The reality of his words hit me hard. Because even though he understands why I had to leave and focus on what I wanted, his perspective makes a lot of sense too.

I don't want to look back on my life and regret making work my only priority. If it was all about proving to myself I could stand on my own two feet, I've done that. I've been hustling to create my own agency, and I did it.

So why am I still working nonstop instead of enjoying the freedom that comes with being my own boss? Although I have an assistant, I could hire more help or take on less work.

Do I use work as an excuse to avoid not being happy in other aspects of my life?

Is it possible Warren's right about filling a void?

Before coming here, I would've said absolutely not.

But when's the last time I went out with friends where we didn't talk about our jobs? Or make friends who weren't in the publishing industry? They're more like acquaintances if I'm being honest. They only know me in a professional sense, not my personal life.

Would Hayes work less if I asked him to? Go to the theater, travel the world, make friends in other countries.

I honestly don't know that he would.

But Warren wouldn't even leave Tennessee for me.

Finally moving my feet, I walk to the kitchen and find the divorce papers I've been asking him to sign for years. And there on the last page is his signature.

This is what I wanted and why I came here in the first place.

He...*let me off the hook*. We had two more dates planned and now it's...*over*.

I should be relieved.

But then why does it feel like he ripped out my heart and stomped on it?

I put them back in the manilla folder, grab the rest of my things, change out of his T-shirt, and do the walk of shame back to my parent's house.

If my mother's upset with me for not coming home last night, she doesn't show it. Neither does my father.

They're at the breakfast table like every morning, and when I wave to them, neither acknowledge that I'm still wearing my dress from last night. And most definitely look wrecked. Mascara rubbed off. Hair in a messy bun.

Tear-stained cheeks.

"Freshen up and come eat, honey," is all my mother says when I go toward the staircase. "We have some things we need to discuss about the weddin'."

My voice is too hoarse to speak, so I nod, then make my way to my bedroom. I'm waiting for the reality of what happened to hit me. That he's signed the papers and it's possible I'll never see him again. We fought with each other but he didn't *fight* for me the way he said he would. Didn't beg me to reconsider his perspective, which I thought about the entire drive home.

Because I do see it and am now questioning everything I thought I knew.

If Hayes and I were madly in love, we'd want to spend more quality time together instead of only coexisting in the same space. We're basically co-workers, not lovers.

Warren and I could never keep our hands off each other. Physical touch was our love language. That and quality time.

When I'd come home during college breaks and holidays, we were inseparable. He rarely worked late unless there was an emergency, and if there was, he always insisted on making it up to me. Even for those few months after I graduated and we lived in a trailer behind his parent's house, we ate dinner together every night and spent the rest of the evening glued to each other's sides. Sometimes we'd go out, other times we'd stay in, but it didn't matter because as long as I was with him, I was happy.

And maybe that scared me.

Maybe I thought I had to run off and work toward a goal so I wasn't dependent on yet another person. My parents made sure I was dependent on them, never allowed me to get a job, and my husband offered me the same privilege. He wanted to take care of me. But I didn't want to feel trapped.

I'd heard of women in their forties or fifties who suddenly were on their own after years of raising babies and taking care of the households to be left for a younger version of themselves. They had nothing to show for their life because they hadn't worked and even a college education wasn't enough to get them employment. I knew I had my parent's money as a backup if I were to ever end up in that situation, but that's the thing—I didn't want to depend on their money. I wanted to do things myself and prove I was capable. They never let me try. Everything was handed to me.

I needed to be able to look myself in the mirror and make myself proud.

Marrying Hayes won't change that. I doubt anything would change between us. He'd rather go on a book tour than plan our honeymoon.

Once I've showered and changed into clean clothes, I dig around my old bookshelves for a box I know I stored in there. Behind my books, I find it.

I decorated the lid when I was fifteen. It's covered in glitter glue and mini polaroids with the words MAISIE + WARREN 4 EVER written in the center. It's adorable but has definitely seen better days.

Carefully removing it, my heart squeezes at what's inside. It's been years since I've looked through it.

We couldn't use our phones in class, so we'd write each other little notes and pass them between blocks. We took a million selfies and photos from dances. There has to be a dozen movie stubs from the drive-in and movie theater in another town.

Being under twenty-one, there wasn't much to do outside of the ranch or resort.

It's basically a time capsule. When life was simple and loving each other came easy.

I unfold one of the notes and realize it's the piece of paper he wrote his vows on.

Maze,

You know when it's been raining for days and you feel down because the weather's so gross? Then it finally ceases, the clouds clear the sky, and the sun beams down on your skin for the first time in a week. You inhale the country air, and the smell of spring flowers and freshly mowed grass hit your senses. Calmness rushes through you as the view in front of you takes your breath away. That's how I feel every time I look at you.

You captivate me.

You make me breathless.

You remind me there's always something to look forward to during the gloomy days because the sun always returns, and when it does, it comes in the form of unconditional love and happiness. And that's you.

I can't imagine my life without you in it and I hope I never have to.

You're my whole world and I'll never stop loving you.

This isn't till death do us part.

It's until the next lifetime where you and I exist together.

I will always seek you out, no matter who or where I am.

You're my soulmate now and for eternity, wherever that exists, I'll always wait for you.

The sleeve pressed against my face is soaked by the time I finish reading.

How the hell did I let him go?

Warren's words are as true today as they were seven years ago on our wedding day. It's why he chose being alone over moving on. He'd rather wait until we find each other again in another life than be happy with someone else in this one.

I flip through a few more photos, smiling as the memories resurface, and remembering how good things were then.

I don't know if we can rewrite history, start fresh and try to get it right a second time, but as Warren said—I don't want to look back on my deathbed and wonder about the what-ifs. I'd regret it forever.

Once I've wiped my face and put everything back in the box, I head downstairs to meet my parents. Dad's reading the news on his phone and Mom's flipping through a magazine, barely touching her food.

"Darlin', I found the perfect shoes for you to wear with your reception dress. Let me know what you think…" She reaches for her phone without making eye contact.

One wedding dress wasn't enough for my mother. No, I

needed a ceremony gown and a reception dress, which means two sets of shoes and jewelry to go with each.

I sit across from her, pushing in my chair as the chef sets my plate down in front of me.

"Thank you," I murmur, but my appetite is gone.

"How stunnin' are these Louboutin's?" She holds up a photo of sparkling strappy ankle heels. "They're gorgeous on their own but won't take away from your dress."

"They're nice," I say, picking at the fruit in front of me. "I'm not sure I'll need 'em though."

"Of course you will. The other shoes are flatter, so you'll want a heel with the silkier dress. It'll accent your legs, too."

"I meant 'cause I'm not sure there's gonna be a weddin', Mama."

My dad finally acknowledges me and lowers his phone long enough to gape at me. "Whaddya mean?"

"I told Hayes I'm still married..." Since my father doesn't know I've been spending the past week with Warren, I tread carefully on how to tell him.

"Why would you do that?" Mom snaps. "You said Warren was gonna sign the papers."

I swallow down the blade lodged in my throat. "He did."

"Then what's the issue?" Dad asks.

"I don't want to sign 'em," I admit.

"Don't be foolish, Maisie." Mom tsks, reaching for her mimosa. "This is what you wanted. You're engaged to Hayes."

"I'm aware," I bite out. "But I learned he knew I was married this whole time 'cause he hired a PI when things were becomin' serious. He never said anythin'."

"He did a background check on you?" My dad's brow lifts.

When I nod, my mom waves him off. "So what?"

"So he proposed to secretly push me to get divorced instead of tellin' me he knew and wanted me to do it."

"He doesn't wanna share you, sweetie. Can you blame him?"

"People who love each other aren't supposed to lie to one another, Mom. We both kept secrets from one another for three years."

"Yeah, but it's not that big of a deal. He wants you to be his wife, not some other man's. That's understandable."

"What else did he find on you?" Dad asks.

"As far as I know, that's it. Why?"

"Does he know about your trust fund?"

I take a sip of my water before my mouth goes dry. "I never told him, but that doesn't mean he doesn't know about it or at least assume I have one. I haven't touched it myself."

"You may want to let him know so he's not surprised when he sees it in the prenup," Dad says.

"What prenup?"

This is the first time I'm hearing of one.

"I suggested our lawyer write one up," he states. "Considerin' how long it took to get Warren to sign the papers, I don't want you goin' through that again."

"He's never goin' to sign that," I blurt. "He's old fashioned as it is."

"Sure he will." Mom grins confidently. "It protects him, too."

"Considerin' his IP and copyrighted works, he won't want to put that at risk, so if he wants to marry you, he'll agree to protectin' both of your assets."

"That..." I shake my head, unable to comprehend this. "That ain't a marriage. Separatin' things as if we're already on the verge of splittin' up. Why bother at that point?"

"Honey, it has nothin' to do with how you feel for each other.

But you both had lives before enterin' each other's, and there's nothin' wrong with protectin' it."

"Warren didn't go after it. What makes you think Hayes would?"

"Well…" Mom snickers. "Warren isn't Hayes."

Exactly.

"Warren's entitled to half of it though, right? We never signed a prenup."

"Our lawyers would make sure his claim never saw the inside of a courtroom. If he went that route, he'd risk his family's ranch."

"You'd go after 'em?"

"If he contested the divorce, yes. We'd fight and keep him in court for longer than he could afford."

"Daddy!" I drop my fork.

"It's not personal, sweetheart."

"It is to me!"

"Does it matter anyway?" Mom shrugs. "He signed the papers and once they're filed, it'll only take a couple months to go through, and you'll be in the clear for the weddin' date."

It matters because I'm realizing how heartless my parents truly are. Warren has every right to contest the divorce to get his fair share and for them to so easily threaten his family's livelihood doesn't sit right with me.

Warren wouldn't anyway, so it's hypothetical, but my parent's true colors are alarming.

"I'm callin' it off," I blurt when my parents are in the middle of a discussion. "Cancel everythin'."

Mom's gaze shifts to me with deep frown lines around her lips. "Maisie…let's not be rash."

"I'm not marryin' another man while being in love with someone else."

"You're what?" Dad raises a brow, seemingly unaware. "Since when?"

I shift uncomfortably but then straighten my spine to tell him the truth. "I think I always have been. Long before I came back here. But it took a few days to realize it."

Mom purses her lips, disapproving of my outburst. "She's been spendin' time with him."

"Warren?"

"Yes, Daddy. Every night since last weekend."

"Oh." He meets my mom's eyes and they share a look. "Does Hayes know this?"

"Yes, and he basically told me to make a decision by the time he arrives on Saturday or he'd make it for me."

"Apologies for interruptin' sir, but you have a call," one of the housekeepers reluctantly enters the dining room. "In your office."

When he leaves, I'm ready to bolt too.

"Hayes will be here in two days. Don't make any decisions until you see him," Mom says, lowering her voice. "It's easy to reminisce with an old flame when it's the two of you. But you'll remember how much you love Hayes too once he's here."

Doubtful. But I nod anyway, no longer in the mood to argue.

That doesn't mean these two days can't continue as planned.

Warren still owes me two dates and I'm going to make sure he follows through.

chapter seventeen

Warren

GOING to work after such a disastrous morning feels wrong. There's no way I'll be productive but it beats sitting at home alone. I need to get out of my office today and work up a sweat. Something to keep my mind off her.

I close my laptop and go in search of Bodie. I find him with Ricky and Colton.

Of course.

"Hey! He's alive." Bodie cracks up.

"I'm surprised y'all are too."

"So, how'd it go last night?" Colton waggles his brows.

"Not great." I shift my gaze to Bodie. "I'm gonna work in the pasture today."

"We were about to unload the hay and straw bales from the trailer."

"Delivery arrived?"

"Yeah, a few minutes ago."

Oh shit. I'm usually the one who signs off on it.

"Don't worry, I checked it over," Bodie says, pulling on his gloves. "If you wanna help, we're goin' to the loft now."

I nod, rushing to my office to grab my gloves and then meet them outside.

The loft's above the stables, half for hay, the other half for straw, which means we're constantly going up and down the stairs until it's full. We keep a stock of each in a stall for easy accessibility, but someone has to restock it when it gets low.

We recruit a couple other ranch hands and manage to finish within an hour. I'm drenched in sweat, but it felt good to stay busy and do some physical work.

For the rest of the morning, I switch between mucking stalls and checking emails. Bodie knows something's up, but he doesn't pressure me to talk about it. Honestly, I'm not sure what to say or if I want to admit I failed.

But I do need to get it off my chest without fear it'll get back to the rest of my family.

WARREN

I signed the papers.

SILAS

Already? I thought you had seven days?

WARREN

Change of plans.

SILAS

I can leave work early if you need someone to
drown your sorrows with, or if you prefer
another route, I'll drive us to a strip club.

I snort. No way his fiancée would care for that.

WARREN

Thanks, but I think I'd rather drink alone.

SILAS

Oh come on. That's never a good sign. If you're gonna get stupid drunk, at least let me witness it.

WARREN

Thanks for the support, asshat.

SILAS

Kidding! But seriously…you can't drink with your chickens again. That's next level depression.

WARREN

That was one time! Plus, I like my chickens more than most people.

SILAS

Maybe we should explore why that is…

WARREN

No thanks, Dr. Matheisen.

SILAS

I would make a badass therapist, wouldn't I?!

I shake my head.

WARREN

Actually, I need to restock my firewood pile. So I'll probably do that instead.

SILAS

Is that code for something?

WARREN

No, it means I'm low on wood.

SILAS

In the middle of May?

WARREN

It gets chilly at night up in the mountains.

Which is true...I rarely turn on my furnace since I prefer the ambience of the fireplace.

SILAS

Alright, well call me if you chop off your leg
and need a ride to the ER or whatever.

WARREN

How thoughtful.

SILAS

That's why I'm your best friend!

Chopping wood until I can't feel my arms sounds like the perfect way to clear my mind.

Before I can leave early for the day, Ricky tells me a horse ran off after its rider hopped off and forgot to tie it up.

Most of our horses are trained well enough to stay put, so something must've spooked it.

The guides are also trained to stay with our guests and call for help instead of chasing after them.

"Bodie tackin' up a horse to go look for it?"

"He's out with another guest."

"Shit. Okay, I'll go.

I grab Priest and get him ready, then take off on the trail behind the stables. It takes me three hours to find her. *Lilith.*

Of-freaking-course.

"C'mon you hellion."

She lets me approach without issue, but she's irritated and timid. That's when I realize she's injured. There's blood coming from a nasty gash on her front left leg.

"What'd you get into?" I ask softly, carefully sliding my hand down but not touching the wound. She punctured it on something sharp.

Most likely one of those posts Bodie was supposed to dig up.

Grabbing my phone, I go to text Bodie to call Dr. Warner since she'll need to get looked at, but footsteps approach from the other side of the clearing.

A loud whistle, most likely to get Lilith's attention, and a slew of curse words.

"Oh fuckgoddammitshitfuck."

"Bodie?" I call out.

Priest whinnies at the sound of branches cracking. I rub along his neck to settle him down, but it's Lilith who flips out before I can grab her reins. She bucks, something I've only seen her do twice, and nails me right in the chest.

I go down before I'm able to stop myself and lose my breath. My head hits something hard, and I groan at the impact.

"Warren!"

Bodie's voice in the distance grabs my attention, but when I open my mouth, nothing comes out. I'm gasping for air, unable to call out for him.

The pain in my chest starts to intensify and my head pounds at whatever I landed on. I try to focus on my breathing and slowing it down before I have a full-on panic attack.

"Oh shit, dude." Bodie comes into view, kneeling beside me. "Callin' for help right now."

He pulls out his cell, but I'm struggling to keep my eyes open.

How the hell did this happen? I've been around horses my whole life and should've kept Priest further away from Lilith once I realized she was injured so we weren't within kicking distance.

"Stay awake. You're okay." He shakes my arm, putting the phone to his ear. "You're gonna be fine, Warren. You're in shock and knocked the wind out of yourself."

I try to shake my head. It feels worse than that.

"Leave me here," I mumble.

Wouldn't that be poetic? I'd rather die here alone than face the heartache I've been avoiding all day.

"What're you talkin' about? I'm not goin' anywhere."

He talks to someone, requesting immediate help, but the reality is we're a few miles from the stables. Even if an ambulance rushed here, it'd take them thirty minutes to arrive and find us.

"Lilith's hurt," I barely mumble.

"Lilith? Yeah, she took off when I rushed over. I texted Colton already to come find her. He'll call Dr. Warner to examine her injury."

My vision goes blurry and it gets harder to suck in a breath although my heart's racing.

"Bodie."

"I'm right here."

"Tell her I love her," I force out the words with all the energy I have left.

"Warr—"

Darkness takes over before he can finish shouting my name.

There's a theory that when it's your time, your favorite or most cherished memories flash through your mind, but I didn't realize I'd be able to hear her voice and feel her touch before I go.

Talk about torture.

chapter eighteen

TRYING to focus on reading and returning emails when all I want to do is go back to Warren's is brutal. But I'll have a much better time knowing there isn't a pile of work waiting for me.

Assuming he'll want me to stay.

Each day since I've been home, my mom's brought up something about the wedding. One day, picking out the Save the Date's, another was about the music, and today the shoes.

That's partly why I flew down here so it was easier to make decisions with the coordinator, but my heart's no longer in it.

I need to tell Hayes but doing it over the phone feels wrong and disrespectful, especially when he's coming in two days.

As I'm closing my laptop to take a snack break, Hayes sends me a text—the first since our last conversation.

HAYES

Hi, darling. I'm struggling to get these last
chapters finished and decided to rewrite a
couple before writing the ending. I don't think
I'll be done before Saturday, but I still want to
see you in person, so I rescheduled my flight
for Tuesday. I want to be able to have a clear
head when we talk and I will once my book is
turned in.

I don't have it in me to even be surprised.

HAYES

This doesn't mean I'm not going to fight for
you. I've been thinking a lot the past twenty-
four hours and told my publisher I'm cutting
the book tour short, so when I get there we
can plan our honeymoon. I'd rather spend that
time with my wife and I should've considered
that months ago.

Okay, now *that* does surprise me.

Twist my engagement ring, I contemplate how to respond,
but before I can, a new message pops up.

WARREN

Hey, Maisie. This is Bodie. Warren got hurt at
the ranch. I'm in the ambulance with him now
on the way to the hospital. I don't know what's
going on between y'all, but he told me to tell
you he loves you before he lost
consciousness, so I figured you should know.

I gasp for air, squeezing my throat as I reread his message
three times.

He told Bodie to tell him he loves me before he passed out?

Fuck, that kills me.

> MAISIE
>
> Which hospital?

As soon as he replies to tell me where to go, I'm halfway out the door.

> MAISIE
>
> On my way. Is he okay?

> BODIE
>
> His vitals are all over the place but he's breathing. Lilith kicked him in the chest and he went down hard. Smacked his h**ead.**

Holy fucking shit.

That's not good.

> MAISIE
>
> Is he awake? Can he talk?

> BODIE
>
> No, he passed out when I was on the phone with 911. The EMTs hooked him up to oxygen and gave him something because his blood pressure was spiking. But he hasn't opened his eyes.

> MAISIE
>
> Shit. Okay, I'm heading there now.

> BODIE
>
> I'll text or find you in the waiting room when I find out anything.

> MAISIE
>
> Thanks, Bodie.

My heart pounds and mind races with panicked thoughts as I try to focus on driving. Of course, nothing is close in these rural towns. The closest hospital is over thirty minutes away.

When my phone rings with my mother's name on the screen, I quickly answer since she'll continue bugging me until I do. And I don't need her draining my battery right now.

"Yeah, Mom?" I answer, choking on the tears streaming down my cheeks.

"What's wrong? Why'd you leave in a hurry?"

I quickly wipe my face. "Warren got hurt at work and the ambulance is on the way to the hospital," I blurt in one long breath. "And before you say anythin'—"

"I wasn't."

"Good. 'Cause I'll never forgive myself if the last conversation we had was us fightin' and him thinkin' I didn't love him."

"I know, honey. I'm sorry to hear he got hurt. Keep me updated, okay?"

"Sure, Mom."

"Maisie…" She sighs. "We want you to be happy. That's all we've ever wanted for you."

"Even if that means movin' here and stayin' married to Warren?"

"Yes," she replies instantly. "Of course."

Although she can't see me, I nod because although I'm nearly thirty, it's nice to hear my parents will support my decision regardless of what they wanted me to do.

"I'm glad ya came around," I say, trying not to sound bitter. "Hayes isn't comin' until Tuesday now, so I'll tell him then."

She's quiet for a moment and I think I've hit a dead zone until she speaks up. "We can hire someone to go to New York and pack up your things if you'd rather not see him after that."

That probably shouldn't make me smile, but knowing they'd do that for me, is how they show love.

"Thanks for offerin', Mom, but I need to handle this myself. You and Daddy can't keep bailin' me out." Like with the divorce attorney and drafting the papers. "I'll be okay and figure it out."

"Alright, well, let me know if you change your mind. Especially knowin' Hayes hired a PI to spy on you. Who does that?"

I roll my eyes at the irony of her being Team Hayes only a few hours ago. But I think this is her *trying* to be on my side and support my decision.

"And not to be pushy or overstep, but once y'all talk and it's for sure canceled, I'll take care of everythin' with the coordinator."

Now *that* I'll let her handle. She needs a project to stay busy or she won't leave me alone.

"I appreciate that, Mom. Thank you."

At the very least, talking to her helped calm me long enough to drive to the hospital without speeding.

"I'm almost there, so I'm gonna let you go. But thank you talkin' to me so I didn't panic too much."

"You're welcome, sweetie. Let me know when there's an update. I'll add him to my prayer group."

"Thanks, I'll be sure to tell him that."

He'll wonder if he woke up in a different timeline where my mother's concerned for him.

Truthfully, I'm wondering the same.

When I get to the waiting room, some of Warren's family members are already seated and now I'm concerned if they'll want me here or not.

"Maisie!" Posey jumps up from her chair and rushes toward me, wrapping me in a hug before I can even speak.

"Hi," I squeak. "How's he doin'?"

She pulls back, brushing her fingers over my cheek where my mascara probably ran down.

"Still waitin' for an update. Bodie's pacin' the hallway outside his room since they won't let anyone in. Last I heard they were gonna take him to get a CT scan for his head and chest."

I follow Posey to where Warren's parents and Bellamy are waiting. Mrs. Langston smiles before wrapping her arms around me.

"Hi, sweetie." She squeezes my hand. "Glad you came."

"What exactly happened?"

Posey explains what Bodie told her and although some of it's confusing, I get the gist of it. Having firsthand experience with that demon horse, I can't help feeling bad she got hurt and is probably scared.

"How's Lilith?" I ask.

"Colton's still lookin' for her. She might be in worse shape than Warren thought," Bellamy explains, sitting next to their dad.

"Or worse now after runnin' off," Posey adds. "She was already off-trail in a rockier area."

"Oh shit."

"If she's not in good shape, the vet will put her outta her misery. He's already there waitin' to see if Colt finds her," Mr. Langston explains.

"Wait, what's that mean?"

"It's too hard to say for sure, but he'll assess once he examines her," Mrs. Langston clarifies, but my gut tells me that's not what her husband meant.

If Lilith doesn't make it, Warren will feel horrible. Although he acts like a hard-ass, he's a softie for his horses, and knowing he's part of the reason she took off while injured, he'll blame himself.

We sit and make small talk while we continue waiting. Eventually, Warren's aunt arrives in a panic. She was already down a manager and couldn't leave until the next one came.

"What's takin' so long?" She paces and then goes to the nurse's station. It's sweet she loves her nieces and nephews like they're her own children.

"The doctor's on his way out now," I overhear and instinctively stand, everyone else doing the same.

Bodie's the first to come out followed by an older man.

"Is he awake?" Posey whispers to Bodie, but he shakes his head, and my heart drops.

The doctor calmly introduces himself while everyone impatiently waits.

"We're running a variety of tests to evaluate Warren. Because he was kicked in the chest, there's a risk of blunt thoracic trauma—which can range from minor bruising to life-threatening internal injuries. He may have a concussion, but until he's awake, we can't properly assess his neurological status. The initial CT scan doesn't show any hemorrhaging or structural brain injuries. It did reveal some bruised ribs, so he was lucky not to have any fractures. The blow to his chest most likely triggered a trauma response—either from pain, panic, or both. If he was already in distress at the time, that could have compounded the reaction and led to the spike in his blood pressure. For now, he's breathing on his own and we're monitoring his vitals closely."

Everyone's so quiet—all I can hear is the blood rushing in my ears and my pulse throbbing in my neck.

"So he's gonna be okay?" Posey's the first to speak.

"He's not gonna die?" Bellamy asks.

"Apart from any unforeseen complications, he should be fine. But until he wakes up, we won't know about his neurological status."

"Is it normal he still hasn't?" I ask.

"It can take some time," he replies gently. "His body and brain are still recovering from the trauma. Sometimes we need extra time to heal, but we're watching closely to make sure there's no hidden swelling or bleeding that'd be causing a delay in him waking up."

"Can we see him?" Mrs. Langston asks.

"Yes, but only a couple people at a time. His nurse will come out and bring y'all back."

"Thank you," Mr. Langston says, shaking his hand. "Appreciate it."

"Of course."

It's another twenty minutes before a nurse comes out and then Mr. and Mrs. Langston go to his room first. I'm anxious as hell, itching to run in there and shake him awake so I can tell him I love him and to fight like hell. The doctor implied he's going to be fine and that he's lucky because it could've been so much worse, but I can't help the fear building that there's always a chance for things to take a turn.

Posey and Bodie go next, but they return disappointed because he still isn't awake. After them, JoJo and Bellamy check on him but return with the same outcome.

Once it's my turn, I ask if anyone else wants to come with me because I feel awkward taking up time that they could be sitting with him. But Mr. Langston says he has to get back to the ranch, so Bellamy and Posey tag along with him. Then it's just me, his mom, and aunt.

"Go ahead, sweetie. He's in room sixteen. Take as long as you need," Mrs. Langston encourages when she notices me hesitating. I already said goodbye to the others, so I nod and walk down the hallway.

My heart beats out of my chest when I enter his room and find him sleeping peacefully. He looks so calm while I'm trying not to panic.

I pull up a chair next to his bed and weave my fingers through his. They're ice cold, so I cover my other hand over both of ours.

"I can't help thinkin' I'm to blame for some of this," I admit softly.

After we fought this morning, he was probably distracted, stressed, or both. As far as I'm aware, this hasn't happened before because Warren's good at his job. Always has been.

"I'm so sorry, Warren. For everythin'." Tears cloud my vision, so I close my eyes and rest my head against our combined hands.

After a few minutes of silence, I can't take it anymore. I hate that he probably can't hear me, but I speak anyway.

"Do you remember that box I kept our notes, photos, and other mementos from high school? I kinda forgot about it until I came back and saw it on my bookcase. Anyway, I went through it and found the vows you wrote on our weddin' day and cried over every word you wrote. I can't believe I forgot how beautiful it was. Maybe I blocked it out so I could push away my feelings after years of tryin' to move on. Rereading it was heartwrenchin' now knowin' how much you truly meant your words. I can't believe I was able to walk away after that. It actually makes me sick and mad at myself. I had my reasons at the time, but still, it blows my mind."

I look at his eyes, willing them to open, and frown when they don't.

"I can't help thinkin' there's a reason for everything that's happened. Maybe we needed the time apart so I could stand on my own two feet and get clarity on what truly makes me happy. Maybe we woulda ended up in a bitter divorce had I stayed and resented you. I hate thinkin' that I woulda but knowin' who I was in my younger twenties, it makes me wonder. Or worse, you woulda resented me. Kinda surprised you don't already. You'd have every right to."

"Warren would never resent you."

I nearly jump out of my chair at the voice behind me.

Spinning around, I find Silas in the doorway. I haven't seen him since I've been back, but wow, he's changed a lot. Both of his arms are covered with ink and his dark facial hair isn't new but it's thicker than Warren's.

"Holy fuck, you scared me." I press a palm to my chest and feel how fast my heart's racing.

He pushes off the wall and walks inside. "Sorry, I was tryin' to figure out a way to let you know I was here."

"That was one way to do it," I say in an aspirated laugh.

He stands on the other side of Warren. "Bodie called me a bit ago, but I was an hour out of town, so I rushed here as soon as I could. Any update?"

"Not really. Just waitin' for him to wake up."

Silas grabs the extra chair and takes his other hand.

"Hopefully me being here doesn't traumatize him more."

"No, he'd be happy you're here. I don't know what happened between y'all but he texted me this mornin'."

That makes me tense. "What'd he say?"

"Not much, honestly. Just that he signed the papers and when I asked him about havin' seven days, he said there was a change of plans. I offered to leave work early so we could hang out but he said he wanted to drink alone. I shoulda pushed him to take the afternoon off instead, but he mentioned choppin' wood to restock his pile, and I stupidly cracked a joke about callin' me if he needed a ride to the ER. Ya know, presumably 'cause he was gonna be choppin' wood while angry and drunk."

"Oh my God…" My eyes stretch wider with each sentence he speaks.

The guilt on his face makes me feel bad.

"He shouldn't be handlin' an axe while drinkin' anyway," I say, comforting him the best I can.

"I doubt he was gonna or I woulda intervened. Most likely he woulda been out there until his arms hurt or drank alone with his chickens."

"He does have a weird obsession…as if he gave birth to 'em and they're his children."

Silas chuckles, and so do I. It feels good after crying most of the afternoon.

"You met 'em yet?" he asks.

"No, he was supposed to introduce 'em to me before our date tonight." I rub the pad of my thumb over his knuckles.

"Indiana Jane is my favorite. She's spunky."

I can't help the burst of laughter that falls out of my mouth. "And I thought Kelly Cluckson was clever."

"He let me name two: Cluck Skywalker and Princess Lay-a."

I grin, his nerdiness from high school showing. "Very cute and fittin'."

"I thought so. Except Warren hasn't let me play with 'em since the last incident."

I arch a brow. "Do I even wanna know?"

"To be fair, Bodie started it."

"Of course he did."

"The chickens are already crazy on their own but add in drunken tag where we run around the coop until one of us trips makes 'em extra crazy."

The corner of my lips twitch. "I'm startin' to understand why Warren no longer allows it."

"He acts like we hurt 'em when it was 'em who kicked our asses."

I open my mouth but then a groan grabs my attention.

"Are y'all seriously talkin' shit about my chickens while I'm unconscious?"

I jump to my feet, the chair scraping across the floor, too in shock to be subtle or quiet. "Warren?"

"Shoulda known talkin' about 'em would wake you up," Silas taunts, grinning wide.

"Mhm. Stop flirtin' with my wife." Warren glares.

I can't stop smiling and crying happy tears.

"How do you feel?" I ask, softly rubbing over his hand.

He grunts, trying to reposition himself. I reach for his pillow, helping him sit up more. "Like I got kicked in the fuckin' chest by a twelve-hundred-pound horse."

"Smacked your head too," I clarify, readjusting his blankets.

He winces as if he just realized it hurts.

"Glad you're awake, man" Silas pats his shoulder. "Gonna send a text to your family so they know." Silas reaches for his phone on the table. "And I'll tell your nurse."

"Can you tell his mom and aunt too? They're in the waitin' room."

"Sure thing. Be right back."

Once we're alone, I sit and lean in closer. "You scared me."

"Sorry 'bout that." His voice is strained, and he seems a bit out of it, but overall, he's talking normal.

"Everyone's been worried sick about you."

"I have no doubt. My family's gonna be insufferable now."

"How long have you been listenin'?"

He reaches for me, grabbing my hand and linking his fingers through mine. It sends a wave of electricity down my spine, and I beam at him.

"Since the moment you started talkin'," he says, making me wonder if he heard everything or since Silas entered. "My brain was still too foggy to comprehend I needed to open my eyes and move my lips to speak."

"Don't worry about talkin' if you're too tired. Rest as much as you need," I reassure him, keeping my eyes on his.

He nods once, speaking softly. "I'm so glad you're here."

"Of course." Every nerve cell in my body explodes with relief.

"I'm kinda surprised," he says cautiously.

"Well…" I grin hesitantly. "You still owe me two dates."

There's so much I want to tell him, starting with how I'm still in love with him and that I'm not filing those divorce papers— assuming he'll give me a second chance after our fight this morning. But that discussion can wait until he's feeling better and stronger.

The corner of his lips twitch. "Does this count as one?"

I chuckle, sniffing and clearing my throat. "Not a chance, cowboy."

chapter nineteen

Warren

I'VE NEVER FELT MORE my age than trying to get out of a hospital bed.

It's not the first time I've had bruised ribs, probably won't be the last, but it's the first time a horse kicked me in the chest and knocked me on my ass.

My ego might be a little bruised too.

After I got a neurological exam, the doctor had me stay overnight to monitor my blood pressure and the trauma to my head. Luckily, no concussion, but I woke up in the middle of the night with it pounding so they gave me some meds for it.

"Mom, I'm fine," I insist for the hundredth time.

"You might be, but I'm not. You scared me to death so I'm seein' that my oldest son has everythin' he needs."

She hasn't left the hospital and insists on fussing over me. Meanwhile, I'm dying to go home so I can be alone with Maisie since we haven't had any alone time to talk. Mom and Aunt JoJo hogged me most of the evening, but we've been texting.

I was equally shocked and relieved to hear Maisie's voice

next to me. Even more surprised she still wants the last two dates I owe her after our fight and signing those papers. But after she blamed herself, I made sure she knew this wasn't on her. It's mine for not taking my own advice about not being in the kick zone.

After she kept yawning, I told her to go home and sleep since the room they put me in only had a small couch. They would've brought in a cot but she wouldn't have been able to sleep well with the nurses constantly coming in and my mother asking me if I needed anything every five minutes.

"I need my own bed and a six-pack."

And my wife next to me.

She tsks. "You can't drink if you're takin' meds."

I'd hardly consider Tylenol to be a big concern, but she's probably right. I slept with ice packs on my ribs most of the night, so that's helped with the pain, but I'm stiff and sore as shit. Hospital beds weren't designed with larger men in mind.

I'm waiting for the nurse to return with my discharge papers and then I'm getting the hell out of here. The staff has been great, but I'm uncomfortable. I need a hot shower and clean clothes.

I'm also anxious about Lilith.

My memory's still a little foggy on the events because it happened so fast, but it's obvious she was in distress and scared so I don't fault her.

She shouldn't have been allowed to go out on the trails. She needed more desensitization and training, so this is on me, and it's now something we're going to be assessing on a monthly basis. Thank goodness none of the guests got hurt or we'd be looking at an even bigger issue.

Colt finally found her but she's in rough shape. Dr. Warner

worked on her leg wound, but he's concerned about infection and it getting into her bloodstream. For now, it's a waiting game to see how she responds to the meds and if they can keep her stable and comfortable so she doesn't bear weight on it.

"Hey, son." Dad enters, handing mom a bag. "How ya doin'?"

"Fine. Ready to go home."

He wraps an arm around me, patting my shoulder. "Aunt JoJo's at your house now gettin' it ready."

Great.

"Doin' what exactly?"

"She put on clean sheets and stocked your fridge with food from the restaurant. A couple lasagnas and some chicken cordon bleu."

Well shit, that sounds fucking delicious after only eating pudding cups and apple sauce.

"What about my chickens? Did she—"

"Bodie did. He said he got everythin' taken care of," Dad replies, but there's a hint of amusement in the way he says it.

That means the little shit stole my eggs

Posey and Bellamy walk in giggling and looking suspicious.

"Where'd y'all go?" Dad asks.

"Sorry, we got distracted by all the cute doctors in the hallway." Posey smirks, waggling her brows. "I think they're doing rounds but they should be doing *me* instead."

"Wouldn't be surprised if you got knocked up from the way one of 'em was starin' at your ass." Bellamy snorts.

"Girls..." Mom scolds.

"So glad we could have this little family reunion in my hospital room while I'm already sufferin'," I deadpan, wishing I was already home.

"Oh lighten up...you're alive and have all four limbs." Posey pokes my arm.

"Too bad he didn't lose his dull personality," Bellamy taunts.

I groan, leaning back against the pillow. "Why're you here again?"

"Dad made me."

Figures.

Finally, the nurse returns with my discharge papers and I've never signed anything faster. Of course, they don't let you walk out, I have to be wheeled out.

"I'll get the truck and meet y'all at the front doors," Dad says, giving Mom a quick kiss.

"Shotgun!" Posey calls out, following behind him.

"No way! Your choice in music sucks," Bellamy calls, chasing after her.

"They're not allowed in my house," I mutter to my mom. "So please drop 'em off somewhere. Preferably the town over."

She sits in the chair next to me. "Don't let 'em fool ya. They were very worried about you."

"Mhm."

They were probably fighting over who'd get to move into my house if I died. If I were a betting man, I'd put my money on Posey. She's little and petite, but she fights dirty. With us only being two years apart, we'd wrestle as kids and while I'd be careful not to hurt her, she'd bite my arm and shove her knee in my gut once I was distracted by the pain.

"So while we have a minute, tell me what's goin' on with Maisie and you."

"Later, Mom." I groan, not at all wanting to talk about it. At least not until I get to discuss things with her. After I signed the papers and left, I was fully prepared to never hear from her again. I understood her points and didn't want to stand in the way.

But when I heard her voice and felt her touch, I've never been more relieved. She cared enough to be here and even if we only get a few more days together, I'm taking them to spend every minute with her. I'd rather end things on a positive note than the way we did yesterday morning.

WARREN

I'm about to leave the hospital. Can you meet at my house?

MAISIE

Sure! Your family won't mind if I'm there?

WARREN

You being there is the only way my mom will leave.

MAISIE

So you need me as a buffer?

WARREN

No, I just need you.

I've never been more grateful to be in my own home again. Maisie was already inside waiting for me, which I appreciated. It gave my mom the hint to go home and hopefully rest since she was up most of the night too. She reassured my mother she'd make sure I took it easy and rested, but by the look my mom gave me, you'd think Maisie told her we were going to fuck all night long.

"What do you wanna do first? Eat? Sleep?" she asks, following me into my bedroom.

"Shower," I say, already unbuttoning my jeans and walking toward the bathroom. "Then, eat and lay in bed."

"Okay. I can put one of JoJo's dinners in the oven."

She goes to leave but I stop her.

"You're not gonna help me?"

"With what?"

I smirk, lowering my zipper. "Takin' a shower."

She crosses her arms, holding back a grin. "You can't bathe yourself?"

"I won't be able to stretch my arms to scrub my back…" I mimic trying to but wince when the stretch makes my ribs ache. "Not sure I can even pull off my shirt."

"You're pathetic." She laughs, coming closer to help lift my shirt over my head.

Her wide smile drops when she looks at my chest. I assume she's looking at the massive bruise forming, but then she touches my chain.

"Your wedding band?"

Glancing down to where she's holding it between her fingers, I nod. The inscription inside is our wedding date and initials.

"Too dangerous to wear it at work, so I always kept it on a chain. I'd usually put it back on my finger once I got home, so you probably never realized."

"I thought you took it off in your truck and put it back on after work. I didn't know you wore it like this."

"I wanted it close to my heart."

"And you've been wearin' it around your neck this whole time?"

I tilt her chin, meeting her teary-eyed gaze. "I rarely ever let it outta my sight. It means as much to me today as it does the day you gave it to me."

The evening we went swimming, I took it off so it didn't freak her out with it only being our second date. I also didn't want to risk losing it in the water. The staff removed it at the hospital for my CT scan, but once I was allowed to change out of the gown and into my clothes this morning, I put it right back on.

"Warren," she says softly, swallowing hard. "I'm gonna need you to gimme permission to kiss you."

I lick my bottom lip, tilting my head at the unexpected question. "You never need permission for that, Maze."

The corner of her mouth curves up deviously. "Too bad you're injured."

Grabbing her waist, I pull her to my chest and dip down until my lips are half an inch from hers. "Don't play with me."

Her breath hitches but she's braver than before. Fingers slide into my waistband and she brushes her fingers against my bare skin, making me the breathless one.

"Get in the bath so I can scrub your body."

My brow arches, contemplating her suggestion. "Are you joinin' me?"

She smirks, tracing her finger over my exposed hip. "I will if you're a good boy."

My eyes go impossibly wide.

She's never said those words to me before.

My dick takes notice and jerks in response.

"Fuck, Maze." I cup her cheek, tempted to lean in and claim her mouth. "I'll give you anythin' you want."

Taking my hand, she leads me into the bathroom and turns on the bath water. Realization dawns on me the tub's finally getting used for what it was originally intended for and a part of me is nervous as fuck. I'm not sure what's going through her head and don't want to overstep her boundaries. All I know is she wants the dates I owe her, which might not happen until I get some rest, but regardless, I'm elated as hell she's here.

"Do you need help gettin' 'em off the rest of the way?" she asks.

"I can probably manage, but I'd much rather you do it for me."

She pushes off the vanity, desperate to touch me or perhaps taking pity on me. I move my hands out of the way so she can slide my jeans down my legs and then step out of them. She looks up at me between her lashes and I signal with a nod for her to keep going.

My cock's imprint is more than obvious but she doesn't flinch when she reaches up and pulls my boxer briefs down. I try desperately to tame my boner but the vision of her kneeling in front of me is confusing my brain.

This wasn't supposed to be sexual, but fuck, I want her lips wrapped around me more than I've ever wanted anything.

"That's a very interestin' piercin'. Did it hurt?"

"Fuck yeah it did. Silas dared me. We took a few shots first to take off the edge."

"*We*? He's pierced too?" she asks, standing to her full height. Without her heels, she's a head shorter than me.

"Yep. Except he got a different one."

She arches a brow. "How very manly of you two."

"You seem very curious about it."

Her shoulder lifts, feigning disinterest. "Get in the tub. I'll grab your soap."

"Yes, ma'am." My lips quirk up when a hint of a blush hits her cheeks.

I can't remember the last time I've been in here, but I clean it regularly when I do the rest of the bathroom. I'm glad it's finally getting used.

"Any preference on which one?" She holds up two options.

"You pick."

She sets one down on the ledge and then moves to grab some more supplies. A washcloth and my two-in-one bottle for my hair.

"How's the water feel?" she asks, turning it off before it gets too full.

"Really nice."

Would feel even better if she were pressed up against me.

Sitting on the ledge, she dips the washcloth into the water and adds a generous amount of soap to it.

"Be honest, how bad is the pain?" she asks, softly rubbing over my arm.

"On a scale of one to ten, probably a five."

She nods, intently focusing on washing across my chest and other arm.

"My ribs are tender and muscles are stiff, but nothin' a good night's rest can't cure."

"Any news on Lilith?"

I tell her the latest update and she frowns.

"I hope she makes it."

"She will," I say confidently, resting an arm on the other ledge. "She's strong and spunky, like you."

"Not sure if that's a compliment or not."

"It is." My eyes track her every movement and when her hand lowers down my stomach, underneath the water, I inhale a sharp breath.

She pauses. "That hurt?"

"No." She hasn't touched me like this in so long, my heart's threatening to explode at how desperate I am for more of it. "You can keep goin'."

She continues washing me, adding more soap as she does. Shifting closer, she reaches around me to get my neck and shoulders.

"Mm..." I unintentionally moan as she digs into my muscles. "Fuck, that feels good."

My eyes fall closed as every inch of my body melts into her touch.

"If you wanna move forward a little, I can get your lower back," she says softly.

I bend my knees and slide away from her to give her better access, the cool air hitting my skin causes me to shiver.

"One second..." Her voice is distant so I assume she's grabbing something else from the shower, but then the water ripples and bare legs come into view around my waist.

Is she...

"Finally decided to join me, huh?" Looking over my shoulder, she's plastered to my back.

"No peekin'..." The washcloth finds my skin again as she continues scrubbing.

"You seriously expect me to sit here while you're naked behind me and not look?"

"Yes...you're supposed to be takin' it easy."

"That's...impossible." My hands grab her calves on each side of me and I playfully squeeze. If she's touching me, I need to be touching her.

"You're the one who said your mobility was limited, so don't be gettin' any ideas."

Her taunting voice has my dick growing hard.

"I'm long past that, darlin'. Your nipples are etched into my skin at this point."

She pushes them harder into me, and I cough out a laugh. Now I know she's torturing me on purpose.

I slide one of my hands up her leg, bending my arm back until I can reach further up her thigh.

"Uh-uh, what did I say?" She swats it away.

"I've been a very good boy...so you should reward me for my restraint."

"Not while you're on bed rest."

"Who said anything about that?" I pout. "Half of me is still very functional."

She snorts, reaching over my hips and toward my abs. "I have a sneakin' suspicion which half."

Glancing over my shoulder so I can see part of her face, I smirk. "Keep goin' and you'll find out for certain."

chapter twenty

Maisie

MY HANDS HAVE a mind of their own when I do just that. Inching closer between his legs, I find a very thick and hard erection. Slowly, I slide my fingers up his shaft and am careful when I reach the piercing.

I wonder how it'd feel inside me.

Especially with my own piercing.

Fuck, that's a dangerous thought to have when he's on limited physical activity.

"Maisie…" he groans out my name like he's praying for mercy.

Knowing how long it's been and how no one else has touched him like this makes me want to pleasure him even more. Unfortunately, I don't have super long arms so my grip is weak trying to hold onto him.

Instead, I use the washcloth as my helper to reach around and slide up the other side of his length. He must like it because his fingers dig into my calves as another moan vibrates from his throat.

When his chest rapidly rises and falls, I can't help lowering my lips to the nape of his neck. I flatten my tongue and lick him.

"Shit, Maze. I should be the one touchin' and kissin' you." He tilts his head toward the other shoulder, giving me easier access.

"Not tonight. I'm takin' care of my needy little patient," I whisper in his ear. "So let me help you relax."

I continue rotating my hands over his cock and around his thighs. My fingers tease and massage every inch of skin I can reach.

Warren's trying so hard to control his breathing. I can't help worrying it's hurting his ribs.

"If I'm causin' you more pain, tell me."

"Definitely not." He shakes his head, tilting it to the side toward me.

My eyes catch his and he lowers his gaze to my lips.

"Whaddya need?" I ask since he's close and I want to help him get there.

"Your mouth."

His hand reaches up to cup my face and then we're in a heated battle of tongues and teeth. It's hot and desperate, like a sweet craving you've been fighting, and suddenly, it's within your grasp and you finally taste it. *Inhale* it.

It's all-consuming.

My hands stall for a moment while my brain catches up with the rest of me. His lips move with mine, sucking and tasting like I'm his lifeline.

"Sit in front of me, Maze," he says, breaking the kiss and I realize how stretched his neck is trying to reach me.

There's no easy way to maneuver around him without putting my whole crotch in his face, so I step out of the tub before climbing in again. He slides back, giving me more room to sit across from him.

"That's…*new*." His gaze lowers below the water.

My cheeks heat. "Saw that, did ya?"

He grabs my waist, sliding me closer until my legs are on top of his. My calves slide around his waist, pressing his erection between our bodies.

"Careful," I say, gripping the edge of the tub so I don't put any pressure on his chest. Thank goodness there's enough room for us or it'd be awkward and uncomfortable. Being able to both fit was the reason I wanted a deep tub in the first place.

"I'm fine, Maze." His palms lower to my ass, pulling me tighter against him. "Can I touch it?"

"The piercin'?"

"Mhm. I wanna see your reaction."

I swallow hard and nod, but I already know it's going to be my undoing. We've always been explosive in the bedroom and as much as I want to relive those moments with him, I'm nervous it won't live up to the expectations he's built up in his head all these years we've been apart.

But when his finger slides between my thighs and brushes over my clit, all those fears fade away. Our chemistry and feelings toward each other is what made it so good between us in the first place.

Once I realized those feelings still existed and I stopped fighting it, that same spark returned.

"What made you do this?" he asks in a deep, raspy voice that has me clenching my pussy.

The pad of his thumb rubs over it, stealing a gasp from me when he does it again.

"Bachelorette party gone wrong," I admit, breathing faster. "We all got somethin' pierced. I contemplated gettin' my nipples done, but those take too long to heal."

"Mmm…" He groans, his lips hovering over my ear. "You made a good choice. This is like a built-in teammate to help you come even harder."

My hips involuntary arch into his hand, seeking his touch. I wrap my arms around his shoulders, needing more.

"Put your fingers inside me," I beg, burying my face in his neck.

"Patience, my love."

My heart rate spikes at the term of endearment he used when we were younger and I'd forgotten how much it turned me on.

"I thought you were a good boy who gave me whatever I wanted…" I taunt, hoping he'll cave and finger fuck me the way I need.

"I will…if you beg for it."

Pulling back, I meet his burning gaze and he smirks like a cocky asshole.

Fine, if that's what it's going to take, I'll do it.

"Warren, *please*," I say almost breathlessly. "Make me come."

"That's my good girl." His cock jerks between us. "You have no idea what those words do to me."

He circles my clit a few more times before pressing into my opening with two fingers. I lift slightly to give him more room and then slide down on them.

I let out a heavy sigh of relief.

"Goddamn, you're so tight." He captures my mouth, sinking his tongue between my lips and breathing in my moans. "Fuck yourself on my fingers, baby."

And I do.

My body rides his hand like I'm a starved and desperate woman. When his thumb reaches up and teases my piercing, a shockwave washes through me, and I explode harder than I have in years.

"Holy shit," I gasp out the words, unable to control the way my body shakes. Either from the water turning cold or the adrenaline high, but either way, it's intense.

"Are you okay?" He cups my face, and I frown at the loss of him inside me.

All I can do is nod.

"Yeah, I very much like your little piercin'." His teasing tone makes me chuckle. "You look so perfect and wrecked for me."

Once the high wears off, Warren helps me out of the tub and we rinse off in the shower together. We make out most of the time we're there but when I offer to help him out with his *massive* problem, he insists I don't need to.

However, I can't stop thinking about twisting my tongue around those barbells and wrapping my lips around the tip.

Once he's dried off and pulls on clean boxer briefs, he slips into bed and tells me to join him. I packed a bag with extra clothes but decided to only put on an oversized T-shirt and panties.

"Feelin' okay? Did you want me to grab an ice pack or your meds?"

"Nope, I'm great."

When I climb in next to him, he wraps an arm around my waist and yanks me closer. Then he dips down and captures my lips. "Would be even better if you stayed right here with me all night."

"Hm...that can be arranged." I wrap my arm low on his stomach, teasing the hem of his shorts. "But only if you listen to doctor's orders."

He groans in my ear. "Then you better stop tryin' to touch my dick 'cause it's very aware of your presence."

"You shoulda let me take care of it in the shower, then."

His mouth sucks my neck and I hum at how good his scruffiness feels scratching over my skin.

"I'm tryin' to take it slow," he murmurs. "I don't wanna risk movin' too fast and losin' you again."

The hurt in his voice makes my heart stop, and I freeze. "I'm not goin' anywhere, Warren."

He lifts his head, meeting my gaze. "You're not?"

"I haven't figured everythin' out yet, but I don't wanna leave you again. Hayes is flyin' here next week and I planned on talkin' to him then."

"So you're mine for a few days?" He arches a brow, grinning.

"Hopefully more, but yes. I'm here to be your personal nurse."

"Mm..." His hand slides down my back until he grips my ass. "First a naked sponge bath and now you're half-naked in my bed? I think you're tryin' to gimme a heart attack. Not very *professional* of you."

"Sorry, Mr. Langston..." My fingers skim over his erection, feeling how hard he is for me, and he shutters. "I can't help myself around you."

I can't remember the last time I felt this ravenous and desperate.

The fact I didn't bother to pack my laptop and work supplies tells me how mixed up I had my priorities. I used my job as an excuse instead of facing reality that I wasn't as happy as I tried convincing myself. I've given more tasks to my assistant and got a job listing up so I can hire more help. It'll help me grow as an agency and give me more time to focus on what's important—a work-life balance that doesn't consume my whole world.

"You're not playin' fair, Mrs. Langston." He nips my lower lip, his other hand reaching up to cup my breast over my shirt.

I full-on blackout when he says those words.

Fuck, that's so hot.

"You can't tell me to take it easy when you're teasin' me like that." He arches his hips, pressing his cock harder into my palm.

"Warren…" I breathe out his name. "Call me that again."

It takes a moment for him to realize what I said but then he grins against my neck, feathering kisses toward my ear.

"Mrs. Langston…my fuckin' gorgeous wife."

Without giving me a chance to react, he pulls me on top of him, and I immediately lift up so I don't bear weight on his chest.

"I'm fine, baby. It's a bruise not a bullet hole," he reassures. "Now turn around."

"W-what? How?"

"Climb over me and stick your ass in my face. That way there's no pressure on my chest."

"You want to eat me from behind?" I haven't been in that position since the last time we did it years ago.

He gives my ass a hard swat in response.

But then that means I get to finally taste him.

I carefully rearrange myself until my legs are on either side of his head and his cock is inches from my face.

"Like this?" I arch my back, feeling a bit self-conscious and wondering if I remembered to shave this week.

"Perfect…" His palms slide up my thighs and he squeezes. "Fuckin' hell."

I can tell how affected he is by the bulge is suffocating in his boxer briefs. Rubbing gently over him, I ask, "Can I?"

"Yes, be careful of the piercin'. It makes everythin' extra sensitive."

Oh, is that so?

I push down his shorts until he's exposed, hard and weeping for my touch. When I slide my tongue over him, he slides my panties to one side and inhales deeply. One finger swipes through my slit before he flicks his tongue out and tastes me.

For someone who hasn't been with a woman in seven years, Warren's not hesitant or gentle when he devours my pussy. Licking and sucking, he's a man on a mission to make me come all over his face.

I'm trying my best to focus on the cock in front of me, but every touch he gives me has my body on fire. I can barely breathe when he presses the tip of his thumb in my ass.

"Oh my God…" I moan around his tip between my lips.

Wanting to cause him the same pleasure, I deep-throat him as far as I can and slide my hand between his thighs until I find the spot underneath his balls.

He groans against me and lifts his hips against my mouth. When I hollow my cheeks, I continue teasing his taint and twirling my tongue around his length. When I sink even further down, I choke but don't stop.

"I need you to come, Maze." He digs his fingers into my skin before his tongue slides up into my crack and then back down to feast on my clit.

Holy fuck.

He finds the perfect rhythm and my movements stall as the buildup intensifies. Every lick, suck, and bite has me on edge.

My eyes roll to the back of my head. "I'm so close…"

When his finger breaches my hole again, I shatter around him and gasp for air. This position makes it awkward since I can't squeeze my thighs or grind against him, but he holds me in place while I cum on his face.

As soon as I can breathe again, I swallow him down until I'm choking on his release.

"Jesus Christ…" He growls, his legs shaking underneath me. I grin proudly that I'm the only woman who's ever had him this way and made him make those sounds. They're intoxicating and I can't believe I'd gone so long without them.

Climbing off him and turning around, I crawl up the bed and crash against the mattress next to him.

He chuckles, pulls up his shorts, then leans over on his good side to wrap an arm around me.

"Your pussy tastes better than I remember. I'm afraid I'll get addicted to it now…" He brings up his hand, brushing wild strands of hair off my face, and tilts up my chin. "You doin' okay?"

Laughter bubbles out of me. "I haven't come that hard in so long. I'm numb from the waist down."

"Not surprised, baby. You made a fuckin' mess on me."

Peeling my eyes open, I smile wide at the evidence on his lips and chin. Flattening my tongue, I lick up his face and giggle when he pokes my side.

"No ticklin'!" I laugh when he does it again. "No fair, I can't get even."

He grabs a fistful of my hair, yanks me closer, then crushes his mouth to mine.

On second thought, I'll take it if it means he rewards me like this.

chapter twenty-one

Warren

I CAN'T HELP WATCHING Maisie as she sleeps next to me.

So beautiful and peaceful.

I'm scared I'll blink and she'll be gone.

But I trust when she says she's not leaving this time. Yeah, it might get ugly once Hayes is here, but I'm prepared to fight like hell if I need to.

Last night, after lying in bed for a couple hours, we got hungry. We warmed up one of Aunt JoJo's dishes and snuggled in bed before passing out.

It's been so long, I almost forgot how good it felt to have her warm body next to mine. Legs tangled together, her wild hair in my face, and her little sleepy noises purring in my ear.

I'm in paradise.

But then I'm woken abruptly with eager lips wrapped around my cock—now I'm in fucking heaven.

"Maze?" My eyes are half-open as I reach for her head between my legs.

She pops off me. "Are you expectin' someone else down here?"

I chuckle at her jealous scowl. "Do you even have to ask?"

"Then the next time you say my name, you better be screamin' it, not questionin' it."

Good God.

"Fuck, Maze." My cock twitches. "That's a filthy little mouth you've got."

She raises her brows before sinking back down on my shaft.

I don't last long with the way she twists her tongue around my barbells or her little eager moans as she goes as deep as she can.

"Come up here," I demand, spent from the intense orgasm, but not willing to let her go without returning the favor.

"Up where?"

"Hold onto the headboard and sit on my face so I can lick that sweet pussy."

She wiggles her way up my body and when she lifts her T-shirt, I'm met with bare skin.

"No panties, huh?"

"Didn't want the restriction."

"Thank God." I hoist her up to where I want her, perfectly over my mouth, and eat her like a starved man. "Fuck, you taste good."

My words come out muffled but she moans out my name in response.

I love flicking her piercing and the way she squirms against me. Knowing I'm the reason she's about to lose her mind gets me hard all over again.

"Right there, don't stop."

My hands find her waist and help her rock back and forth

over my tongue. Little sucks and nips between her folds and over the crease where her hips meet her thigh have her going wild.

"Yes, so close! *Oh my God...*" She thrashes, thighs squeezing my head as she grinds over my face and her sweet juices coat my tongue.

Her body relaxes and then it's as if she realizes she's sitting on my chest, she sits up. "Did I hurt you?"

"It wouldn't matter if you did. I'd risk my life to keep my face between your thighs."

She snorts, climbing off me and lying on her side next to me. "It's darker today."

Leaning up, I spot the ugly bruise and shrug. "Guess you'll have to kiss it until it's better."

"You wish, cowboy." She quickly smacks her lips against mine. "I need a hot shower and food."

"I can help with both of those..."

"No shower shenanigans until you're healed. But since I can't cook for shit, you're on breakfast duty."

I poke her side, making her squeal. "You're no fun."

"I'm startin' to remember that keepin' you alive was a full-time job. If you weren't being reckless at work, you and Bodie were playin' tractor chicken."

I full-on belly laugh, which makes my ribs ache, but shit. I'd forgotten about that.

"That was his idea," I remind her.

"And you were supposed to tell him it was a bad one."

"I tried! He called me a coward."

"He was twelve!"

"As his older brother, I had to teach him a lesson and prove him wrong." I shrug, sitting up and sliding out of bed.

My parents were pissed when they found out, especially

since we both got our tractors stuck in the ditch and needed a third tractor to pull us out.

She shakes her head. "That's nothin' compared to the numerous shit you and your cousins got into each time they came to visit."

That reminds me I should text Landen back. He sent a text and I forgot to respond. The girl he's been crushing on fell off her horse during a barrel race competition and lost part of her memory on the same day as my incident. I haven't had the chance to tell him about it.

But I do remember one of his messages said she woke up with no recollection of him and apparently has a major crush on him.

I'd laugh if it wasn't so insane.

Before she can go into the bathroom, I stand and pull her in for a kiss. "Good mornin'."

She giggles against me. "I need to brush my teeth."

When she pulls away, I yank her back and tilt her chin. "I think we're past worryin' about mornin' breath."

"Just admit you like the taste of your cum on my lips."

"You got me." I wink, then capture her mouth and slide my tongue in. "But I much prefer the taste of yours."

While Maisie showers, I brush my teeth and get dressed before going to make breakfast and catch up on my texts. Landen and I've talked more than usual while we discussed what to write to the parole board. It'll be another month before we find out if they approve or deny her. The waiting sucks, especially for Talia and Tucker's families, but it'll be nice once they know for sure.

LANDEN

Bodie told me you got your ass kicked by a
horse? You good?

Of course Bodie would say that. Such a punk.

WARREN

Bruised up, but I'm alive. How's your new
girlfriend?

LANDEN

Dude, it's weird. Everyone's freaking out how
nice she's being to me. Kinda making me
wonder if she's messing with me on purpose
and this is one of her pranks to fuck with me.

WARREN

Wouldn't that be hilarious…

LANDEN

Yeah…so hilarious.

I laugh, knowing how long he's liked her and now she finally does, but he probably can't trust it since her memory will probably return at some point and she'll remember she hates him.

WARREN

I'd roast you harder but I'm in too much of a
sex-induced coma to try.

LANDEN

EXCUSE ME???

Please tell me with your wife.

I roll my eyes.

WARREN

Yes, obviously.

LANDEN

With bruised ribs too? Impressive.

I snort, shaking my head at where his mind automatically went.

We text a few more times before I switch to Silas since he's been messaging me since last night.

SILAS

If you don't respond, I'm gonna assume you died.

WARREN

Not dead.

SILAS

Fuck, there goes three hours writing up your obituary.

WARREN

Hold onto it, I guess?

SILAS

Good idea.

Now that you've come up for air, how are things?

I give him a brief update with my ribs and Maisie so he stops worrying. Then I find some meds and swallow them down. After last night's and this morning's activities, I'm probably a bit more sore than I should be.

Still, nothing I can't handle.

SILAS

That's great, dude.

Oh, not that you asked but…

Oh God.

WARREN

I'm scared.

I continue cooking while I wait for his response, grabbing meat and veggies from the fridge and cracking eggs into a bowl.

SILAS

I took your advice and planned a spontaneous drive out into the woods with Aundrea. Got into the backseat and accidentally kicked the door open while we were in the middle of it. Ended up with a tick on her ass and a million mosquito bites. She's pissed!

I blink at my phone screen.
He has to be joking.

WARREN

I didn't say take her to the woods.

SILAS

Didn't you?

WARREN

I said a SECLUDED area. Why would you take her to the woods? That's where wild animals and murderers hide.

SILAS

That's what she said! Fuck.

WARREN

You're gonna have to make it up to her now.

I finish making our omelets, put a couple slices of sourdough bread in the toaster, and add fresh fruit on the side.

"Somethin' smells delicious in here." Maisie nearly skips into the kitchen, looking adorable in my old resort T-shirt and distracting me from what I was doing.

"Are you tryin' to kill me?" My gaze lowers down her body and when staring at her isn't enough, I fist the fabric across her chest and yank her toward me.

She drags her teeth over her bottom lip and bats her eyelashes innocently.

"Wearin' my clothes again, Mrs. Langston."

Her breath hitches, eyes beaming at my words. "Now you're tryin' to kill *me*."

Smirking, I hover my mouth above hers, waiting for permission. "Am I allowed now?"

"Yes, brushed and flossed."

"You used my flosser?" I arch a brow, amused.

"And rinse."

"Fuck, that's hot." Before she can respond, I capture her lips and slide my tongue between them, exploring how fresh and clean she tastes.

I manage to break away and tell her to sit so we can eat.

"Mm...this is so good," she says around a mouthful of omelet.

Odd as it sounds, I love watching her enjoy food. She doesn't make eating a priority because of work, so I feel pride she's devouring it.

"I'm glad you like it."

"You keep this up, I'm gonna gain like ten pounds."

"So?"

"A week," she adds, and I snort.

As we eat and chat, I tell her we'll go feed the chickens after and she can finally meet them.

"After all the horror stories I've heard of your chickens, I'm scared. What if they pluck my eyes out?"

"They won't." Grabbing her empty plate and putting it on top of my own, I stand and bring them back to the kitchen.

"But what if they do?" She follows, standing next to me at the sink. "Will you still want me? How will I work if I can't read my clients' manuscripts?"

Amused at the unlikely possibility, I cup her chin and grin at her cute frowny face. "I will be madly in love with you with or without eyes. And I'll quit my job so I can stay home and read all their books to you. But you'll never have to worry about that 'cause I'd let 'em attack me before they'd get to you."

Her eyes water, and I worry I said something wrong. "Are you okay?"

Nodding, she swallows. "That was unexpectedly sweet."

"You're surprised?"

"That's the thing. I know you'd do those things, but I'm not deservin' of that from you, so it gives me conflictin' feelings."

"Too bad you don't get to determine what I do for you."

She pouts, narrowing her eyes. "Have you always been this stubborn?"

"When it comes to you, baby? Absolutely."

I don't give her time to argue before my lips are back on hers. She melts into me and I inwardly smile at how easy it's been to fall into old habits.

"And I didn't wait seven years to let you doubt my feelings. I don't expect you to share the same ones I have after movin' on with your life, but I'm a patient man. I'm not goin' anywhere."

I take Maisie outside once she's in the right attire and fill up the feed buckets so she can help. Although she's weary, she acclimates easily as she follows my directions.

"Oh God, that one has it out for me. I can tell..." She stands frozen with a bucket clutched to her chest. "She looks murderous."

Chuckling at her dramatics, I lead her toward the coop.

"Chick Jagger is harmless. She loves to eat, but she won't hurt you."

"I dunno...I think she's plottin' something against me."

"C'mon, let's go."

Once I check their water, we spread their feed and watch as they eat.

"Wanna collect their eggs?"

Maisie eyes the group of them cautiously before following me inside the coop.

"You need to relax, babe."

"I've seen videos online of chicken attacks!"

It's hard not to laugh at how serious she is.

"If there's any of 'em to worry about, it's Chucky."

"The rooster?"

"He's the aggressor."

"And you're just *now* tellin' me?" she whisper-hisses, shifting in circles to look for him.

"I plan to get more eventually, so you're gonna have to become friends."

"*More*? How many eggs do you get a day?"

"One from each, so six total."

"That sounds like plenty."

I chuckle at her panicked tone, but she'll come around eventually. "I plan to cook for you regularly, my love. We're gonna need more eggs."

"Well it's hard to argue when you say sweet shit like that."

Laughing, I point to their nests. "Go look, city girl. Time to country you back up."

chapter twenty-two

Maisie

I CAN'T REMEMBER the last time I've felt this way.

Truly content and happy.

And I know it's only been a week since Warren and I have been going on these "dates" but being back here has reminded me to slow down. Enjoy life again.

Minus the chickens currently chasing after me.

"Stop runnin'!" Warren calls out, but he's crazy if he thinks I'm going to stand around and let them get me.

I'm not sure which one I pissed off, but she didn't like Warren kissing me. The moment he did, she came after me and I booked it.

The gate is closed, so I quickly open and shut it behind me once I'm on the other side.

My heart's beating out of my chest as I try to catch my breath.

"Maze…" Warren stands on the opposite side of the fence and I swear he's laughing at me. "They're not gonna hurt you."

"That one wanted to…" I point to the one trying to peck its way through the chicken wire to get to me.

"They'll get used to you."

I give him a look like he's insane for thinking I'm ever willingly going back in there.

"They're possessive of you in some weird-chicken kinda way." I walk backward toward the house. "I'm goin' where it's safe."

He pinches his lips like he's holding back. "Gimme a few and I'll meet you inside."

I wash my hands as soon as I'm in the kitchen and wait for my racing heart to slow down. As I dry them off, a text alert pops up on my phone. I never replied to Hayes' last messages because it was right before Bodie told me about Warren, and I haven't figured out how to respond.

> **HAYES**
>
> Hi, darling. I know you must be upset with me or maybe you just need time with everything going on, but I wanted to make sure you knew how much I miss and love you. I'm so close to writing the end of this book and I can't wait to celebrate with you and spend quality time together.

My stomach drops.

I have conflicting feelings about our conversations from this past week. To finding out he hired a PI, to him knowing I was married this whole time, to proposing to push me to get a divorce, and then the back and forth of saying I needed to make a decision or he'd make it for me but that he'd fight for me.

It's a lot.

But I don't have room to complain when I didn't exactly tell him the truth either.

We're both at fault.

Not really a way to start a marriage.

I'm still wearing my engagement ring because it feels weird to take it off after all this time. Not because I'm doubting my decision, but I need to give it back when I see him in person.

Assuming he won't chuck it at my head.

These new circumstances have me thinking about my favorite book even more since Warren asked me about it. How one decision or chance meeting can change everything and it's not always about the choices you make, rather the ones you don't, that can haunt you.

MAISIE

Glad to hear your book's almost done. I have a lot to say, but I prefer to do it face-to-face when you come here.

HAYES

That's fine. I can't wait to see you.

There's no way to respond to that so I don't. I lock my phone and set it down on the counter.

If I didn't keep most people at arm's length, I'd have girlfriends to talk to about this. Most of my friendships from my industry are surface-level. We talk shit mostly, but it rarely turns personal. Even if it did, I probably wouldn't share much anyway. One of my biggest fears was people associating me with my parent's money and assuming everything got handed to me instead of putting in the hard work to get where I am. Their financial support helped but it's not why I'm good at my job.

But the publishing industry can be cut-throat, which is a lot of keeping your friends close but your enemies closer. With social media, it's easy to see which ones run their mouths and ones who engage versus those who know to keep it professional.

I put my assistant in charge of posting when our clients have upcoming or new releases. Other than that, I stay offline.

"Maze?"

"In the office," I call out.

He appears moments later.

"Whaddya doin' in here?"

"Just lookin'."

"Hm." He presses his chest to my back, dipping his mouth to my ear and wrapping his arms around me. "Think you might wanna decorate it?"

"I'm not much of a designer, but I could try. What kind of theme or color scheme do you want?"

His lips press softly against my neck. "Not for me, love. Decorate it for you."

I spin around in his hold, lifting my gaze to his. "You'd just… give me this room?"

"I thought we went over this…" He cups my cheek, brushing the pad of his thumb lightly across my skin. "I built it for you."

I already told him I'm staying, but I still can't wrap my brain around him building this house inspired by my dream board. Even more mind-blowing is that he lived in it alone for all these years.

"It doesn't feel real," I admit softly. "I have a hard time acceptin' I deserve it or you."

"Leave that guilt behind. You chased your dreams and that's nothin' to feel bad about. We're different people now. If you're stayin', we get a fresh start. No more dwellin' about the past."

Nodding, my heart explodes at his sweet words. Besides

being surprised he waited this whole time for me, I'm shocked another woman didn't scoop him up. Not that he would've given them a chance, but…

Wait.

"Has another woman ever pursued you? You said you didn't sleep with anyone else, and I assumed that meant you didn't date either. But surely there's been interest?"

"There was."

I wait for him to elaborate but when he doesn't, I continue, "That's it? You're not gonna tell me?"

"There's nothin' to tell. They'd flirt a little and make it obvious they wanted me to ask 'em out, but I made sure to let 'em know I wasn't available."

"Even though, technically, you were."

"I wasn't."

"But really…"

"Not in my mind."

"Okay but—"

His mouth crashing down on mine shuts me up, but when his tongue massages mine, I completely forget the words I was about to say.

Warren lifts me up under my knees and I almost panic because he's not supposed to be doing any heavy lifting, but then he sets me down on top of the desk. Standing between my thighs, he deepens the kiss and I feel his thickening length between us.

"Did you do that so I'd stop talkin'?"

"Yes," he murmurs, lowering his mouth down my neck and panting into my skin. "Doesn't seem to have worked though."

I huff a laugh, tightening my legs around his waist.

"How many women?"

"None, Maze. You know that."

"No, how many flirted and wanted you to ask 'em out."

"Why's it matter?"

I can't explain it. The raging jealousy builds in my chest at anyone ever getting to experience him the way I do. He's truly one-of-a-kind and knowing he waited for me makes him an even more rare gem.

"It just does," I tell him instead of admitting it.

He blows out an aspirated breath. "I dunno, maybe a dozen or so?"

"A *dozen*?" I gasp, leaning back far enough to meet his eyes. Here I was thinking like five. "Gimme their names. All of 'em."

He furrows his brows, chuckling. "Half of 'em are probably married by now. The rest I have no idea. They were mostly strangers I'd meet when I'd go out to the bar with Silas or at rodeos."

"Well, you're restricted from those areas from now on."

He crosses his arms, taking a cautious step back. "Is that so?"

"Yes, it is."

If he knows I'm acting unreasonable, he doesn't call me out on it. This fiery heat between us feels new yet so familiar that I'm aware of what a catch he is and I don't like the idea of another woman being interested.

And yes, given the circumstances, I have no right to have those feelings, but I'm only a girl remembering how in love she was with the boy she fell for at fifteen.

"Would you feel better if the next time it happens, I tell 'em I have a wife and that if she even smells that another woman was near me, she'll come for blood?"

"Next time?" I glower, huffing but secretly enjoying that he's playing along. "And yes I would. Let 'em know I have pepper spray."

He barks out a humorous laugh, tilting my chin until his gray eyes pierce mine. "I will never let a non-relative woman near me ever again."

"Good. That's all I needed to hear."

With a devilish smirk, he gives me a sweet kiss. "For our date tonight, I'm cookin' you dinner, so I need to run to the grocery store. Do you wanna come?"

"Can I pick out the wine?"

"Absolutely."

I grin. "Then let's go!"

Who knew grocery shopping with my estranged husband would feel so *normal*?

In New York, I'd typically pick up items as we needed it from a nearby market since neither of us cooked much. It's been years since I was inside a large grocery chain, but somehow, it was fun.

While I pushed the buggy and followed him throughout the store, he talked about what he was making and all the ingredients he needed for it. We grabbed more fruit and yogurt for smoothies since that's easy enough for me to make. Then we did some damage in the bakery section before grabbing a couple bottles of Cabernet Sauvignon for the Beef Wellington.

"It takes a while to prep and cook, so I have to start as soon as we get back," he tells me as he pulls out of the parking lot.

"I'd offer to help, but I will only get in your way and slow you down."

He smirks, glancing at me from the driver's side. "Don't worry. I've only made it once so fingers crossed I don't screw it up or we'll be eatin' those frozen pizzas instead."

Once we're home, I help him bring in the bags and then unload the items on the counter since I have no idea where he prefers to put everything.

"Well...what else can I do to help?" I ask, looking around the kitchen.

He steps closer and kisses the top of my head. "Nothin', I'll take care of it. You relax. Watch TV or read. Take a bath. Whatever you want. Dinner should be ready by six."

That's four hours from now.

"You sure you should be standin' that long?" I look down at his chest.

"I'll take breaks if I need to, but don't worry about me."

Well that's easier said than done, but I take the hint and get out of the kitchen so he can work.

Since I packed my kindle in my purse, I browse for a new book since I haven't been able to read for fun in years, minus earlier this week. Once I've downloaded a few, I run the bath water and dig around for some salts and soap.

Although I showered this morning, soaking in the tub sounds too good to pass up.

Sinking deeper into the warmth, I groan at how good it feels against my muscles. I found some bubble bath, so when I move, they float around me.

I prop my feet up and grab my kindle from the table, then click on the first book about a grumpy hockey player and his rival enemy he's hated since childhood—who obviously fall in love.

A girl could definitely get used to this.

I'm not sure how long I stay in here, but once I get to fifty percent of my book and the bubbles have disappeared, I rinse off and get out.

I wrap a towel around my body and another one in my hair, then dig around my bag for clothes. I packed one longer dress that I should've hung up, so I find a clothes hanger and let it hang from the door while I take my time getting ready.

Warren doesn't have a hair dryer, but I was smart enough to pack my cosmetic bag so I can at least brush my hair and put on some makeup while it air dries.

While I listen to music and wait for the moisturizer to soak into my skin, I text my brother since the baby shower is tomorrow. We haven't seen each other this week, but I'm hopeful I'll get to chat and spend time with them during or after the party.

MAISIE

If you're having a girl, Gracelyn's a really pretty name :)

I chuckle because he'll recognize my middle name and most likely give me shit for it.

AARON

And curse her with a personality like yours?
That'd be child abuse.

Yep, I knew it.

MAISIE

You mean an AMAZING one like mine! Collins
already said it's on the list of potentials.

AARON

She was just trying to be nice.

MAISIE

Liar!

AARON

If it's a girl, we're giving her a cool name.

MAISIE

Cool? I'm too afraid to ask.

AARON

Yeah…non-traditional and unique.

MAISIE

Oh God. You're not gonna name your baby
something weird like Pickles or Maroon,
are you?

AARON

Great, I showed Collins and she likes
Maroon…way to go.

I snort, almost dropping my phone on the bathroom vanity.

MAISIE

HAHA…You better pray it's a boy.

Once I've finished my hair and makeup, I put on my dress
and a pair of heels. Although we're not going out, the fancy meal
he's making merits a fancy dress.

"Fuck. Me."

I jump at the gravelly voice behind me.

Warren's gaze is focused on my ass when I turn around.

"Is it too much?" I ask, flattening my palms down the tan and floral print.

He stalks toward me, taking notice of the slit that goes up my thigh and rubbing his hand over it.

"I've never seen anythin' more breathtakin' in my life." He cups my chin but doesn't lean in like I want. "And you definitely took my breath away."

How has this man who's made me swoon at least thirty times this week continue to make me blush?

"I'm so glad you approve 'cause I wore it for you."

So you can take it off me later…

But I keep my horny thoughts to myself.

"These are cute." He plucks at the off-the-shoulder Chiffon fabric that connects to the spaghetti strap.

"It's especially cute rumpled up on the floor," I say in the most innocent voice I can muster.

His soft gaze turns heated and then he's lifting me up and tossing me over his shoulder.

"Warren!" I squeal, holding onto his ass for support. "Watch the hair! Wait, you're not supposed to be liftin' anythin' for seventy-two hours!"

His chest vibrates with laughter before he carefully drops me onto the bed. When he cages his arms on either side of my head and hovers above me, my stomach flips.

"So does that mean come Monday, you're mine to do whatever I want with?"

Dammit, why did I have to remind him that he was on restrictions?

"There's plenty I could do to you that wouldn't require you to do any heavy liftin'." I smirk, lifting my knee to rub between his legs and feeling his thickening erection.

"That's..." He licks his bottom lip, shaking his head. "...a very temptin' offer, my love. But I need to shower and then I'm feedin' you since you never remember to eat. After that, we're gonna dance and have some dessert."

Oh damn, that sounds romantic as hell.

Before I can respond, he dips down and presses a gentle kiss to my just-glossed lips.

"Mm...taste delicious too." He winks, then pushes off the mattress, making me the breathless one.

While Warren showers, I continue reading my book, but once he comes out dripping wet in only a towel, it takes all my restraint to hold back.

"You're such a tease..." I groan.

Instead of taking pity on me and changing in the bathroom, he drops the towel, revealing his tight bare ass.

"I swear to God..." I pout, no longer able to focus on my kindle. "This is my punishment, ain't it?"

Flaunting every perfect inch of his body I want to run my tongue over.

"Just a temporary one," he says over his shoulder, then smirks before continuing, "Until I can reward you, that is."

Sweet Jesus.

How does this man have so much restraint?

I suffer in silence while he gets dressed, attempting to read my book but looking over the words to stare at him.

And of course, it doesn't get better when he puts on black jeans with a slutty ripped knee hole. Then he pairs it with a black button-up shirt and tucks his wedding-ring chain underneath it.

When he's finally ready, he grabs my hand and leads me into the kitchen. The meat is still cooking but we also grabbed some appetizers, sides, and desserts.

"Taste this." He holds out a combo I've never seen before. Even watching him put it together had me questioning his taste.

"What is it?" I eye the piece of shrimp sitting on top of a cucumber slice.

"Avocado shrimp cucumber." He moves it closer and my nose wrinkles.

"Try it," he insists.

I open my mouth and take the bite.

"You're gonna have to get used to my cuisine 'cause there's no New York delivery here."

"Ha-ha," I mock around a mouthful.

But then I taste it, and surprisingly, don't hate it.

"Okay, that wasn't bad." I swallow it down, shocked I didn't gag on the mix of textures. "I'll try another."

His smug smirk makes me roll my eyes at him being right.

He works on the side dishes while I tell him about the current book I'm reading.

"Does this one end in a happily-ever-after?"

"I hope so! After all the sex scenes, they better end up together."

His lips twitch as he arches an amused brow.

Maybe that's why I'm so hard up. That damn book got my hormones in overdrive.

When the meat's done and he cuts into it, I'm legit impressed.

"I can't believe you made that. Looks so good." The aroma of the tenderloin and mushroom layer has my stomach growling.

He plates it with roasted green beans and mashed potatoes before setting them on the table with lit candles.

I'm on the verge of an orgasm when I take my first bite.

"You're never allowed to stop cookin' for me."

"Wouldn't dream of it." He winks.

I can barely move by the time we finish eating, but it was so worth it.

"I'd offer to help clean up, but you're gonna have to gimme three to five business days to recover." I should've stopped eating after the first slice he gave me, but it was too good not to have a second.

"I'll take care of it." He kisses the top of my head.

"Then I'll be no better than your siblings you call freeloaders." I stand, grabbing my empty plate and wine glass.

He chuckles, grabbing the dishes from me when I meet him at the counter. "I'd much rather cook and clean up for you, so don't worry. They steal my food like little vultures and then leave a mess before sneakin' out."

I laugh, clearing the rest of the table. "They love you, though. They feel safe stealin' from you 'cause you let 'em without repercussions."

"So you're sayin' I should be meaner?"

"No!" I giggle. "But maybe change where you keep your hideaway key."

I rinse off the plates and hand them to Warren to load the dishwasher. Then we put the leftovers in the fridge and he pulls out the frozen turtle cake to thaw.

"I'll be ready to eat that in twenty-four hours."

He snickers. "Then dance with me while your stomach settles."

"Okay, but no promises not to throw up."

"Were you always this dramatic?" he taunts, taking my hand and bringing me to the middle of the living room.

He opens his vinyl record player and puts on jazz. The

fireplace is already crackling but since he opened a couple windows, it's the perfect temperature inside. And with the dim-lighting, it's the most romantic I've seen this room.

"Probably but you were too in love with me to notice or care." The words fall out of my mouth before I can stop them and I wince at saying the L word on his behalf. "Shit, that came out wrong."

He pulls me against his chest, wrapping one arm around my waist and cups my chin with his other hand. His lips meet mine for a tender kiss. "But you're one-hundred-percent correct 'cause I'm still deeply in love with you, Maze. Nothing's gonna change that."

I rest my palm over his racing heart, tightening my other arm around him and meet his sincere gaze.

"That's a relief 'cause you did exactly what you set out to do even though I was hell bent on provin' you wrong."

"And what was that?"

I lower my gaze, biting my lower lip before meeting his soft eyes again. "That you could have me second-guessin' my decision and remind me what being in love with you felt like. Except you were wrong about one thing..."

His heartfelt smile drops and the skin between his brows creases. "What thing?"

Grinning, I reply, "That it'd take seven days."

chapter twenty-three

Warren

MAISIE'S GAZE meets mine and when she says those last words to me, I melt into her. Every inch of my body is covered in goose bumps as I try to control my racing heart. This is all I've ever wanted since the moment she left, and I'm scared I'll wake up and it'll all have been a dream.

Drawing her lips to mine, I part them with my tongue and taste the lingering wine on hers.

I know what she's implying, and that's good enough for me, but a part of me needs to hear those words to confirm.

"Say it, baby," I plead against her mouth. "*Please.*"

"I love you," she whispers before meeting my gaze. "And it only took four days to realize I'm still head over heels, crazy in love with you that I can't believe I ever forgot how it felt. But that's just it—I didn't, not really. I compartmentalized my feelings in an attempt to move on 'cause livin' with a shattered heart was unbearable. So I convinced myself you had moved on and that I needed to as well. But comin' here, findin' out you hadn't, and rememberin' how easy it was to love you made me realize what I'd left behind."

"Fuck, Maze." I try to hold back my emotions. "I've waited seven years to hear those words. But I'd be lyin' if I didn't say I'm terrified you'll change your mind again."

At least until Hayes is out of the picture for good and the knot in my stomach goes away.

"I don't blame you for not fully trustin' me. Not sure I'd trust me either. But I'll spend the rest of our lives provin' it to you."

I dip my mouth to hers again, this time going slow and steady, swaying to the music. She tightens her hold on me, and I gently cup the back of her neck, never wanting to let her go.

If it wasn't for this damn physical activity restriction, I'd carry her ass back to my bed, strip her naked, and kiss every inch of her until she begged me to make love to her.

We continue dancing as we make conversation and kissing in between. My heart's never felt so full and content.

And I'm hoping like hell I never have to go through losing her again because there's no way I'd survive it a second time.

Waking up with Maisie's limbs tangled in mine will never get old.

Even listening to her little snores brings me peace.

My house's been quiet for far too long and my bed empty for even longer. It only took a couple nights to get used to it again.

After we ate dessert last night, we snuggled in bed, she read some more of her book, and then we passed out.

Well…after I gave her an earth-shattering orgasm with my tongue.

After she read more spicy chapters of her book, I had to prove to her the real thing was better than reading about it.

She'll be gone for several hours today to attend her brother and sister-in-law's baby shower. I'd go with her since it's a co-ed party, but showing up with her estranged husband would put the spotlight on us instead of the parents-to-be, so I'll be here getting things ready for our final date.

However, it won't be the last. I'll continue to date my wife until I'm no longer able to breathe.

"Just a few more minutes…" I beg, burying my face in her neck when she tries to slide out from the covers. I tighten my grip around her stomach, pulling her closer.

"Mm…" She hums, taunting my morning wood by rubbing her ass against me. "Let me take care of that for you."

Before I can stop her, she spins around and slides her hand down to my aching cock.

"Maze…" I groan, my breath hitching at her rubbing me over my shorts. "Don't start somethin' you can't finish."

"I've got a few minutes to spare…" She taunts, lowering down my body as I shift to my back and then she settles between my thighs.

I lift my hips so she can slide my shorts down, but as soon as my dick comes into view, her lips wrap around it.

"Holy shit…" I gasp, her eager tongue twisting around the tip and barbells before she sucks it back into her hot mouth.

I grab a fistful of her messy hair so I can see her gorgeous face. She wraps her fingers around the base of my shaft, squeezing and stroking as she swallows me down.

"Fuck, baby. You take me so fuckin' good. Just like that…"

When she lifts her glassy eyes to meet mine, I nearly drown her in my cum. Goddamn, she's a dream.

She bobs on my dick like she's as starved for it as I've been for her. It doesn't take long for my heart to explode and the warmth to build down my spine. I spill down her throat, moaning through the intense release.

My back flattens on the mattress, no longer able to hold myself up, but her tongue licks me clean. Then she so generously slides my shorts back up.

I almost laugh at the comedic way she does it.

"That should hold you over until I return." She towers over me, resting her palms on the bed beside my head. Then she smacks her lips against mine, but I'm too sated to pull her back for more.

"That'll be what I think about all day now…" I groan.

"Good, I like being on your mind."

This time I do reach up and cup the back of her neck, pulling her down just above my mouth. "My love, you always are. I'm madly obsessed with you."

She sinks down on top of me but shifts half her weight onto the bed to avoid my ribs. Although they're feeling much better, I wouldn't care if she crushed me at this point as long as it meant I got to taste her.

When she moans against me, I cup her ass and pull her up closer.

"You better prepare yourself for tomorrow night. The moment I get you alone and rip off your clothes, there'll be no mercy."

"Goddamn you." She grinds into me. "How're you gonna say that when I have to get ready to leave?"

I give her ass another tap, then arch my hips into hers. "And that should hold *you* over until then."

After Maisie left, I showered and got ready for the day. I need some help getting things ready for tonight, so I texted Colt to borrow a projector and screen they make available for the guests at the resort. If someone wants to watch a movie on a large screen, staff will set it up for them.

However, I want it so Maisie and I can watch a movie in the bed of my truck like we were supposed to at the drive-in. But in the privacy of my own driveway where I can touch my wife without getting an indecent exposure violation.

"Hey," I say when I find Colt in the waiting area of The Branch Haven. It's where most of the resort items are stored, but I need his master key to get what I need.

Next to him are the rest of our siblings.

"What're y'all doin' here?" I ask, suspicious of their intentions considering they all look like they're up to no good.

"We're bondin'..." Bellamy says, but I'm not buying it.

"Is that so?" I cross my arms. "Without me?"

"Figured you were *too busy* to spend time with us..." Posey's snarky tone makes me roll my eyes.

"When has that ever stopped you from buggin' me?"

Bodie snorts. "They're only here to get info about you and Maisie."

"Dude!" Posey and Bellamy scold him at the same time.

"As if he doesn't know you're a couple of gossips." Bodie

shrugs but then looks at me. "So? Are you gonna tell us how things are goin'?"

I humph at how eager he sounds and how nosy they all are.

"They're goin' fine."

"Just *fine*? Yeesh..." Posey's eyes widen before darting to Bellamy.

"Oh, and your datin' life is goin' so well?" Bodie snickers. "Tell 'em about the last guy you scared away."

"Hey, it's not my fault all these *men* are insecure babies."

I purse my lips. "What'd you do?"

"This guy was goin' on and on about how hot and tall he is, and that he gets it from his dad, who's like six-foot-five and supposedly some hotshot lawyer. He wouldn't shut up about it, so I told him to show me proof."

"And then what?" I ask.

"He sent me a picture of a very handsome older gentleman in a three-piece suit lookin' fine as hell." She pinches her lips as if she doesn't want to say her next words. "And I replied, *smash*."

Everyone bursts out laughing, and I shake my head.

She sighs. "Yeah, he blocked me after that."

"Well, I can confidently say my relationship is goin' much better than that."

"So y'all back together?" Bellamy asks eagerly.

"Technically, yes. But she needs to break it off with her fiancé when he arrives in a couple days."

"That's not weird or anythin'." Posey grimaces. "But she's movin' back here?"

"We haven't discussed all the specific details but yeah. She needs to pack up her things and get 'em shipped here. I already have an office she can use, so she'll be able to work while she waits for the rest of her stuff."

"I'm still in shock you won her back over in less than a week," Bellamy says.

"Are you sayin' I have no game or what?" I ask, pretending to be offended.

"Pretty much. All I saw you do is sulk and growl at anyone who tried to flirt with you," she replies.

"You look happier," Posey says, smiling. "So she better not hurt you a second time or—"

"She won't," I say confidently, but hoping I'm right.

We chat for a few more minutes before Colt helps me bring the projector and screen to the back of my truck.

"I'm gonna give you the same speech I give the guests…" He says, closing the tailgate. "The projector cannot withhold your weight, therefore, do not lean on it, put too much pressure on it, or use it as a wall with your body or anyone else's."

I laugh at how professional he's trying to sound, no doubt the same voice he uses on the guests. "So basically you're tellin' me not to fuck against it?"

"Correct, so please don't." He smirks. "Or there'll be an added fee to your bill."

I spend the rest of the afternoon getting things ready. Although we have leftovers from last night's dinner, I make some finger foods and snacks to eat while we watch the movie. We have to wait until it's dark so we can see the screen, but it should be easy enough to set up. The projector will sit on top of my truck while I set up the screen on the ground. It has a stand so I'll be able to adjust the height as needed.

When Maisie walks in hours later, she looks exhausted. Without speaking, she kicks off her heels, lowers the zipper of her dress, and lets it pool to her feet before climbing on the bed where I was waiting for her.

I open my arms and she snuggles against me.

"Long day?"

"Soooo many people. I'm tapped out on socializin' for the next month."

I chuckle, feeling her pain. Leaning over, I kiss the top of her head. "I missed you."

She peers up at me, smiling. "Missed you too. It was weird havin' to be so fake."

My brows crease. "Whaddya mean?"

"Everyone knows I'm engaged to Hayes, so everyone was gushin' over my ring and asked about weddin' details."

"You didn't tell 'em?"

"No, I didn't want to make it a big deal on Aaron and Collins' special day. It woulda felt wrong to announce that I'm callin' it off before I tell Hayes in person. Plus, my mother loves being the center of attention. I couldn't dare take this being her first grandchild away from her." She rolls her eyes, but I hate that everyone thinks she's with another man.

"Does this mean instead of sendin' out Save the Dates we can send out Still Married cards?"

A laugh bubbles out of her.

"My mom's head would explode." She licks her lips, contemplating. "Let's do it."

"You did all this while I was gone?" She looks inside the truck bed filled with pillows, blankets, and a picnic basket. It's parked in the middle of my driveway, so if she falls asleep, I can easily carry her inside.

"I thought it'd be a nice way to relax after a hectic weekend."

"I love it." She stands on her tiptoes, pressing her lips to mine. "What movie are we watchin'?

"Well...the resort has limited options, but I picked one I thought you'd like."

I help her up and she kicks off her shoes and snuggles under the blankets. She's in a knee-length flowy purple skirt and white blouse, looking every bit overdressed, but sexy as hell.

Once we're situated and have our snacks in front of us, I turn on the movie from my Bluetooth.

10 Things I Hate About You begins playing and as soon as the music plays, she squeals.

"Oh my God! I haven't seen this in so long!"

"I knew you'd love it." She only made me watch it once a month during our high school years.

"Julia Stiles! My first girl crush."

I chuckle, shoving some popcorn into my mouth. "Mine too."

She nudges me, laughing.

"Ms. Perky writin' an erotic novel is so much funnier now that I'm a lit agent. And more disturbin' that she's doing it in a school filled with minors."

We both grimace.

"Aww...Heath Ledger. Rest in Peace to my first heartthrob."

She grabs one of the Pigs in a Blanket I made and moans when she takes a bite.

"Jesus Christ, that was so inappropriate..." Her eyes widen at the guidance counselor talking about a bratwurst.

I enjoy every bit of her commentary as we continue watching. She used to do the same thing as teens when we'd watch a movie. Even at the theater she'd lean over and whisper in my ear, but I loved hearing every thought that came to her mind. It was always entertaining as hell.

"The endin' always makes me teary-eyed. Her readin' the poem in class in front of him and the way he watches her cry, then surprises her with a Fender Strat and admittin' he fell for her...*gah!* They don't make movies like that anymore."

"My favorite is the way she tries to scold him about how he can't just buy her gifts every time he screws up and keeps kissin' her to shut her up."

"Hm...that's where you got it from." She playfully glares.

"Shhh..." I cup the back of her neck, bringing her mouth to mine and sinking my tongue between her lips.

"Oh you're so busted, cowboy!" She laughs, trying to shove me away, but it only encourages me to add more of my weight over her.

Kissing my way down her jaw and neck, I grab her wrist and trap it above our heads. "Never heard any complaints from you before."

"Well...you are a very good kisser."

I smirk before gliding down her body. Lifting her shirt, I suck on her skin and then continue until I'm between her thighs. My legs hang off the tailgate, so I climb off completely, and grab her ankles so she's within reach.

"Jesus," she squeals when I bring her to the edge and props herself up on her elbows.

I kneel in front of her, spreading her legs wider. "It's Warren, baby. Say my name when my tongue's inside you."

Sliding her panties to the side, I lick up her slit and suck her clit into my mouth. Feeling her squirm and panting makes my dick so hard, it strains behind my zipper, and I'm tempted to release it just to give it relief.

"Oh fuck…" She gasps out her words. Her hand reaches for me, knocking my backward baseball cap off so she can tangle her fingers through my hair. She tightens her grip, pulling at the strands and cries out again when my own groans vibrate against her.

With my palms holding her thighs open, I lift her hips slightly to angle my mouth and tongue inside her deeper.

"Warren…anyone could see us out here," she says as if just realizing we're out in the open. It's pitch black besides the lights near the front door and the moon shining down on us.

"I'd never let anyone see what's mine, baby. Don't worry." I continue devouring every inch of her pussy, kissing between each thigh, and when she's on the verge of exploding, I add two fingers inside.

"Right there, I'm so—" Her words turn into a breathy gasp, and with her back arched and legs shaky, she comes on my face.

"Fuck, Maze." I groan, licking up her mess.

Before this week, I was starved for her, and now I can't get enough. Hearing the pleasure slip from her lips and feeling her body react to me is enough to make me cum in my pants.

"Get up here and lie down," she demands. "And no arguin'."

Her stern voice makes me chuckle. "Yes, ma'am."

She wastes no time climbing over my thighs and yanking my jeans and shorts down. Her hot mouth inhales my cock, swallowing it down her throat until I can't hold back anymore.

"Goddamn, you drained everythin' outta me," I say between trying to catch my breath.

She crawls up my body and taps my lips. The fire in her eyes tells me I better obey, so I do.

As soon as I open my mouth, she spits in it, and I swallow it down. "Such a filthy girl." Then I crush my cum-flavored lips to hers.

chapter twenty-four

Maisie

ALTHOUGH I SLEPT like a baby after Warren drained every ounce of energy out of me, I hate waking up and him already being gone for work.

I vaguely remember him kissing me goodbye and telling me he put my breakfast in the fridge for me to warm up later.

That man is obsessed with making sure I eat, but it's another reason I love him. Even though it's Monday and he'll be at work all day, his mind is making sure my needs are met.

Since I still haven't gone home to my parent's house, I'm without my laptop, so I schedule a video chat with my assistant. I need the distraction while I attempt to shave every inch from the waist down. And hoping Warren doesn't mind me using his razor.

"Why do you sound out of breath?" Taylor asks.

I propped my phone up and angled it toward the ceiling so she doesn't get an unwanted show.

"'Cause tryin' to shave between my cheeks is like doin' gymnastics without stretchin', or ya know, being flexible."

"I-I'm sorry I asked." She giggles.

Grabbing my phone, I readjust it so she can see my face. "Not as sorry as I am for you havin' to hear about it."

"Well…good luck? Besides that, how're things going?"

I haven't told her much since I was being cautious of people finding out the truth, but since I'll be moving here, I had to explain myself.

"Great." I beam. "Incredible, honestly. It feels too good to be true and I'm waiting for the impendin' bomb to come and blow it all up."

"Don't think like that. You deserve to be happy and we can have virtual cocktail hours, so don't worry about me." We used to meet up once a week, so that's something I'll miss.

"I appreciate that, Tay. I'm just a nervous wreck until I can talk to Hayes, officially cancel the weddin', and get my things moved here. It feels so quick but not at the same time."

"It is quick but that doesn't mean it won't work out. My little sister eloped after knowing her husband for only six days! Talk about insanity."

"Wait, after less than a week?"

"Yep…and got knocked up six weeks later."

"Sweet lord."

I finally manage to maneuver my foot up on the counter and spread wide enough to shave lower. Oh God, that feels weird. Too bad there's not a local waxing salon or I'd be face down ass up right now letting someone else do it.

"Trust me, our parents weren't happy about it either. But they've been together for five years and have two kids together."

"Damn. I guess when you know…"

"So they say." She sighs, rolling her eyes and I laugh. She

hasn't found anyone to settle down with yet but I have no doubt she will.

"Warren has two brothers if you wanna move here," I taunt. "Although they're young and immature."

She snorts. "The thirty-five-year-olds aren't any better up here."

We continue talking while I shave my legs and between my thighs, then I lotion every inch of my skin. I soaked in the bathtub earlier and finally finished the book I was reading.

Before hanging up, we discuss some of the resumes that have come in. I'm excited to hire more help to give me more time to focus on a work-life balance. Warren deserves that from me, and so do I.

My body shouldn't feel like I'm fifty because I stay in one position for too long. Even though my desk can raise so I can stand while working, it still wreaks havoc on my back and hips.

"Good luck with everythin'. Keep me updated," she says and then we say goodbye.

I'm not sure what Warren has planned for us this evening, especially since his lifting restrictions are over, but I want to be prepared. It feels like we've waited an eternity instead of a few days.

WARREN

I should be home in a couple hours. Any ideas what you'd like for dinner?

I smile at his message, deciding to tease him a little.

MAISIE

As long as it involves me being naked underneath you, I don't really care what we eat.

WARREN

Fuck, that was unexpected. My employee,
Nicky, was standing over my shoulder so I
could show him something on my laptop
screen and read your message before I could
swipe it away.

Oops.

MAISIE

You mean Ricky? Also, my bad.

WARREN

No, they're brothers. He was on his
honeymoon last week and today's his first day
back to work.

MAISIE

They're brothers and their names rhyme?

WARREN

Yep.

I can't help laughing because I just know Warren gives them
shit for it.

MAISIE

That's what I get for trying to sext my husband
at work. Thank God I didn't send a photo of
my recently-shaved pussy.

My phone rings three seconds later.

"Hello, husband," I purr.

"Maze..." His tone is firm, and I wince.

"He was still standin' behind ya, wasn't he?"

I hear laughter in the distance and a groan from Warren.

"Yeah, he was."

"Shit. Any chance he'll pretend he didn't read that?"

He sighs, breathing out roughly. "Highly unlikely."

"Alright, so no more naughty textin' while you're at work."

"You can in about five minutes when I kick his ass outta here so he gets to work."

"In that case, prepare yourself, cowboy."

"Gimme your best, wife."

Ooh, I'm going to make him regret those words.

After hanging up, I make him wait longer than five minutes so he can suffer in anticipation. If I had any lingerie with me, I'd tease the shit out of him, but for now I have to improvise.

I lie naked in the middle of the bed and cross my legs so he can see my piercing just enough to notice I'm bare. Then I angle my phone high up so he'll be able to see the skin that meets under my breasts but no nipple shot.

A glimpse of what'll be waiting for him when he gets home.

After taking a few shots, I send him my favorite one with a text.

MAISIE

Since you're handling dinner, I'll take care of dessert 😌

I wait impatiently for his response, wondering if he got sidetracked or busy with work and hasn't been able to check his phone.

Deciding to grab my Kindle, I get under the covers and grab the next book in the series I was reading.

Before I can finish the first chapter, the front door opens and slams shut. I jump at the booming sounds of boots storming down the hallway and then the bedroom door whips open.

"Jesus, you scared the shit outta me. I thought Bigfoot was comin' for me."

Without a word, he closes the gap between him and the bed, throws off the covers and grabs my ankles. Then he yanks me down the mattress toward him.

"That was quite the photo you sent me…" His deep growl has me aching to squeeze my thighs but he's hovering about me and standing between my legs.

"Did you like it?" I smirk, losing the grip on my Kindle and leaning up on my elbows.

"I did," he says with amusement. "So much so I had to leave work before someone saw my ragin' boner."

My eyes drop to his crotch and the grin that forms across my face is lethal. I love that I did that to him.

He cups my chin, bringing my gaze up to his. "And now you're gonna pay for that little stunt."

"Oh no…what a hardship that'll be."

Leaning in, he nips at my lower lip. "Such a sassy fuckin' mouth."

"You love it." I slide my tongue out and his eyes track the movement. "Why aren't you naked?"

He snickers, kneels on the floor, then brushes his nose up my thigh. "'Cause I'm supposed to be at work right now."

"And yet, you're not. So strip, cowboy."

"Hm…maybe I'll torture you instead the way you're torturin' me." His finger breaches my pussy, slowly sinking inside.

Fuck, that feels good. I'm so wet, he easily adds a second.

His torturously slow movements bring me close to the edge before he pulls back and restricts me from my orgasm.

"Warren, *please*," I whine after the third time he edges me.

"Mm, you beg for me so sweetly, baby. I'm almost tempted to

give in, but I want you so needy for it that by the time I return, I'll have you squirtin' before I even give you my cock."

He pulls away, standing to his full height, and I hold out my hand, trying to grab him. "No! How dare you?"

Tilting my chin, he presses a tender kiss to my lips. "It'll be worth the wait, my love. I promise."

My pussy weeps, and I nearly cry at the loss of him.

"You're so gonna pay for this," I weakly threaten, plopping back on the mattress with a huff.

"I'll be home at five." He winks and then walks out of the bedroom.

Warren's lucky there's less than two hours until he's due back because the way he left me ready and wanting is pure torture.

I manage to get dressed so I'm not walking around naked, although I'm sure he wouldn't mind, but I'm not taking the risk of one of his siblings or parents randomly showing up.

Instead of staying in bed waiting for him, I go downstairs to the library and snuggle up in the chair while I read. It's hard not to think what it'll look like in a couple months. My books on these shelves. Books I've read as a teenager and into adulthood. Books of authors I represent.

It's still hard to comprehend that he built this for me.

But I'm grateful for it.

At some point, I doze off and wake up to the smell of something delicious cooking upstairs. Warren must be home and he didn't come get me.

Knowing him, he probably showered first and then started dinner. The man is nothing if not predictable in sticking to his schedule, which now includes making sure I eat.

Going upstairs, I find Warren standing in front of the stove, shirtless in only a pair of joggers and looking every inch irresistible. I wrap my arms around him, plastering my chest to his back, and squeeze.

"That smells so good whatever it is," I say, pressing a kiss between his shoulders.

"Smothered pork chops," he informs me, spinning in my arms and cupping my face. He dips down and brushes his lips against mine.

"Mm...a girl could get used to this." I melt into him, sliding my hands over his bare stomach. "Why didn't you wake me?"

"You looked so peaceful sleepin', but I was about to since the food's almost done." He twists a strand of hair behind my ear, giving me the sweetest smile. "I liked findin' you down there. Panicked at first when you weren't in the usual places but seein' you in the readin' chair I got for you made me stupidly happy."

"How do you always say the sweetest things?" I lean into his touch, wanting more. "And why aren't we naked right now?"

His deep chuckle sends a thrilling shiver down my spine.

"Well..." He lifts me by my ass and my arms wrap around his neck as he sets me down on the other countertop. I almost scold him about lifting me before I remember the restriction timeframe is over. The bruises have faded more, which makes me feel better about him manhandling me. "I'm gonna feed you first. You said you were handlin' *dessert*, right?"

I snicker, tightening my thighs around his waist and pulling him closer. "You're already halfway naked, so let's skip right to it." Sliding my fingers underneath his waistband, I lick my lower lip, hoping he takes the bait.

His eyes track the movement before shoving his thumb between my lips. "Suck, baby."

I gladly do as he says, twirling my tongue around his digit before hollowing my cheeks and sucking on it.

"Fuck, you do that so good. Such a greedy girl." His whispered groan has my pussy weeping for him to touch me.

As my hand slides deeper in his joggers, I discover he's not wearing any shorts underneath. My eyes widen with heat as I inch closer to his thickening erection.

"Patience, darlin'." He removes his thumb before lowering his mouth to mine. "Dinner's ready."

My head falls back with a whimper. "I've been plenty patient, especially after that little stunt you pulled this afternoon."

His easygoing grin turns feral, a flash of pride beaming between his eyes. "I've waited years for you, Maze. Another thirty minutes won't kill us."

Him maybe. I might actually stroke out from the way he constantly makes my heart race.

Warren helps me off the counter and tells me to go sit at the table, even though I offer to help set it. He catches me staring at his slutty pants, displaying exactly what's available underneath the fabric, and chuckles.

He brings the food over with two glasses of wine, and I can't even be disappointed because I'm starving and everything looks so perfect.

Before taking the seat across from me, Warren stands behind my chair and wraps his hand around my throat. Then he tilts my head back and squeezes before claiming my mouth with his.

He licks and sucks my tongue, devouring me like a starved man, and knowing damn well what it's doing to me.

It's one of the hottest things he's ever done.

"Enjoy your dinner, baby." He presses his lips to my neck and then releases me.

I'm left panting and eager as he sits across from me, a smug smirk planted on his face.

"Tell me about your day," he says once our plates are filled.

I talk to him about the new book I'm reading and the other events that took place while he was gone, talking to my assistant, taking a long bath, shaving every inch of my body. His fork clanks against the plate when I go into detail about that last part.

"And how was yours?" I ask with amusement. "Did Nicky recover?"

He scoffs. "That little shit tried to use it against me to get more days off. We already put him and his new wife up in one of the domes for the week with the stipulation he came into work each day."

"You're makin' him work during his honeymoon?"

"He only gave me four days' notice and should be grateful I gave him one week off to go to Mexico. He'll survive."

"They probably never left the room anyway."

"That's what I said!"

We both laugh, and I remember ours after we got married.

"Would you wanna go on one with me?"

"On a honeymoon?"

"Yeah, like a couples getaway to reconnect. Maybe after I move back?"

I don't know why I'm nervous asking but Warren's so comfortable here, and I get the feeling he doesn't leave very often.

He reaches across the table, interlocking his fingers with mine. "I'd love to."

Then he brings my hand to his lips and kisses my knuckles. "Where would you wanna go?"

"Considering I haven't traveled much myself, I'm open to almost anywhere. Somewhere on the water would be nice."

We continue talking about ideas, which is somehow a distraction from the wild thoughts consuming me and eating our food. He made roasted garlic potatoes and glazed carrots for the sides, which were as delicious as the meat.

"I'm gonna have to take up workin' out, runnin', or somethin' 'cause you're feedin' me way too good." I lean back, holding my stomach. With the amount of food he makes, I won't be able to fit in my clothes anymore.

Warren stands, collecting our empty dishes. "Eatin' is good for you, my love. Especially when you're carryin' our baby."

"W-what?" My jaw drops before I can pick it up.

"Well...eventually, right?" he asks, walking to the sink. "We always talked about havin' kids at some point. Is that no longer somethin' you want?"

"Yeah..." I nod and go into the kitchen. "I do want kids, but—"

"We don't have to rush, Maze." He cups my jaw, sounding so sincere, it almost breaks me. "Whenever you're ready."

Hayes made it known he was too old to become a first-time dad and knew he'd be too busy to be one, so although I'd always wanted to be a mom, I accepted that it wasn't going to happen. The whole idea of getting pregnant and having babies always appealed to me, but I let that dream go in order to be with him.

I hadn't realized until this moment that I no longer had to "Does that mean you're ready now?"

"I am when *you* are," he clarifies, lining my lips with his.

When his tongue massages mine, tingles radiate my skin, and I arch my body closer to his. His heart thumps against my racing one, making it even harder to pull away so I can speak.

"Warren..." I whisper his name but it comes out as a moan.

"I know, baby," he whimpers, pressing his erection into my lower stomach.

Oh fuck.

Our lips draw together and when he pulls me up, I wrap my legs and arms around his body, keeping us fused. The movement of his body has me holding onto him tighter and anticipating his next move. He walks us into the bedroom, his lips gliding down my neck before gently placing me on the mattress.

When he towers over me, I reach for his joggers, but then he grabs my wrists and flattens them above my head.

"I swear to God," I cry out. "If you're gonna tease me again, I'm kickin' you in the balls."

His menacing chuckle vibrates against my skin when he sucks below my collarbone. He pulls my arms together, wrapping one hand around both wrists, and lowering his other hand before sliding it underneath my shirt.

"Stop worryin', sweetheart..." he murmurs, licking a path up my neck as he cups my breast under my bra. "I'm gonna ruin you in the best way possible."

chapter twenty-five

I SHOULD GET a medal for the level of restraint I've practiced over the past week and a half every time Maisie begged for more. Although teasing her has led to some incredibly hot moments, I'm dying to be inside her and reconnect as husband and wife.

Seeing how greedy and desperate she is for it makes me want to give her everything she needs and more.

I want to *own* her. Take her.

Give her pleasure she's never experienced before.

Every inch of my body wants to consume her the way she's consumed me for years. I want to bury myself in her and never come up for air.

With my knee on the mattress between her thighs, I slide up until it rubs against her pussy. She arches into it before rocking her hips.

"Warren," she whimpers.

Bringing my mouth down on hers, I seek out her tongue before sucking on it.

"What do you need, baby? Tell me."

"Fuck me, *please*. I'm desperate."

"Mm..." I growl, pleased to hear how hungry she is for me. "You want my cock, darlin'?"

"God, yes." She nods eagerly. "Inside me."

"Then take it, wife." I release her wrists and her fingers fly to the waistband of my joggers.

I stand with both feet on the floor as she pulls them down and frees my erection. She wraps her mouth around the tip, flicking the barbells with her tongue before sliding down my length.

Fisting the hair at the back of her head, I help guide her so she doesn't choke. I'm so damn hard, I won't last if she doesn't slow down.

"Maze..." I warn, pushing back. "Up."

She pops off me, getting to her feet, and I crush my mouth to hers, unable to resist tasting her. I grab the hem of her shirt and slide it over her head, breaking our kiss momentarily before I devour her again. Reaching around, I unclasp her bra and let it drop to the floor.

Lifting her up, I place her back on the bed, then yank her leggings and panties down. Fully naked, I spread her thighs and press my mouth between them.

Every inch of her is soft and smooth, and I waste no time sinking two fingers inside. I lap at her clit and tease the piercing between my lips as I thrust in deeper.

Feeling Maisie squirm beneath me and moan my name drives me insane. Nothing's changed in that area.

Her grip tightens in my hair and the breathy whimpers from her mouth turn into screams when she gets close to the edge. But I pull back before she can fall over.

"Warren, no!" she whines, trying to shove my head down.

I chuckle at her eagerness and press one last kiss to her clit.

"Baby, I'm gonna burst if I don't get inside you," I admit urgently.

"Then *hurry*…"

I open my nightstand for the three-pack of condoms my father so awkwardly donated. I would've bought my own but might as well use these first.

Maisie stares while I sheath myself and crawl on the bed, kneeling between her spread thighs. She sits up on her elbows when I push her legs back, opening her wider.

"Tell me if it hurts," I say, referring to my piercing, then press my lips to hers for a quick kiss.

Grabbing my cock, I slowly breach her entrance and ease inside.

Fuck. This is what heaven feels like.

"Look how perfect we fit together," I murmur, staring down between us. "Fuck, Maze."

"Keep goin'. I can take it." Her pleading eyes are impossible to resist, so I give her what she wants. Her breath catches when I bottom out. "Yes, right there."

Pulling back, I admire how wet she coats me before sinking back inside her tight cunt. "Look at you takin' my cock so damn beautifully."

She blushes at the praise, muttering, "Don't fuckin' stop."

Towering above, I slam into her, over and over. My fingers grip her hair, holding her head up to meet my lips.

"Warren, oh my God…" she cries out, her nails breaking the skin as she scratches down my arms.

"I know, baby." I nip the skin beneath her ear. "You're squeezin' me so good."

Wrapping an arm around her waist, I flip us over so I'm on my back. She adjusts quickly, pressing her palms on my chest before she settles her weight evenly, and my heart nearly bursts at the sight of her on top of me.

"That's it, baby. Ride me as hard and fast as you want." I smack her ass, encouraging her to go at her own pace.

"Oh fuck, do that again."

I love when she's vocal and tells me what she needs. I willingly give in, squeezing her ass cheeks before giving them a couple more hard slaps.

Palming her breast, I lean up and lick a nipple before sucking it into my mouth. "Goddamn, your tits bouncin' in my face is so fuckin' hot."

When her pussy squeezes my cock, I pull her down to my chest so the friction can rub against her clit, and I can claim her mouth. I lift my hips to match her pace and drive into her.

"Deeper...I'm so close."

I flip us over again, but this time, I tell her to turn and get on all fours so I'm behind her. But I don't give her what she wants right away.

Sinking lower, I spread her cheeks and lick from her clit to her tight hole.

"Oh God..." She writhes, arching her back.

"Ride my tongue," I demand with a quick smack on her ass.

She slides a hand between her thighs, rubbing her clit, and I groan against her pussy as I tongue-fuck it.

Getting to my knees, I pull her up slightly so her back's pressed against me, and shove two fingers between her lips.

"Get 'em nice and wet, sweetheart."

She does, sliding her tongue between each digit, before I sink them inside her. "Gonna stretch you out nice and good to take my cock from behind. Think you can take it?"

"Mm-hmm." She nods eagerly. "Go as hard and deep as you can."

I tilt her head until my lips crush hers.

"Don't be gentle...gimme everythin' you have."

Nipping at her earlobe, I inhale her sweet scent and groan. "You don't want sweet 'n slow?"

She swallows as if she's hesitant to tell me.

"Say it, Maze. I'll give you anythin'."

"Be rough with me. *Use* me. All that hurt and sadness you felt over the years. Give it to me."

"Fuck, baby. I don't wanna hurt you like that."

"But I want you to. I *need* you to." The way she looks at me has me in a puddle at her feet. So desperate and hungry for it.

"You gonna beg for it?" I taunt, wanting to hear how badly she wants it.

"Yes, I'll do anythin'." She nods fervently. "Punish me for ever leavin' you. Ruin me for any other man."

God. Fucking. Dammit.

"Jesus Christ, Maze." I bite down on her neck, making sure she's properly branded. "By the time I'm done markin' you from the inside out, you'll forever feel me with each step you take."

"Please, yes..."

"Face down, baby. And hold onto somethin'."

Rubbing my cock down her crack, I smack it against her pussy a few times before sliding inside. It's so tight, I can hardly control myself, but I'm not coming until she's squirted all over me first.

My fingers bruise her sides as I impale her over and over,

reaching deeper with each thrust, and when I adjust my angle, hit that sweet spot inside her.

"Ohfuckohfuckoh*fuck*," she mutters into a pillow.

I slap her ass, making her scream out again.

"Such a good fuckin' girl for me," I growl, unable to control my own moans.

"Shit, you're deep," she breathes out, arching lower.

"And you're takin' it so good, baby." I stare at my cock pounding into her and squeeze her hips harder.

Feeling her wrapped around me, panting and shaking, makes something inside me snap. Years of wishing for this, thinking it'd never happen again, makes me possessive as hell. I never want another man breathing around her, nevertheless, touching her.

"Warren, please. I'm so close. Let me come…"

"Tell me you're mine." I thrust my hips harder the way she wants.

"I'm yours," she promises.

"You wanna come?"

"Yes…so badly."

Grabbing around her waist, I pull her up so we're glued together.

"You think I should let you after the way you broke me?" I growl in her ear.

Her breath hitches and she shakes her head. "It'll never happen again."

Even after everything, I believe her.

"Fuckin' beg me, Maze." I reach down and tease her clit. "Beg me not to stop right now and keep it from you."

"I'll do anythin', please." She moans when I find that perfect rhythm. "*Pleasepleaseplease*."

"On your stomach, baby." I help guide her down but then

turn her to the side and settle in behind her body. Propping up her leg, I slide in deep without having to hold myself up. "Now breathe."

I cradle her head, bury my face in her neck, and drive into her. Sliding my hand down, I rub over her piercing, and moments later, she cries out.

"Thatta girl, come on my cock," I murmur in her ear, wrapping my fingers around her throat so I can feel the pleasure vibrate through her.

A gasp followed by full-body shaking has me teetering on the edge of losing it.

"Holy. Shit." Her body melts against me.

I kiss along her neck, soaking in every minute. "I'm almost there, love. Roll on your back."

When she moves, I straddle her waist and remove the condom.

"Show me your tongue," I demand, rubbing over my shaft.

Leaning up on her elbows, she obliges, and I continue stroking. The view of her is all it takes. The tension snaps in seconds and the build-up from the way she took me unravels. I growl through the release, making a mess of her face and throat.

"Fuck, that's hot."

She glances down at her chest and swipes her fingers through it before sucking on it. "Well...at least your aim got a little better. We'll work on it."

I huff a laugh, collapsing to the side of her. Cupping her face, I crush my mouth to hers. "That was so worth the wait, baby."

She nods, still trying to catch her breath, looking wrecked and sated. The pulse in her throat beats erratically against my palm.

"I'll grab some water and then we can rinse off in the shower."

I move to get up but she stops me. "Wait."

"You okay?"

"Just wanted to tell you how much I love you."

This time when I brush my lips over hers, it's steady and slow. "I'll never get tired of hearin' you say that. I love you so fuckin' much."

Once we're hydrated and clean, I tuck Maisie into bed. She looked so exhausted, I didn't want to keep her up.

I go to the kitchen and finish wiping down the counters and putting the leftovers in the fridge. It's hard to believe she's only been back for less than two weeks and she already fits perfectly in my life. Things started out bumpy, and I know we still have some obstacles to overcome, but I'm ready to go through them with her.

Because when I said forever and till death do us part, I meant every word.

chapter twenty-six

Maisie

I'M HALF dead when I wake up the next morning, but in the most delicious way possible. I welcome the ache because it reminds me of the night before and how amazing we were together.

In all our years together, I've never seen him so unhinged and possessive before. Our sex life was amazing before, so I knew, or rather, hoped it'd be easy to fall into those same habits with our refound chemistry.

But it was so much better.

He had this animalistic urgency to claim me, but with a gentle and tender force about it. Always slowing down to kiss me right before he impaled me, over and over again, making me cry out for more. The depraved way he licked and sucked on my skin and this insatiable need to consume me was unlike anything I'd experienced before.

He dominated every inch of my body, flipping me into different positions and feasted on me like a starved man.

It felt like we'd never been apart, anticipating each other's movements and rocking together until we came undone.

There was no ounce of skin left untouched by his mouth or hands. I admire the red markings he left on my neck and ass, ones I wish were permanent. His eager growls edged me closer as he sucked the life out of me, tasting every inch he could reach.

Waves of pleasure shot through me each time he rubbed over my clit piercing, but when he squeezed the sides of my throat, it made everything more intense. I couldn't get enough of it the same way he couldn't get enough of touching me. Every pull of my hair and smack on my ass triggered a lust-filled explosion.

He was unstoppable.

Even the slower and tender moments were needy and desperate.

And it turned me on even more knowing only I got this side of him.

Only me.

I made him feral in a way I hadn't seen in years.

Perhaps the wildest part is he made me come alive in a way I forgot how to. He knew exactly what I needed and what to do to get me there.

That doesn't just happen with anyone. Very rarely.

Our connection only works because of our intense history and how easy it was to remember how in love with him I am.

But he was right, the wait was worth it.

I step out of the tub, wrapping a towel around my body and one in my hair. It was soothing to soak my sore muscles in the hot water and relax for a while before all the chaos begins.

Hayes is supposed to arrive at some point today. He emailed me his flight plans but I told him it'd be a better idea if he got a rideshare from the airport to my parent's house instead of me picking him up. I don't want the first time we get the chance to talk in person to be while I'm driving.

I will always love him for healing something inside me he didn't break, for supporting me in my career, and for loving me the way he did during a time I needed it. But not every person you fall in love with is meant to last forever. Sometimes it's a temporary destination on your journey to something new.

Before I can get dressed, there's a loud knock at the front door. Assuming it's someone for Warren, I ignore it. Or try to at least.

"Maisie!" More pounding. "I know you're in there!"

Oh God.

It's my mother.

Tightening my hold on the towel, I rush toward the living room and then whip open the door.

"Mom, hi."

I saw her two days ago at the baby shower, but now she looks less than thrilled to see me.

"Get dressed, we need to go."

"Go where?" I ask, moving back to let her inside.

"Home." She turns toward me once I close the door. "The Save the Dates have gone out."

My eyes widen. "*What*? They weren't scheduled to go out for two more months! How'd this happen?"

The look on her face isn't one I see very often, sad almost. *Sympathy.*

"Hayes called Nicola and told her y'all wanted 'em to go out early. Instead of confirming with me, she went ahead and did it."

"Oh my God!" I shout, trying to wrap my head around what the fuck is happening.

Why the hell would he do that?

"Don't worry, she's fired."

"Great, but now what?" I walk down the hallway to find some clothes so I'm ready to face Hayes the moment he arrives.

"Now we do damage control…" She follows me into the bedroom where I'm already digging into my bag. "Sign the divorce papers."

"Wait." I freeze before finding her gaze on me. "What're you talkin' about? I already told you I'm not signin' 'em and am movin' back here."

"Well, plans change. Now everyone thinks you're gettin' married in four months so unless you want a media crisis on our hands, you're gonna have to make up."

I blink, unbelieving of the words coming out of her mouth. "Excuse me?"

"Oh don't act like this little affair isn't pre-weddin' jitters." Her gaze shifts to the bed that's still a messy heap of twisted sheets. "What you and Hayes have is worth fightin' for and it's clear he's not ready to let you go."

This coming from the same woman who five days ago was horrified to hear he'd done a background check on me, but as soon as there's a threat to her reputation, she does another one-eighty.

"I'd rather lick a hot skillet than marry a man just so you can avoid humiliation."

"Maisie, be reasonable."

"*Me?* Do you hear yourself?" I pace the room, trying to wrap my head around what the hell is happening. "Mama, I've always tried to make you and Daddy happy and proud of me, but there ain't no way I'm gettin' married to that man. He knew I was gonna tell him it's over, especially after I told him I wasn't sure I could sign the papers and needed to talk to him in person, so he purposely sent those out to play mind games. And y'all are gonna let him win if you take his side."

"Five-hundred Save the Dates went out…how do you expect me to explain to our closest friends and families that suddenly the weddin' is canceled?"

"I really don't care." I huff, waving my arms around. "Get a banner plane and let it fly over the city: Callaway Wedding Canceled. Bride Went Back to Her Husband."

She scoffs, not entertained by my lashing out. "Now don't be ridiculous."

"They'll figure out when the invitations don't go out. Who cares?"

"Your father, for starters. How's it gonna look to his business associates to find out his daughter's wedding's been canceled?"

"Half of 'em should worry about their own marriages instead of mine. The other half's children don't even talk to 'em anymore 'cause all they care about is money and their reputation. Would be a shame if you entered that half," I snap.

She stomps over and slaps me hard across the face. "You watch your mouth."

I'm frozen, shocked, unable to breathe at the reality of her hitting me.

She's never done that before.

"You need to come home and take care of this. Preferably before Hayes does."

She walks out without another word and I'm left reeling from what took place.

Begrudgingly, I get ready and repack all my shit that's made a mess across the bedroom and bathroom. Once I'm able to move in, I'll be much more organized.

Then I make the bed and clean up the best I can. Warren knows I'm meeting with Hayes today, but I was hoping to talk to him before I left.

When he doesn't answer my call, I drive over to the stables to check if he's in his office.

"Sorry, Maisie," Bodie says. "He's guidin' some guests on a trail ride since no one else was available at the time. Should be back in half an hour."

"Shit..." I chew my lower lip, tapping my foot nervously against the cement. "I have to go home and deal with some stuff. I was hopin' to see him before I left, but I guess I can text him."

"He probably doesn't have service, but you can try."

"Well just in case, can you tell him I was here? Let him know I'll call him as soon as I can."

"Sure, no problem."

"Thanks, Bodie."

"Wait." He stops me before I can walk out. "Everythin' okay with you?"

"Yeah..." I try to sound convincing. "My fiancé, er, ex-fiancé, isn't makin' things easy with breakin' off the engagement, so I just need to put out a couple fires."

"Well..." He stands taller. "If you need a third-party to come kick his ass, you know where to find me."

I bark out a laugh, appreciating the offer. "I'll definitely let you know."

Once I'm in my car, I send Warren a text to let him know I stopped by and that I have to get home so he doesn't worry. As expected, it doesn't go through, but hopefully he'll see it once he's back to the stables.

My mind runs nonstop on the drive home. Besides my mother who doesn't have a compassionate bone in her body, I'm furious with Hayes for the stunt he pulled. He knows how my parents are and how they'd push me to keep the wedding date if it meant they didn't have to go through the embarrassment of explaining why it was called off.

He also knows I don't like disappointing my parents, even as awful as they can be sometimes, but the girl who needed their praise and acceptance is no longer the girl he'll see today.

Being back here brought me so much needed clarity. It's as if I've been living in a fog for the past seven years, but it finally lifted, and I can see clearly again.

My country roots, the people I once considered a second family, the never-ending views and fresh mountain air are what I'd been missing. I was living my dream each day but not really *living* the way that fed my soul.

Warren reminded me what I truly needed.

And there's no way I'm letting it go after realizing it.

chapter twenty-seven

Warren

IT'S BEEN two fucking days and I've barely spoken to my wife.

She reassures me she's handling her parents and Hayes, but I'm worried they're trying to wear her down. The moment Bodie told me Maisie stopped in before she left, I've been spiraling. I got her text but she didn't reply to me for hours. She said she'd call later to explain everything and when she did, I nearly lost it.

Especially the part where her mother slapped her.

And then to find out that motherfucker sent out their Save the Dates in hopes she'd be forced to change her mind.

Over my dead fucking body.

She reassures me his tactics aren't going to work and that her parents are trying to figure out how to cancel it without a lot of press attention. Since they're uppity rich fucks, everyone in the area knows their name. Her parents care more about their image than their own daughter's desires and that makes me want to go scoop her up and haul her ass back here where she belongs.

I texted her three hours ago and she still hasn't replied. Assuming the worst makes my blood pressure spike.

It doesn't help that Lilith had a setback. She got an infection and the antibiotics aren't working. Dr. Warner put her on a different medication, so now we wait and see if it helps or not.

Adding to that, I can't stop thinking about Hayes sleeping in the same house as her.

Eating at the same table.

Getting her attention and within touching distance of *my wife*.

Fuck it.

I can't do this anymore.

"Where're you goin'?" Bodie asks when he sees me stalking toward the exit.

"To get my wife back."

My tires spin out and spit gravel when I press the gas pedal to the floorboard. I need to change out of my work clothes and grab a couple things before I drive to her parent's. Hopefully my heart will slow down before I get there because right now I'm exploding with anger.

It's only a twenty-minute drive but I make it in fifteen.

When I ring the bell and their butler or whoever the hell he is answers, I walk right past him without waiting for permission.

"Sir! You can't—"

Ignoring him, I keep walking until I hear voices coming from the dining room.

"Warren?" Maisie gasps, quickly standing from her chair and almost knocking it over. "What're you doin' here?"

"I came to ask you the same thing. It's been two days, Maze. I want you home."

"We aren't finished," the man sitting across from her says.

"Hayes, quiet," Maisie snaps, coming closer.

I cup her face, needing to touch her. "You haven't been respondin' to my messages. I got worried," I say softer this time.

"I'm sorry. We're in the middle of...negotiatin'."

My brows furrow. "Negotiatin' what?"

Her shoulders slump and she sighs. "When I moved in with him, he added my name to the lease, so he wants me to pay my half until it's over."

"Okay." That doesn't sound too bad. "What else?"

She blows out an uneasy breath and I already know I'm not going to like it. "He wants to get compensated for pain and sufferin'."

"Come again?" I shift my gaze to the pitiful man at the table. "For what exactly?"

Hayes decides that's his cue to stand and enter the conversation. "For not being forthcoming about already being married while we dated for over three years. For leadin' me on to think we had a future. For the backlash I'm gonna get from having to announce the wedding is canceled."

"Backlash from what?"

"My career," he snips. "I made it known I was engaged and now I face the humiliation of it ending."

I roll my eyes. He acts like he's the goddamn king.

Pretty bold for a guy who looks like Posey could fight one-handed.

"If I don't agree to it, he'll go to the press to purposely humiliate me, which will have huge repercussions for my career."

"And this family's reputation," Mrs. Callaway adds.

Oh, God forbid...

"And you call yourself a man? Fuckin' pathetic," I spit out, then turn toward her parents. "Y'all are so worried, you dish out the money. You have enough of it."

"He wants my trust fund," Maisie blurts, and my neck nearly snaps when I look from her to Hayes. "It's worth one point two million."

My fists tighten at my sides. "He's not entitled to that!"

"In return for his silence and havin' to deal with the potential backlash," she explains with annoyance. "But my parents are tryin' to negotiate a lower amount, which is why it's takin' so long."

My jaw threatens to break at how hard I'm clenching it. God, I hate this. And for what? Because he got his feelings hurt?

Join the fucking club, asshole. I lived without her for seven years and would've never thought about touching her money.

Wait a minute...

"She can't sign off on her trust fund without my permission," I say and her father sits taller as if he's finally tuned into the conversation. "We're married, so half that trust fund is legally mine. And I ain't agreein' to shit."

Everyone's eyes widen at the realization.

That's right. They can all fuck off.

I cross my arms, widening my stance. "You can bargain with me now, *Hayes*. Because without me, you ain't gettin' a cent."

"You'd risk her name gettin' dragged?" Hayes asks.

I casually lift a shoulder, but I'd never let that happen if I can help it. "You're not the only one with connections on how to cover up a scandal. I'd rather spend her entire trust fund on hirin' someone to drag you through the mud than let you get a piece of it."

"Warren, he knows a lot of people in the industry and

media." Maisie's tone sounds defeated as if she's already given up on fighting about it.

"Good…they're about to call him a homewrecker who tried to blackmail you in return for hush money. I'm no attorney, but I'm pretty certain extortion is illegal, and if found guilty, a serious felony charge. Imagine how that'll look to his fans and agent." I frown, feigning concern. "Now, I'm not well-versed in the publishin' industry, but I'm gonna assume that'd be considered bad press, yeah? And doesn't that risk *his* career more than yours?"

I shrug again as if I'm too dumb to understand.

"Bellamy, she's my youngest sister—" I eagerly explain to Hayes as if he cares. "She handles the marketin' for the resort and is really excellent at her job. Hell, she has us booked out a year in advance. Anyway, she has a lot of connections too in gettin' news and press releases out to the public. Probably won't even take long. Once it circulates locally, it'll get picked up by a national outlet…"

He doesn't need to know I'm bluffing my ass off, but I'll do whatever it takes to protect my wife.

I pull out my phone as if I'm about to text her when Hayes speaks up. "Wait."

Raising a brow, I pause.

His gaze ping-pongs between mine and Maisie's before clearing his throat. "She covers her half of the lease for the next six months and gives me back her engagement ring."

My gaze shifts to Maisie and she gives me a subtle nod.

Reaching over, I squeeze his shoulder until my fingers dig through his skin. "Now, was that so hard?"

His jaw tenses as narrowed eyes glare at me.

The bastard had no clue who he was up against until I showed up. Hell, I should've come two days ago and put him in his place, then I could've had her home with me already.

"I'll have our lawyers draw up the papers immediately," Mr. Callaway says, and for the first time in probably ever, he smiles at me.

Who knew this was all it took to finally get some respect from my in-laws? Not that I need it because fuck them.

"Speakin' of her engagement ring…" I release my hold on him and dig into my pocket. "Found it on the floor. Fucked it right off her finger when I had her bent over on my bed."

Gasps echo throughout the room and then Hayes' fist meets my jaw in a forceful punch. It knocks me off my axis, and I stumble back into the wall, knocking into one of their framed art pieces.

"Hayes! The hell is wrong with you?" Maisie screeches, standing between us. "Warren, are you okay?"

I rub a hand over my chin, stretching it out to ease the pain. When I move to hit him back, Hayes holds up his hand to block me and then swings but ends up nailing Maisie in the face instead.

"Oh shit!" Before his knees can hit the floor, I pull him by his shirt and slam him into the same wall.

"Are you tryin' to meet God?" I pull him back just to push him into the wall again. "I hope you have life insurance, motherfucker!"

"It was an accident!" He tries getting out of my grip, but I don't let him.

Maisie's groan catches my attention and I drop the asshole to the floor to tend to her.

"Baby?"

One of the housekeepers approaches with an ice pack. I quickly thank her, then lift Maisie into my arms and carry her out of there.

chapter twenty-eight

WARREN SETS me down on my bed and presses the ice pack to my cheek before I lean back on the propped-up pillow. He's enraged, but I'm relieved he's here.

I should've looped him in sooner, but dealing with Hayes and my parents at the same time was mentally draining. I was ready to sign off on my trust fund to get it over with and so he'd go back to New York. But since Hayes went and had the Save the Dates sent out early, my father wanted to negotiate now that my parents have to figure out how to announce the whole thing's been canceled, on top of paying for a big event that's no longer happening.

I guess I should thank my father for not letting me give in or Warren would've been too late on his threat to call Hayes out.

"I'm fine," I tell him when he glares at where Hayes accidentally hit me.

"I'm gonna kill him."

I roll my eyes although it hurts to do so. "You did kinda

provoke him with that ring stunt. Not that I blame you, but he didn't mean to hit me. He was aimin' for you."

He rubs his fingers along his jawline as if it's still sore. "He meant to punch me the first time, though."

"I know, but the last thing you need is to go to jail for assault. Not that I wouldn't bail out my husband, but it wouldn't be a great fresh start for us." And would only add to the rumor mill that's bound to happen once everyone knows we're back together.

He tips my chin, studying where I'm sure a bruise is forming. It happened so fast, I didn't even have time to react or get out of the way.

"I love when you call me that," he murmurs, brushing the pad of his thumb along my other cheek.

Grinning, I set the ice pack down so I can lean in and kiss him. "Thank you for comin'. I'm sorry I didn't respond to you but now you know why. A few minutes before you showed up, my dad threatened to shove his boot up his ass."

Warren snorts. "Does that mean he's finally found someone he hates more than me?"

"Daddy doesn't play around with money or blackmail, that's for sure. He already called his attorney several times. If you hadn't shown up, Hayes woulda become a missing person's case."

"Now that's a good idea."

I playfully shove his arm. "Warren!"

"If there's one thing your father and I have in common it's doin' whatever it takes to protect you. Hell, we could bond over diggin' his grave. Although I can't really see your dad gettin' his hands dirty. He'd probably make me do it while he micromanages and scolds me for doin' a shitty job."

"Jesus Christ." I shake my head. "You're more insane than I realized."

"Only when it comes to you, my love." He tips my chin, softly pressing his lips to mine.

"And I'm afraid to say it runs in the family. Bodie offered to kick his ass if I needed him to."

That makes him laugh for the first time. "Bodie woulda throat-chopped him and then kneed him in the balls. He's a dirty fighter like Posey."

"So you're all unhinged? Bless whoever makes an honest man outta Bodie."

"I doubt it'll be anytime soon."

Warren glances at my dresser and notices the lid with our names on it. "Is that the box with our notes and photos?"

"Mm-hmm. I was goin' through it again last night."

Rereading all our notes, reminiscing over the photos, and overall wishing he was with me.

"To make sure you were makin' the right decision?"

I can't tell if he's being serious or if he really thinks I was having second thoughts.

"No, 'cause I missed you." I frown, grabbing his hand. "I'm sorry if I made you doubt my feelings."

"It's not that, Maze. I've been goin' stir crazy for two days not knowin' what was goin' on. Not hearin' from you or gettin' to see you made me fear the worst, like he was sweet-talkin' you into stayin' together or somethin'. I dunno."

He hangs his head, and I hate that I'm the reason he was so stressed.

I bring my hand to his face, forcing him to look at me. "I apologize for not lettin' you know sooner. I wanted to handle this on my own. I got myself into this mess and it was my responsibility to take care of it, so I didn't want to involve you when things were going so well between us."

He takes my hand, kissing across the knuckles. "But that's my job. We're a team. Let me help, or hell, fight your battles for you."

"Well, you kinda did without permission." I snicker, but I'm not mad about it.

"You left me no choice," he quips. "And now you know— ignore me and I'll burn down the world lookin' for you."

My erratic heartbeat pounds even harder at the, although probably unintentional, sexiest thing I've ever heard him say.

"Duly noted." I smirk.

When there's a knock on the door, my mother enters, looking more cautious than usual.

"You okay, honey?"

"I'll live." My eyes track her suspicious movements. She's been more worried about their reputations than listening to what I want.

"I was hopin' we could talk..." Her gaze shifts to Warren for a split second. "Alone."

Warren abruptly stands, facing her. "From now on, you'll speak to her through me."

"Pardon me?"

"You think you can slap my wife and get away with it?"

Oh fuck. Fuckfuckfuck.

"I've already apologized for that."

Actually...her direct quote was, "I didn't mean to slap you."

That's as much of an apology she'll ever give me.

Warren crosses his arms, widening his stance. "Say whatever you came to say. I'm not leavin' her with you."

My mother clears her throat, looking more uncomfortable

than I've ever seen her. "Fine," she bites out, folding her hands in front of her. "The lawyers are on their way with the paperwork you and Hayes need to sign. With that, if you and Warren are gettin' back together, your father and I would like y'all to sign a postnuptial agreement to protect your trust fund so this doesn't happen again."

That has me jumping to my feet. "No."

"If he loves you the way he claims, there shouldn't be an issue. Plus, it protects him, too. He owns property on his family's ranch I'm sure he wouldn't want our family going after."

Of course they dug into his business.

I'm not surprised considering he reminded them we didn't have a prenup and he's entitled to half of it. Warren would never go after it anyway.

"I'm not askin' my *husband* to sign anything. That's absurd."

"I'll do it," Warren blurts before my mother can open her mouth to argue with me. "If that's what it'll take for you to leave us alone and let us be happy, I'll sign."

"You don't have to!" I yank his arm to turn him toward me and find his hardened gaze. "They can't force us."

"I trust you a hundred percent, baby. One piece of paper agreein' I won't go after your money is no sweat off my back. Before I started buildin' the cabin, I bought the land from my parents so it was in my name, but the minute I can, I'm addin' yours too. If somethin' happens between us, I'd gladly give it to you. Take it. It's yours. I built it for you."

"You built it for *us*, remember?"

He cups my face with both palms and leans down until he's a breath away. "Yes, and if you're not there with me, it has no value anyway."

Warren's words from a week ago still play on a loop in my mind.

Truthfully, I resent my parents for guilting him into agreeing to it, especially since they think they *won* some kind of one-sided game. But Warren doesn't seem one bit fazed by it. I should've known he wouldn't. He's never cared about their money or the entitlement it gives them.

As soon as I signed both agreements, I packed up and left. Kissed my parents on the cheek and told them not to contact me until I reached out to them.

Their priorities don't align with mine and there's no reason to pretend we're on good terms when we aren't. They'll have to get a complete personality facelift if they want to be in my life again.

Fortunately, Warren's family has welcomed me back with open arms and have proved once again why I've always loved being around them.

In the agreement that Hayes signed, he had to ship all my belongings here, and it's due to arrive this weekend. Once Bodie overheard me telling Warren, he let their sibling group chat know it was all hands-on deck to help me unpack. Considering all my books from my parents' house were delivered yesterday, I appreciate the extra help.

I'm most excited about putting books on my new shelves and organizing them. Hell, that part might take me the longest.

I'm officially going back to work full-time on Monday. I'll get my office set up and decorated before then so I can focus on reading and finding a couple more employees to help grow the business.

It's been a nice break, even with Warren at work during the day, because I never took the time to relax and read for fun. I think I've read five books this week and am in the middle of an audiobook that I listen to while I'm in the bath.

Hayes texted me the day he shipped out my boxes to let me know when to expect them but then he actually gave me an apology for sending out the Save the Dates and going after my trust fund. I apologized too for how things ended and not being truthful, or faithful for that matter, then I wished him the best in his career and finding a partner more suitable for him.

Though, I wouldn't be surprised if he'd be content living alone and staying single. His work came first and I don't see that changing anytime soon.

But overall, things could've ended worse.

Assuming he didn't cover my belongings in hot wax or something before shipping them to me.

"Hey, Maisie!" Bodie greets me when I enter the barn. "Warren's in his office."

"I came to visit someone else today," I tell him, grinning.

"Is it me? I know I'm irresistible, but I think you're too old for me."

"You idiot." Warren's voice comes from behind and the distinct sound of him hitting Bodie over the head.

Warren meets me in front of Lilith's stall.

"How's she doin' today?" I ask, petting her nose.

"Much better. The meds are finally workin' and she's been eatin' and drinkin' normal."

I smile wide, brushing my fingers over her mane. Although

she tried to kill me a few weeks ago, we've bonded and moved past the near-death experience.

"Hopefully she'll be up for ridin' again soon."

"You?" He chuckles. "Let's not get ahead of ourselves."

I arch my back, pressing my ass into his groin. "Excuse me, cowboy? You implyin' I dunno how to ride?"

He grabs my hips, stopping me from rubbing against him. "No, I'm sayin' unless you have a death wish, you're not allowed to ride her. She needs more trainin' and it'll be a while before she's up for that."

I frown. "As long as she's healin' though."

Warren reaches around me and pats her nose. "She's a fighter."

"So how's your day goin' so far?" I ask, wiggling my ass against him once more.

"It's a whole lot better now." He wraps a hand around my waist, pulling me into his thickening erection.

"Feels like it's *really* better."

"Maze…" He growls in my ear. "I'm not finished with work for another three hours, so you better stop that."

But where's the fun in that?

"Or you could take me into your office and you could *finish* right now."

Expecting him to say no, I'm taken off guard when he grabs my hand and pulls me into a different room. By the time he locks the door, I'm pressed against it with Warren's tongue in my mouth.

He works the buttons of his shirt until he frees it from his body. My palms slide up his rock-hard stomach and I dig my nails in his chest before scratching them back down.

"Fuck, Maze. We have to be fast. Be a good girl and bend over the saddle stand."

He doesn't have to tell me twice.

I do as he says and wait for him to position himself behind me.

"Good thing you're wearin' a skirt."

"Yeah...what a coincidence," I drawl, snickering over my shoulder.

"You're a naughty girl, Mrs. Langston." He smacks my bare ass when he realizes I'm wearing a thong.

I shake my hips, impatiently waiting as I watch him lower his jeans and boxer briefs.

He slides up my shirt so my back's exposed and then holds out his palm in front of me. "Spit."

I do as he says and then he strokes his cock a few times before sliding inside me. Sighing with relief, I arch into him as he sinks deeper.

Since I'm on birth control and I didn't want us to have to use condoms, I got STI testing done to be reassured we were safe going bare. It's always been explosive between us, but it's even better with nothing between us. When he reaches around to rub my clit piercing, I gasp at the friction.

Wrapping his other fist around my hair, he pounds harder and goes so deep, I nearly fall to my knees.

"Such a perfect, tight cunt. Fuck, I'm not gonna last if you keep squeezin' me like that."

I purposely squeeze harder.

A crack on my ass is my reward, and I yelp at the pleasant burn.

"Holy shit..." I try to keep my voice down just in case, but he makes it nearly impossible when he's so good at finding my sweet spot.

"Come on my cock, baby." He grunts in between thrusts, trying to control his breathing so he doesn't finish before me. "I'm so close."

When he grips my hip, I slide my hand between my thighs and continue circling my clit.

"I'm right there. Don't stop," I beg.

One more thrust and I'm done for.

I moan into my palm, trying to hold back and then he grunts, spilling inside me.

"Christ," he huffs out a laugh when he starts sliding out. "You're a mess."

"You wrecked me." I collapse against the saddle.

"Don't move," he demands before shoving two fingers back in. "Gonna make you walk outta here still filled with my cum."

"Warren," I whisper-hiss over my shoulder. "The fabric barely covers anythin', it's not gonna stay inside."

"Shoulda thought about that before comin' in here to tempt me."

When he's satisfied with his handiwork, he puts my thong back in place, lowers my shirt, and turns me around to face him.

"There." He winks, tilting my chin to press his lips to mine. "Now you'll have no choice but to think about me the rest of the afternoon."

chapter twenty-nine

Warren

GOING HOME for lunch to eat with Maisie is my favorite part of my workday.

Even after two months of her officially moving in, I never get tired of seeing the evidence of her in our house. Her books stacked in random areas, laptop usually left open on the coffee table, and an abundance of self-care products scattered over the bathroom counter.

Honestly, I couldn't love it more.

We've formed a nice routine in the evenings. I shower after work, start dinner, and then after a few attempts of telling her to come eat, I pick her up out of her desk chair and haul her ass to the table. I keep the fridge stocked with snacks and protein smoothies so she remembers to eat during the day.

Afterward, we go outside and feed the chickens.

All *twelve* of them.

For someone who hated them at the beginning of summer, she was quick to ask if she could name them. And because she's a bookworm at heart, gave all six chicks Disney princess names.

Now I'm walking around shouting at *Cinderella* and *Belle* to stop fighting while *Aurora* and *Tiana* chase after *Ariel* and *Jasmine.*

Going from six to twelve is a fucking shitshow.

But I wouldn't have it any other way.

On the weekends, I've been teaching Maisie how to cook. It's slow going, but she's trying. Minus the Salsbury steak incident where she managed to burn it on the outside while the inside was still rare.

In between all the chaos, I've been planning Silas' bachelor party since I'm his best man and he's getting married soon. Aundrea gave strict instructions on what he was allowed or not allowed to do, so we're basically left with going to a gay bar so "women won't hit on him."

But I wouldn't be surprised if she shows up there just to make sure.

Most likely, we'll end up drunk and taking turns on the mechanical bull.

"Sweetheart? Where're you?" I walk into a quiet and dark house. Her car's in the driveway, so she must be downstairs reading. We're going away this weekend, so hopefully she started packing before getting lost in her book.

But when I flick on the lights, people jump out from behind the furniture and scream, "Happy Birthday!"

The living room spills out with family and friends. But my eyes scan the area for her.

When she finally emerges with the biggest smile on her face, I playfully shake my head. "Oh hell, you did not."

She wraps her arms around my neck and pulls me in for a kiss. "Were you surprised?"

"Uh, yeah. How in the world did you plan this without me knowin'?"

"I'm very sneaky." She waggles her brows. "And had lots of help."

I walk around with Maisie and thank at least fifty people and my siblings for coming and cramming into my house. My mom gives me a knowing look like she's also behind this little surprise and then Aunt JoJo congratulates me on joining the dirty-thirties club.

I'm shocked when I see Landen and Ellie. Even after she lost and regained her memory, they fell in love and are now engaged. With how obsessed he is with her, I wouldn't be surprised if they get married right away.

After we sent in our letters about Angela to the parole board, we later found out they approved her anyway.

It was a major blow, but Landen's been handling it well given the circumstances.

"I can't believe y'all made the drive up here." I pull him in for a hug. It's been a while since we've seen each other. "I get to finally meet the woman who's had a hold on you for the past four-plus years."

"That so?" Ellie gloats and smirks at Landen. "Tell me more."

We all laugh.

I like her already.

Once I introduce her to Maisie, we chat for a few minutes before continuing to give Bodie and Colt shit for keeping a secret from me.

"Happy birthday, man!" Silas smacks my back, hugging me hard.

"Thanks, I'm glad you came." I look around for his other half who never lets him out of her sight. "Where's Aundrea?"

He scratches his cheek and averts his gaze. "She had plans tonight. But she sends her best wishes."

He's lying.

But I'm not sure why.

I'll get it out of him later.

Another face I'm surprised to see is Maisie's brother and his wife. Not that we aren't on friendly terms, but they have a newborn baby.

"Hey, how's my nephew?" I ask, peeking through the blanket to see his face. He's sleeping against Collins' chest.

"He breastfeeds every two hours and only sleeps when I hold him," Collins says. "So, as long as I don't have to eat or shower, he's great."

I chuckle. "It'll get easier, hopefully, some day."

Maisie hands me a drink and I take a sip when Aaron says, "He's gonna need a cousin close in age, so chop chop. It's been long enough."

I nearly spew my beer all over the baby, coughing it up when it goes down the wrong way.

"Aaron!" Maisie playfully smacks him. "I'm not ready to share my husband yet."

"You okay?" Collins asks when I can't catch my breath.

I clear my throat, finally getting it together. "Yeah, great."

Maisie and I continue mingling, grabbing food and chatting with everyone. I'm still in shock she pulled this off without making it obvious she was up to something. My birthday's on Sunday, which is why we're going to Nashville for a little getaway.

"You pulled off quite the party, Mrs. Langston," I drawl, holding her against me once the last guests leave.

Mom and Aunt JoJo stayed to help clean up and then I kicked them out since we're leaving in the morning.

Tucking loose strands behind her ear, I lower my lips to hers. "Now I need to one-up you."

"Why can't you just let me have this? You're always cookin' and takin' care of me. I wanted to do somethin' special for you."

I grab her chin, giving the tip of her nose a little kiss. "You did, my love. Thank you again."

She smacks my ass. "You're welcome, old man."

"*Old man*? You're gonna be thirty soon, too."

She puts her finger over my lips. "Shhh."

Instead of arguing, I lift her up and carry her ass to bed where I spend an hour thanking her.

"Silas?"

I rub the sleep from my eyes and squint to conceal them from the bright sky.

"Hey, sorry it's so early. Can I come in?"

"Yeah, of course." Stepping back to give him room, he enters the house and then I close the door behind him. He doesn't seem like himself. "Everythin' okay?"

I haven't seen him since my birthday party two weeks ago. His bachelor party is next Saturday, so we've been making plans over text. On top of getting ready for his wedding, Landen and Ellie decided to give us a thirty-day notice they wanted to get married at the Willow Chalet, so it's been all hands-on deck getting ready for that.

"Not really." He follows me into the kitchen where I'm making breakfast. "This wasn't somethin' I wanted to tell you over the phone."

"Shit, that sounds serious." Crossing my arms, I lean against the counter as he takes the stool behind the breakfast bar. "What happened?"

"Aundrea called off the weddin'."

Considering she didn't come for the party, I assumed they got into a fight or something or she didn't want him to have a bachelor party, but damn, I didn't expect this.

"Shit, dude." I drop my arms. "Do you know why?"

He explains everything while I finish frying bacon and sausage links. I feel for him, especially with how close they were to getting married, and how much he loved her.

But I'm afraid the problem is she loved the *idea* of him more than him as a person. Always wanting him to change or act a certain way. Practically keeping him on a leash. Forcing him to work with her dad and live a lifestyle that matched hers.

Maybe I should've seen it coming.

But by his distraught voice, he hadn't either.

"Yeah, so...now I'm out of a job and place to live," he continues when I make him a plate of scrambled eggs.

"Two hot men in my kitchen and the delicious smell of food? Have I died and woken up in a romance novel?" Maisie struts in wearing one of my work T-shirts, adorably clueless of our tense conversation.

"Mornin', baby." I give her a quick kiss. "Aundrea and Silas broke up."

She inhales a loud gasp. "Oh my gosh, I'm so sorry." Wrapping her arms around his shoulders, she gives her best attempt to hug him.

"He needs a place to crash for a bit," I tell her. "We could set up an air mattress in the library or living room until he finds his own place."

"I don't wanna be an inconvenience," Silas argues. "I can stay at a motel."

"Absolutely not." I shake my head, making Maisie a plate of eggs and meat. "We'll figure it out."

"What about Posey?" Maisie asks, and I subtly shake my head, but she ignores it. "She has a spare bedroom and did I hear you need a job? She was just tellin' me she's still lookin' for extra help at the goat farm."

"Maze...that's not a good idea," I tell her carefully.

She doesn't remember their feud.

Or rather, their one-sided feud.

"Why not? It's perfect! He doesn't wanna sleep on an air mattress anyway."

I glance at Silas who looks conflicted. "She'll never agree to it."

She furrows her brows. "How come?"

I remind her how they always fought like siblings in high school, and ever since, she refuses to be around him. Though I never knew exactly why she hates him so much. I always assumed it was because he picked on her like a little sister while she crushed on him.

"That was years ago. Surely she's still not upset about it."

"Trust me, she is." Silas stabs a piece of sausage. "She hasn't talked to me in years."

"*Years?*" Maisie gasps. "That can't be right."

"It's true," I confirm. "Posey deemed him enemy number one. Anytime he's around, she leaves or blatantly ignores him."

Maisie's quiet for a moment, stewing on our words.

"Hm...I'm gonna call her. Doesn't hurt to ask."

She pulls out her phone, and although I know it's about to be a shitshow, I don't stop her.

"Good mornin' my favorite sister-in-law," Posey singsongs.

At least she's in a good mood. *For now.*

"Hello to *my* favorite sister-in-law," Maisie says, grinning. "I have a big favor to ask."

"Okay, shoot."

"It'd mean a lot to both me and Warren, so please remember that."

"You're pregnant? And you want me to be the godmother? I accept!"

Maisie snorts. "No, not quite. We have a friend who could use a place to stay while they look for an apartment, so would you mind a roommate?"

"Depends. Who is it?"

Maisie pauses briefly. "It's Silas."

"Are you fuckin' kidding me? Not happenin'. Please tell me you're jokin'." Her voice goes up an octave with each fuming word. "Did your asshole husband ask you to fuck with me?"

Yep, there it is.

"Posey, I'm being serious. Aundrea broke up with him and he has nowhere to go."

"That's literally not my problem. He can sleep with the goats for all I care."

"Posey," I drawl, deepening my voice. "He can hear you."

"Motherfuckers! I hate y'all."

"It's fine," Silas blurts. "I'll figure somethin' else out."

"Time to get over your unrequited crush, Posey. You're the most forgivin' person I know. Why can't you let this go?"

The line goes silent.

"Posey?" Maisie cautiously asks.

"It wasn't unrequited," she murmurs so softly, I almost don't hear her.

My eyes snap to Silas, confused by what she means. His cheeks redden and he averts his gaze.

"What the fuck does that mean?" I bark. "Please tell me it doesn't mean what I think it means."

Did they...were they...*no*. There's no way.

But I was going through my own shit when Maisie left for college and even after, so it's possible I missed the signs. I guess? In high school, I was obsessed with spending time with Maisie as much as I could, but I also made time for Silas, and he would've told me if something was going on between them. *Right?*

"It was a long time ago," Posey says. "I have valid reasons for hatin' him, but if you wanna know why, ask him."

Then she hangs up.

Silence fills the air and my glare doesn't leave my best friend who's pretending to be more interested in his food than our conversation.

"Told ya she wouldn't agree to it," he finally mutters.

My tongue flicks the inside of my cheek as I try to calm my racing heart. "You have a lot of explainin' to do."

He blows out a breath. "It's not what you're thinkin'."

Maisie scoots in closer to Silas, a wicked grin on her beautiful face. "Tell me everythin' and leave nothin' out."

I snort, rolling my eyes at how nosy she is. No wonder her and Posey get along so well.

"But please limit any gross details..." I hold up my palm, assuming the worst. "As her brother, I don't wanna know *everythin'*."

"Well I do, so you can plug your ears." Maisie grins, focusing her attention on Silas. "Start at the beginnin'."

After an exhausting thirty minutes of Silas sharing the story and Maisie interrupting to ask him follow-up questions, I'm torn between kicking his ass for keeping secrets from me or feeling bad he's really shit out of luck on getting back on her good side.

"You need to apologize," Maisie tells him. "Make amends. Not 'cause you need a place to stay, but because it's overdue and you owe her one. And you never know..." She smirks at me. "Sometimes apologies can lead to somethin' more."

chapter thirty

Maisie

SPENDING our first Christmas together since getting back together is all I've been able to think about for the past couple months. I couldn't wait to start decorating the cabin so I started after Halloween weekend.

Garland and lights wrapped around the deck, wreaths on the doors, white lights hung across the roof, and an inflated Santa in his sleigh with the reindeer on the lawn. Warren and his brother's put up colored lights around each tree in the front yard.

The chickens hated it at first, but they've come around now.

And the inside looks like a true Christmas cabin explosion— red bows, two themed trees, more garland and lights, singing Santas, and stuffed reindeer.

It's the first time as an adult I've been able to decorate a house that's truly felt like a home.

I've already told Warren we're not taking it down until Valentine's Day.

Maybe St. Patrick's Day if he lets me.

It's also the first time I've taken off work completely for the second-half of December. Even set up an away message on my email that I'd return after the New Year.

Nothing is more important than spending this time with Warren and his family.

Warren has to work during the day, as usual, so I've been baking and cooking with his mom and Aunt JoJo. I even surprised him by making dinner a few days ago and it was actually decent.

Not fancy like the meals he makes, but I'm working on it.

I always find time to read but being able to binge a whole book in one sitting while rotting on the couch is my new profound love.

"May I interrupt your book for a moment of your attention?" Warren drawls overly dramatic as he walks into the living room. I'm sprawled out in my oversized sweatshirt, fireplace heating my legs and bare feet, and a half-filled mug of hot chocolate on the coffee table.

He's lucky he's so damn sexy or I'd tell him to go away.

"I suppose so…" I mock.

"I wanted to give you an early Christmas gift since the next few days are gonna be chaotic with family events."

"I thought we were exchangin' gifts on Christmas mornin'?"

"We are but this one is extra special and deserves its own moment."

Curious, I sit upright and make room for him next to me.

He reveals a wrapped book-shaped item from behind his back.

I reach for it but he quickly pulls it away before I can grab it. "Hold on, grabby hands."

Pretending to pout, I wait impatiently.

"I had to dig into a couple of your contacts to make this happen, so please don't be mad about that. I think it'll be worth it once you see what it is."

"My contacts? Like who?"

"Your agent friend, Jessica, and she got me into contact with someone else, who gave my email to the author."

"Oh God, what'd you do?"

And how in the world did Jessica keep this a secret from me?

Even though she's Hayes' agent, we remained friends, which I'm grateful for. It was a bit of a shift after moving here and adjusting my schedule. Although I enjoyed the in-person networking, I can still network virtually and fly there for special conventions or fairs.

But I'm no longer making it my only focus and working toward a better work-life balance.

Warren smiles before leaning in to kiss my cheek. "Merry Christmas, baby."

He hands it over, a paperback for sure, but when I rip it open, I'm truly shocked.

Even more when I open it to the first page and find a handwritten letter from the author.

Dear Maisie,

I'm so honored to hear this is your favorite book! Considering how much you must read, it feels extra special to me and these characters. Your sweet husband politely begged for a signed copy (like I was going to say no to you of all people) but he mentioned how you two bonded over the open-ended ending and how he wondered what happened after, so I typed up a bonus epilogue for you to read. It's a few years in the future so hopefully you'll get some of your questions answered. I struggled to write the second book for years, so I stopped trying, but getting your husband's kind and personal email re-sparked the joy I felt writing this story in the first place. So I owe you both a huge debt of gratitude because now I feel ready to continue writing the next book and making it even better than before.

All my love, xo

I'm in tears by the time I finish reading her note. There's an envelope tucked in the back with the bonus epilogue she wrote, but then I notice something else.

"Did you annotate this?" I flip through the pages of highlighted sentences and sticker tabs.

"Yeah, I wanted to read it anyway, so I thought I'd include some of my commentary while I did. I added a tabs key so you know what the colors of each one mean."

I don't know whether I should panic that he wrote in a signed edition or be overwhelmed that he read my favorite book and included his thoughts on it.

Maybe both.

But leaning more toward how thoughtful he was for finding a way to reach out to her and getting this copy. I'll cherish it even more knowing he wanted to read it because he knows how much I loved it.

"This means so much, babe. Thank you. I can't believe you managed to read this without me knowin'. How long have you had this?"

"Well, I had to one-up you from my birthday surprise." He grins. "I mostly read it in my office between tasks. Took me a while, but I loved it. Might've teared up a few times."

Chuckling, I pull him in for a kiss and hug him tightly to my chest. "I can't wait to reread it with your notes. Do you wanna read the bonus together?"

"You have no idea how much restraint it took not to peek at it."

I laugh and then we settle in next to each other while I unfold the typed pages and read it aloud.

And within minutes, we're both tearing up again.

"Wow...she killed this. I can't wait for the full book whenever she releases it."

"Me too. You'll probably read it faster than me, but it'll be fun to read the same thing together."

"This is truly the best gift I've ever received. Thank you again."

He tips my chin and brushes his lips to mine. "Anythin' for you, my love."

I carefully set the book down on the coffee table before straddling his lap and wrapping my arms around his neck.

"So glad you begged me to take your name over nine years ago."

"I did not *beg*..." He clarifies, almost insulted. "I strongly insisted."

"And I happily agreed." Smiling against his mouth, I grind against him, feeling him thicken between my thighs.

"Maisie Langston..." He growls my full name as he buries his face in my neck, causing a shiver down my spine. "Do not start somethin' you can't finish."

"And who says I can't?" I taunt him more by rubbing over his hard length. "I'd like to properly express how grateful I am."

He groans as I continue rocking my hips. "Then pull out my cock."

My body hums at his demanding voice.

I lower to my knees on the floor and eagerly yank his pants down. As soon as I get into position, I grab the base of his shaft and wrap my lips around him. Instead of drawing it out, I see how fast I can get him there.

"Fuck, Maze." His heavy breathing echoes in my ears and I beam at how easily I turn him on.

When I slip my other hand between his legs and find that tender spot behind his balls, he thrusts in deeper.

"Shit, baby. I'm close. Oh fuck..."

Hollowing my cheeks, I continue stroking him and sucking around his piercing. Moments later, he's groaning through his release and filling up my throat.

Instead of swallowing, I climb up his body until I'm hovering above him and tap his lips with my *you know what to do* expression. Without fail, he opens wide and spit his cum in his mouth.

Slamming my lips to his, I sink my tongue between them and taste how good we are together.

Warren slides his hands between us and pulls up his pants, then hauls me over his shoulder before standing.

"What're you doin'?" I squeal, holding tightly to his ass.

"Gonna fuck you in the library and then tuck you into bed."

I snort. "Wait, not in front of the Santas!"

My library was the first to get bombarded with Christmas decorations.

He smacks my ass, then takes the steps downstairs. "After what I'm about to do to you, we'll both be on the naughty list."

epilogue

Warren

FOUR YEARS LATER

"MY GOD," I drawl, walking into the bathroom and finding my hot wife soaking in the tub.

"About time you got home." Maisie grins. "Join me?"

I'm already unbuttoning my jeans. "Don't have to ask me twice."

I had errands to run in town or I would've been home a lot sooner.

Once I sit behind her, I pull her against my chest and wrap my arms around her swollen belly. Gently rubbing over her bump, I hum at how beautiful she looks carrying our baby.

"I wonder who she'll look like," Maisie says, leaning her head back on my shoulder.

"Hopefully you. Although, instead of being weak against one girl, it'll be two."

She chuckles, shivering against my stubble when I press my lips along her neck.

"And I have no doubt she'll be wrapped around your finger," she adds.

"Her mother certainly is." I slide a palm up between her breasts and rest it around her throat, then tilt her chin to claim her mouth. "And I wouldn't have it any other way."

"Mhm…" She moans, wiggling her ass.

"Careful," I growl. "That's how we got here in the first place."

"Then it's a good thing we're addin' extra bedrooms to the house."

As soon as we found out we were expecting, I recruited my dad, brothers, and Silas to help me add a couple extra rooms to the back of the cabin. They're almost finished and then we'll get the nursery ready. Maisie's already buying clothes and stocking up on diapers, which are mostly taking over her office.

I'm proud of how well she's managed and grown her business. She has two assistants and three agents working for her now. Although she works hard, she's learned to take time off and enjoy our life together.

It's all I've ever wanted for us.

And now I couldn't be happier to be growing our family.

"Have you added any more baby names to your list?"

Last I checked, she had fourteen listed, in order from most favorite to least, but it changes every few days based on her mood.

She tucks in her lips and looks away from me.

That's a yes.

"Well…do I get to hear 'em?"

She lists off five more she found online that I don't *hate* but none are really hitting for me.

"There's one more I considered but I'm not sure how you'll feel about it."

"Okay, tell me."

"I was rereadin' your annotations in my book the other day and the sister's name popped out at me. When I read her book, I also thought it was cute, but then I dunno…it stayed in my head and I kinda love it now."

The continuation of her favorite book released last year, but she was able to read an early copy of it. Then she let me read it and it was as good as the first, maybe even better since you got to see both so happy.

"Birdie…" I try out the name, loving the way it sounds aloud. "I really like that."

"You do?" Her gaze finds mine. "What about a middle name?"

"Hm…Grace or Gracelyn if you want her to have yours? Otherwise, could we give her Aunt JoJo's name? She would be so honored."

"Birdie Josephine," she says slowly, a smile covering her face. "That's perfect."

"However…" I contemplate mentioning it. "Kids might call her BJ or tease her about it once they learn what it means."

Maisie nearly growls at the thought. "It's a good thing she'll have a dad with two brothers to teach her how to kick their little asses."

A laugh bubbles out of me as I press my lips to her temple. "That's my girl. Teachin' our baby how to fight back before she's even outta the womb."

After I rub some bath scrub over her body and we rinse off in the shower, we change into some comfy clothes, and I start making dinner for us.

Maisie comes into the kitchen and sits at the breakfast bar with our memory box that has since been upgraded to a much larger one. We celebrated our ten-year wedding anniversary two years ago with a vow renewal ceremony at the Willow Chalet.

It was important for me to give her the wedding she had always wanted, so we took a ton of photos, made a new wedding album, and hung up more pictures in the house.

Now our memory box is filled with our past before and after we reunited. The most recent addition being our ultrasound photos of our first child.

And yeah, I'm hopeful we'll have more than one.

But I'll be happy either way.

Getting to spend the past several years as a married couple and getting to know each other again isn't something I'd give up for anything. Things happened exactly the way they had to so we ended up here and more in love than ever.

"What're you doin'?" I ask, watching her flip through the baby book she picked out a couple months ago.

"I want to write a message to the baby about the moment we decided on her name." She beams, grabbing a pen. "And that if the kids tease her, she has our permission to beat 'em up."

"You are *not* puttin' that in there."

"Oh yes I am!" She writes aggressively, and I don't even attempt to stop her. It'll be something funny to read years from now.

"Don't forget we're babysittin' for Nicky and Darla tomorrow night," she reminds me when I set her plate down in front of her. "The terror twins."

She shudders and so do I.

"And who got us into this mess?" I arch a brow. "Pretty sure I'll be busy."

Doing literally anything else.

No one's more shocked than me that those two not only

stayed married all these years but then got pregnant with twin boys right after their honeymoon.

"Like hell you will be. Unless you mean busy helpin' me with 'em."

"You volunteered us," I remind her.

"Darla cornered me at the grocery store, talkin' all about their anniversary. I couldn't say no!"

"Well, then you better call Posey and Bellamy for backup."

"Warren Grady," she scolds. "This'll be good practice for us."

"Startin' with toddlers? I don't even know what to do with 'em."

She breathes out a breathy laugh. "Whatever it takes to keep 'em alive."

Read Warren & Maisie's bonus scene on my website:
brookewritesromance.com/bonus-scenes

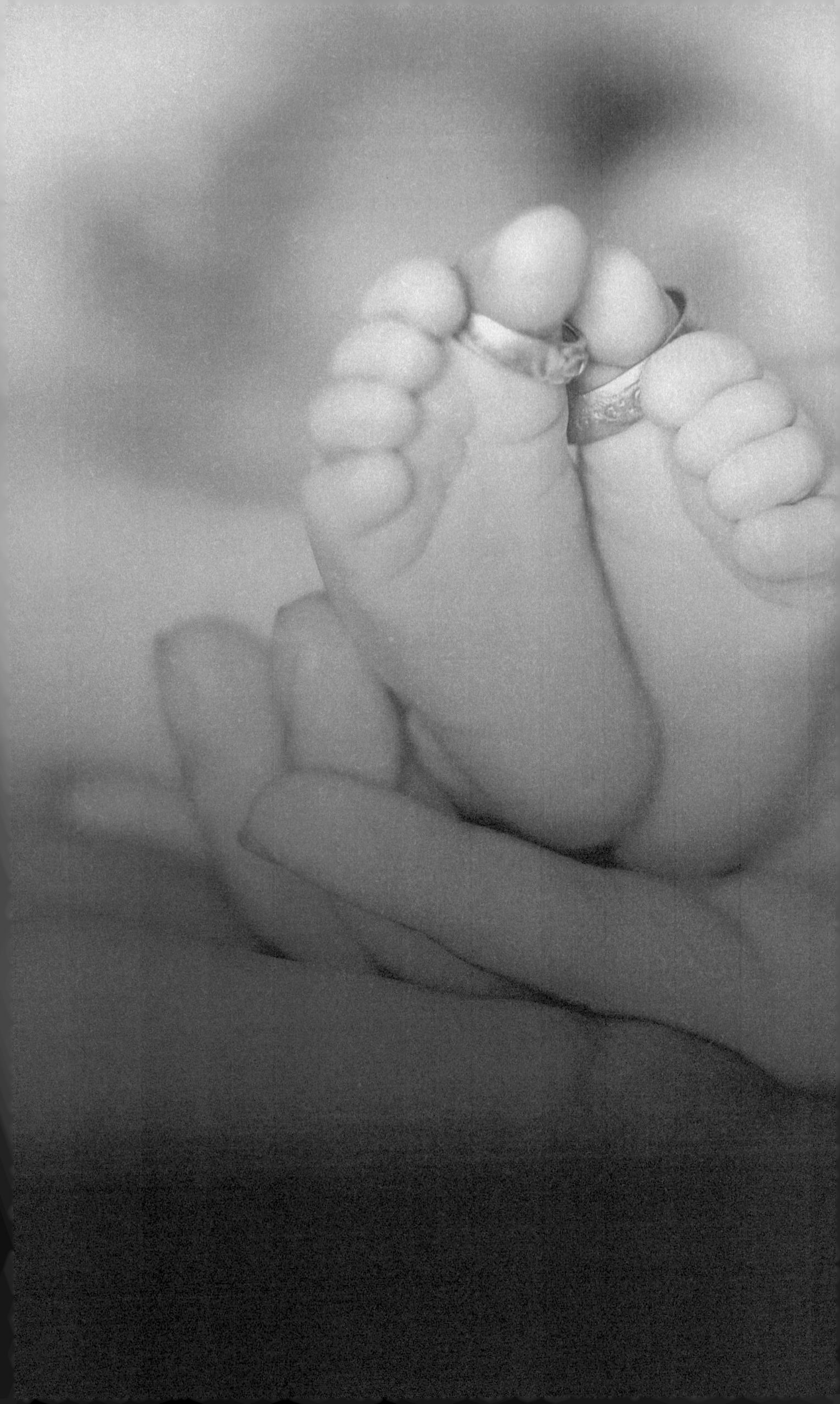

baby announcement

Birdie Josephine Langston was born five days past her due date, causing her Mama to perform outrageous activities to do whatever it took to get her out—including but not limited to: eating spicy foods, hiking up the mountain in ninety-degree weather and almost passing out, strenuous sex, and bouncing on a yoga ball until she nearly peed herself—and when none of those worked—her husband put her on bedrest. Birdie finally debuted at the end of summer weighing seven pounds, three ounces, and was twenty-inches long.

Daddy, Mommy, and baby are all doing amazing and are happier than ever.

next in the willow branch mountain series

Read Silas & Posey's story next in Take My Love

A forced proximity stand-alone from small-town romance author Brooke Montgomery about a heartbroken man who finds himself without a job or place to live and the country girl who owns a goat farm with an open position and spare bedroom...

I've crushed on my brother's best friend since I was twelve. He never gave me a second glance until I was dared to kiss him.

The following summer, we drunkenly hooked up at my brother's wedding. Finding out he had no memory of our night together made it my dirty little secret.

I spent years avoiding him, but then he shows up at my goat farm needing a job and place to live after his fiancée calls off their engagement. Reluctantly, I agree to give him a chance.

But that doesn't mean I have to make it easy on him.

Keeping things strictly platonic between us, I suggest he date again to get over his ex. When he needs a plus-one, I offer to be his wing woman.

After a night of drinking, I stupidly confess the reasons guys keep breaking up with me and he offers to help me instead.

Lines blur when "just roommates" turn into roommates with benefits, but I'm still determined not to let him break my heart a second time.

Even if it seems inevitable.

about the author

Brooke has been writing romance since 2013 under the *USA Today* Bestselling Author retired pen names: Brooke Cumberland and Kennedy Fox, and now under the Amazon top 100 Bestselling Author pen names: **Brooke Montgomery** and **Brooke Fox**. All together, she's published over 65 books.

She writes books that she loves reading about the most—cinnamon roll heroes with dirty mouths who are obsessed with their women. She enjoys writing small town romances with big families and happily ever afters!

When she's not writing, you can find her reading or listening to audiobooks. watching hockey, or cooking. Sometimes all three at once.

Learn more on her website at
www.brookewritesromance.com

www.ingramcontent.com/pod-product-compliance
Lightning Source LLC
Chambersburg PA
CBHW030736310726
48969CB00005B/1234